Goodbye Days

ALSO BY JEFF ZENTNER

The Serpent King

Goodbye Days

a novel

Jeff Zentner

CROWN
NEW YORK

Text copyright © 2017 by Jeff Zentner
Cover art copyright © 2017 by Jarrod Taylor

All rights reserved. Published in the United States by Crown Books for Young Readers, an imprint of Random House Children's Books, a division of Penguin Random House LLC, New York.

Crown and the colophon are registered trademarks of Penguin Random House LLC.

Visit us on the Web! randomhouseteens.com

Educators and librarians, for a variety of teaching tools, visit us at RHTeachersLibrarians.com

Library of Congress Cataloging-in-Publication Data
Names: Zentner, Jeff, author.
Title: Goodbye days / Jeff Zentner.
Description: First edition. | New York : Crown Books for Young Readers, 2017. | Summary: "The heart-breaking and at times humorous look at one teen's life after the death of his best friends and how he navigates through the guilt and pain by celebrating their lives—and ultimately learning to forgive himself" —Provided by publisher.
Identifiers: LCCN 2016008248 | ISBN 978-0-553-52406-2 (hardback) | ISBN 978-0-553-52407-9 (glb) | ISBN 978-0-553-52408-6 (epub) | ISBN 978-1-5247-1956-2 (intl. ed.)
Subjects: | CYAC: Grief—Fiction. | Guilt—Fiction. | Best friends—Fiction. | Friendship—Fiction.
Classification: LCC PZ7.1.Z46 Go 2017 | DDC [Fic]—dc23

Printed in the United States of America
10 9 8 7 6 5 4 3 2
First Edition

Random House Children's Books
supports the First Amendment and celebrates the right to read.

For my beautiful Sara.

My color of the winter clouds at night.

My right blue music.

Death steals everything except our stories.

—JIM HARRISON

Chapter One

Depending on who—sorry, *whom*—you ask, I may have killed my three best friends.

If you ask Blake Lloyd's grandma, Nana Betsy, I think she'd say no. That's because when she first saw me earlier today, she grabbed me in a huge, tearful hug and whispered in my ear: "You are not responsible for this, Carver Briggs. God knows it and so do I." And Nana Betsy tends to say what she thinks. So there's that.

If you ask Eli Bauer's parents, Dr. Pierce Bauer and Dr. Melissa Rubin-Bauer, I expect they'd say maybe. When I saw them today, they each looked me in the eyes and shook my hand. In their faces, I saw more bereavement than anger. I sensed their desolation in the weakness of their handshakes. And I'm guessing part of their fatigue was over whether to hold me accountable in some way for their loss. So they go down as a maybe. Their daughter, Adair? Eli's twin? We used to be friends. Not like Eli and I were, but friends. I'd say she's a "definitely" from the way she glowers at me as if she wishes I'd been in the car too. She was doing just that a few minutes ago, while talking with some of our classmates attending the funeral.

Then there's Judge Frederick Edwards and his ex-wife, Cynthia Edwards. If you ask them if I killed their son, Thurgood Marshall "Mars" Edwards, I expect you'd hear a firm "probably." When I saw Judge Edwards today, he towered over me, immaculately dressed as always. Neither of us spoke for a while. The air between us felt hard and rough as stone. "It's good to see you, sir," I said finally, and extended my sweating hand.

"None of this is good," he said in his kingly voice, jaw muscles clenching, looking above me. Beyond me. As though he thought if he could persuade himself of my insignificance, he could persuade himself that I had nothing to do with his son's death. He shook my hand like it was both his duty and his only way of hurting me.

Then there's me. I would tell you that I definitely killed my three best friends.

Not on purpose. I'm pretty sure no one thinks I did it on purpose; that I slipped under their car in the dead of night and severed the brake lines. No, here's the cruel irony for the writer I am: I wrote them out of existence. **Where are you guys? Text me back.** Not a particularly good or creative text message. But they found Mars's phone (Mars was driving) with a half-composed text responding to me, just

2

as I requested. It looks like that was what he was working on when he slammed into the rear of a stopped semi on the highway at almost seventy miles per hour. The car went under the trailer, shearing off the top.

Am I certain that it was my text message that set into motion the chain of events that culminated in my friends' deaths? No. But I'm sure enough.

I'm numb. Blank. Not yet in the throes of the blazing, ringing pain I'm certain waits for me in the unrolling days ahead. It's like once when I was chopping onions to help my mom in the kitchen. The knife slipped and I sliced open my hand. There was this pause in my brain as if my body needed to figure out it had been cut. I knew two things right then: (1) I felt only a quick strike and a dull throbbing. But the pain was coming. Oh, was it coming. And (2) I knew that in a second or two, I was about to start raining blood all over my mom's favorite bamboo cutting board (yes, people can form deep emotional attachments to cutting boards; no, I don't get it so don't ask).

So I sit at Blake Lloyd's funeral and wait for the pain. I wait to start bleeding all over everything.

Chapter Two

I'm a seventeen-year-old funeral expert.

The plan was we'd finish our senior year of high school at Nashville Arts Academy. Then Eli would be off to Berklee College of Music to study guitar. Blake to Los Angeles to pursue comedy and screenwriting. Mars hadn't figured out where he was going. But he knew *what* he would be doing: comic-book illustration. And I'd be heading to Sewanee or Emory for creative writing.

This was *not* the plan: for me to be waiting for the funeral of the third member of Sauce Crew to begin. Yesterday was Mars's funeral. Eli's the day before.

Blake's funeral is at his small, white Baptist church—one of about 37,567 small, white Baptist churches in the greater Nashville area. It reeks of graham crackers, glue, and old carpet. There are crayon-drawn pictures of Jesus, resembling a bearded lollipop, handing out blue and green fishes to a multitude of stick figures. The air-conditioning doesn't work well in the early-August heat and I'm sweating in a navy-blue suit my sister, Georgia, helped me pick out. Or rather, Georgia picked it out herself while I stood there, dazed. I came out of my stupor briefly to express that I thought I was supposed to get a black suit. Georgia gently explained that navy was fine and I could wear it after the funeral. She always forgot to say *funerals*. Or maybe she didn't forget.

I sit in the back of the church, forehead resting on the pew in front of me. I watch the tip of my tie sway to and fro and wonder how humans got to a place where we said, "Whoa. Hold on. Before I can take you seriously, you need to hang a brightly colored strip of narrow pointy cloth around your neck." The carpet is blue and flecked with white. I wonder who designs carpet. Whose life's calling this is. Who says, "No! No! It's not right yet! It needs . . . specks of white! And then my masterpiece is complete!" I mull over this stuff because the world's reliable absurdity is one of the few things that can distract me, and I welcome distractions right now.

My forehead aches from resting on the hard, smooth wood. I hope I appear to be praying. That seems a church/funeral-appropriate thing to be doing. Plus it saves me from having to make small talk (which I despise under the best of circumstances) with the people making a hushed, sorrowful buzz around me, a swarm of mourning locusts. *Isn't it terrible. . . . What a loss. . . . He was so young. . . . He was so funny. . . . He was . . . He was . . . He was.* People take

5

shelter under clichés. Language is powerless enough in the face of death. I guess it's asking too much for people to veer from the tried-and-true under such circumstances.

There's a huge crowd. Blake's extended family from East Tennessee. People from Blake's church. Friends of Nana Betsy's from work. A bunch of our classmates from Nashville Arts. I'm friendly with most of them, if not friends. A few come by and quickly express sympathies before moving on, but they mostly leave me alone and I'm grateful. That is, I'm grateful if they're leaving me alone for compassion's sake and not because Adair has already persuaded them that I'm a killer.

There's a rustle beside me, the cushion of the pew depressing, a warmth, and then the sunlit perfume of honeysuckle. If any smell stands in defiance of death, it's honeysuckle.

"Hey, Carver."

I look up. It's Jesmyn Holder, Eli's girlfriend. Ex-girlfriend? They never broke up. They'd been dating for maybe two months. She has dark circles under her eyes. She wears her grief like dust on her face.

"Hey, Jesmyn."

"Can I sit here?"

"Sure." *Glad there's at least one future classmate Adair hasn't gotten to yet.*

"I guess I'm already sitting here."

"I heard someone say once that it's easier to ask forgiveness than permission."

"You here alone?" Jesmyn asks. "You were at the other two with a girl."

"That was my sister, Georgia. She had to work today. Sorry we didn't really talk at the other two funerals."

"I wasn't in a chatty mood."

"Me neither." I tug at my collar. "Is it super hot in here?" In general, I'd rather be bitten on the nuts by a Komodo dragon than make small talk. But sometimes you do what you have to do.

"Yeah, but my Filipino genes are fine with it," Jesmyn says.

We sit quietly for a moment while she surveys the crowd. "I recognize a lot of these people from the other two."

I lift my head slightly. "Some go to NAA. You still planning on going?"

"Of course. You didn't think I was going there because of Eli, did you?"

"No. I mean, I don't know. No."

"Two girls from NAA got into Juilliard's piano program last year. That's a huge percentage. That's why I decided to go even before I met Eli."

"I'm glad you're coming still. I didn't mean anything."

"It's cool. Anyway, this seems like a weird thing to talk about right now."

"Everything seems weird to talk about right now."

"Yeah."

At the front of the room, Nana Betsy shambles, weeping, toward Blake's cedar casket to run her hand along its smoothness once more before the funeral starts. I did that before sitting down. The smell of the cedar. Sharp and clean. It didn't smell like something that should be buried under the dirt. It was closed. You don't let people see how someone looks after something like the Accident. So perched atop the casket lid on a wooden stand there's a photo of Blake. He purposely made it ridiculous. It's a department-store portrait; Olan Mills or Sears studio or something. He's wearing a thrift-store sweater from the 1980s and pleated khaki pants. He's holding a huge, grouchy-looking Persian cat. He didn't own a cat. He literally borrowed one for the photo. Pure Blake. A genuine and radiant grin covers his round face. His eyes are closed as if he blinked. He thought photos where people were blinking were hilarious.

I couldn't help but smile when I saw it. Even under the circumstances. All Blake had to do was walk into a room and I started preemptively laughing.

"How come you're not here with your parents?" Jesmyn asks, drawing me out of my memory.

"They're in Italy for their twenty-fifth anniversary. They tried to come home, but they had trouble getting tickets and my dad had to deal with a lost passport. They're coming home tomorrow."

"That sucks."

"Why aren't you sitting with Eli's parents?"

Jesmyn crosses her legs and picks a piece of lint off her black dress. "I was. But Adair was giving me a supercrusty vibe. And then I saw you sitting here looking really lonely."

"Maybe this is how I always look."

She brushes a lock of her reddish-black hair from her face. I smell her shampoo. "Imagine my embarrassment if I came over here to show you kindness and you didn't need it."

"Adair won't be happy with you showing me kindness."

"Yeah, well. I guess life is about risk."

I rub my eyes. My exhaustion is beginning to set in. I haven't slept more than a few hours in the last three days. I turn to Jesmyn. "Have you talked to Eli's parents or Adair much since the accident?" I realize, even as I ask, that I have no idea where Jesmyn herself stands on the whole blame thing. Lack of sleep has lowered my inhibitions such that I'm asking questions that might lead to answers I'm unready to hear.

She opens her mouth to answer when the service begins. We bow our heads as Blake's pastor prays and then offers words of comfort from the gospels. It reminds me more of Mars's huge funeral at New Bethel AME Church than Eli's small private service at Connelly Brothers' Funeral Home. Eli's parents are atheists, and it was the first funeral I'd ever been to that didn't once mention God. Seventeen years old and the breadth of my funerary experience probably rivals that of people twice my age.

Six members of Nashville Arts's a cappella choir perform a requiem. They did this at Mars's and Eli's funerals too. Tears streak Jesmyn's face like an atlas of rivers. She holds a wadded-up tissue and dabs her eyes and nose, staring straight ahead. I don't understand why I'm not crying. I should be. Maybe it's like how it's sometimes too cold to snow.

One of Blake's uncles reads First Thessalonians 4:14–17 in his thick East Tennessee accent. His large hands tremble. His voice wavers. *For we believe that Jesus died and rose again, and so we believe that God will bring with Jesus those who have fallen asleep in him. According to the Lord's word, we tell you that we who are still alive, who are left until the coming of the Lord, will certainly not precede those who have fallen asleep. For the Lord himself will come down from heaven, with a loud command, with the voice of the archangel and with the trumpet call of God, and the dead in Christ will rise first. After that, we who are still alive and are left will be caught up together with them in the clouds to meet the Lord in the air. And so we will be with the Lord forever.*

A fly lands on the pew in front of me and rubs its back legs together. This fly is alive and Blake is dead. The world brims with pulsing, humming life. Except for in the wooden box at the front of the room. There everything lies still. And what caused this stillness was the most banal, routine activity on my part. Texting my friends. The human equivalent of a fly's rubbing its back legs together. It's just something we *do*. It's not supposed to kill your three best friends.

Nana Betsy limps to the pulpit to deliver the eulogy. She has bad knees. She takes a long while to gather herself before speaking. Her hands are empty, as though she planned to say whatever was in her heart. The look on her face says that there's too much to choose from.

I try not to breathe too much or too loudly in the silence. My mouth is dry and I have a headache forming at the base of my skull. My throat aches as if I have something caught in it. The precarious wall I've built—that we all build to protect others from enduring the spectacle of our grief—is beginning to crumble.

Nana Betsy clears her throat and speaks. "Blake's life

wasn't always easy. But he lived joyously. He loved his family. He loved his friends. And he was loved by them."

Down comes the wall and out pours the swirling, gray sea it contained. I put my head in my hands and rest my elbows on my knees. I press the heels of my hands over my eyes, and tears seep hot around the sides. I'm trembling. Jesmyn's hand is on my shoulder. At least the ache in my throat is gone, as though it were an abscess full of tears that I lanced.

"Blake was funny," Nana Betsy says. "If you knew him, he made you laugh at some time or another."

Tears stream down my wrists and dampen my shirt cuffs. They dribble onto the blue carpet with white flecks. I think for a second about all the places I've made a small part of me. Now a tiny piece of this church holds my tears. Maybe after I'm dead, they can cut up the carpet and extract my DNA from my tears that have soaked into the carpet and resurrect me. Maybe that's what the resurrection will be.

"Think of him every time someone makes you laugh. Think of him every time you make someone laugh. Think of him every time you hear someone laugh."

I draw a deep breath that hitches and shudders as the air enters my lungs. It's probably too loud, but I don't care. I sat in the back for a reason. I don't sense anyone turning to look at me, at least.

"I can't wait for the day that I see him again and throw my arms around him. Until then, I know he'll be sitting at our Savior's feet." She pauses to compose herself before finishing. "And he's probably making Jesus laugh too. Thank you all for coming. This would have meant a lot to Blake."

The funeral ends. I stand to serve as pallbearer. They didn't ask me to be Mars's or Eli's pallbearer.

Jesmyn reaches up and touches my hand. "Hey. Do you want a ride to the cemetery?"

I nod, grateful, sagging into myself. Like I've awoken from one of those dreams where you cry and soak your pillow. Your grief is animal, formless, unhinged in the illogic of dreams. You wake up and don't remember what you were crying about. Or you do, and you were crying because you've been offered a chance at redeeming yourself. So when you realize it was a dream, you keep crying because your shot at redemption is another thing you've lost. And you're tired of losing things.

I help carry Blake's casket to the hearse. It weighs a thousand pounds. I had a science teacher ask us once: "What weighs more? A pound of feathers or a pound of lead?" Everyone said lead. But a few hundred pounds of best friend and casket don't weigh the same as a few hundred pounds of lead or feathers. It weighs much more.

⊞ ⊡ ⊞

It's a short walk from the front of the church to the waiting hearse, but in the sultry afternoon heat, I'm soaked when I get to Jesmyn's battered Nissan pickup.

"Sorry, my AC doesn't work," she says, sweeping piano books off the passenger seat.

"Don't you die of heat every time you drive anywhere?"

"That's the best way you could phrase it?"

"Don't you suffer extreme discomfort but not literal death every time you drive anywhere?" I get in and roll down the window.

We drive without speaking for most of the ride, the muggy air washing over our faces. My cheeks are gritty with dried salt.

When we're a few blocks from the cemetery, Jesmyn asks, "Are you okay?"

"Yeah," I lie. A few seconds pass. "No."

Chapter Three

Sauce Crew.

Every group of friends needs a name. We were Sauce Crew.

Sophomore year. Close enough to the end of the school year that we're in a perpetual state of giddiness. It's a Friday night and we've just attended Nashville Arts's production of *Rent*. It was great. But on a Friday night in spring—each of us surrounded by our three best friends—it could have been the worst train wreck of a steaming turd (work with me on the mixed metaphor) imaginable and we'd still have been euphoric.

So we're at McDonald's stuffing our faces.

"Okay," Mars says through a mouthful of hamburger, apropos of nothing: "What if you had to classify every animal as either a dog or a cat?"

Eli spews soda out his nose. We were already laughing at the question, and now we're laughing at Eli mopping Mountain Dew off the Wolves in the Throne Room T-shirt he wore as if it were grafted to his chest.

Blake is gasping for air. "What are you *even talking about*?"

Mars reaches over to dip a french fry in my ketchup. "No, no, all right. Check it out. Raccoons are dogs. Possums are cats. Squirrels are—"

"Hang on, hang on," Eli says.

"Dude, Mars," Blake says, "raccoons are clearly cats. Possums are dogs."

"No, hang on," Eli says. "Any animal you can't train is a cat. You can't train a raccoon. Cat. You can't train a possum. Cat."

"Wait, how do you know you can't train a possum?" Mars asks.

"You can train a cat," I say. "I've seen YouTube videos of cats using a toilet."

Now all three are howling, struggling to breathe. Blake is doubled over. "Please tell me when you ditch out on us to write, you're sitting at home watching cats piss and shit into human toilets and pumping your fist—*Yeah! Cat using human toilet!*"

"No, but I just come across them. Through life."

Tears stream down Mars's face. " 'Through life.' Blade said 'through life.' Oh my God. Oh my God."

Get it? Carver? Blade? Blake had come up with the nickname. It's funny because I dress like a guy who wants to be a writer and whose older sister works at Anthropologie and helps dress him. Guys who meet this description don't generally go by "Blade."

"Okay, guys. Ferrets. Ferrets are long cats," Eli says.

"I've seen a trained ferret, so you can definitely train a ferret," Blake says.

"To use a human toilet?" Mars asks.

"I didn't know there were ferret toilets," Blake says.

"If it's true that you can train a ferret, then I take back what I said, because ferrets are definitely cats," Eli says.

"Okay, seals," I say.

"Mmmmm, cat," Mars says, staring off thoughtfully.

Eli looks incredulous. "Wait, *what*?"

"You can for *sure* train a seal, bro," Blake says.

"No, hang on," Eli says. "I think Mars is implicitly saying seals look like cats to him."

Mars pounds the table, rattling our trays. "They do. They have catfaces. Also they love fish. Cats love fish. Seals are watercats."

We're getting dirty looks from other diners. We couldn't care less. Remember? Young. Alive. Friday night in spring. A feast of junk food spread before us. Best friends. We feel like lords. Everything seems limitless.

Blake stands and finishes his drink with a rattling slurp. "Gentlemen, I need to"—he makes air quotes—"urinate, as it were. If y'all will excuse me. When I return, I expect to have some resolution of the seal-cat issue."

Mars slaps me on the back. "Better go with him so you can film it."

"You don't understand, man," I say. "I'm only into cats that way." Peals of laughter from Mars and Eli.

We're well into our discussion of whether grasshoppers, jellyfish, and snakes are dogs or cats when we realize it's been a while since we've seen Blake.

"Yo, fam, check it out." Mars points at the children's playground adjacent to the McDonald's. Blake is pitching back and forth on one of those rocking horses mounted on a thick spring. He's waving furiously at us, like a little kid, and whooping.

"Look at that asshole," Eli murmurs.

"He shame," Mars says.

"Wait, what?" I ask. *He shame?* That's not a thing people say. You're missing like three words in that sentence, including a linking verb."

"I'm making it a thing. Someone does something stupid? He shame. You do something stupid? You shame."

I shake my head. "That will never be a thing."

Eli gathers unopened packets of Blake's chicken nugget sauce and hands a couple to Mars. "Come on, we gotta blast him."

I hurry to keep up as they dash outside.

"Blade, you film," Eli says. I also throw like a guy who wants to be a writer.

Blake rocks, whooping, laughing maniacally, whipping around an invisible cowboy hat and waving at us.

We grin and wave—Eli and Mars waving with one hand, handfuls of sauce packets behind their backs—watching him for a second while I film on my phone.

"Okay," Mars says under his breath, still grinning and waving furiously. "Count of three. One. Two. *Three*."

He and Eli stop waving and lunge forward, hurling sauce packets. Mars has a good arm. His dad used to force him to do all kinds of sports. Eli has this rangy athleticism. He'd have probably been a decent basketball player if he could put down his guitar long enough and if he weren't so allergic to keeping his long, curly black hair out of his face. A teriyaki and a BBQ each score a direct hit on the horse's head, causing them to burst open and spray Blake. His joyous whoops turn to cries of indignation. *"Awwwww, no way, you assholes! Gross!"*

Mars and Eli high-five each other and then awkwardly high-five me. I suck at high fives. They collapse on the ground in hysterics, rolling around.

Blake walks up, arms outstretched, dripping with sauce. Mars and Eli hurry to their feet. Blake starts chasing them in turn, trying to wipe sauce on them. He's much too slow, even with them breathless from laughter. Finally he gives up and goes to the restroom. He returns, dabbing his shirt with a wet paper towel.

"Y'all are so damn funny. The damn Sauce Crew."

"We should call ourselves that. Sauce Crew," Eli says.

"Sauce Crew," I say somberly, extending my hand, palm down.

"Sauce Crew," Mars says in his terrible English accent and puts his hand on mine.

"Sssssssssssssauce Crewwwwwwwww," Eli says, in a boxing announcer voice, and puts his hand on Mars's.

"Sauce—" Blake starts to put his hand on Eli's but then playfully slaps him on the cheek and goes for Mars. They both giggle and dodge while trying to keep their hands together. "Sauce Crew," Blake says, and puts his hand on top of Eli's.

"Saaaaaaaaaaaaaauce Crew!" we shout in unison.

"Did one of you donkey dicks film it at least? I want to put it on my YouTube," Blake says.

⊞ ⊞ ⊞

I watch them lower the third member of Sauce Crew into the ground.

I am Sauce Crew now.

Chapter Four

It's late afternoon when Jesmyn pulls up to my car, and the sun sifts through leaves, making them glow green. My head is pounding. I realize it's not only because of the tension I'm carrying, but also because I've barely eaten all day.

We sit there for a moment, the heat pressing down on us like a vise. After a day of ceremony, I can't seem to even get out of the truck without some.

I rest my arm on the windowsill. "Thanks. For sitting by me during the funeral and driving me to the cemetery. And standing with me at the cemetery. And then driving me here." I pause. "Sorry if I'm forgetting anything."

"No problem." Jesmyn's voice sounds washed out.

I reach for the door handle but stop. "I never asked how you're doing."

She sighs and lays her head on her hands, which rest on the steering wheel. "Shitty. Like you."

"Yeah."

She wipes away tears. A few seconds of sniffling pass. Then the slow returning creep of guilt, taking the baton from grief and exhaustion. It resembles that moment when you're hiking and you step into an icy creek. It takes a second for the frigid water to seep in and soak your socks. Maybe you've even managed to pull your foot out of the water already. But then there's that wet chill spreading around your foot, and you know you're going to be miserable for the rest of the day.

I've allowed myself to assume, because of her kindness, that she doesn't blame me. What if all her kindness has nothing to do with that and everything to do with trying to persuade herself not to hate me? I can see convincing yourself not to hate someone by investing kindness in them.

I'm too spent. I have no energy for the truth; no place left to put it.

"Anyway, thanks again." I open the door.

Jesmyn pulls out her phone. "Hey. I don't have your number. School's starting in a few weeks, and I need all the friends I can get there." This sounds like an epiphany coming to her even as she says it.

"Oh. Yeah. I guess I'm not super close with anyone there anymore either."

We exchange numbers. Maybe this was the ceremony I needed. Some tiny ray of hope.

It's dawning on me how lonely this school year will be. Sauce Crew was so tight. We were our own universe. No one alive is in the habit of thinking to call me on a Saturday night. But my bigger problem is Adair. She always wielded outsized social influence at NAA—way more than Eli ever did. Way, *way* more than me. If she never stops hating me, many people are going to follow her lead just to stay in her good graces.

"Well," Jesmyn says. "At least we're done with funerals."

"That's something, I guess."

"See you later?"

"Yeah. Later."

Now comes the hard part. When we can't lose ourselves in regimented programs for our grief. When we're alone with ourselves.

But the day's not over for me yet. Nana Betsy invited me to stop by her house, where they were having a low-key potluck dinner to send the relatives from East Tennessee home with full bellies.

I squint against the dazzling light while I rummage for my keys and consider how blithely bright the day is.

The spinning world and the burning sun don't care much whether we stay or we go. It's nothing personal.

⊞ ⊟ ⊞

"Hey, Lisa," I say to one of the NAA a cappella members passing in the parking lot on the way to her car.

"Oh. Hey." She's suddenly transfixed by her phone. She's one of the people Adair was talking to before the funeral started. And as far as I know, she never bore me any special ill will before now. *Yep. This school year is going to rule.*

I'm about to get into my car when I see a youngish bearded man in khakis, a dress shirt with the sleeves rolled up to the elbows, and a loosened, skinny tie approaching.

"Excuse me. Sorry, excuse me," he calls, waving. "You Carver Briggs?"

At least someone wants to talk to me. "Yeah."

The young man is carrying a notebook and a pen. He has what looks like a digital recorder in his shirt pocket.

He extends his hand. "Darren Coughlin, with the *Tennessean*. I've been covering the accident from the beginning."

I shake his hand reluctantly. "Oh." *So you're the one responsible for the article printed a few days ago, telling the world that this was a texting accident and making everyone point at me.*

"Hey, I'm really sorry about the circumstances. I'm working on a story about the accident, and Judge Edwards referred me to you. He said you might have some information about it? They were your friends?"

I rub my forehead. This is literally one of the last things on Earth I want to be doing right now. "Can we do this another time? I don't really want to talk."

"I get it, and I'm not trying to be insensitive, but the news doesn't stop for grief, you know? I'd like to get your side before we go to press."

My side. I suck in a breath. "Um, yeah. Best friends."

He shakes his head. "So sorry, man. Do you know anything about what might have caused the accident?"

23

"I thought you already had an idea."

"Well, seems like it was texting, but do you know who Thurgood—"

"Mars."

"Excuse me?"

"We called him Mars."

"Okay, do you know who Mars was texting with?"

My stomach folds around the jagged edges of the question. My sweat cools. *Yes, as a matter of fact I do.* "I—I'm not sure exactly. It might have been me."

Darren nods and scribbles notes. "Were you texting him at around the time of the accident?"

He might be trying not to come across as brusque and uncaring, but he is, and it's making me jittery. "I—maybe?" My voice is diminishing.

"Are you aware of any criminal investigation into the accident?"

I shudder like a buzzing wasp just landed on my neck. "No. Why?"

He shakes his head nonchalantly. "Curious."

"Have you heard anything?"

"No, I'd just be surprised if there weren't an investigation. Three teenagers, texting, you know."

"Should I be worried?"

Darren keeps scribbling notes. He shrugs. "Probably not."

"I mean, a couple of cops talked to me right after and I told them that Mars and I were texting that afternoon. But they didn't, like, arrest me."

"Yeah, I don't know." Darren clicks his pen.

"Could you maybe not write that I might have been texting Mars?" I'm smart enough to know both how futile this request is and how bad it makes me sound, but I sometimes do dumb stuff.

He looks up. "Man, I can't—"

I chew on a fingernail. He never finishes the sentence.

Darren raises his pad again. "So, what time were you—"

It suddenly occurs to me how little I have to gain by continuing this conversation, and how much I have to lose. "I gotta go. I gotta—"

"Just a couple more questions."

"No, sorry, I have to be at Blake's house. His grandma wanted me to come." I sit down in my car and close the door. I have to roll down the window to breathe in the stifling heat.

Darren rests his hand on the windowsill. "Look, Carver, I'm sorry to be doing this right now. I really am. But this is news. And the news doesn't wait for people to mourn. So you can either tell me your side of the story or you can wait to read it in the paper. But either way."

"I don't read the paper." I turn the key in the ignition.

He fishes a card from his shirt pocket and hands it to me through the window. "Anyway, man, here's my card. Drop me a line if you remember something or if the police start asking questions."

I toss the card on the passenger seat.

"Can I get your number?" Darren asks.

"I'm late." I roll up the window. Darren gives me a you're-making-a-mistake look, as though I didn't know I already had.

Acid bubbles up and scalds the back of my throat as I drive to Blake's house.

◩ ◩ ◩

Blake Lloyd is surely the only student in the history of Nashville Arts who secured admission on the strength of his public farting. Okay, not *just* public farting, but that was by far the most popular part of his oeuvre.

Blake was a minor YouTube celebrity. He made comedy videos—skits, observations, impressions, etc. He'd thicken his accent and country it up. What really got people's attention, though, was his willingness to embarrass himself publicly. He'd trip himself at the grocery store and take out a display of cereal boxes while his pants fell down (he always cleaned up his messes). He'd step in dog poop barefoot. He'd walk into Green Hills Mall, the snootiest mall in Nashville, shirtless (and he did *not* look like he worked out).

And then there was the public farting. In movie theaters. During a quiet scene. *Puuuurp*. Then a pause. Then another one. Longer. *Priiiiiiiiip*. He always kept a straight face. One of his most popular videos was one where he rips ass at the library and he hasn't even gotten the whole thing out yet when the librarian bellows, *"EXCUSE YOU."*

In the months before the Accident, though, he had upped the ante to public farting in midconversation. So he's talking with a prim hobby-shop clerk, acting the perfect young

26

gentleman, and midsentence, he cuts one. The lady tries to be polite, because we all make mistakes, but she can't help an involuntary grimace. But then he goofs out another—it sounds like a pig's squeal. *Brrrrrrp.* And now she's certain it's no mistake.

"Do you need the restroom?" she asks icily.

"Ma'am?" Blake says.

Now this may not seem the sort of portfolio that would get you into a competitive arts school (please note: if you say "competitive arts school" fast, it sounds like "come pet at a fart school"). But Blake was smart. He studied comedy. He listened to people talk about it and pick it apart, analyzing it on podcasts and in essays. He knew his craft and was serious about it. He knew how to intellectualize it and frame what he was doing to make it attractive to the admissions committee. So he wasn't a bored kid farting in public for laughs on the Internet. He was *a performance artist, actively violating the social contract and confronting those in public spaces with the reality of bodily function.* He was challenging people, forcing them to question the artificial barriers we construct between ourselves and our bodies. He was subverting expectations. He was sacrificing himself; laying it on the line. *He was creating art.*

Plus, come on. Farts are always funny. Even to admissions officers.

I get to Nana Betsy's house and let myself in. There's a laptop set up as you walk in the front door, and it's playing Blake's videos. So amidst the somber hush of conversation, you hear the occasional flatulent toot emanate from the laptop speakers, followed by chuckling from the groups of two or three people alternating standing around the laptop.

The photo of Blake that rested on top of the casket now sits on the coffee table. The house is warm in the way of confined spaces full of people. It smells of potluck food and the aftershave and perfume that men and women get as presents from grandchildren.

I pause in the living room for a second, unsure of what to do. Nobody acknowledges my presence. A gust of guilt buffets me, so powerful it makes my leg bones feel like they're resonating to some low frequency. *You filled this house with mourners. You created this occasion.* I have that feeling when you think everyone is staring at you even though you can see they aren't.

I spot Nana Betsy in the kitchen, talking with her brothers. Our eyes meet and she motions for me to come in. I enter the kitchen and Nana Betsy, without interrupting her conversation, points me to the adjacent dining room, where steaming slow cookers, casserole dishes, and disposable aluminum pans crowd the table. Cold grocery-store fried chicken. Squash casserole topped with Ritz crackers. Turnip greens with chunks of pork. Little smoked sausages swimming in BBQ sauce. Mac and cheese with the top baked brown.

It's strange that this is the best we can do. We don't even have a special ceremonial mac and cheese to mark someone's passing from this world. We only have the normal stuff that your mom feeds you on any given day when someone you love hasn't died.

I pile food precariously on a paper plate, grab a clear

plastic fork and a red Solo cup of sweet tea, and find a corner of the living room. The couch and most of the chairs are taken, so I sit on an ottoman and eat, trying to make myself invisible, carefully balancing my cup on the carpet. I have to force down each bite through a constricted throat. Hungry as I am, my body is telling me I'm unworthy. Replaying my conversation with Darren in my mind every few minutes also doesn't help.

People bump into each other, interacting. Fish in an aquarium. The men wear wrinkled, ill-fitting sport coats and sloppily tied ties. They look uncomfortable, like beagles wearing sweaters.

I finish and I'm about to stand when Nana Betsy shuffles in. A woman rises from the rocking chair, and she and Nana Betsy share a long hug and kiss on the cheek. Nana Betsy bids her farewell and tells her to take a plate of food for the road. Then Nana Betsy drags the rocker beside me and sits with a soft groan. She looks bone weary. Her eyes normally dance. Not today.

"How you doing, Blade?"

Nana Betsy was the only person on Earth outside of Sauce Crew who called me Blade. The nickname tickled her to no end.

"I've been better."

"I hear you," she says.

"Blake's funeral was beautiful." I'm saying it without conviction. I'm not even fooling myself. A beautiful funeral for your best friend is a species of drinking a delicious poison, or being bitten by a majestic tiger.

Nana Betsy sees right through me. "Oh, baloney," she says gently. "A beautiful funeral would have been Blake making everyone laugh once more. One his mama was at."

I hadn't wanted to ask about that. But Nana Betsy says it with a certain yearning, something she wants off her chest but she needs someone to ask her about it.

"Do you know where she is?"

She blinks away tears. She folds her hands on her lap, prayer-like. "No," she says softly. "I don't hear from Mitzi but once every couple years. When whatever man she's taken up with leaves her high and dry again and she needs money to feed her habit. She'll call from some motel in Las Vegas or Phoenix on a disposable cell phone. I have no number for her. No address. No way to reach her. On top of everything else, I guess I'll have to hire someone to track her down so's I can tell her Blake is gone."

"Man." *What do you say to that?*

"Thing is, she'll be devastated even though she's never been interested in being a mother to him."

A weighty silence. A blessed fart from the laptop. Nana Betsy laughs through her tears. "I miss him so much. I don't know how to live without him. I'm not even sure how I'll weed the tomato garden with my knees bad as they are. Blake always did it for me." She produces a handkerchief and wipes her eyes. "I loved him as my own."

It's several seconds before I can speak; I'm swallowing the sobs trying to claw their way out of my throat. "I don't think I'll ever laugh again."

Nana Betsy leans over and hugs me. She smells like dried

roses and warm polyester. She doesn't seem to have a single sharp edge. We hug and rock side to side for a second or two.

"I better keep making the rounds," Nana Betsy says. "You're a good friend. Please don't be a stranger."

"I won't. Oh, my mom and dad wanted me to tell you again they're sorry they couldn't come. They tried to make it home from Italy, but they couldn't in time."

"You tell them I understand completely. Bye, Blade."

"Bye, Nana Betsy."

Before I leave, I take a last look around. I remember the occasions Blake and I sat in this living room planning his next video. Playing video games. Watching a movie or some sketch-comedy show.

I wonder if the actions we take and the words we speak are like throwing pebbles into a pond; they send ripples that extend farther out from the center until finally they break on the bank or disappear.

I wonder if somewhere in the universe, there's still a ripple that's Blake and I sitting in this living room, laughing ourselves silly. Maybe it'll break on some bank somewhere in the vast sky beyond our sight. Maybe it'll disappear.

Or maybe it'll keep traveling on for eternity.

Chapter Five

When I get home, Georgia greets me at the door with a huge hug, squeezing the breath from me.

"How was your day in the scented candle mines?" My heart's not remotely in the joke—one of our regulars—but I make it as a halfhearted nod to normalcy.

I feel her half smile on my cheek. "If I pretend that's still clever, will it cheer you up?"

"Maybe."

She pulls back and takes my hands. "Hey. You hanging in there?"

"Define 'hanging in there.' I'm alive. My heart's beating."

"Time's the only thing that can touch this."

My sister is only a little older than me, but she's sometimes wiser than her years. "Then I want to go to sleep and wake up a decade from now."

We stare at each other for a second. My eyes well with tears. It's not sadness or exhaustion this time. It's Georgia's goodness. I'm a total baby in the presence of unalloyed kindness. I choke up when I see YouTube videos about people donating a kidney to a stranger or saving a starving dog or something.

"I know you miss them," Georgia says. "I'll miss them. Even Eli constantly trying to look down my shirt."

"Once Mars drew a picture of you in a bikini as a present for Eli."

She rolls her eyes. "Did you at least defend my honor?"

"Of course. I mean, it was a really good picture, though. Mars was good." I choke up.

Georgia gives an oh-you-poor-thing wince and hugs me again. "There's some lasagna left."

"I ate at Blake's."

"Mom and Dad called while you were at the funeral. They were checking up on you. Call them."

"Okay." I hesitate before spilling. "So—a reporter ambushed me after the funeral."

Georgia's face sours. "*What? A reporter* wanted to talk to you after the funeral of your best friend? Are you shitting me? The hell?"

"Yeah. He was superpushy. Like"—I imitate Darren's voice—" 'Well, Carver, I gotta write about this, and the news doesn't wait for grief, so if you wanna tell me your side, you better.' "

She rears back, folds her arms, and does that pissed-off thing with her lips that absolutely only girls of a certain age can do. "What's this dipshit's name?"

I know the look on her face. It's the look she used to get every time I told her about kids picking on me in middle school, just before she went to "sort things out." "Please don't. I guarantee it'd make things worse."

"For him." (She isn't wrong.)

"For me."

We stand at an impasse. She sniffs at me. "Speaking of news: you kinda stink."

"I was wearing a suit all day and it was superhot, but whatever."

"Go shower. You'll feel better."

"I'm despondent and I apparently smell like gross balls. How could I possibly ever feel better than I do now?"

⊞ ⊞ ⊞

Georgia's right; I'm improved when I get out of the shower, dry off, and flop naked on my bed. I stare at the ceiling for a while. When I tire of that, I dress in a pair of khakis and a button-down shirt with the sleeves rolled up.

I open my blinds, letting the peach-hued dusk cast long shadows in my room. I sit at my desk and open my laptop. Glowing on the screen is the story I'm working on. Any illusion I have of losing myself in that, though, quickly vanishes.

I live in a part of Nashville called West Meade. My street has an unusual characteristic: a train track running behind it on a raised berm. Trains come by every hour or so. In the distance, I hear a train whistle. I watch the setting sunlight strobe between the train cars as they pass behind the 1960s-era houses directly across the street from mine. I pick up my phone to call my parents, but I can't. I'm not in the mood to talk to anyone.

And suddenly I have the overwhelming sensation of swirling down the drain of a bottomless melancholic boredom. Not the please-kill-me-when-will-this-class-be-over sort. The sort where you realize that your three best friends are, at this very moment, experiencing the afterlife or oblivion, while you sit on your ass watching a train pass as your laptop screen darkens and goes to sleep.

Darkens and goes to sleep. That's what happened to my friends. And I have no idea where they are right now. I have no idea what's become of their intelligence, their experience, their stories.

I'm a casual believer in God. My family goes to church at St. Henry's maybe four or five times a year. My dad says he believes in God enough to make himself suffer over it but not enough to make anyone else suffer over it. My belief has never been tested in this way. I've never had to examine myself to decide whether I *truly* believe that my friends are currently in the presence of some benevolent and loving God. What if there is no God? Where are they? What if they're each locked in some huge white marble room with blank walls and they're there for eternity with nothing to do, nothing to see, nothing to read, nobody to talk to?

What if there's a hell? A place of eternal torment and punishment? What if they're there? Burning. Screaming in agony.

What if I'm going there when I die for killing my friends? What if Nana Betsy has no power to forgive and exonerate me?

I feel like I'm watching something heavy and fragile slide slowly off a high shelf. My mind swirls with mysteries. The eternities. Life. Death. I can't stop it. It's like staring in the mirror for too long or saying your name too many times and becoming disconnected from any sense of yourself. I begin to wonder if I'm even still alive; if I exist. Maybe I was in the car too.

The room dims.

I'm tingling.

I've fallen through ice into frigid black water.

I can't breathe.

My heart screams.

This is not right. I'm not fine.

My vision narrows, as if I'm standing deep in a cave, looking out. Spots form in front of my eyes. The walls are crushing me.

I'm gasping. I need air. *My heart.*

Gray, desolate dread descends on me—a cloud of ash blocking the sun. A complete absence of light or warmth. A tangible, mold-scented obscurity. A revelation: *I will never again experience happiness.*

Air. I need air. I need air. I need air. I need.

I try to stand. The room pitches and tosses, heaving. I'm walking on a sheet of Jell-O. I try again to stand. I lose my balance and fall backward, over my chair, thudding on the hardwood floor.

It's one of those nightmares where you can't run or scream. And it's happening to me this moment in the dying light of this day of dying. *AND I AM DYING TOO.*

"Georgia," I croak. *AIR. I NEED AIR.* My pulse thrums in my temples.

I start crawling toward the door. I can't stand. *"GEOR-GIA, help me. Help me."*

I hear Georgia open the door. "Carver, what the shit? Are you okay?" She sounds like she's calling down a well. Her bare feet slap on the floor as she runs to me.

Her hands on my face. I gasp. "Something's wrong. Something's wrong."

"Okay, okay. Breathe. I need you to breathe. Are you hurt? Did you do something to yourself?"

"No. Just happened. Can't breathe."

"Did you take anything? Drugs?"

"No."

She stands up and presses her hands to the sides of her head. *"Shit. Shit. Shit.* What do I do?" she says, more to herself than me. She kneels beside me again and slings my arm over her shoulder. "Okay. We're going to the ER."

"Nine-one-one."

"No. We'll get there faster if I take you. Come on. Up."

With a grunt, she helps me to my knees. I'm seeing double.

"Okay, Carver, I need you to try to stand and I'll support you. You're too heavy for me to lift."

I make it to my feet, where I sway drunkenly. I put one foot in front of the other until we're outside. Georgia sits me in the passenger seat of her Camry and runs inside for her phone, her wallet, a pair of sandals for her, and a pair of shoes for me. I want to puke. I close my eyes and try to breathe through the nausea.

While I wait, I wonder if it's annoying God to be missing the last member of Sauce Crew in his collection. I wonder if dying right now wouldn't be the worst thing in the world. It would certainly solve a lot of the problems I foresee in the immediate future.

⊞ ⊞ ⊞

When we arrive at the St. Thomas West Hospital ER, about ten minutes from our house (with Georgia exceeding the speed limit by twenty-five miles per hour), I'm breathing easier and I'm less queasy. My vision has opened up a little, my heartbeat has slowed, and in general, I'm a lot less certain I'm going to die, which comes as a strange disappointment.

I'm able to walk into the ER on my own. While I'm filling out paperwork, Georgia pulls out her phone and starts scrolling through her contacts.

I pause mid–check mark. "Are you calling Mom and Dad?"

"Of course."

"Don't."

"Carver."

"What? Don't worry them. Plus it's probably the middle of the night in Italy."

"I *know* you aren't stupid."

"I'm serious. Just . . . we'll tell them when they're home."

"Okay. We are sitting in the ER after you *fully* had some weird deal. I'm calling Mom and Dad. End of story."

"Georgia."

"We are not, like, debating this. I wonder if I can legally

give consent for you to be treated. Fortunately, they don't seem to care about parental consent at the ER."

Georgia's a sophomore biology major at the University of Tennessee, with plans to go to medical school. She's probably loving this on some level.

"No answer," Georgia mutters. "Hey, Mom, this is Georgia. I'm at St. Thomas ER with Carver. He had some sort of . . . episode after the funeral. He's doing okay now. Call me."

I slump in my chair and stare forward.

Georgia finds my eyes. "Why are you so weird about opening up to Mom and Dad when you're vulnerable?"

"I don't know. It's embarrassing."

"They want to be a part of your life. So many kids would kill to have our parents."

"Can we not talk about this now? I feel shitty enough." She's right, but I can't deal with yet another kind of guilt.

"Well, we might be waiting awhile."

"Let's find something else to talk about."

"All I'm saying is that when we're down, we need the people who love us."

"Got it."

"*Got it,*" Georgia says, mimicking my voice.

I'm feeling better now, less like I'm facing imminent death or confinement to some dread-filled limbo. Only exhaustion mixed with shapeless anxiety. Which I guess is my new normal. Too spent to experience much embarrassment, though, which is a relief.

It's several minutes before a nurse comes to talk to me

39

about my symptoms and take my blood pressure. They run an EKG. A little while after that, the doctor comes to see us. She gives off a reassuringly chipper go-ahead-try-to-shock-me aplomb even though she doesn't look much older than Georgia. It's weird to imagine Georgia wearing scrubs and treating people in a few years. She'll probably try to guilt-trip all her patients.

"Hello, Carver. Dr. Stefani Craig. Nice to meet you. Sorry you're not doing well. Tell me what's going on."

I describe what happened. Dr. Craig nods. "You paint quite the picture." She clicks her pen, looking over my chart. "Have you been under any extraordinary stress lately?"

"You mean besides my three best friends dying in a car accident last week?"

She stops clicking her pen and freezes, her brisk confidence abruptly vanishing. "My God. The texting accident? I read about that in the *Tennessean*. I'm so sorry. I can't imagine."

"I was at a funeral a few hours ago."

She winces and sighs. "Well. The timing, the symptoms, your EKG: it's a textbook panic attack. I had a roommate in med school who got them around finals. They're common among people who've experienced a traumatic event. Or three. Normally, they happen a little later and at more unexpected times, but you may be wired differently."

"So—"

"So physically you're a healthy seventeen-year-old. You're not going to die from this. You may never even have another panic attack as long as you live. But you've had

40

psychological trauma and it's important to work through it. There are medications, but I'd prefer any such prescription come from a mental health professional. You have insurance. I'd look into who takes your plan and see someone. That's my official recommendation."

"We have someone," Georgia said.

I look over at Georgia. She mouths, "Later."

"Great," Dr. Craig says, extending her hand. "Anyway, you're good to go. Carver, all the best. Again, I'm so sorry for your loss. What a difficult thing to deal with, especially at your age."

Especially at my age. I bet this is something I'm going to be hearing a lot in the days to come. I shake her hand. "Thanks."

She hurries off to deal with people who are actually hurt and not merely crazy. I wonder if I would have preferred that there be something physically wrong with me. Something you could heal with a cast. Stitch up. Excise. My mind is all that makes me special. I can't afford to lose it.

We sign some more paperwork and leave. Georgia's phone rings as we're walking out in the parking lot. I listen to her side of the conversation. "Hey. . . . No, he's fine. It was a panic attack. Said they're normal during stressful— Right. . . . Yeah. . . . No, don't. We're literally leaving this minute. We'll talk when y'all get home. . . . Just— I know. . . . I know. . . . Yeah, I'm gonna talk to him. No, I said *I'll* talk to him. Okay. Okay. Love you. Have a safe flight and don't stress. We'll see you at the airport. Okay. Hang on."

"Is that Mom?"

"Telemarketer. I swear, these guys."

"Hilarious."

Georgia hands me her phone. "Here. She wants to talk to you."

My mom sounds distraught. She puts me on speaker with my dad. I summon all my strength to tell them I'm okay; that I'm going to be okay. I tell them I'll see them soon.

Georgia unlocks her car and we get in. It's dark out, but the car is still warm and it comforts me like a blanket.

I recline in my seat with my eyes closed, further sapped by the effort of trying to seem as fine as possible for my parents. "Sorry to make you bring me here for nothing."

Georgia puts her key in the ignition and starts to turn it but stops. "It wasn't nothing. You had a panic attack. You didn't know if you were having a heart attack or what."

"I want this day to be over. I want this life to be over."

"Carver."

"I'm not going to kill myself. Chill. I just wish I could go to sleep and wake up when I'm eighty."

"No you don't."

"I really do."

"We need to discuss what the doctor said. About talking to someone. And you don't talk to Mom and Dad. You're Mr. Secret Agent High School Boy with them."

"I'll talk to you."

Georgia starts the car and backs out. "That won't work. First off, UT starts in a couple of weeks, so I won't be here."

"We can talk on the phone."

". . . Second, I don't have the training to deal with this stuff. Dude, this is serious. Therapists are the real deal."

"Mmmmm." I lean my head on the window and stare out.

"Remember when I hit that rough patch senior year? After Austin and I broke up?"

"You seemed depressed."

"I was. And I was having eating issues. I went to see a therapist named Dr. Mendez, and he was way cool and helpful."

"You never mentioned that."

"I didn't want to advertise it."

"I don't want him to tell me I'm crazy."

"So you'd rather *be* crazy. Look, he won't tell you that. Plus they won't even let you be a writer if you've never needed to be in therapy."

"I'll think about it."

"I'm here for you, Carver, but you need to see Dr. Mendez."

"I said I'd think about it."

I don't say anything more on the short drive home. Instead, I reflect on frailty. Mine. Life's.

I want to live unburdened again.

Chapter Six

My parents look wan and battered when Georgia and I pull up to the airport. I guess it makes for a nice symmetry with my hollow, vacant-eyed appearance. The muscles of my face feel like they forgot how to form a smile. But I try anyway as I get out and make as if to help my parents load their suitcases in the car, mumbling, "Hey, Mom and Dad." My dad catches my wrist and pulls me to him. So hard it would seem rough if I didn't know better. He hugs me like I've just been pulled from rubble.

"If we had lost you. If we ever lost you," he whispers in a hoarse, tear-clogged voice.

That he can talk at all means he's doing better than my mom, who hugs me from behind—they've got me in a sandwich—sobbing. I can feel both of their tears, warm on my face and dribbling down my neck. And if I'm being honest, a good amount of those tears are my own.

"Missed you," I say.

We hug like that until an airport police car pulls up behind our car and tells us over his PA that we need to move.

I sit between my mom and dad in the backseat while Georgia chauffeurs us. Except for my mom asking me how I'm doing, and my responding, "Not great," we don't speak on the ride home. Instead, my mom pulls my head down to her shoulder and strokes my hair.

⊞ ⊞ ⊞

Where are you guys? Text me back.

I awake with a wild gasp, my pulse galloping. My sheets are drenched with sweat, my face tight with the salt of dream tears. I used to love crying in dreams for some reason—the release of it, maybe, crying in that savage way that you won't let yourself do when you're conscious. Waking up with your eyes wet like puddles after a midnight thunderstorm. That was when I wasn't crying for anything in particular.

I guess guilt doesn't sleep. It only eats.

Chapter Seven

I sit at my desk, staring at a blank document on my laptop screen. I'm supposed to be working on my college admission essay, something I've procrastinated about all summer, until exactly one week after the last of my three best friends' funerals. Maybe not the most solid idea.

I wish I had to work today. I was employed part-time, shelving books at a huge used-book/CD/DVD/record/video-game/all-sorts-of-other-stuff warehouse near my house called McKay's. I've worked there the last few summers, but I usually quit a couple of weeks before school starts. I regret doing that this year.

It's not that I love shelving books as much I love simply being surrounded by them. I need the not-interacting-with-anyone-ness of it. I need mindless repetition. I need the vanilla-dry-leaves-tobacco-air-conditioner-mold scent of it in my nose. Even though it reminds me of the Accident. That's where I was when it happened. That's why I wasn't in the car.

I start to text Jesmyn. We've been casually texting for the last week. She probably won't respond. She mentioned that she's teaching piano and practicing all day. I'd love to watch her play sometime.

My mom interrupts me midtext. "Carver," she calls. "Come here. Hurry. Judge Edwards is on TV."

A spasm of adrenaline seizes my chest. My bowels become a swirling vortex. *This can't possibly be good.* I jump up, banging my knee, and run in on trembling legs. My mom, dad, and Georgia are gathered around the television, standing.

Judge Edwards looks stern, wearing an expensive-looking gray pinstripe suit that fits him like he grew it and a blood-red tie. He's speaking into a reporter's microphone. ". . . And so, to send a message to the community and to young people about the perils of texting friends while driving, I would call upon the office of the district attorney to open an investigation into this matter and weigh criminal charges."

"Have you spoken personally with the district attorney?" the reporter asks.

"No, ma'am, I have not. I do not believe that would be appropriate or transparent. I would not want to be seen as interfering with the district attorney's prosecutorial discretion. I trust she will exercise that discretion appropriately to see that justice is done."

I want, quite frankly, to crap in my pants. My mom

covers her mouth with both hands. My dad's expression is stony. He folds his arms and runs his hand over his face. Georgia stares at the screen as if she wishes she could shoot streams of sulfuric acid from her tear ducts into the TV and inundate Judge Edwards, turning him into smoking goo.

"If the district attorney declines to seek an indictment, or even if she does seek one, will you be pursuing civil action against the fourth juvenile involved in this incident?"

"We are not, uh, foreclosing anything; not taking anything off the table. Our primary concern is and will always be the safety and well-being of our youth." He nods firmly. *That's all, folks. Nothing left to see here.*

"Thank you, Judge Edwards. Phil, back to you."

"Thanks, Alaina. A tragic accident and a grieving father . . . Davidson County Metro officials have decided *not* to approve . . ."

I tune out the anchor's drone. I collapse onto the couch and hold my head in my hands. "Oh my God. Oh my God," I murmur over and over. Everyone is mute. I can hear Georgia breathing through her nose. It's not the sound you want to hear.

She stabs her finger at the TV, voice quavering with rage. "Okay, *that*? That is *utter fucking horseshit*." Her voice rings off the walls in the still room.

"Georgia," Mom says softly.

Georgia's eyes blaze. A lioness in a tank top and yoga pants. "No. Don't *Georgia* me. That is total and complete *nonsense*. Does he not get it? Does he not grasp that it was *his* dumbshit son who caused this? And he wants *Carver* to go to jail?! No. I'm sorry. No." She shakes her head in a way that would put cartoon dollar signs into a chiropractor's eyes.

We're all still stunned. Unspeaking.

Georgia looks at each of us in turn, seeking our eyes. Looking for our spirits. Our fight. "Carver, give me your phone. I'm calling His Honor's honorable ass right this second, and I'm telling him to go ride a bike with no seat."

"Georgia," my dad says.

She extends her hand to me with a snap. "Give it to me." She sounds close to tears.

"I don't have his number in my phone," I say softly, dazed. "Only Mars's cell phone." And then I add in a whisper: "Obviously I have Mars's cell phone."

"Georgia, calm down," my dad says. "He is a *judge*. You call him and curse him out, you'll go to jail."

"Then what?" she says. "What are we going to do?"

Dad takes a deep breath and rubs his eyes. His hand trembles. "I don't know. I—I don't know." He looks at my mom. "Lila, call your brother and see if he can recommend a good criminal lawyer in town."

The words "good criminal lawyer" are three knees to the ballsack in quick succession.

Mom returns to their bedroom for her phone, but not before I see tears welling from her eyes and tracing down her cheeks in shining trails.

"I start school in three days," I murmur. I'm as paralyzed as when I heard about the Accident. It's like I've left my body and I'm watching myself receive the news. I try to take a deep breath. *Please don't have another panic attack. Not here. Not now.* I hear my mom from her bedroom, talking to her brother Vance, a business lawyer in Memphis. She's trying to sound casual and failing spectacularly.

Georgia sits beside me. I can tell she's consciously trying to be calm and soothing. She rubs my back. "Carver. Just— don't worry. We're here for you."

My dad embraces me. He smells of dryer sheets and black pepper. "Listen, pal. We're—you're going to be okay, all right? We'll hire the best lawyer in Tennessee if we have to."

"I'll drop out of college and work full-time to pay him," Georgia says, her jaw set.

"No, *I* will," I murmur.

"Nobody's dropping out. We'll handle this," Dad says.

"I'm telling y'all right now, straight up? If this remotely turns into a thing, I'm packing Carver's ass in my trunk and driving him to Mexico. I do not give a shit." Georgia becomes very country when she's angry. Which is funny, because she's a big-city girl, born and raised in Nashville.

Mom returns. She's struggling for composure. Her eyes are red and weepy. She sighs and speaks quietly to my dad. "Callum, I talked to Vance. He said he'd ask around to see who some of the best criminal lawyers in Nashville are. He said all we can do is wait."

"Wait. Oh, that's nice. That's going to be fun for Carver, his senior year of high school, while he's applying to colleges and doing without his three best friends. Waiting for the ax to fall," Georgia says. "This is such massive bullshit."

Leave it to Georgia to say exactly what I'm thinking. Well, all but the massive bullshit part. I wonder if I don't deserve to atone with my freedom. If someone or something isn't finally coming to collect some great debt I've incurred. Which would make this whole situation not massive bullshit at all, but normal-sized, small, or even nonexistent bullshit.

My head spins. "I'll be in my room." I need to brood.

My mom, dressed in her physical therapist's scrubs, hugs me and kisses me on the cheek. "You're not alone in this. We're standing by you."

"Carver, you want to go see a movie or something to take your mind off stuff?" Dad asks.

"It won't help. Thanks, though."

"I'll be in the den, then, working on my syllabus," Dad says. "If you change your mind."

"Emma's dad is a lawyer," Georgia says. "I'm going to call her."

I go to my room and sit on my bed. I text Jesmyn. **Are you free? I need someone to talk to.** While I definitely believe that spelling and grammar count, even in text messages, I'm not normally so formal. But it somehow felt weird to be any less so. Also, I'm already wishing I didn't end that sentence with a preposition. Also, what if I offended her by saying "someone to talk to," as if any warm body will do? Shit. Also, did it sound needy to say "I need someone to talk to"? I mean, of course it did. By definition it did.

No response. Not surprising.

I pace. That doesn't help.

I pray in my heart. But as I said, I'm only a casual believer, so while it helps me a little to have covered that base, it doesn't help a lot.

I drop and start doing pushups. I haven't done a pushup since junior high PE class. My arms burn. I manage ten before I have to rest. Then I start in on some more. I don't understand why I'm doing this. But it's helping a little.

"Carver?" Georgia's voice from the doorway startles me midpushup. I wish I'd closed my door all the way.

I jump up and clap the dust off my hands. "Hey."

"I talked to Emma and she's going to talk to her dad."

"Cool."

"What were you doing?"

"Pushups."

"Why?"

Sometimes you learn things the moment they come out of your mouth, like the information was hiding there, safe from your brain. "In . . . case I go to jail, I want to be able to protect myself."

Georgia shakes her head and her eyes fill with tears, but she says nothing. My heart is thudding. She hugs me. "I have to work in a little bit. Otherwise I'd hang with you all day."

"At least I didn't have another panic attack, right? I'm going to Percy Warner."

Percy Warner Park is about a ten-minute walk from my house and encompasses acres of forest and miles of trails. Sometimes, the only way I have of dealing with stuff is to be around things more ancient than me and my sadness; things that will forget me.

Maybe when I get home, Jesmyn will have texted me.

⊡ ⊡ ⊡

They're all doubled over on Eli's couch, their controllers at their sides, laughing over my latest, especially ignominious demise.

"Did you see where his body fell?" Blake says, wiping tears.

"Look, shitlords, my parents won't let me have a game console. And I have a life, so I don't sit around practicing video games twenty-four/seven. So I suck. Whatever," I say.

But my explanation only invites louder guffaws.

"Blade's spinning in circles, shooting, and throwing grenades wildly until someone comes up behind him and clocks him with the butt of their rifle," Mars says.

"Imagine if he were really in the army," Eli says.

"No, please, everyone pile on the big video-game loser," I say. "Anyway, Mars, you should be a lot better, like genetically. Wasn't your dad a Marine or something?"

Mars snorts. "Yeah, he led a Marine company in the first Gulf War. Won the Bronze Star and a Purple Heart for some shit he won't talk about. Stop trying to change the subject from your sorryness."

Blake stands up and starts quickly spinning in a circle, making tossing motions. "Here's Blade: '. . . and a grenade for you, and a grenade for you, and one for you, and let's don't forget *you*,'" he says, in an exaggerated singsongy preschool-teacher voice. They're all practically pissing themselves laughing.

"What if Blade applied his video-game skills to other stuff?" Mars says, trying to catch his breath.

"Like if he were a waiter," Eli says.

"Eat a bag of elephant buttholes, y'all. A gigantic old-timey burlap sack full of elephant buttholes. With an elephant butthole printed on the side like a dollar sign," I say. They howl.

Mars stands up. "Here's Blade as a waiter. He stands in the middle of the restaurant throwing everyone their food: 'Here're some rolls for you! And some coffee for you! And some meat loaf for you! And some . . .'" He hesitates.

"He can't remember any more food," Eli says. "Mars's forgotten food."

"It's hard to think of food when you're on the spot," Mars says. "Hurry, name a food right now. Go. Name a food."

"Grilled cheese sandwich," Eli says immediately.

"Name another one," Mars says. "Hurry. Quick. Name another food. Any food. Go. Come on. Name a food. Do it."

"Uh—soup," Eli says.

"Another. Quick!" Mars says.

"Uhhhhhhhhhhhh."

We all crack up.

This is what I was doing at around this point last year. I'm not sure it was exactly three days before school started, but it was close.

As I walk among the trees, sweating, I dwell on my possibly

impending prosecution. I think about Jesmyn. I wonder if I'll be able to think the same way on walks around a prison exercise yard. But mostly I recall that time Sauce Crew laughed together. One among many; it wasn't anything special.

I'm not sure why this moment burns like a torch in my memory, but it does.

◻ ◻ ◻

When I get home, Jesmyn still hasn't called or texted. But Darren Coughlin has left a message on my phone asking me to comment on what Judge Edwards said. I guess he tracked down my number somehow. I don't tell my parents and I don't call him back. What would I say? *I sure hope I don't go to jail even though part of me is convinced I deserve to. I'm sorry I killed my friends. I'm sorry.*

Chapter Eight

It's eleven-thirty; I'm almost asleep when my phone buzzes.

It's Jesmyn. Sorry just got your text. Practicing all day. Still need to talk?

I dial her so quickly, I drop my phone. I manage to pick it up as she answers.

"Hey," I say softly.

"Hey," she says. "What's up?"

I lie on my bed and put my hand over my face. I groan-sigh. *"Ahhhhgh.* I'm freaking out right now."

"Why?"

"Did you hear what happened?"

"No."

"Okay, Mars's dad is a judge."

"The superintense guy?"

"Exactly. So this morning, my mom calls me in; they're watching the news. And there's Mars's dad on TV and he's saying he wants the DA to investigate the accident maybe for criminal charges." My voice starts trembling at the end. I've cried in front of Jesmyn before, but no need to make it our new thing.

"Wait, what?! *Criminal* charges? What did you even do? You didn't shoot them. That's crazy."

One more person who holds me blameless. And an important person at that—my only friend left in the world. My racing blood slows. The tremor departs from my hands and voice.

"I don't know what'll happen," I say. "We're going to talk to a lawyer, in case."

"If you need me for anything, I can testify or whatever. I'll be like *Objection.*"

I giggle. "Pretty sure only the lawyer can say that."

"No way. I want in on the objection action."

"So yeah. There's my cool life. What did you work on today?"

She sighs. "A Chopin nocturne that I'm considering for my Juilliard audition. But maybe not anymore. I might switch to Debussy. Or I might do something totally different."

"Oh, I mean, how you not gonna do Debussy if you can do Debussy? Come on."

She giggles. "Shut up."

"Who's your favorite composer?"

"Oh, please. Why don't you ask me which is my favorite finger."

"Which is your favorite finger?"

"Hmmmmm. Middle, actually. Right hand middle."

"See? Favorite composer."

"No. That was a bad analogy. Who's your favorite writer? See?"

"Cormac McCarthy. Easy."

"Crowmac McWhothy?"

"Oh, come on."

"Shermac McCathy?"

"Dude. Stop." I can't believe she's managing to cheer me up after the day I've had.

" 'Cormac' is an alien's name."

She would have made a great honorary member of Sauce Crew. " 'Jesmyn' is an alien's name."

"No, seriously. Doesn't 'Cormac' sound like a Martian name?"

"Okay, it does kinda. Which works because he's from Planet Awesome. Have you seriously never heard of him?"

"Nope."

"Well, we gotta fix that. Where do you stand on cannibalism?"

"I would say . . . opposed? Generally opposed?"

"How about reading about cannibalism?"

"If it's a good story. If I'm, like, invested in the characters."

"All right."

Something lifts from my chest as we talk. As if I were

lying under a pile of stones, and someone is removing them one by one. An oh-so-gradual lessening.

We talk into the early morning. I have to plug my phone in. We both get so sleepy that by the end, we say each other's name every once in a while, to fill the interlude between topics. To make sure we're both still there.

Chapter Nine

My parents sit at the kitchen table having coffee and cereal when I stumble in. They look at me as though I told them I have an invisible friend who tells me to collect knives and save my pee in jars.

"Hey, sweetie," my mom says. "We heard you up in the middle of the night."

I rub my face. "Yeah. Couldn't sleep."

"You should rest today," my dad says. "School starts soon and you haven't been sleeping well. And this Judge Edwards thing can't be helping."

"I can't sleep anymore today. Plus I'm going to go help Blake's grandma weed her garden and do whatever else."

My mom hands me a bowl of cereal. "You still haven't talked to us at all about everything. It's been a week since

Blake's funeral. It's not healthy to bottle things up. If you won't talk to us, we want you to talk to someone."

"I've been through this with Georgia. I'm fine."

My dad tries to speak gently. "You're not fine. People who are fine don't go to the ER with panic attacks." He sounds frustrated. I can't really blame him, but he frustrates me too sometimes, so fair is fair.

"That happened once."

"Are you working on anything new? Any new stories or poems?" my mom asks. "That seems like it would help."

"No." Being asked the question while I'm totally blocked up certainly doesn't make me feel better. Maybe my muse was in the car with Sauce Crew.

As we sit there together, I can sense their minds turning, trying to take advantage of the opportunity. Looking for the right words. I know what the air feels like around people who are trying to find perfect words and coming up empty. So I eat quickly and stay mum.

As I go to brush my teeth, my dad says, "We love you, Carver. It's hard to watch you hurting."

"I know," I say. "I love you guys too." *And if it's hard to watch me hurting, imagine how the hurting feels.*

⊞ ⊡ ⊞

"Okay, check it out, y'all. Squirrel rodeo," Blake says.

"What, like we're going to ride the squirrels?" Mars asks.

"Yeah, we're gonna ride the squirrels. No, numbnuts, here's how it works. You see a squirrel by the side of the path, and you move to steer it onto the path. Then you follow it slowly. Not too fast, or it'll bolt and you'll lose. Every time it starts to go off the path, you move and cut it off, so it keeps going on the path. You have to keep it on the path for eight seconds. Squirrel rodeo."

"Just when I'm afraid we've reached the limits of your hillbillyness, you dig down deep," Mars says.

"At least he's not suggesting that we catch the squirrels and eat them," I say.

"*Yet,*" Mars says. "He's not saying that *yet.*"

"Y'all are never going to make the professional squirrel rodeo circuit with that attitude," Blake says.

"Listen, bruh, I signed up for a peanut butter and banana milkshake from Bobbie's Dairy Dip. I did not sign up to chase no damn squirrels with my last week of summer vacation."

"What if your dad could see you chasing squirrels around Centennial Park?" Eli asked.

"He'd be like, 'Thurgood? To *what end* are you chasing these squirrels? How will the chasing of these squirrels advance your studies and learning? Are you pursuing excellence in the chasing of these squirrels? Your grandfather did not march with Dr. King so that you could chase squirrels.'" Mars delivers these lines in an imposing, staid tone.

We crack up because Mars is exaggerating only a little.

Blake raises his hand for us to shut up and approaches a squirrel by the side of the asphalt walking path. "Here we go," he whispers, phone out and filming. He carefully herds the squirrel onto the path. For about seven seconds, the squirrel trots in front of him. Blake maneuvers to cut off each attempt by the squirrel to veer off the path until finally it bolts. He groans. We laugh.

For the next fifteen minutes, we all try our hand at squirrel rodeo while Blake films us. None of us is very good, but we enjoy ourselves.

Finally we sit under the shade of a tall oak, sweating in the close afternoon heat. Blake edits videos and posts them to his YouTube. Eli texts someone. Mars sketches. I work on a story on my phone.

"New tradition," I say after a while. "At the end of every summer before school, we grab some Bobbie's Dairy Dip, come to Centennial Park, and play squirrel rodeo." If Sauce Crew had official positions, mine would be Keeper of the Sacred Traditions. I love the idea of the families we choose having all the features of familydom, including traditions.

"A tradition to rival Christmas and Thanksgiving," Mars says.

"Way more fun than Christmas and Thanksgiving, dude," Blake says.

"What about when we're in college?" Eli asks.

"We'll do it while we're all home over the summer," I say.

We hang out that way in the relative cool of the tree-formed shadows splayed across the grass, the sunset a purple fire in the leaves. The cicadas hum in our ears like the Earth vibrating.

There's that feeling that you'll never be lonely again.

That every time you speak, someone you love and who loves you back will be listening.

Even then I knew what I had.

Nana Betsy takes a while to come to the door after I ring the bell. "Blade? To what do I owe this pleasure?" It's been a week since Blake's funeral and she still exudes rumpled bereavement. I'm familiar with this from looking in the mirror. Inside the house behind her, it's messier than I've ever seen it. The lawn is overgrown.

I pull my dad's work gloves from my butt pocket. "You said Blake helped you with the weeding and it was hard for you to do. So I'm here to help you weed the garden and do whatever else."

"Oh, heavens." She waves her hand. "You don't need to do that. I can pay a boy from the neighborhood a few dollars to do it. But come in. Pardon the mess."

"I do need to do it." I meet her eyes. "Please."

She fixes her genial, even gaze on me. "No you don't." She says it softly but firmly.

"Yes I do." And suddenly I want to cry, so I pretend to cough and look away. I have a flash urge to tell her about the possible DA investigation. As quickly as it comes, I quash it. I can't bear her thinking of me as a criminal.

She lets me compose myself before she answers. "All right. Let's go in the backyard. I'll show you what needs done. Meanwhile, I'll run to the grocery to pick up a few things to make fresh lemonade and feed you lunch. You deserve better than the week-old leftovers I've been living on."

I really don't. "You don't need to do that."

"Blade. This is not up for debate."

We go into the backyard. She shows me where to weed. She gets me a basket for the ripe tomatoes. She shows me to the lawn mower and gas, and how to use it. She drives off to the store, and I set to work.

The salt of sweat burns my eyes in the syrupy, stagnant midmorning heat, the sharp, herbaceous scent of tomato vines in my nose. I lose myself in the mindless rhythm of the work. I forget about Judge Edwards. I forget about Adair. I forget about Darren. I forget about the Accident. Maybe this is good practice for when I go to prison and I'm cleaning up the highway in an orange jumpsuit. *Bend down. Yank. Toss to the side. Bend down. Yank. Toss to the side. Bend down. Yank. Toss to the side.* At first I use my dad's gloves, but my hands are getting all sweaty so I cast them aside. My hands turn brown with dirt and green from the broken weeds. I don't even notice Nana Betsy returning.

I'm halfway through mowing the lawn when I see her waving to me from the porch. I cut off the lawn mower.

"Lunchtime! Bring in some of those fresh tomatoes."

I grab a few of the biggest and reddest ones and step into the blessed cool of the air-conditioned house, thoroughly wiping my feet.

"In the kitchen," Nana Betsy calls.

I start to enter the kitchen, but for some reason, I can't make myself. I want to go back outside and keep sweating; keep punishing my body. I want to feel hunger and thirst. I don't want Nana Betsy to give me comfort and refreshment.

"Come on now," Nana Betsy calls again.

I break my reverie and walk directly to the sink, scrubbing

the dirt and weed juice from my hands. On the kitchen table sits a loaf of white bread, a jar of Duke's mayonnaise, salt and pepper shakers, a pitcher of fresh-squeezed lemonade clinking with ice, a serrated knife, and two plates.

"Sit down," she says, pulling out a wooden chair from the table. "Nothing fancy, but to my mind, there's not a thing on God's Earth better than a fresh tomato sandwich on a hot day."

"I agree." My sodden T-shirt sticks cold to my torso in the air-conditioning.

Nana Betsy picks out one of the nicer tomatoes and cuts it into thick circles. She slathers mayonnaise on a couple of pieces of bread and lays some of the tomato slices on one of the pieces. "I'll let you do your own salt and pepper." She makes one for herself.

"Mmmmm," she says, getting up to fetch a roll of paper towels for us to use to wipe the pink tomato-mayo juice from our hands and faces. "Fresh tomatoes taste like sunshine, don't they?"

"Mmmm-hmmm," I say, taking a sip of the sharp, tangy lemonade. It makes my salivary glands ache. "They taste like summer." *Or they're supposed to. I don't deserve this and so it tastes like sand on my tongue, even though it's a perfectly fine sandwich.*

"That's exactly what Blake always used to say. He loved tomato sandwiches."

"Blake kinda loved all food."

Nana Betsy chuckles. "That he did."

"Once, Blake and I were over at my house, and we were

66

starving, but neither of us had any money to go buy some-thing to eat. And our fridge was full of all this gross kale and stuff because my parents were on a health kick. So we went through my kitchen for something we knew how to cook. We found a pack of spaghetti, but we didn't have any sauce. So we ate it with ketchup and mustard."

Nana Betsy snorts and covers her mouth. She's shaking with laughter.

"So anyway," I continue, "I take maybe two bites, but Blake? He loves it. Eats the whole rest of the bowl. And he goes 'Blade, Blade, we should make this a new food. We should call it hamburger spaghetti. Hamsghetti. We should sell this idea.' And I go 'Blake, the only reason you find this edible is you're so hungry. This is totally gross.' "

Nana Betsy is sniffling and wiping tears, but they're tears of laughter. For a moment, I don't feel guilty anymore. The smallest taste of redemption. And it's sweet on my tongue.

"Boy, between the two of us, we really had Blake's num-ber, didn't we?" Nana Betsy says.

I catch an errant drip of tomato juice. "Yeah."

"Funny how people move through this world leaving lit-tle pieces of their story with the people they meet, for them to carry. Makes you wonder what'd happen if all those peo-ple put their puzzle pieces together." Nana Betsy takes a big bite and stares off, looking contemplative. "I have a crazy idea. *I* think it's crazy."

"Go ahead."

"Something I most regret is that I never got to have a last day with Blake. Nothing fancy. No climbing Mount Everest or skydiving. Just doing the little things we used to love to do together. One more time."

She rocks gently and closes her eyes for a second. Not as if sleeping. As if meditating. She stops rocking and opens her eyes. They've regained the tiniest glimmer they had before all this, and it's the only ray of hope I've felt in the last month. As if happiness is something that you can never extinguish entirely, but that lives smoldering under wet ashes.

"What if we were to have one last day with Blake? You and I."

"I'm not sure I follow."

"I mean we get together and have the last day that Blake and I never got to have; the one that you and Blake never got to have. We put our pieces of Blake together and let him live another day with us."

I feel like I'm halfway to my car with something I've shoplifted, and I hear a security guard yelling for me to come back. "I mean, I—I don't know if I could—I—"

She's sitting forward now. "Course you could. First off, you two were thick as thieves. Bet you knew him in ways I didn't."

"Maybe."

"And I bet I know plenty about him that you didn't."

"Definitely."

"Second of all, Blake's let me read your writing."

"He did? What?"

"The story that takes place in East Tennessee after a volcanic eruption kills most everyone off. I loved it. I'd meant to say something earlier."

"Wow."

"Point is: if anyone can write Blake's story again for one more day, it's you."

"But. Are you sure you want *me*?" *Because I wouldn't want me.*

"I'm sure. Who else could do it?"

Deep trepidation knots my guts. "I don't know."

"You don't have to answer now. Think about it. What's the worst that could happen? It wouldn't be exactly like having Blake. But we can't have Blake. So maybe we can have this."

Her eyes are gentle. There's less distance in them than the last time I saw her. I don't want to say no. But I can't bring myself to say yes.

"You don't owe me a thing," she says. "If you can't do this, I'll understand. Maybe I'll wake up tomorrow morning and think it's a bad idea or that I can't handle it. But will you consider it?"

"I will. I promise." I study her face for any sign that I've broken something. I see none. At least there's that. "Thanks for lunch. I better finish the mowing."

Nana Betsy leans across the table and hugs me for a long while, her hand on my cold back. "Thank you," she whispers.

⊞ ⊞ ⊞

I lie on my bed, still wet from the shower, with my fan blowing on me. I find this soothing. It conjures up getting out of the wading pool when you're a carefree kid and letting the sun dry you.

I plan my night. Most have been spent sitting around watching Netflix with Georgia. But she's going out with friends. I suddenly realize how quiet and barren my life has become. How little my phone beeps with a new text or call. How many solitary nights lie ahead of me.

I don't want to be alone. Normally I'm fine with it. But not tonight. My mind turns to my sole possibility for company.

I start to text Jesmyn but equivocate. *Is this weird?* We've had a sort of emotional connection, but was it somehow conditioned on the moment? On the detachment of texting and talking on the phone?

Under other circumstances, I might have agonized more. But loneliness breeds a desperate courage—the what-do-I-have-left-to-lose? kind. I text her before I can reconsider.

Hey. Want to hang out tonight?

My phone buzzes. Totally. What time?

I sigh in relief. **7? I can pick you up.**

Cool. 5342 Harpeth Bluffs Drive.

It's like I finally opened the seal on a jar of salve.

I go to the kitchen and warm up some grocery-store rotisserie chicken I find in the fridge.

"What are you up to tonight?" Georgia asks. She sits at the kitchen table, texting, dressed to go out.

"Hanging out with a friend," I say through a mouthful.

"A man-date or—"

"No, Jesmyn. Eli's girlfriend. The girl you saw with Eli's parents at Mars's and Eli's funerals."

"The hot one? You should've introduced me."

"She and I have gotten closer since then."

"What're you guys doing?"

"I have a couple of ideas. Mostly talking."

This is the point when Georgia would ordinarily be teasing me. Mussing my hair. Trying to give me a wet willie. And I wish she would, because that would be a concession to normalcy. It sounds weird to say out loud that I'm hanging with my deceased friend's girlfriend. I need Georgia's teasing to tell me it's okay.

Instead, she gives me an aw-isn't-it-great-that-your-life-is-moving-forward pat on the shoulder. "It'll be healthy to talk with someone."

My mom walks in. "Hey, honey. How's Betsy doing?"

"Fine," I mumble through a bite. "Sad."

"Dad and I are watching a movie tonight. You're invited."

"I'm going to hang out with a friend tonight."

Her face registers pleased surprise. *I didn't know you had any other friends.* "Do we know him?"

"No."

"Okay. If you change your mind or get home early, we're here."

"I appreciate it."

Georgia's giving me a look, so I scrupulously study my plate until I'm done eating.

❖ ❖ ❖

Jesmyn lives in Bellevue. It's about fifteen minutes from my front door to sitting in front of her house in one of the treeless, anonymous tracts of new housing that dot that part of Nashville.

I'm fifteen minutes early. I'm chronically early places. I'm used to waiting for things to start.

I sit in front of Jesmyn's house until seven, listening to music and wondering what Eli thought when he pulled up here for the first time. This neighborhood couldn't be more different from Eli's. He lived in Hillsboro Village, near Vanderbilt University, in a beautiful old house on a tree-lined street. I wonder for a second if he can see me sitting in front of his girlfriend's house. I hope that if he can, he can see into my heart and see how much I wish it were him sitting here instead.

At exactly 7:02 (I've learned it unnerves people when I walk up right on time), I knock on Jesmyn's front door. A tall white guy with thick gray hair answers.

"Oh . . . sorry, I might have the wrong house," I say.

He smiles. "Are you looking for Jesmyn?"

"Yes."

"I'm Jesmyn's dad. Jack Holder. Nice to meet you."

We shake hands. "I'm Carver Briggs. Good to meet you."

"Come in."

Her house is spacious, clean, and white. White ceilings, white walls. The scent of berries and green apples. The hardwood floors gleam. Everything looks new. A huge grand piano occupies part of the living room.

"You have a beautiful house," I say as I follow him up a carpeted staircase.

"Thanks," Mr. Holder says. "We only completely unpacked a month ago. We've been here since about mid-May, right after Jesmyn's school let out."

"What brought y'all to Nashville?" I ask.

"Position with Nissan. Realizing that the Madison County school system was probably not the springboard to Juilliard that Jesmyn needed."

We walk down the hall. Mr. Holder turns to me. "So . . . were you friends with Eli?"

"Best friends." I knew I'd get the question, but it still stings.

"I'm so sorry."

"Thank you." I wish I could gather into a stadium every single person on Earth who'd ever be inclined to express their sympathies for my loss at any time. Then, at the count of three (and perhaps the firing of a cannon), everyone would express their sympathies simultaneously for thirty seconds. I would stand in the middle of the field and let the sympathy wash over me in a tidal wave. And then I'd be done once and for all with the slow trickle.

"To a father, no guy is ever good enough for your daughter. But I always thought Eli seemed like a nice and talented young man."

"He was."

We walk up to an open bedroom. Mr. Holder peeks his head in and knocks on the doorjamb. "Jes? Honey, your friend is here."

I peek around him. Clothes are strewn everywhere. Concert posters cover her walls. Modern music, classical music, new posters, vintage posters. Jesmyn sits at a synthesizer connected to a laptop with a cable. I hear the hushed thumping of keys as she plays with her eyes closed, headphones on. Her face has a beatific expression—so different from her mournful look when last I saw her, which was at the funeral. I regret interrupting. She jumps at the sound of her dad's voice. She glances over at us and then at her laptop. She hits the space bar, pausing what appears to be a recording program. She pulls off her headphones and sets them on top of her synthesizer.

"Hey, Carver. Sorry, lost track of time."

"No worries," I say.

Mr. Holder leans against the wall.

"Seriously, Dad?" Jesmyn says.

"Jes."

She rolls her eyes. "We're gonna be up here for like two minutes while I put my shoes on."

I blush. "I can wait downstairs—"

"No, it's fine. Carver, it's a pleasure," Mr. Holder says. He holds up two fingers to Jesmyn with a cautionary lift of the eyebrows. "Two minutes and I'm coming back up." He goes downstairs.

Jesmyn rolls her eyes at his back. "Sorry."

"Dads be daddin'." I nod at the laptop. "What are you working on?"

She waves it off. "Oh . . . it's—I write and record songs. Just a thing I'm trying. Come in. The clock is ticking, apparently."

I step over a pair of jeans and sit on her bed *(the bed Eli used to sit on)*. "I thought you only played piano."

"It's all I do well. Eli said you write."

"Yeah. Not songs or anything. That's my dad's thing. I

74

write short stories and poems and stuff. I want to write a novel someday."

"He said you were good."

"I don't know."

"You got into Nashville Arts."

"Yeah."

Jesmyn walks to her closet. She faces away as she sits and pulls on a pair of socks and her battered brown cowboy boots. This is how I'm used to seeing her (if you can be used to seeing someone you've seen maybe seven other times). Not in funeral black. A flowy, white sleeveless blouse and cutoffs. Her fingernails and toenails are painted two white, one black, one white, one black. Piano keys.

It casts a shadow on my heart that these are the circumstances under which I'm watching a beautiful girl ready herself to leave the house with me. In an ordinary existence, this moment would hum with endless possibility. It would be the precise second when the supernova of love is born. Something you tell your grandkids about: *I remember when I went to pick up your grandma for our first date. She wasn't ready yet. I got to see her playing her keyboard for a second or two, looking like a leaf slowly falling; drifting on the wind. She stopped and I sat on her bed and watched her find a pair of clean socks. She grabbed the straps on the sides of her cowboy boots and sat on the floor, pulling them on, leather creaking. Her room smelled like her honeysuckle lotion and some sort of heady incense that smelled both new and ancient to me. I watched her making these everyday movements, and even in such an ordinary moment she was extraordinary.*

This moment is a cruel parody of that. It doesn't belong to me. There's nothing beginning here. We're bidding something farewell; laying one more thing to rest.

I hope someday it feels right again to pick up a girl and get ice cream and eat it at a park.

I hope there are beginnings in my future.

I'm tired of burying things.

I'm tired of the liturgies of ending.

Chapter Ten

We sit in my car outside Jesmyn's house.

"Do you have something in mind?" Jesmyn sits cross-legged in the passenger seat. Girls are light-years ahead of guys in sitting-on-car-seat innovation.

"Kinda, yeah. You down with Bobbie's Dairy Dip?"

"Never been."

"Your dad said y'all just moved here. I remember Eli mentioning that."

"Yep, from Jackson, Tennessee. Few months ago."

"Do you like Nashville?"

"You kidding? There's music everywhere. I belong here."

"So Bobbie's Dairy Dip is an ice cream place. We used to get peanut butter and banana milkshakes there."

" 'We' meaning you and Eli, Mars, and Blake?"

"Yeah. It was kind of a tradition."

"Both the Southerner and the Filipino in me dig the sound of peanut butter and banana milkshakes."

I start the car and pull away. My mouth outruns my brain. "So I didn't realize—"

"What?"

Shit. "You're adopted."

She cocks her head quizzically. "Wait . . . what?"

"Uh."

She turns in her seat. "What—what are you saying?" she asks softly.

I'm slack-jawed.

"My whole life is a lie," she whispers, her face solemn. "My obviously white dad and mom are not my real parents?"

I'm still speechless.

She laughs. A clean, bright, and silver sound, like wind chimes. "Come on, dude," she says. "Does 'Jesmyn Holder' sound like a Filipino name to you?"

I can't help but join her laughing. "I'm not an expert in what's a Filipino name and what isn't."

"*Holder.* As in the English word for one who holds something."

"All right. Well."

"Well."

"Were your ancestors way into holding stuff or what?"

"I guess? Like . . . swords or geese or horseshoes or whatever old-timey people were into holding."

"Whatever it was, they were into holding it enough that that's what everyone thought they should be named."

We pull up to Bobbie's. "So what's your deal, ancestry-wise?" she asks, not moving to unbuckle her seat belt.

"My dad is Irish—like literally from Ireland—my mom is some mix of German and Welsh or something."

"Really? Your hair and eyes look too dark to be Irish."

"My dad says we're called 'Black Irish.'"

"Does your dad have a cool accent?"

"He's lived in America for a long time, so it's pretty faded, but yeah."

A stab of guilt steals my breath. Eli isn't here because of me, while I joke around with his girlfriend and talk about who we are and where we came from; while we partake of a tradition that should have been Eli's. I beat down a wave of queasiness and dread. *Please, God, not here. Not now. Not a panic attack in the Bobbie's Dairy Dip parking lot with Jesmyn Holder sitting cross-legged in the passenger seat of my Honda Civic.* I stare forward and inhale deeply. And again. And again. Jesmyn's voice snaps me back.

"Hey. Carver. Are you okay?"

I look over at her but can't form words. I'm trying to decide how honest to be, but my mind isn't working right.

"You look pale," she says. "Everything cool?"

I nod unsteadily and take another deep breath. "Yeah. Just . . . a thing. I'm cool."

"You sure?" She unbuckles her seat belt.

I start to say yes but surging nausea cuts me off, so I give a thumbs-up.

⊞ ⊞ ⊞

By the time we get our milkshakes, I'm better.

"Did Eli ever tell you about squirrel rodeo?" I ask, pulling out of Bobbie's parking lot and driving toward Centennial Park.

Jesmyn gives me the expression you would expect from someone just asked about her familiarity with something called "squirrel rodeo."

"I'm guessing not," I say. "We had this tradition where after we got milkshakes, we'd go to Centennial Park and play squirrel rodeo. It's a game where you try to steer squirrels along a path."

"I can't imagine why Eli didn't brag to his cool girlfriend about this," she says.

"It's more fun than it sounds."

"Is that even possible?" A hint of a smile at the corners of her mouth.

I smile and we drive on.

"So," I say after a while. "How are you?"

"I've been having trouble sleeping," she says.

"Same. I wonder if I'm ever going to feel normal again."

"I was talking about it with my mom. She lost a friend in college. She said it takes time. There's not a pill you can swallow or anything."

Even if there were such a pill, I'm not sure I'd let myself have it. I'm not sure I would feel deserving.

"So your parents are pretty good to talk to?" I ask.

"Definitely."

"That's cool."

"Do you talk with your parents?"

"Not really."

"Why?"

"I mean, they're great parents and they're always telling me I can talk to them. I just don't. Too weird."

She licks a drip from the side of her cup. "Do you have anyone to talk to? Obviously we're talking, but . . ."

"Yeah, my sister Georgia. We're tight. But she starts up at UT like a week after our school starts."

"I wish I had siblings closer in age. I have two older brothers, Bo and Zeke, but they're ten and twelve years older than me."

"Wow."

"Yeah, they're married and have kids and stuff. They don't even live around here. I'm basically an only child."

It's dusk when we arrive at Centennial Park. We start walking.

"All right, squirrel rodeo time," I say.

"What am I supposed to be doing?"

I explain.

"So I have to keep the squirrel on the path for eight seconds?" Jesmyn asks.

"That's right."

We pass people holding hands, having picnics, taking engagement photos, kissing, throwing babies in the air. Summertime parks are where the most vibrant displays of living go on. I wonder if watching people live is something that will ever again fade into the background for me.

I examine Jesmyn's face for some clue of what she's thinking. I'm unable to read her yet.

She busts me. "What?"

"Nothing."

"Do I have something on my face?"

"No."

"Okay," she says softly, pointing at a squirrel by the side of the path, its tail twitching. "Start the clock." She moves carefully and steers the squirrel onto the path. It jumps a few feet and stops. She pursues it with quick, fine steps, her cowboy boots making a clip-clopping on the pavement, like little hooves. The squirrel leaps along the path a few more feet and starts to veer off to the right. She cuts it off and it keeps moving along the path.

I watch her in the yellow haze of the declining day. She moves with a certain natural rhythm; maybe because she's a musician. It's a relief to find beauty in something.

She turns back to me, smiling. "How long?"

"What?"

"Dude, you were supposed to be timing me."

"I had a panic attack," I blurt out, unclear on why I chose this exact moment to confess this.

Her smile dims; a cloud covering the sun. "What? Like while you were timing me?"

"No, no. The night of Blake's funeral. I had a full-on panic attack. My sister took me to the hospital and everything."

"Holy shit, Carver." She motions to a nearby bench and we sit.

"I'm okay now. The doctor didn't even give me any medicine."

"What was it like?"

I start to answer but pause to let a couple with a stroller pass by. "Being buried alive. Falling through ice."

"What are you going to do to treat them?"

I lean forward and run my fingers through my hair. "Maybe I'll—I don't know, actually. Maybe see if they keep happening, and if they do I'll talk to someone, I guess."

"Like a psychiatrist or something?"

"I don't really want to."

"It's what I'd do if I were you."

"Are you talking to someone? Professional?"

"Not besides my parents. But I would if I were having panic attacks."

We sit there for a while without saying anything.

"I'm sorry this night's turned into such a bummer," I say. "It was supposed to be fun. Getting back to normal a little bit. Doing the tradition."

"You knew Eli. Did you think all our dates were rainbows and ponies and ice cream?"

"No."

"Not that this is a date."

My face reddens. "I know."

Thankfully, Jesmyn doesn't acknowledge my embarrassment. "We talked about real shit that matters. I'm not scared to have genuine conversations."

"Me neither."

"Then this friendship has a shot, I guess."

"I hope."

We settle into a comfortable silence and watch the sky

darken, the sun setting. The breeze is soft, as though the day's breathing is slowing before it sleeps.

When I finally speak again, it's not to fill the lull but because I want to talk. "Blake's grandma invited me to spend one more day with her. I guess we'd do the things she wishes she and Blake had gotten to do together for his last day on Earth. Try to re-create his personality or story or whatever."

"How would that work?"

"Never done one."

"That sounds tough. Like emotionally."

"Oh, I've considered that."

"Are you gonna do it?"

"Not sure." I want to tell her how hungry I am for some absolution. But that would be an admission of guilt, and right now, that's my secret, a box of snakes under my pillow. I also want to tell her how afraid I am that I won't be able to do Blake's story justice and that's what's making me hesitant.

A few moments slip by. "You ever been to the beach in November?" I ask.

She shakes her head.

"I have. Once. My aunt got married on the Outer Banks of North Carolina. In November. Georgia and I were so excited to be going to the beach. We packed swimming suits and everything."

"Isn't it way cold?"

"Our parents tried to tell us that, but we didn't listen. Anyway, we get there and everything is closed. Nobody around. The beach is freezing. But you couldn't tell how cold the beach was by looking. There aren't leafless trees there or anything. The ocean looks the same; everything looks the same. So it could be summer, except that the beach is deserted and everything's closed. It's a really sad and lonely feeling."

Jesmyn tucks a stray lock of hair behind her ear. "I bet."

"That's me now, inside. Beach-in-November."

Jesmyn stands. "Come with me."

"Do you want to go home?"

"No, to where we can see the skyline. I'm still not used to getting to see skyscrapers every day."

We walk to the other side of the park, where we have a view of Nashville's skyline, twinkling in the humid distance. Jesmyn sits in the grass.

"Not worried about chigger bites?" I ask.

"Not really."

I sit beside her. "I'd hate for us to have any unshared tribulation."

"I can see why Eli liked you so much."

"You can?"

"Yeah. You use words the way a musician uses surprise chords in a song."

"That a good thing?"

"I'm not going to insult you after you've enriched my life by showing me squirrel rodeo," Jesmyn says with a half smile.

"Did you and Eli talk about music a lot?"

"Does ninety percent of the time count as a lot?"

"Talking with me must be pretty beach-in-November."

She shakes her head and stares at the buildings, rising bone white into the sky. She looks distant. Haunted.

I study her face. "Sorry if I said something dumb."

"You didn't."

"What then?"

She keeps her eyes fixed on the skyline. She takes a deep breath. "I'm scared. School starts in two days and I'm not sure I'm ready anymore."

"Me neither."

"Even with Eli gone, I have one more friend going in than I expected. But I'm still terrified."

"I have a lot fewer friends than I expected. So I get it."

Jesmyn shifts position, sitting cross-legged. She picks at blades of grass. "And now I'm scared of dying before I do all the things I want to do in life. Seventeen years isn't enough. There are so many pieces I want to learn. I want to record albums and perform. I never used to obsess about dying."

"Me neither. I sometimes look at my bookshelf now and think about how someday I'm going to die without ever reading a lot of the books there. And one might be life-changingly good and I'll never know."

Jesmyn reaches over and gently picks a ladybug off my sleeve. "Will you go with me on the first day of school? Like walk into the school with me?"

"I was going to ask you the same thing."

Jesmyn lies on the grass with her hands behind her head. I stay sitting.

"I have an idea," she murmurs.

"Yeah?"

"We should make a rule that we only spend some of our time talking about the past."

"Probably a good idea." I'm glad she suggested it, because I don't feel like I have the right to.

"It doesn't mean we care about them less. It just means that we still have to live."

On the street adjoining the park, a car passes, blaring music from open windows. A group of seven or eight Vanderbilt-aged kids walks past, giggling and chattering. A father and mother stroll by on the path, the father carrying an exhausted toddler on his shoulders.

Night descends as a falling blanket. The city is a constellation of lights, each one representing a hand that turned the lightbulb. A hand attached to a mind containing a universe of memories and myths; a natural history of loves and wounds.

Life everywhere. Pulsing, humming. A great wheel turning. A light blinks out here, one replaces it there. Always dying. Always living. We survive until we don't.

All of this ending and beginning is the only thing that's infinite.

Chapter Eleven

I text Jesmyn almost immediately after arriving home from dropping her off. **I had fun tonight.** I should wait. I don't want to come off as a weirdo. But also I'm now keenly aware of how important it is to tell people what you want them to know while you can.

After a few seconds: Me too.

Let's hang again soon, I reply. **It felt good to talk.**

Definitely, she replies.

A liquid rose-gold warmth—whatever color is on the opposite end of the spectrum from the color of aloneness—fills me briefly.

And then I wonder if Eli, wherever he is, can see me texting his girlfriend, talking about what a blast we had hanging out without him. I hope he can't. I wouldn't want him to get the wrong idea.

Chapter Twelve

I'm sitting at home; it's morning on the day before school starts. I'm psyching myself up for our meeting with my lawyer in a few hours and this weird surge of bravery comes over me. I feel ready to tell Nana Betsy *Yes, I'll do it. I'll do the goodbye day. I'm strong enough to handle it.*

I drive out to her house, park, walk up the driveway, and make it all the way to the door. Then I completely chicken out. It's like my courage was playing a prank on me.

I consider knocking on the door anyway and seeing if she needs any help with anything and not mentioning the goodbye day. But I'm scared she'll bring it up. She'll read the cowardice on my face and smell the stink of guilt on me. So I slink away, hoping maybe she'll forget ever suggesting it.

Chapter Thirteen

The lawyer's oak-paneled waiting room smells like leather chairs, musty paper, and cigarette smoke on clothes from whoever was here last. Dotting the walls are paintings of golfers and hunting dogs with various fowl in their mouths. Generic waiting-room magazines (*Sports Illustrated, Time, Southern Living,* etc.) sit on an end table, but none of us are reading. On the whole, it's a fairly shitty way to spend the last afternoon before school starts, but I seem to be in the "fairly shitty way" business lately.

I sit between my mom and dad. My dad shifts in his seat and keeps crossing and uncrossing his legs. My legs bounce while I rest my elbows on my knees and stare at the weathered hardwood floor. My mom lightly rubs my back. Her touch calms me a little. Thank goodness Georgia is at work. She'd be riled up and riling me up right now.

The only sound in the room is the clicking of the receptionist's perfectly manicured fingernails on her phone screen as she texts.

▨ ▨ ▨

"Lawyers, bruh," Mars says, pulling up the seat across from me.

"Yeah," I say.

"Naw, for real, though, dude. I would know."

"Your dad."

"And my brother. Don't forget my brother too. Just like my dad. Man, they would team up on me, lawyer my ass in the most mundane circumstances you can imagine."

"Like?"

"Oh. We're playing a board game and my dad's like, to my brother, 'Marcus, you cannot make that move,' and my brother's like, 'Yes, I can, because if you examine the structure of the rules generally, they express the implicit intention that I should be able to make this move,' and my dad's like 'Blah blah, but if you go beyond the text of the rules as written, blah blah, I don't even know.'"

"Let me guess: whichever one of them won the argument, you lost."

"Ding ding."

"So here I am, sitting in a lawyer's office, waiting for him to tell me how he's going to argue with another lawyer to try to save my dumb ass. And whichever one of them wins, I'm going to lose. To some extent."

"Correct."

"One of them might win, but I'll lose."

"That's what I'm saying."

"You're a real help, dude."

"I try."

"This sucks."

"I know." Mars gives me that lopsided smile of his and adjusts his glasses.

"We maybe should have gotten together and tried to avoid this mess."

"I'm already avoiding it."

"Good point. So how you doing, man? Everything good where you are right now?"

But he's already gone.

⊞ ⊞ ⊞

A door opens at the end of a short hall, and a guy who resembles an anthropomorphic coyote, with icy blue eyes and facial tattoos, swaggers out. He looks like an outlaw. A tall, portly man with shaggy, longish white hair, wearing a gray pinstripe three-piece suit, follows him.

"Mr. Krantz? Carver Briggs is here," the receptionist says to the white-haired man.

Mr. Krantz comes around the receptionist's desk, hand extended. We stand as he shakes our hands.

"Folks, Jim Krantz. Call me Jimmy. Pleasure. This way." He has a syrupy drawl.

We enter a small conference room with a round mahogany table, bookshelves full of green and tan law books with gilt lettering, more leather chairs, green-shaded lamps, and more hunting and golf pictures.

"Sit, sit." Mr. Krantz gestures. He pulls out a chair, sits with a grunt, whips a pair of reading glasses onto his nose, and pulls out a legal pad and an expensive-looking gold pen. "All right, folks. Tell me what seems to be the matter."

I sit there, mute. My dad clears his throat and tells Mr. Krantz about the Accident and Judge Edwards's call for the DA to open an investigation. Mr. Krantz grunts and takes notes. Then he leans back in his chair and nods at me. "Okay, son. Tell me about this accident. What was your role, if any? I remember reading about it in the paper just after it happened, but I don't recall that they said exactly what caused it. Something about texting?"

My legs start bouncing again. I hiccup acid, clear my throat, and take a deep breath. "I was at work. Um. I was supposed to hang out with my friends, Blake, Mars, and Eli. They were coming from Opry Mills Mall, where they'd gone to an IMAX movie. They were going to swing by my work and we were going to go to the park and hang out. So I texted Mars, 'Where are you guys? Text me back.' That's all it said."

Mr. Krantz doesn't look up from his note-taking. "Who was driving?"

"Mars. Edwards."

"That's Fred Edwards's son?"

"Right."

"Did Mars text you back?"

"No, but there was a half-finished text to me on his phone when they, um. When—"

"Okay, I gotcha," Mr. Krantz says softly, looking up from his pad. "Now Carver, everything we talk about in here is

93

strictly protected by attorney-client privilege, which means nobody can force you to tell them what we discuss. That goes for your parents too, because they're necessary parties to your defense. And that privilege exists so that we can be completely open and honest with each other, so I can best defend you if it comes to that, all right?"

I nod.

"So I need to ask: were you aware, when you texted Mars, that he'd probably text you back?"

I feel like I do that moment right before I'm about to slip on ice. I try to blink away the tears welling up in my eyes, but some spill. "Yes."

"Were you aware Mars was driving at the time?"

"Pretty sure," I whisper. It hurts to say this in front of my parents. I know I'm letting them down.

"Why text Mars and not one of your other friends in the car?"

"Um." I'm crumbling.

"If you need a minute."

"Um. Because Mars always answered texts the quickest. Even if he was driving. I was being impatient. I wasn't thinking." A tear splats on the green carpet of the conference room and slowly expands. My mom rubs the nape of my neck.

"Okay," Mr. Krantz says softly, and leans back in his chair. He sets down his pen, pulls off his glasses, and chews on one of the earpieces for a moment, apparently deep in thought, allowing me to pull myself together. Or at least try.

"It's obvious he didn't intend to hurt anyone," my mom says. "This is ridiculous."

"Well," Mr. Krantz says, still chewing on his glasses. "Yes and no." He rises, walks to a bookshelf, and pulls down a green volume. He puts his glasses on and leafs through it quickly. He sits.

"Folks, I won't sugarcoat. Under Tennessee law, there's an offense called criminally negligent homicide. Used to be called involuntary manslaughter. Criminally negligent homicide happens when someone takes 'a substantial and unjustifiable risk' and 'the failure to perceive it constitutes a gross deviation from the standard of care that an ordinary person would exercise under all the circumstances as viewed from the person's standpoint.' "

I don't fully comprehend what he's saying, but I understand what "unjustifiable risk" and "gross deviation" mean. A purple spasm twists my stomach.

"Can you translate?" my dad asks, rubbing his forehead. "I'm a damned college English professor and you lost me."

Mr. Krantz whips off his glasses again. "Means if you got a pretty good idea that you're doing something that could get someone killed, and you go ahead and do it, you're on the hook even though in your heart you never intended to kill anyone. This is sort of the hot new thing in prosecution. Up in Massachusetts, they tried to pin manslaughter on a girl who encouraged her friend by text message to commit suicide. Similar idea here."

My insides are trying to crawl down my leg. An almost aggressive silence hangs in the room like a plume of nerve gas.

"So it's not ridiculous. And the state's best bet to prove it will be to wrangle Carver into saying exactly what he told me. But he doesn't ever need to do that, because the Fifth Amendment protects against self-incrimination." Mr. Krantz eyes me with a hopeful glimmer. "You haven't told anyone what you told me, have you?"

I shake my head. "Not exactly."

Mr. Krantz raises an eyebrow.

"After Blake's funeral, a reporter tried to talk to me. Said Judge Edwards referred him to me."

"And you told him . . ."

"That I didn't really know what happened. That I was texting with Mars the afternoon of the accident."

Mr. Krantz chews on the end of his glasses and chuckles ruefully. "Edwards. That crafty son of a bitch. He knew he might get you to voluntarily incriminate yourself, and because a reporter isn't law enforcement, it would come into evidence at trial. Anybody else?"

"No."

"You got a girlfriend?"

"Uh . . . no. I mean. No. I have a friend who's a girl. She's just a friend, though."

"Don't tell her anything."

"Okay."

"What are the chances the DA won't file charges at all?" my dad asks.

Mr. Krantz blows out, his cheeks puffing. "That Judge Edwards can be a scary character."

"We noticed," my mom says.

"There's some delicate stuff going on here politically. The DA, Karen Walker, is up for reelection next year. She needs

Davidson County's black vote to win. Edwards holds tremendous sway with that voting bloc. Plus Walker's people are in front of Edwards day in and day out. So politically, this issue is two for the price of one. She makes it into Edwards's good graces, and with it comes the black vote and she can grandstand about the perils of teen texting. Maybe even garner national attention. Sets herself up for a senate or gubernatorial race someday. She's a winner the minute she indicts, even if she tries Carver and loses. And there's an old saying that a good DA can indict a ham sandwich."

"That is some bullshit," my dad says in a low, trembling voice. I've never heard him use that tone before. It makes me afraid, hearing him afraid.

"Yup," Mr. Krantz says.

"What do we do now?" my mom asks.

Mr. Krantz leans forward with his elbows on the table, hands clasped in front of him. "We wait. See what the DA does. Meanwhile, Carver, you do not talk to *anyone* about this without me present, understood? The cops ask you your favorite color? I don't want you answering until I'm sitting next to you."

"Okay."

"And in the meantime, Carver lives under this cloud," my dad says.

"Pretty much," Mr. Krantz says. "It's a shit show, no doubt."

"Is there any good news?" my mom asks.

Mr. Krantz reclines and clasps his hands behind his head, sucking at a tooth. "Carver wasn't in that car."

We wrap up our meeting and leave. Dad walks on my right side, Mom on my left. I'm hanging my head. "I'm sorry, Mom and Dad."

My dad puts his arm around me. "You have nothing to apologize for. You did not intentionally hurt anyone."

"Accidents happen," my mom says. "Even terrible ones."

"This must be costing a ton," I say.

"Don't worry about that," my dad says.

"How much *will* this cost?"

"It doesn't matter," my mom says.

"It matters to me."

"You have enough to worry about," my dad says, removing his arm from my shoulder and rubbing the back of my head.

I was just curious, but now I *need* to know. "I got us into this mess. I think I'm entitled to know."

My dad dodges my eyes. "Look. Keep your mind on school, get good grades, stay on top of scholarship applications. That's how you can help."

I stop walking. My parents make it a few steps farther before turning back to me. "How much?" I ask quietly. With my face, I try to tell them I'm not taking another step until I get an answer.

My dad looks at my mom. She gives him an ambivalent "if you must" nod. He wipes his hand down his face. "When all is said and done, hundred, hundred fifty is what they told me."

Something bright and hot detonates in my mind. *"Thousand?!"*

"That's if it goes to trial and we lose and need to appeal," my mom says.

I close my eyes, dizzied. "But still."

"We'll borrow against the house if we need to," my dad says.

"We could lose our house?!"

"Let's cross one bridge at a time here," my dad says.

"Don't think that way," my mom says. "We need to think positively."

How's this: I am positively fucked.

⊞ ⊞ ⊞

I flop on my bed and text Jesmyn. **Well, that sucked gray, smelly rhino ass.**

After a few minutes, she texts me a frowny face followed by Big hugs. Want to talk about it?

Basically, they could charge me with negligent murder.

Seriously????? Shit.

Yeah. Oh, and this will cost a bazillion dollars, so my family's going to end up homeless, too.

If I were there I'd give you a huge hug.

I would gladly accept said hug.

Tomorrow morning. When I come to pick you up.

Deal.

Chapter Fourteen

It's 7:17 a.m. on the first day of school at Nashville Arts. Jesmyn is supposed to be here in three minutes. I've been awake since 3:57 a.m. If there's a hell, I imagine existing there in a perpetual state of having woken up two and a half hours before you need to be somewhere. And that's even without the anxiety over maybe going to prison and the knowledge that today will be the air on the exposed nerve endings of my loss. I'm going to be reminded more today of Sauce Crew than at any point since the funerals. And I don't know how I'll react.

Those are the cons. On the pro side, Jesmyn will be here in three—no, two—minutes. And I'm excited to see her even though (because?) she's part of the reason I couldn't sleep.

I sit in my room, finishing the last couple of bites of a Pop-Tart. I brush some crumbs from my bed. Georgia sticks her head in.

"First day of schoooooool," she says. "Looking sharp."

I have my normally untucked button-down shirt tucked into my khakis. I'm wearing a blazer. My hair is neatly combed. As neatly as it'll go, anyway. "I gotta represent on the first day," I say around a forced smile.

"Oh, you're reppin' *hard*. Doesn't school start at eight? You better head."

"Jesmyn is picking me up."

"I'm happy y'all are hanging out even though I don't know her."

"Me too. You'd dig her."

"It blows about the circumstances, but . . ."

"Yeah."

"How you doing this morning?"

"I've been up since four."

Georgia leans against the doorframe. "Holy shit, Carver."

"I couldn't stop my brain."

"You're the only seventeen-year-old boy on Earth with that problem."

I shrug. "Well."

"Couldn't you even, like, spank it to get back to sleep? That's a thing dudes do, right?"

"What if I told you I tried that twice and it didn't work."

"*Ewwwww!* You are the grossest."

"*You brought it up.* Serves you right."

Outside, Jesmyn's battered white pickup pulls up to the curb. I see her bend down as if rearranging things.

I jump up from my bed and grab my bag. Georgia steps away from the doorway to let me pass.

101

"Come here," I say. "Come give your little brother a huge hug."

She recoils and lifts her leg as if to kick me. "Sick, no. Keep your jizzy hands away."

I put my finger to my lips to shush her, even though Mom's in her bedroom. "I was totally kidding."

Georgia hugs me gingerly, wincing.

"No I wasn't," I murmur midhug.

She pushes me away. "Don't be such an actual, literal hog around Jesmyn."

I contort my face into a cheery grin and speak in a robotic voice. "We here at Carver Industries value your feedback! Your comments are important to us! Unfortunately, we are not accepting personal criticisms at this time!"

"The cool thing about that joke is how it never gets old."

"The cool thing about your face is how it never gets old."

"Okay, well, this has been fun. Have a great first day, dingus."

"I'll try. Bye, Mom!" I call in the direction of my parents' bedroom.

My dad's already left for work at Belmont University. Today was his first day back too. My mom comes out of her bedroom, where she's been preparing for work, and meets me at the front door as I'm leaving. She hugs me and kisses me on the cheek. She's perfumed with the sort of no-nonsense lotion that smells like pleasant chemicals but works really well. "Have a good day, sweetie." There's a wistful tinge to her voice. It wouldn't surprise me if she were remembering the two mothers and one grandmother who aren't bidding their boys farewell today for school.

I take off my blazer on my way down my front walk, remembering that Jesmyn's AC doesn't work. I open the door and get in. It's a lot cleaner than the last time I was in it. It looks like she vacuumed. I smell vanilla. Jesmyn is wearing tight black jeans and black ankle boots with a blue denim western shirt. Something about how immaculately she's put together makes my gently seething nervousness roil. *Oh, right. School really is starting today.* Not that I'd forgotten, but . . .

"Miss Punctuality," she says. "Go me. And now for that hug I owe you." She leans over and we embrace for several seconds. It simultaneously takes the edge off my nervousness and hones it to a new sharpness.

"You look nice." I sit back and buckle my seat belt. She drives off.

"Thanks. I'm surprised I even fit in these jeans right now. My mom made my favorite breakfast and I completely pigged out."

"What was it?"

"Biscuits and gravy, grits, country ham. Fresh-squeezed orange juice."

"That's funny that's your favorite breakfast."

"Why?"

Oh, shit. Shoulda thought before speaking. "Because—"

"Because I'm of Asian descent and therefore it's funny that I enjoy Southern food? I'm from Jackson, Tennessee, dude. Racist."

My stupid mouth. "No, I'm sorry, I totally didn't intend it that way. I mean, maybe I did a little, but I swear I wasn't trying to be an asshole."

She laughs. "I'm just giving you shit. That is racist, though."

"I really didn't mean any offense."

"Don't worry about it."

"I say dumb stuff when I'm nervous."

"At least it's not your first day at a new school in a new city." She pauses with a smirk. "Full of racists."

"I deserve that." I roll down my window the rest of the way and rest my elbow on the sill. "It's *because* it's not a new school that I'm nervous. Everybody knows what happened. Everyone's going to be staring and whispering probably." As I say it, the bubbling inside me begins to boil faster.

"Eli said people are generally pretty cool there."

"They are. Mostly." *Mostly when Adair isn't turning the screws on them, though.* I angle a vent blowing tepid air toward my face. "Ever notice how every time we hang out, we're both sweating our asses off?"

"We've always hung out in August."

"Good point."

"You had Sauce Crew. Now you have Sweat Crew."

I let the words melt on my tongue. She's joking, but I relish their taste. "Sweat Crew. Yeah."

"Do we have any classes together?" she asks. "Let's see."

I pull out my schedule. "I have AP English lit, creative writing, writing critique group, lunch, AP history, teacher's aide, and AP biology. How about you?"

She starts to pull out her schedule. I instinctively put my hand over hers. "Not while you're driving."

"Don't worry," she says softly. "I was giving it to you so you could read it."

She gives it to me, and I read: music theory and sight-reading, piano performance, lunch, show choir, calculus, yoga. "Yeah, not much similarity here." This is no surprise. I rarely had classes with Eli, Blake, or Mars. Eli was always music heavy and Mars was always drawing/painting heavy. Blake and I sometimes had writing classes together, but then he had his A/V stuff that I didn't.

I tuck her schedule in her bag. "Do you want to hang out at lunch?"

"No, I'd rather have that moment when I'm walking through the lunchroom with my tray and nobody will let me sit with them."

"She'll be here all week, folks. Don't forget to tip your waiter."

She turns up the volume on her stereo. "This is one of my favorite songs."

"What is it?"

" 'Avalanche' by Leonard Cohen."

"I've never heard of Leonard Cohen."

Her expression is abject disbelief. *"Whaaaaaa—* Dude. We *gotta* fix that. You're a writer. He's like *the best* writer."

"I'm a little dumb about music. I listen to whatever people—Eli, Georgia, whoever—introduce me to."

"Okay, then you're going to start listening to music I introduce you to."

"Deal. What's funny is that my dad used to be a song-writer. That's why he came to America and moved to Nash-ville. He even had a medium hit in the nineties."

"Are you serious?"

"Yep.

"Come on."

"It was called 'When My Heart's Torn Up.' Bowie Lee Daniels cowrote it and performed it."

She pounds the steering wheel with both palms. I notice that her fingernails are painted in the NAA school colors: blue, except for her ring fingers, which are painted yellow. *"I've heard that song a million times.* I used to have to line dance to it in grade school PE."

"Sorry."

"No, it's cool. You said he *used* to be a songwriter?"

"He teaches English at Belmont now."

"I want to meet him."

"Someday."

We pull into the NAA parking lot and my heart starts pounding. I'd lost myself in our conversation. Jesmyn navigates to a parking space, parks, and turns off her truck.

She sits there for a second. "Hey. While we're talking music. Have you ever heard of Dearly?" She sounds slightly tentative.

"Yeah. I haven't listened to him much. Georgia's a big fan."

"We have a lot of work ahead of us," she mutters, shaking her head. "Anyway. I have two tickets to his show at the Ryman in October." She hesitates for a moment. "I was going to go with Eli. Do you want to go?"

Inwardly, I'm screaming, *Yes, yes, of course.* Meanwhile, my mind is saying, *Ahem. Now you're actually taking something that belonged to Eli. It's only a concert ticket and he's not around anymore to use it and he'd want a friend to have it, but nevertheless, you are taking something that belonged to Eli and using it to have a good time with his girlfriend while his ashes sit in an urn.*

"Yes," I say, as a lightning pang of remorse seizes my stomach. I swallow it down. "I'd love to."

⊞ ⊞ ⊞

We're standing in the parking lot outside NAA's front doors, gathering our will to enter the modern, boxy, glass-and-steel building with reclaimed-wood accents. We have probably ten minutes before the first day of junior year starts.

"Come on," Blake says. "We gotta make an entrance. People will expect it."

"Of *you*," I say.

"I'm not going to walk in first day of school and fart or something," Mars says.

"Yeah, I'm not looking like an asshole potentially in front of Olivia," Eli says.

"Because that ship hasn't sailed," I say.

Eli grabs me in a headlock and starts noogie-ing me. "Dude, stop, you're messing up my hair. Dick." I break the hold and pull away.

Blake stands between us, arms outstretched. "Okay, when you guys are done playing grabass"—he pronounces it *grahboss*—"I want to go over the plan."

I smooth my hair. "Listening."

"So we're gonna walk in—we'll all be walking in slow motion—"

"Dude, that's lame," Mars says.

Blake raises his hand in a pleading gesture. "No, listen. Then I'll do my plan. But y'all can't laugh or anything. You have to keep walking. Cool?"

We groan and roll our eyes. "Okay, cool," we all say, as if it's a great imposition, even though we're dying to see what Blake cooked up. I know I am.

We wait for a space between people walking in, and then we go. Blake's in front; we're dispersed behind him. It's hard to walk in slow motion, but we do it. Through the glass doors. People milling around in the entryway, chatting, stop to stare. At NAA, you stare when you see Blake Lloyd has something up his sleeve.

Slightly ahead of me, I see Blake's pants start to sag precariously. Then they're off his butt. Then they're down around his knees. He's having trouble walking. We're trying to play it straight and keep up our slow-motion stride. Mars covers his face with his hand in slow motion. Then Blake's pants are around his ankles. He's wearing tighty-whities.

He breaks slow motion and jumps forward a couple of steps, then stumbles, arms flailing, and skids onto his front. While falling, he hurls his backpack along the floor ahead of him. It's unzipped. About twenty issues of *Cat Fancy* magazine slide across the floor, fanning out.

We've completely broken character, and along with

everyone else, we're watching Blake scuttle around on the floor like a crab on ice, grunting and wheezing, trying to stand. We're howling with laughter. He almost makes it up but puts his hand on a *Cat Fancy,* slips, and hits the deck again. He goes around on his hands and knees, red-faced, gathering his magazines, tighty-whities gleaming.

Finally he makes it to his feet, pants still around his ankles. He addresses the cackling throng, which includes Adair and her friends. "Hey, everybody. First day, huh?" There's a weighted pause as people suppress giggles to hear what Blake will say/do next. And of course: *phthththththththththt-phphphphph.* He rips one, sharp and stuttering, with a certain full-bodied richness at the finish. The crowd goes bonkers. Full-on applause.

It was as sublime a piece of choreography as I've ever seen. I couldn't tell how much of it was planned and how much was improvised. Blake has a unique talent for making planned things seem spontaneous and spontaneous things seem planned.

The still-tittering crowd disperses at the bell and hurries to class. We're high-fiving Blake.

"I gotta admit, bro, that was good," Mars says, wiping tears. "You pulled through."

"Two thumbs up," Eli says. "I saw Adair filming."

"Make sure you talk to her. I want video," Blake says.

As we head to first period, I notice Blake walking oddly. "Hey, did you hurt yourself?"

"No, no." A pause. He's clearly making a concerted effort

to sound nonchalant. "I don't guess any of you guys have an extra pair of clean underwear you're not using right now, do you?"

■ ■ ■

"This building is so fancy," Jesmyn says. "It looks like it belongs in L.A. or something. My last school looked like it belonged in . . . Jackson, Tennessee."

"Uh-huh," I say.

"You totally weren't listening," she says.

"No, I was."

"Liar."

I take a deep breath. Dread has started to seep down my body—indigo-purple dye injected into my brain, dispersing through my bloodstream. "I was thinking about something else."

"Them?"

I nod.

Her hand weighs light and warm on my shoulder, over my backpack strap. I'm vaguely aware of the people flowing around us into the building while we stand like sticks jammed in a creek bed. I hold my blazer wadded up in my hand. What I thought made me look cool and authorial, I now realize, makes me look funereal.

"You're not alone, at least," she says. "Neither am I. That's something."

"We should probably go in. It's about to start."

"Well. Shall we?" Jesmyn asks.

"We shall, I guess," I say, as though she suggested walking onto the thin ice of a frozen lake.

The smell of gentle (art school parents can be pains in the ass) industrial cleaning chemicals assaults my nose. Soft green sage and cedar, rather than electric-cough-syrup cherry and neon-laboratory pine. It's a smell I used to love because it signified the possibility and promise of a new year. I enjoyed first days of school. When I had Sauce Crew. The scent puts my memory of last year's first day in sharper relief. And that heightens my sense of festering dread.

The entryway atrium is a hive of activity. There's a perceptible hush as Jesmyn and I walk in. Like somebody turned a volume knob down an eighth of a turn. People try to continue their conversations, but I see the abrupt shift in topics as they eye me sidelong. On their faces: *There's Carver. What do we do? Do we talk to him? Do we sully ourselves by associating with him?*

Then I spot Adair, flanked by three of her friends. She catches my eyes and stares jagged icicles at me. She mutters something to one of her friends. I imagine: *Look, there's Carver showing up on the first day of school with his dead best friend's—my brother's—girlfriend. I wonder if he even waited until my brother was ash before trying to move in.*

I have a slow-motion sensation again, but this time it's not intentional. It's not funny. Blake isn't slightly ahead of me, nudging the waistband of his pants downward.

I sense Jesmyn at my side. I'm vaguely aware she's said something, but my ears only catch whispered snippets from the crowd. *There he is. . . . Seems okay. . . . Haven't heard . . . Eli's girlfriend . . . Don't know her name.* Then I hear Adair clearly through the murmurs and mutters. "Great day to be alive, huh?" she says to one of her friends.

I suddenly can't imagine even one moment of happiness here all year. An invisible anaconda winds around my chest, squeezing, crushing. My heart strains against the pressure. My throat clenches. A sheen of sweat forms on my forehead like an ice slick on a bridge. My mouth is parched.

And then, as if pushed by an unseen hand, my head turns involuntarily to the right. There, in a glass display case normally used to showcase student awards, paintings, drawings, photographs, and other creations, are photographs of Blake, Eli, and Mars against a black background. The words "In Memoriam" float spectral and silver above them. *Look, see Carver's creation. His magnum opus. Isn't it funny that the one piece of writing he ever did that most impacted people's lives was a lethal text that said,* Where are you guys? Text me back.

"Carver?" Jesmyn says, sounding as if she's distant from me and echoing down a cavernous marble corridor. She lightly touches my left upper arm. But I don't acknowledge her because the following thoughts command my full attention: *I need air. My picture should be there too. I need air. I will never be happy again. I need air. I'm going to jail. I need air. Adair hates me. I need air. Everybody thinks I'm moving in on Eli's girlfriend. I need air. Everybody hates me. I need air.*

My head heaves like I'm on the deck of a ship. Then, that falling-through-ice sensation. That watching-something-heavy-and-fragile-slide-off-a-shelf feeling. Dark spots congregate in my field of vision. I need air. I need air. *Not here. Not now. Not this. Not in front of Jesmyn. Not in front of everyone. Not in front of anyone.* But it's too late to call it back. It built like some awful orgasm; once it tips there's no return.

My blazer slips from my grasp. My backpack slides off and thumps on the floor. My laptop is inside, and I would be more concerned but for the minor fact that *I cannot breathe I'm being buried alive I need to breathe I'm dying.*

Jesmyn faces me now, both her hands on my arms. She's blocking me from the crowd's view. "Carver," she's whispering, "Carver, are you okay? Are you having a panic attack?" I see the horde gathering behind her.

I nod, short and quick, so as not to stir my vertigo. My legs go numb beneath me. My heart thunders. Nausea rises in my gut.

"Out," I wheeze.

"Okay." Jesmyn puts her arm around me and starts to help me turn to leave. As soon as I unroot from my spot, I lurch to the side and stumble a couple of steps, catching my toe. I slip from Jesmyn's light grasp and careen into the wall. My head impacts with a fleshy thud directly below the photos of Sauce Crew. A collective gasp sweeps through the crowd. I imagine this would be embarrassing if my need for oxygen weren't reigning supreme over my need for dignity. *Blake would be proud as he looks down on me.* A few people step tentatively forward, uneasy expressions on their faces. "Call Nurse Angie," someone says. *What a gift this must be for Adair.*

Jesmyn kneels beside me. "I'm here. I'm here for you," she whispers, her lips against my ear, the flower and fruit scent of her hair brushing my face.

She helps me to my unsteady feet and grabs my bag and blazer, and we stumble out the door. I keep my eyes down and try to ignore the slight murmur of disapproval that I'm not waiting for Nurse Angie. Jesmyn's hand grips my upper arm. She has strong fingers, no doubt the result of exercising them for hours each day.

I stop for a second as my stomach heaves.

"Are you okay?" Jesmyn asks.

I take a few deep breaths and nod. Latecomers hustle past, casting me looks of concern. Jesmyn directs them away with her eyes.

I was already sweating in the air-conditioned cool of NAA. Outside is a steam bath. My forehead drips. My shirt sticks to my back like a leaf to a rainy window. We reach Jesmyn's truck after what seems like a mile.

She lowers the tailgate with a rusty clunk. "Here, sit."

I nod quickly, showering the ground with droplets of sweat. I sit with my head bowed, as if praying. *Thank you, O Lord, for this gift I have received: to have an utter shit fit of a panic attack in front of everyone on the first day of school, including the twin of my best buddy who—whom—I killed, the twin who now hates me, and my new (and only) friend, Jesmyn, who happened to be her twin's girlfriend. Give me this day my daily humiliation. Amen.*

Jesmyn rummages in the cab. She comes up with a scratchy gray blanket that smells like hay. She folds it in the bed of the pickup to form a makeshift cot. She rolls up my blazer as a makeshift pillow.

"Lie down." She taps the blanket.

I squint against the brightness as I lie on my back. "I'm sorry for getting your blanket all sweaty," I croak.

"I like you enough, I don't even care if you make my stargazing blanket all gross," she says. "Bend your legs. Good." She slams shut the tailgate. Now I'm hidden from view.

Her head appears over the side of the pickup bed, in my field of vision, her face dark against the shimmering sky. She touches my cheek with a cool, soft hand. "What should I—"

"Go. I'll be okay. I'll call Georgia or figure something out."

"It's the first day and I'm late."

"It's cool."

"You have my number. Text me if you need me. I'll be sly and check my phone."

"Would you try to keep Nurse Angie from coming out here? Say I went home already."

"I got this."

"Thanks."

"No problem. All right, I better go."

"I must seem completely nuts."

"You don't at all. We'll talk." She touches my cheek again and then she's gone. I hear the quick clip-clopping of her running toward the school.

I reach for my phone to call Georgia but decide I'd rather lie here for a few minutes and gather my shit. Not that I plan to try sitting through a full day of classes. I'm too drained. I'm too— *Oh, man, the embarrassment.* That's starting to sink in now. My cheeks burn. Like wearing snowshoes to spread your body weight and keep yourself from sinking in snow, losses of dignity are best dispersed across several people to keep you from sinking. Now I'm alone.

My head throbs. I rub the tender, swelling lump growing on it. My eyes fill with tears. One slides warm down my cheek and falls with a soft pat on Jesmyn's stargazing blanket. Or rather: Jesmyn and *Eli's* stargazing (and what else?) blanket. *I guess that makes two things I've taken from you today, Eli. Your Dearly ticket and your spot on the stargazing blanket. But if it's any consolation, wherever you are, I've paid quite a price today in dignity for both. And I'm sure Adair will make sure I pay even more, if Judge Edwards doesn't get to me first.*

I gaze up into the luminous blue, framed in the metal walls of Jesmyn's pickup bed. Here we all now lie, all four members of Sauce Crew, in boxes. I'm the only one not in complete darkness. I'm counting Eli even though he was cremated. He's in an urn. Which is sort of a box. It's dark inside anyway.

I wonder if there was any moment, as they died, when they were able to look heavenward, as I'm doing now, through the torn-off roof of Mars's car. I was "assured" they died instantly. As though that would soothe me.

I wish it would rain. Torrents. So hard it would cleanse me of worry and trouble; so hard it would lift the stain of death from me and carry it to the rivers and out to sea.

Chapter Fifteen

*B*lake peers over the side of the pickup bed. "Hey, shitlord," he says softly.

"Hey," I say. Eli's and Mars's grinning faces appear next to Blake's.

"That wasn't bad," Mars says. "Not Blake level. But not bad."

"I'm the only thing that's Blake level," Blake says. "But yeah, decent."

"Thanks," I say. "Maybe if it'd been intentional, it would've been even funnier."

"The head smack at the end was what elevated it. That took it from funny to comedy," Blake says. "That's the secret to comedy—you gotta always take the next step."

"But next time," Eli says, "try to do it so you don't actually hurt yourself. It's funnier when people don't worry about your physical safety. Nobody wants that guilt."

"Thanks, dude. That's good advice," I say. "Guilt does blow."

I continue to massage the thickening lump over my right eye. I have a nascent headache from the radiating pain. I can tell it's going to make my eyebrow swell enough that I'll be able to see a tiny bit of it in my upper field of vision, driving me crazy. Turns out there's no real upside to collapsing in front of all your classmates two minutes into the first day of school and boinking your head on the wall. And then my mind is still as I watch a billowing ivory cloud lazily cross the sky. It's a dog. Then it's a frog. The ridges of the pickup bed are starting to dig into my spine. I roll onto my side, pull my phone from my pocket, and hold it for a second. I hear, somewhere in the distance, some shuffling; and then the door slams shut and there's the quick scurrying of feet. Then it's silent except for the far-off drone of car tires and thrumming pulse of insects in the trees; all the invisible life that surrounds me.

I call Georgia.

⌑ ⌑ ⌑

"Carver? Aren't you supposed to be in class?"

"Don't be mad," I say as my voice starts to quaver.

"I won't be, but tell me what's going on."

"I had another panic attack." I can hear Georgia fighting the urge to say *I told you so*.

"Shit. Are you okay?"

"Um."

"And of course you called me instead of Mom."

"Yeah."

"Where are you? Nurse's office or what?"

"Parking lot."

"Okay."

"Look for a white Nissan pickup. I'm lying in the bed."

She laughs and immediately catches herself. "Dude. You are having—"

"The shittiest first day of school ever."

"I'll be there in a few minutes. But I gotta rush; I have work."

"Fine."

We hang up and I lie there with my eyes shut, watching the kaleidoscope patterns on the insides of my eyelids. Finally a car pulls up behind the pickup. I still lie there, even when I hear the door open. I can't take the risk that it's someone other than Georgia. Lord knows I've had enough pratfalls today. I don't need to be jumping out of pickup beds and having spooked strangers call the cops on me.

I hear footsteps and Georgia's face appears over the side of the pickup bed, dark like Jesmyn's was against the brightness. It makes me jump, even though I was expecting her. We stare at each other for a moment.

"Carver," she says softly, and reaches out to touch the lump on my head.

I wince and gently bat her hand away. "Don't."

"How? Well, tell me in the car."

I sit up and wait for the head rush to clear. I'm completely sapped. I struggle climbing out of the pickup bed. I flop down in Georgia's car, rest my head against the headrest, and close my eyes. I realize I left my blazer in the pickup bed but I don't have the energy to return for it.

Georgia sits. "You owe me, dude."

I open an eye and look at her. "Why are you shitting on me? My friends died."

"I'm not shitting on you and you can't keep using your friends as an excuse. I tried to convince you to seek help, but no. Well, guess what." She whips out her phone, scrolls through her contacts, hits one, and holds the phone to her ear as she starts to drive away.

"Who are you—"

"Hi, this is Lila Briggs. I need to make an appointment." She's doing a spot-on impression of our mom's honeyed Mississippi accent. Under any other circumstances, it would be cracking me up. "Yes," she continues. "For my son, Carver. With Dr. Mendez. My daughter Georgia was a patient. First availability . . . okay . . . okay . . . excellent. That *is* lucky. Perfect. Ten o'clock tomorrow."

"Georgia," I whisper, but without conviction. I can admit when I've lost. Still, she casts me a caustic side eye. *Do not even,* her look says. I shrink.

"Okay, great. We'll see you tomorrow. . . . You too. . . . Bye-bye." She hangs up and fixes her eyes on the road.

"Georgia."

"Don't start." Her voice, sharp at first, eases. "I'm sorry; you are not okay. Yes, it's hard to admit when you need help. I know. So I'm going to be a good big sister and help you help yourself."

"Am I crazy?"

"Crazy? No. You're dealing with a lot and you're in pain and sometimes that makes us do bizarre things."

"It happened in front of everybody," I say quietly, staring out the window. A tear slides down my cheek. I brush it away with the back of my hand.

She reaches over and takes my other hand. "When we get home, you need to put some ice on your head."

I nod.

"A week from today I'm going to be in Knoxville, starting school too. I mean, we can talk on the phone and text and stuff, but . . ."

"I know."

"Then you know you need to trust other people and open up. You need to let Mom and Dad in more. You need to be honest with Dr. Mendez. If you can talk to Jesmyn, you need to talk to her. You can't be a dumb cowboy about this."

"Nana Betsy asked me to spend a day with her. Like a last day with Blake, but obviously . . . without him. Sort of a goodbye day for Blake."

"Wow."

"Yeah."

"That sounds intense."

"Very."

"See? Perfect example," Georgia says. "I have no *clue* if that's a wise idea. That's exactly what you should discuss with Dr. Mendez. He's way smart."

"I'm going. You made the appointment. You win. I surrender."

"*Yeah,* you do."

"Can you bust out Mom again?"

"Why?"

"I need you to tell my school I'm home sick."

"I should make you try to impersonate Mom."

"No you shouldn't."

"It would be funny."

"For you."

"That's why I should do it."

"Please?"

She sighs theatrically and makes the call.

We drive the rest of the way home, my mouth stitched shut in defeat. I guess I've finally lost a battle against myself that I needed to lose.

I wish I could have lost it more gracefully.

◫ ◫ ◫

"I gotta run to work. I'm already late. You have keys, right?"

I nod.

"When Mom and Dad get home from work, you're explaining all this to them. You are aware of this, right?"

I nod. "Thanks, Georgia."

"I'm taking you to your appointment. I want to say hi to Dr. Mendez."

"Okay."

She drives off and I trudge up the path to my house. Inside, it's tomblike. I hate the stillness of home-alone-when-you're-not-supposed-to-be. Everything sounds way too loud. The refrigerator clicking on and off. Clocks ticking.

122

The clink of glasses as you remove them from the cupboard. Heartbeats. The rush of blood in your ears.

And that's under normal circumstances. Now, silences feel like absences. Absences feel like loss. Loss feels like grief. Grief triggers guilt. Guilt is a scarlet anguish.

I sit in my room, listening to the house creak and pop, when the overwhelming urge to not be so alone sets in.

I have a text to Jesmyn halfway composed when I re-member: *You have very bad luck when you text people at in-opportune occasions. It does not turn out well for the people you are texting.* And so instead I lie on my bed with a bag of frozen peas over my eyebrow and stare at the ceiling for a while. That turns out to be less fun than you might imagine.

I sit at my desk and wake up my laptop. Maybe I can at least be productive on my college admission essay. Maybe that will assuage my guilt over sitting at home on the first day of school. I lean forward in my chair and start typing.

Ever since I was young, I wanted to be a writer.

Okay. Not particularly original or interesting. But a start.

The possibility of creating new worlds and people fascinated me.

This blows.

Just as this essay is probably fascinating you already. Hey, another kid who wants to go to college and has been fascinated by *[insert interest that would sound attractive to college admissions board]* since he *[insert age or formative experience engaging in said interest that suggests that the interest is genuine and not a contrivance to impress a college admissions board]*. But guess where my love of writing took me. One day I wrote a text message that killed my three best friends. Now do I have your attention? Sure, I've written a few stories here and there, but my masterwork was a two-sentence-long text message that ended three stories. I'm the only writer in the world who makes stories disappear by writing. And who wouldn't want to have such a unique and beautiful creature at their institution of higher learning, eh? So let me into your college and I promise to try not to kill anybody else with my writing. That's assuming, of course, that I'm not in prison by this time next year.

It's probably not the best idea, while you're feeling lower than hammered dog turds, to try to write the essay that's supposed to sell you to a college.

I'm exhausted, but I don't want to rest. I'm restless, but I'm too tired to do anything about it. I want to forfeit these hours of my life and make this day be over.

I'm lying on my bed, reading, when my phone buzzes. That's a much rarer occurrence now than it used to be. I jump up, making black spots appear in my field of vision, and grab my phone. It's Jesmyn.

How are you?

Super embarrassed. Sorry.

No need to apologize.

I glance at the clock. Lunch should be about ending.
I hope you didn't have to sit alone at lunch.

No, Alex Bishop invited me to sit with him and his friends.

My innards clench. Of course. Alex Bishop. If you had asked me to imagine a worst-case scenario for the first day of school, it would have gone in roughly this order: (1) I have a panic attack in front of everyone, including Adair, and make a jackass of myself; thus leaving (2) Alex Bishop to try to worm his way in with Jesmyn on her first day there. Alex is a dancer who's cut a fair swath through the female student body at Nashville Arts, including Adair, as it happens. I am not an Alex fan. Eli hated him. He would have loathed the idea of Jesmyn sitting down at a cafeteria table with Alex. I hate it on Eli's behalf.

Be careful of Alex.

Haha, he seemed nice.

"Seemed" = operative word.

Well you ditched out on me.

Not by choice.

I know. JK.

BTW, I left my blazer in your truck.

No prob, I can swing it by tonight after practicing.

You wanna hang out for a while when you do?

Sure. Sweat Crew represent.

For a fleeting moment, this exchange makes me feel normal again. As if I lead a rich life full of friendship and possibility. The feeling quickly dissipates and my mind returns to thoughts of prison and Judge Edwards, panic attacks and Adair.

I wonder if my life's center of gravity will ever shift back to where tiny moments of forgetting aren't lavish gifts.

◫ ◫ ◫

I'm not crazy about the idea of telling my parents, but I do. They're going to find out eventually now that doctors are in the mix. They seem relieved that Georgia finally prevailed upon me to seek professional help. My mom isn't even mad that Georgia impersonated her to make the appointment. "Dr. Mendez was wonderful for Georgia," she says. I have all the parents-telling behind me when the doorbell finally rings. I run to answer.

Jesmyn half smiles when she sees me. "Hey." Then her eyes stray to the lump on my head and her smile fades. "Oh, dude," she murmurs.

My fingers go to it. "I kept most of the swelling down by icing it. Come in."

"Oh, here's your blazer."

"Thanks."

I lead her back and peek into the kitchen, where my parents are cooking dinner and listening to NPR. "Hey, Mom and Dad, this is my friend Jesmyn. She just moved to Nashville and we go to school together. We met through Eli." That last part sounds strange to say out loud. *Hey, Jesmyn, meet Carver. Carver, Jesmyn. Okay, I'm just going to die and let you two hang out.*

My mom wipes her hands on a dishrag and shakes

Jesmyn's hand. "Hi, Jesmyn. Welcome to Nashville. Do you want to stay for dinner?"

"Oh, thanks, but my parents are planning on me."

"All right."

My dad waves from where he's chopping carrots. "Hi, Jesmyn."

She waves. "Hi. Nice to meet you."

I wish Georgia were here to meet Jesmyn. After the day I've had, I could use some cool-older-sister cred.

We return to the living room. "Want to go for a quick walk? I'm in the mood for walking and talking," I say.

"Sure. I gotta be home soon, though."

"Don't mind getting all sweaty?"

"We're not the Sweat Crew for nothing."

We do start sweating the moment we hit the muggy early-dusk heat. By halfway down the block, my shirt is plastered to my torso. The hazy air is fragrant with grilling hamburgers and cut grass.

"Your dad has a cool accent," Jesmyn says.

"Apparently it was way thicker when he and my mom met. It's faded over time."

"That's too bad."

"Yeah. It used to kind of embarrass me when I was little."

Jesmyn looks aghast. *"What?* That's like the sexiest accent."

"Aggggh! Every girl!"

"Just being honest."

"Just grossing me out." I wipe away a drip of sweat before it can get in my eye.

"You wish you were as cool as your dad."

"I wish I had his accent, for sure. So, not that I wouldn't love to talk all day about how sexy my dad is, but how was practicing?"

Her eyes brighten. "Awesome. The school has a Steinway concert grand. It sounded unreal. I mean, the *action* on that piano is, like, orgasmic. How do I settle for my piano at home now?"

Hey, I understand what that's like—to go from an awesome situation to a far less awesome one. "Oh, yeah," I say. "That piano's action is the best. They say playing it is like dipping your fingers in warm butter."

"Smartass. That *is* what it's like. Speaking of playing, how was playing hooky?"

"It blew. Georgia was basically like 'I told you so,' and I tried to work on my college admission essay instead of sitting around, but I froze up. What did you think of NAA?"

"It was cool but scary. At my old school, I was definitely the best musician. Here, I'm a lot more average. I was listening to some of the others play and they're amazing. But I guess it's good practice for if I get into Juilliard. Everybody was supernice, at least."

"Yeah, how was lunch with Alex Bishop? Did he share his, like, wolf-semen shake or whatever he eats for lunch?" I try to sound light and nonirritated.

Jesmyn gives a little squeal of disgust, giggles, and covers her mouth. *"That's nasty."*

I seize my opening, doing an infomercial-guy voice. "Wolf-seed. The only energy shake containing real, one-hundred-percent wolf sperm harvested from organic, free-range wolves. Guaranteed to endow you with vim and vigor so you can dance all day and night. Order now and receive a container of our shark-penis protein powder . . . *absolutely free.*"

She giggles harder and tries to cover my mouth with her hands. *"Stop. You're going to make me barf."*

I notice how crooked her fingers are; how they would only look right curled on piano keys. They're beautiful.

"But seriously," I say.

"Alex was nice, but he has a shirtless picture of himself as his phone's home screen. Ain't nobody got time for that."

"Eli hated Alex."

Jesmyn's smile dissolves. "Why?"

"Because Adair dated him and he dumped her about a week after she lost her virginity to him."

"Ouch."

"Everyone called them 'the ABs.' *A*lex *B*ishop; *A*dair *B*auer. And also because they both have insane dancer abs. They were an NAA celebrity couple briefly."

"That would explain why Adair kept looking at me like she wanted to sever my jugular with toenail clippers. I thought it was because you and I had been hanging out."

"I'm sure that too. You did not earn any points with Adair today."

"Because I had so many to begin with. She's always been weird to me. Like I was sucking up too much of Eli's life or something."

"She and I were never best friends or anything, but we used to be friends."

Our conversation sputters out as we walk the last few hundred yards to the gates of Percy Warner Park. So we stroll quietly under the thickening forest canopy covering the road, the leaves filtering the sunlight to a pale emerald.

Jesmyn starts to say something but stops herself. I look over at her. She's staring straight ahead. Finally: "Today, when I was practicing, I started crying. Randomly. Like I wasn't remembering Eli at that moment or anything. It's just—like what I was playing unlocked another door in me and stuff came rushing out. Grief is weird. It seems to come in these waves out of nowhere. One minute I'm standing in the ocean, fine. The next minute I'm drowning."

"Sounds familiar."

"I noticed."

I blush. "Thanks for the reminder."

"If you didn't feel their loss, what kind of person would you be?"

"The kind who has a shirtless picture of himself as his phone's home screen and drinks wolfseed?"

"Exactly." And then under her breath: "You are determined to make me yak."

What I'm determined to do is keep making her laugh, because her laughing makes me forget for at least a moment.

I stop and turn to her. "I like talking to you."

"Same," she says, facing me.

"I'm going to miss some of tomorrow too because I'm going to this therapist my sister used to see. Apparently he's good."

"Smart idea," she says.

"Do I seem that crazy?"

"No more than I do for randomly crying while practicing. But you seem like you're hurting."

"I am."

"We both are."

We walk to a nearby fallen log and sit down.

"I want to hear you play the piano," I say.

"Okay. As long as you let me read some of your writing."

"If I'm ever able to write anything again."

"You will. But I'll accept old stuff until then."

"Okay. When we get back, I'll give you something."

We watch some deer appear from the woods and begin to nuzzle around the margins of the meadow, cautiously approaching the middle to feed and sniffing the air.

"You're the best thing in my life right now," I say softly, so as not to scare the deer. "I'm glad we're friends."

Jesmyn shifts position on the log, making herself comfortable and—maybe it's my imagination—sitting closer to me in the process. "Me too."

Chapter Sixteen

The waiting room to Dr. Mendez's office is filled with sleek, modern furniture that still seems somehow organic and welcoming. Copies of the *Atlantic,* the *New Yorker,* and the *Economist* sit on the tables between chairs. Everything is in comforting hues of brown and gray. Nothing looks thoughtless or haphazard.

Georgia sits beside me, texting.

A door opens and out walks a slim man who looks to be in his midforties, wearing a well-tailored beige linen suit with no tie. His tidy beard is gray and his hair is graying at the temples. He's wearing rectangular tortoiseshell glasses.

He glows when he spots Georgia. "There's a familiar face!"

Georgia leaps from her chair. "Can I give you a hug since I'm not your patient anymore?"

Dr. Mendez gestures broadly. "Come here!" After they

break the hug, he assesses her. "You look healthy and happy." He has the faintest hint of an accent.

"I am both of those things. How are Steven and your kids?"

"Well, Aurelia is starting her first year at Harding Academy and Ruben starts at Stanford in a few days. And as for Steven . . ." Dr. Mendez holds up his left hand to show Georgia a silver ring.

She squeals and claps her hands to her mouth. "*Get out.* Congratulations! When?"

He beams. "June, in Sonoma, near where Steven grew up. Georgia, it was beautiful. Even my very Catholic madrecita was there, and I caught her shedding a tear."

"I could not be happier for you two."

"Oh, thank you, thank you." His eyes fall on me. "Now, who have you brought me?"

"This is my brother, Carver."

Dr. Mendez extends a hand. "Carver, it's a pleasure to meet you." His handshake is firm, warm, and generous.

"Good to meet you, Dr. Mendez."

He gestures into his room. "Shall we? Without further ado?"

I walk in. Behind me, Dr. Mendez says to Georgia, "Are you staying? If so, we won't bother with goodbyes yet."

Georgia says she's waiting until we're done.

I look around. More sleek, modern furniture, mixed with antiques. On the walls are framed vintage maps and old botanical prints. It smells like spice and wood—warm, brown, and clean. There are floor-to-ceiling bookshelves filled with books. Diagnostic manuals and other tools of the trade, of course, but also books of photography and painting, fiction and poetry. Leather-bound classics. Books in Spanish and English. I'm impressed.

Dr. Mendez shuts the door and gestures toward two identical brown leather armchairs facing each other, a coffee table with a pitcher of water, glasses, and a box of tissues between the two chairs. "Please, make yourself comfortable."

"I thought I was supposed to lie down on a couch." I'm only sort of joking.

Dr. Mendez laughs. It's a kind, warm laugh. "That's only in the movies. Unless you really want to, and then maybe we can rig up a hammock or something."

I make my way to a chair and sit. "No, it's cool. Sitting upright is fun too. I enjoy sitting upright." I talk too much when I'm apprehensive.

I balance on the edge of the chair, like I'm watching a scary movie, and try to keep my legs from bouncing. I fold my arms and then unfold them. Dr. Mendez's hands are empty. "Don't you take notes?"

Dr. Mendez sits, relaxed, facing me. "I do after the session. I find that if I try to while people are talking, I don't listen as well. Will it worry you if I don't take notes during the session?"

"No."

"Your sister obviously loves you very much."

"Yeah. She's always kinda looked out for me."

"How so?"

"I got a lot of crap in middle school, I guess. I was way

into books, which isn't a recipe for middle school popularity. Anyway, Georgia would stick up for me."

"I noticed you looking at my books."

I blush. "Busted."

He grins and waves off my concern. "Not at all. They're there in the open for all to see. But most people don't seem to pay them much attention. You did. You're a big reader?"

"And writer."

"Is that so? That's fantastic. I have a very boring novel I've been working on for, oh, twenty years. At this point, I enjoy the idea of writing a novel more than I actually enjoy the writing part. What do you write?"

"Short stories. Poems. I have some ideas for novels, but I haven't started anything."

"I hope I haven't dissuaded you by talking about my own struggles with finishing what I've started."

"No."

"Good. So. Let me introduce myself. My name is Raúl Mendez. I was born in Juarez, Mexico, and moved to El Paso when I was quite young. I grew up in Texas, did my undergrad at the University of Texas at Austin, before I came to Vanderbilt for graduate school and medical school. I've been here ever since. Now, have you ever been to a therapist before or did Georgia tell you how it works here?"

"No, not really. I mean, I guess we talk? I tell you about my mother? Find penises in Rorschach tests?" I wouldn't normally make such a joke around an adult I had just met. But he puts me at ease and plus I don't want to talk about heavy, serious stuff for as long as possible.

He laughs. He wags his finger and leans forward in his chair, adjusting his glasses. "Close. You talk; I listen. Sometimes I offer an insight about something you've said or ask you to elaborate on something. But I'm doing my job best when you're talking and I'm listening. I'm not here to give you answers to your problems. I'm here to let you discover answers on your own. So it may be frustrating sometimes that I don't come out and tell you what I think you should do, but I assure you that it's part of the process. Okay?"

"Okay. I guess. I mean, honestly, I don't super want to be here."

"That's normal."

"At least something about me is."

"So, Carver—interesting name, by the way—tell me about yourself."

I take a deep breath and run my fingers through my hair. "My name comes from Raymond Carver. My dad is a huge fan of his stories, so he gave me the name."

"I'm a fan."

"Of the name or of Raymond Carver?"

"Both. It seems you and your father have something in common there."

"We both love to read. He's an English professor."

"Sorry for interrupting, continue."

"Anyway, I'm seventeen and a senior at Nashville Arts Academy."

"Now there's a good school for a book lover. You must be an excellent writer to have gotten in there—I assume it was your writing and you're not also an extremely talented jazz saxophonist." He says the last part with an impish eyebrow raise.

"I am," I murmur.

He starts to get up. "As it happens, I keep a saxophone here for my clients, if you'd like—"

I smile. "I was kidding."

"Me too." His eyes sparkle. He pauses for a moment. "So. How are you?"

I cast my eyes over his shoulder and try to inject nonchalance into my voice. "I'm good. Yeah, doing pretty good."

"I'm glad."

"Yeah." I tap my fingers on the armrest, the way casual people do—the way people who are fine do.

"A lot of the people I see are doing pretty good."

"Then why are they here?"

"They want to be doing better."

"And?"

"Sometimes it helps. Sometimes it doesn't. I like to think it helps more often than it doesn't."

"You're not exactly unbiased."

He laughs. "No. True."

"Does it ever make people worse?"

"Are you dealing with something you're worried about therapy worsening?"

"I don't know."

"Are you currently dealing with something in your life you'd like to talk about?"

I consider saying no. But I guess that wouldn't be entirely plausible since, you know, I showed up for this appointment. "I—had a panic attack."

He nods. "When?"

"Yesterday."

"What were the circumstances surrounding it?"

"Aren't there medications for panic attacks?" I ask.

"There are."

"Then why don't we do that?"

"We will. I'm going to send you home today with a prescription for Zoloft, a drug I've used with success to treat anxiety and panic attacks. But I like to start people on a lower dose, so that their bodies can acclimate, and then it takes some tinkering to get the right dosage. It can take weeks before things are dialed in right. In the meantime, we'll be doing therapy. I've found this two-pronged approach to be the most effective."

"I just wanted to save you some time."

"I assure you my time is not so valuable that you're capable of wasting it."

"That sounds like a challenge."

He smiles. "Do you feel like you're in any physical danger? Like while driving?"

"I mean . . . not really. I know what an attack feels like now."

"Your safety is paramount. If you ever feel that you're in danger, I want to know immediately."

"Okay."

"What happened yesterday?"

I sigh. "It was as I was walking into school for the first day. Lost my shi—stuff."

Dr. Mendez shrugs it off. "Word things however you want. You won't offend me. I've heard it all."

"Lost my shit in front of everyone. Completely freaked out. Fell and hit my head. I went home. I just couldn't— That's why I'm here." It's exhausting to say all this stuff out loud—but surprisingly less so than carrying it around.

"So you have this first panic attack and—"

I break eye contact.

Dr. Mendez pauses. "This is something that's happened before."

I raise two fingers, still not looking him in the eye.

Dr. Mendez nods and sits back, forming a triangle with his fingers. "Have these panic attacks come in conjunction with some precipitating event? Some new stressor in your life?"

He earns points for using the phrase "precipitating event." He seems to have perceived that I don't have patience for people who talk down to me. But that doesn't make me any more excited to talk about said precipitating event.

I stare at the Oriental rug under me because I'm unsure what sort of facial expression is appropriate to introduce the death of your three best friends to a total stranger who you'd prefer not to be talking to. Impassiveness doesn't seem quite right. Smiling is definitely out.

"The stuff we discuss in here, it's super, super private, right? Like you won't tell the police?" I ask.

His face doesn't register even a hint of shock. "Absolutely

private. Unless I have reason to believe that you may be an imminent harm to yourself or others. Anything in your past is strictly between us."

"Okay."

"I don't want you withholding because you think *I* can't handle it. I promise you, I can."

"I've been under a lot of stress lately."

Dr. Mendez doesn't respond.

"I don't really want to talk about why."

He still doesn't respond. Just listens.

"I've barely even talked about it with my own parents."

"Any particular reason?"

"No, not really. They're great parents. I've always just been kinda private with them about my feelings and stuff. I don't know why."

"Parents can be tricky."

This guy is difficult not to talk to. It's like the words are butting past my teeth and lips, going, *Excuse me, guys, if you're not going to help us make it to the doc's ears, we'll just take matters into our own hands.*

I clench and unclench my fists. "A few weeks ago my best friends died in a car wreck. All three of them." I'm still looking at the floor until I say "all three of them," when I look up and meet Dr. Mendez's gaze.

He doesn't flinch. His eyes are an open door. "I'm so sorry," he says quietly. "How awful."

I glance away and rub my face because I'm starting to choke up. I hope he doesn't keep probing. For starters, I'm not ready to talk about how I hold myself responsible; how

Judge Edwards is coming for me. I'm not ready to hear myself saying those things yet. I'm scared it will make them more real to say them out loud. An incantation summoning a soul-sucking demon from a flaming pit.

I breathe through the tightness of my throat. "Yeah. It's bad. So the night of the last funeral was the first. I went to the ER that time. Yesterday, the first day of school, was the second attack. I'm here because I don't want there to be a third."

Dr. Mendez nods. "That gives us a fairly clear idea of where our work should start. So talk to me about what you're feeling right now. If you've had any reflections on the grief you're experiencing?"

It's such a simple question, but I'm completely without an answer. There's something priestly about Dr. Mendez that makes me want to confess. His demeanor is so open, gentle, and nonjudgmental. I seesaw between not trusting Dr. Mendez enough to tell him about how I wear Sauce Crew's death around my neck and not wanting to disappoint him by telling him.

"I miss them."

Dr. Mendez nods but says nothing. He's obviously not the type to nervously fill lulls in the conversation. He'll let silence breathe.

"I . . . forget sometimes that they're gone. It happens right after I wake up. For about five seconds each day. For that little moment I'm free. Then I remember. I also remember sometimes right as I'm trying to fall asleep, and it snaps me awake."

I pour myself a glass of water and take a sip. I'm not particularly thirsty but I don't know what to do with my hands. "This friend of mine—she dated one of my friends I lost—talked about grief coming in waves and at weird times."

"Has your grief taken a similar form?"

"Yes."

"This girl you mentioned; is she somebody who's a source of support and comfort to you?"

"Yeah, she is."

"Do you have other people who can share in your experience of this grief in a similar way?"

"I've talked a little with the grandma of one of my friends who died."

"I've noticed that you haven't said their names. You've referred to them as 'a friend' or 'friends.' Do you find it difficult to say their names?"

"I—yeah. I guess I kinda do."

"Do you know why?"

I ponder. "I'm not sure this is why, but I hate saying their names while talking about them dying. It's stupid, but I'm almost afraid if I do, it'll make it real."

Dr. Mendez shakes his head. "I've seen people who were afraid to throw out clothes or shoes of a loved one, because they worried that by doing so, they would make the death final. Nonnegotiable. What would their loved one do if she came home and needed her shoes?"

My hands tremble, but imperceptibly so. Like one of those weird eye twitches you can't see if you look in the mirror. "Can I tell you their names?" My voice trembles too. I can hear it.

"If you'd like to."

I hesitate. "Blake Lloyd. Eli Bauer. Mars Edwards." I say the names like a benediction. It feels good and it hurts.

Dr. Mendez absorbs them. "Thank you for telling me their names. I can tell how important they are to you; how sacred you keep them."

I'm uncertain why I blurt this out. "So. A while ago I was at Blake's grandma's house, helping her with some of the yard work that Blake was supposed to do . . . before he died. And while I was there, she suggested we have a goodbye day for Blake. I'm wondering if I should do it."

"What's a goodbye day?"

"The way she talked about it, we'd spend a day together doing the things she'd have done with Blake if she'd gotten to have a last day with him. I guess we'd try to give life to his story for one more day. Pay tribute. Say goodbye. I have no idea how it works."

Dr. Mendez sits back in his chair, gazing past me, tapping his lips. "Hmm."

After a few seconds, I say, "So, doctor. Tell me about your mother."

He laughs and leans forward. "If I understand correctly, you would be acting as a sort of surrogate for Blake?"

"Kind of? I mean I wouldn't be wearing Blake's clothes or anything, but . . ."

"No, but it would be the two of you interacting in some

way with his memory. Perhaps the sharing of stories or experiences that would have been meaningful."

"I guess."

He taps his lips again. "Interesting." His brow wrinkles in thought.

"Interesting good or interesting bad? Or interesting that I have to figure out on my own?"

"The latter. Grief is a valley from which there are multiple points of exit. I have no experience with this good-bye day idea, but there are proven therapies that work on a similar principle, where you give yourself a new context for experiencing something. If, for example, you're afraid of relationships, you go and enter a relationship and try to experience it in a new, healthier way. So maybe interacting with Blake's memory in this manner would give you a new context for experiencing his loss."

"So do it?"

"That would be difficult for me to know even if we had talked more. I'd say that's a decision you have to make for yourself. The question is: Do you want to do it? Does it feel right? If so, and it turns out to not be what you hoped, we can work through it. Lesson learned. It's not something that would have occurred to me to suggest, but what occurs to me is not necessarily the benchmark for excellence in an idea."

I continue to mull while Dr. Mendez and I talk about how I'm coping, sleeping, eating.

Our session ends. Dr. Mendez and Georgia bid each other a happy farewell. He wishes her luck with the coming school year. She wishes him the best with his new marriage. I walk out with my Zoloft prescription in hand.

I feel lighter. Not like I've taken off a heavy backpack, but like I've temporarily purged myself of some poison. Empty, hollow, blank.

▣ ▣ ▣

When we get outside, the sky is greenish-gray and the air has a sort of feral vitality, like a storm is coming. A balmy gust whips our faces, and in the distance I hear the metallic clanging of a flagpole's clip against the pole. It's the only sound other than the wind in my ears.

We sit in the car and I abruptly start crying. I have no idea why and Georgia doesn't ask. Maybe it's how forlorn that flagpole line sounded. Maybe it's relief. Maybe it felt good to talk to someone who I thought wasn't judging me. Maybe the grieving don't need a reason to cry. It's open season on crying. A cry-all-you-want buffet.

Georgia squeezes my hand. "Hey."

"Hey." I wipe my eyes. "We need to drop this prescription off to be filled."

"You're brave for getting help."

I blow out the breath I'm holding. "I'm not. I obsess about going to jail. I feel scared and shitty and sad and guilty nonstop."

"I know. But you'll improve. Do what Dr. Mendez says. Be honest with him. Take your meds."

I hope she's right. Maybe Dr. Mendez can help with the

grief, but what about the guilt? Unless he has a time machine. And he sure can't keep me out of jail.

Georgia drives me home after dropping off my prescription at Walgreens. I steel myself for my second first day—half day, I guess—of my senior year.

Even when we arrive home, it hasn't started to storm. The sky feels like a hammer hanging above the earth on a frayed cord.

Chapter Seventeen

Blake, Mars, Eli, and I sat in the last couple of rows of Mr. McCullough's History of Western Civilization class. It was the only class all four of us ever had at once. And whoever let us all be together in the same class should have had his or her ass fired. Mr. McCullough, bless his heart, was so utterly well-meaning, sincere, and humorless. He would endeavor to honestly answer any question, no matter how obviously frivolous. So we had been alternating asking a series of increasingly absurd, smartass questions, trying to break him, waste class time, and stay awake.

Did the Mesopotamians ever have tickle fights?

Was Alexander the Great named Alexander the Fine and Alexander the Pretty Awesome until he had some more victories under his belt? (And did he wear belts?)

Did the Mongols give wedgies to people they conquered?

Would Napoleon have been into motorcycles?

Etc., etc.

So Mars and I are next to each other and Blake and Eli have the two seats directly in front of us. They're turned around, whispering while Mr. McCullough drones on about the Vikings.

"It's your turn, Blade," Eli says.

"Are you sure? I thought it was Mars's turn."

"No, remember? I asked if the pyramids had bathrooms."

"Yeah, he's right," Blake says. "Your turn, Blade."

"Okay, hang on. Gimme a sec."

"The secret is not to overthink," Blake says.

A few moments pass. "Okay, I got it," I whisper.

I raise my hand.

Mr. McCullough peers over his glasses. "Carver?"

"Would the Vikings have been into jean shorts?"

Blake, Mars, and Eli soundlessly erupt. They have their heads down on their desks, their shoulders shaking, and their ribs heaving.

Mr. McCullough clears his throat. "Well, ah, now that's an interesting question. It's, ah, always intriguing to speculate about how ancient peoples would have adopted modern technologies. The, ah, Vikings would make clothing from linen and flax, and because of the scarcity of resources and difficulty in making clothing . . ." He goes on and on. The conclusion is yes, the Vikings probably would have been into jean shorts, at least in the summer, inasmuch as they were functional, durable pieces of clothing that allowed them freedom of movement to farm, sail, and fight.

But I'm not listening. I'm basking in watching my friends laugh. There doesn't seem to be any consequence to anything we do.

⊞ ⊞ ⊞

It's asking for trouble to indulge memory this way before I make my second attempt to enter NAA. At least I don't stand and contemplate before entering. I put my head down and walk forward, ignoring the smiling faces of Blake, Eli, and Mars imploring me—all of us—to remember them. The few people I pass in the halls on the way to the cafeteria nod and smile awkwardly but mostly avoid eye contact.

Then I see Adair exiting the restroom, alone.

In fact, there's no one in the hallway but us. Adair's being alone is an exceedingly uncommon occurrence, so maybe I shouldn't beat myself up for making the idiotic move of calling out her name on impulse, to take advantage of the moment, before thinking carefully about what I'm going to say. I don't know where this impulse came from. Maybe I'm feeling up to doing some good listening after my visit with Dr. Mendez.

She whirls around on her heel—dancerlike—and stalks back toward me. Her eyes are grayer, more tempestuous than the sky outside, against her bloodless face. "What do you want?" Her voice sounds like a knife against a whetstone.

I'm actually grateful when she cuts me off before I can say *I have no idea.*

"That was quite the bit of theater yesterday," she says.

"That was real."

"Now instead of everyone talking about what you did, you managed to change the conversation to your little *episode*. How convenient."

"It wasn't convenient for me."

"What, am I supposed to feel sorry for you?"

"I'm not asking you to."

"You're so generous. Thanks."

"Adair, look." *Don't say, "We used to be friends." Anything but that.* "We used to be friends."

She folds her arms across her chest and laughs, clipped and acrid, blinking fast and eyeing me with an incredulous expression. *"Really?* That's why you stopped me in the hall? To remind me that we used to be on friendly terms?"

"Could we maybe talk about this another time? Like go have coffee or something?" I keep my voice low.

"No."

"Adair."

"I'm serious. You didn't have any shame in currying everyone's sympathy yesterday. Now you're embarrassed to have it out in the hallway?"

"It's not that."

"Of course it is. And you should have thought of that before you stopped me. So. What was going through your head, if anything?"

"I just thought—" My face burns.

"Go on."

"I—"

"Huh? Thought what? What did you *think*?"

"I—thought we could, you know, support each other."

I'm fully aware of how stupid and small I sound. Out of the corner of my eye, I see someone start to enter the hallway and then hastily reconsider. I'm remembering why I was so afraid of people fearing Adair.

Adair's voice turns cloyingly sweet and innocent. She bats her eyes. "Aw. Are you *lonely,* Carver? Is your *life* hard now? Does it suck to be *alive*?"

"I'm—"

She raises her finger. "See, here's the thing: I have plenty of friends. But I only had one brother. If you were so worried about being friendless, maybe you should've had more friends than could fit in one car and maybe you should've been more careful about texting them when they were driving in said car."

"Yeah. You're probably right," I murmur. Her words are flaying me.

"But you're not all alone, are you? You and Jesmyn are becoming friendly, I see."

"Who else do I have? Not you, obviously."

"Whose fault is that?"

"I'm not trying to move in on Jesmyn, if that's what you're implying."

"What a prince."

"Adair."

Her eyes narrow in contempt.

I stand there like a drooling, flustered idiot. "I'm sorry."

Adair draws closer. "For what? Huh? What are you sorry for?"

An apparitional Mr. Krantz floats into my mind. *This is*

dangerous territory. "I'm sorry about Eli and Blake and Mars. I loved them too."

"Well, what did you do to Eli and Blake and Mars that you're so sorry?"

I swallow hard, imagining my Adam's apple looking cartoonish. "Sorry that they're gone. I really miss them."

Adair returns to her cloying sarcasm. *"Aw.* Yeah, Carver. *Me too.* I'm sure it's terrible for you. I mean, Eli and I shared a womb and lived under the same roof for seventeen years, but let's not forget about *your pain.*" Her voice begins to crack and tremble at the finish.

"I'm sorry." My face reddens and heats further. Another person hurriedly slips past us, looking determinedly at the floor. *This will be all over school in about fifteen minutes.*

"You said that already."

"What about Mars?" I ask quietly, my heart collapsing in on itself. *What about Mars? Even you blame yourself more than you blame him. Coward.*

She gives a curt laugh—more of a pointed, stabbing exhale. "Oh, I have plenty to say to Mars too. It's just that, well, he's not here because he's *dead* and you're *not.*"

We stare at each other for a moment. Her gray eyes seethe like molten lead. They burn my mind clear of words. But once more, Adair rescues me from having to say anything.

"I hope you go to jail. I really do. I hope you die there," she says before she turns and walks away.

▣ ▣ ▣

I slip into the buzzing cafeteria and scurry to a corner. I wonder how much of the low hum of conversation is already about my run-in with Adair. I lean against the wall and pretend to check my phone for nonexistent messages from friends, also wondering if any human being has ever had a worse first two days of school. I try to will my blood to absorb back the adrenaline. After a bit, the churning in my gut subsides, the redness leaves my face, and I try to find Jesmyn in the buzzing swarm. She finds me first, sneaking up on me from my left.

"Hey, mister," she says.

I jump. "Hey." We laugh nervously.

Then Jesmyn hugs me. It's the first truly pleasant sensation of this whole day. Her body seems to fit me perfectly. Her cool cheek is against mine and the fluorescent lights of the cafeteria stream through her hair. She smells like laundry detergent and cherry candy. I wish I could enjoy it unreservedly without wondering if Adair saw.

You should tell her. You should tell Jesmyn that Adair is watching us, and that Adair thinks you're moving in on her dead brother's girlfriend. You should give Jesmyn the chance to get out while she still can and make some friends at school. You should let her choose not to be a pariah and a target like you. You should—

"You looked like you needed a hug. So, are you crazy?" Jesmyn asks.

"Rude. What if they said I am? Awkward for you."

"Kidding. Do you feel better?"

There's a good question. Before my run-in with Adair?

Slightly better. And I didn't melt down upon entering the school building, so: "Kind of."

"Kind of?"

"I just had a fight with Adair. Really more her tearing me a new asshole."

"Uh-oh."

"Yeah."

"It'll take time for her. Like all of us."

"A long, long time in her case."

"Let's sit. You bring your lunch?"

"Yeah." I pull out my turkey-avocado sandwich and unwrap it, even though I've lost my appetite. "What are you eating?"

"Peanut butter, banana, honey, and bacon," Jesmyn says, covering her full mouth.

"And I was worried you wouldn't like the milkshakes at Bobbie's. What are you, Elvis?"

"I wish. Speaking of, I'm going to be working on my audition piece after school. I need to start practicing with an audience so I can overcome being nervous about people watching. Wanna watch? You can do homework or whatever; I need somebody in the room."

"I'm flattered! You literally need a pulsing sack of human meat and organs to sit in a chair? And hey! That's what I am!"

She hmphs and pushes me. "And because you said you wanted to see me play sometime, dork. I'm not looking for random dudes to sit and watch me. I could go on Craigslist for that."

Speaking of random dudes, speaking of sacks of meat: I

look up across the cafeteria and spot Alex Bishop. Our eyes meet, and mine say: *No need to pity me, asshole. I've lost a lot of things, but I have this. I'm sitting here beside Jesmyn while she eats her Elvis sandwich and you're not. So kiss my ass.* I'd forgotten how triumph feels. It's great.

I enjoy it for about three seconds before I finally notice Adair scowling at Jesmyn and me and whispering to her friends. Our prior encounter echoes in my ears.

"So?" Jesmyn asks.

"Huh?"

"Wanna watch?"

"Oh, yeah."

"What are you thinking about?"

"Nothing," I lie. "Why?"

"Because you're looking especially Carverish."

I laugh in spite of myself. "What does that mean?"

"Sort of lost."

"Oh, cool."

"No, I mean lost in thought. Like the mysteries of the universe are revealing themselves to you."

I've never gotten used to the idea of people thinking about me when I'm not directly in front of them. "They're not. The more I consider the mysteries of the universe, the less I understand them."

"Is that what you and the therapist talked about? The mysteries of the universe?"

"More the mysteries of my own brain."

"Fascinating," she whispers.

"So sarcastic."

"Only a little. You wanna try a bite of my—" Jesmyn starts to say, when a crack of thunder interrupts her. We can hear it over the chatter. An excited rush sweeps through the throng. Jesmyn's face instantly blooms.

She jumps up and grabs my wrist, yanking me to my feet. "Come on."

"What?" I ask, through a mouthful of sandwich.

"Hurry. We gotta watch it." She's tugging me toward the hallway that connects to the cafeteria. It's made of floor-to-ceiling windows.

We get there and Jesmyn drops my wrist, leaving my skin hungry. She presses her hands to the glass—a child at the zoo, replete with wondrous expression. As if trying to absorb something. A blinding flash of lightning and another deafening crack of thunder. She shudders and giggles.

The rain pounds down in sideways torrents. The wind driving it folds the trees almost in half.

"Whoa," she whispers.

But I ignore the storm and marvel at her rapture. "It's like I'm witnessing someone experiencing something holy."

Her eyes glimmer. "You are," she murmurs, not turning from the window. "I love the energy of storms. They remind me of what powerful forces there are out there."

Another thunderous rumble. I wonder if you can hear thunderstorms in prison.

"If you envision nature as a piece of music, then storms are the movements in that piece," she says.

My session with Dr. Mendez has put me in a listening mood, so I listen without saying anything.

"Do you think I'm psycho?" she asks. It's obvious she doesn't care if I do.

"No. I mean, don't forget that I took you to a park to chase squirrels, so I can't really talk."

The storm gathers in intensity. It's noon but dusklike outside. Another flash of lightning, a peal of thunder, and the lights flicker.

I stand close to her and turn my gaze outward. "Speaking of chasing squirrels, do you remember when we did that and I told you about how Blake's grandma suggested that we have a goodbye day for Blake?"

She turns from the window to me. "I remember."

"I talked with my therapist about that. Asked if I should do it. He left it up to me."

"You gonna?"

"Might help."

"Then you probably should."

A flash of lightning illuminates the side of her face nearest the window. I suddenly become acutely aware of how alive and breathing I am. And I also have the momentary sense—a flash—that even though Mars, Blake, and Eli aren't here anymore to screw around with in Mr. McCullough's history class, now I have something different, which is watching a thunderstorm with Jesmyn Holder, and maybe that's okay. I try to grab onto the feeling, but it's too ephemeral to hold and it disappears into the ether.

Jesmyn gives me a half smile and turns to face the storm.

▣ ▣ ▣

After school, I watch her play. I've never sat nearer to some-one doing something better. She sways and murmurs to her-self while her fingers glide over the keys like wings. She pauses midphrase to pencil in notes on her music.

If Adair should happen to peek in and see, it will only make things worse for both Jesmyn and me.

I should be at McKay's right now, asking for my job back and putting in some hours after school, to pay for my legal defense.

Instead, I watch her play. If I could leave my body and see myself, I likely would resemble her when she was watch-ing the storm. As if I'm in the presence of something hal-lowed and true. Like I'm witness to someone's hidden heart, to some secret ritual. For a while I forget myself and every-thing I carry. The grief. The guilt. The fear.

Whatever mysteries may exist in the universe, or within the recesses of my own mind, what Eli saw in her is not among them.

Chapter Eighteen

I have a Facebook account for the sole purpose of corresponding with my grandma in Ireland. I made her get one because she wouldn't stop forwarding me dumb emails. I get a notification that I have a message from her. As I go to read it, I see the little "recommended pages" bar on the side of my page.

This time, among the usuals, there's a new recommended page: *Prosecute Carver Briggs*.

My heart explodes against my ribs like a rabid animal at the bars of a cage. There's not much on the page yet. It has a brief account of the Accident. It has a few statistics on driving fatalities related to texting. It's shared the main article from the *Tennessean* about the Accident. The post has five likes. Two are from Adair's friends. The page itself has thirty-seven likes.

I close my laptop without reading my grandma's message, get up from my desk, and start pacing. I shut my blinds for some reason. I feel naked and vulnerable.

The thing is that none of the articles about the Accident have identified me by name. This page does. Now any future employer, any school that Googles me, will see this. And that's *if* I have future employers or schools and I'm not in prison.

I guess part of me assumed that someday I wouldn't be stained by the death of my friends.

What a silly thing to assume.

Chapter Nineteen

"Why do you have to leave so soon? UT starts Monday," I say.

We're on the porch. Georgia's car sits low in the driveway, packed full.

"Oh, that'd be fun. Wake up at three a.m. on Monday morning so I can roll up to UT at seven a.m., move in, and then run to my organic chemistry class," Georgia says.

"I don't mean that. But you could leave Sunday. It's Friday."

"This isn't the last you'll ever see of me. I'll be home for the Dearly show in October."

"Let's hang out today. Leave tomorrow."

"I seriously need to settle in."

"You need time to party, you mean," I mutter.

Georgia leans forward and cups her hand to her ear. "Oh, what? I didn't quite catch that. Need what? Did you say 'I need a wet willie'?" She sticks her pinky finger in her mouth and pulls it out dripping. She goes for my ear.

"Georgia, no. Gross. Don't be a dickhead." I catch her wrist.

She cackles, licks her other pinky, and goes for my other ear. I grab that wrist too. She squirms out of my grasp and makes a stab for my ear, glancing off my cheek. She's a Pilates nut and, well, I'm not. So I'm having trouble fighting her off.

"Georgia, quit. Come on. Quit." My arm is shaking trying to keep her other hand away from my ear.

"Okay, okay, truce?" Her cheeks are ruddy. She's having a ball.

"Okay, truce." I let her arms go, already knowing I've been had.

We separate, regarding each other warily. Then, like a striking cobra, before I can even raise my arms halfway, her left pinky is wet in my ear.

I stand there. I'm so defeated, I don't even try to swat her hand away. It's very awkward to make sustained eye contact with somebody giving you a wet willie.

She pulls out her finger. "You're going to be okay." Her voice is gentle.

"Oh yeah?" I want to believe her, but it's hard to imagine.

"You're talking with Dr. Mendez. That's huge. You're taking your meds. That's important. You have Jesmyn, who seems supercool."

162

Jesmyn came to the goodbye barbecue we had for Georgia the night before. "She is cool," I say.

"Don't screw that up, whatever it is."

My heart seizes with guilt. "We're just friends."

"Promise you'll keep seeing Dr. Mendez, even if things don't happen right away?"

"Yeah."

"You can call or text me anytime you need to talk."

"Yeah."

"Will you try to let Mom and Dad in a little more?"

"I'll try."

"My offer to beat Adair's ass stands."

"I know. Both of us don't need to go to jail."

"Carver? Please be careful. Don't hand Judge Edwards anything. Don't say anything you shouldn't."

"Okay."

"Come give me a hug."

I put both hands over my ears and walk into her outstretched arms. Once safely in her embrace, I return her hug. "I don't have that many people left." I try to say it in a jokey way but come up short.

"Hang in there." Georgia gets into her car, waves, and leaves.

I wave as she drives away, my life shrinking again.

▣ ▣ ▣

I almost lose my nerve. My hands shake as I dial Nana Betsy's number.

"Blade," she says, her voice brightening. "How are you?"

"I'm okay. How are you?"

"I'm surviving. Some days better than others."

"I hear you. So—I'm calling because I think we should have a goodbye day for Blake, as you suggested. I don't know how this works, but I want to try."

There's a pause on the other end of the line. "Well, that's wonderful. I guess we'll play it by ear, won't we?"

"That sounds like the way to pay tribute to Blake."

She laughs. "How does the Saturday a week from tomorrow work for you?"

"Should be fine."

"Then we'll start bright and early and go until night. This'll be a true last day with Blake."

"Okay."

"This means a lot to me. It would mean a lot to Blake."

"I hope so."

We hang up and I sit there on my bed for a while, listening to myself breathe. Wondering what I've gotten myself into. Wondering if I'm equal to the task of laying my friend to rest once and for all. Wondering if I deserve any closure that may come of it.

Chapter Twenty

I dream about them again. In my dream we're together and we're doing something happy—I'm not sure exactly what; my dreams aren't always so specific—and I'm relieved that they're not gone. When I wake up, I beg them to linger with me awhile longer, but they don't.

As they have done so many times, they evaporate into the small hours' dark, leaving me alone with my wild grief. With my searing guilt.

Chapter Twenty-One

Every so often in our lives, we face a challenge that seems more than we can bear. I had one of these challenges right before I began my senior year. I had to learn—

I had to overcome—

It taught me—

No. I can't. Sorry, college admissions people, but I really have to quit lying through my teeth on this dumb essay, because I haven't learned. I haven't overcome. I'm having panic attacks and I can't sleep at night. Losing my three best friends hasn't taught me shit other than my capacity for grief and self-loathing.

Tgjjgdssvhjinngdsbnkjmvcdfbnnnbcsdfdkfsfd' apsdofias'dpfosakdf'sapdfjo

I'm gonna delete all this shitty crap and I'm
going to Nashville State Community College, where
I'll study janitorial science. That is if I'm not in the
penitentiary.

I lean back in my chair and growl at the ceiling. This
day wasn't proceeding so terribly until now. I got home
about an hour ago from watching Jesmyn practice. I get hunger pangs now on the days when I don't watch her. And the
music seems to be wrenching open some rusty door in me.
The words are beginning to flow again. Well, trickle. I've got
the first two pages of a new story. That's something, I guess.

A knock. "Come in," I call.

My mom enters, followed by my dad. They wear grave
expressions. My dad is holding a newspaper. My heart starts
thudding.

"Hi, sweetie," my mom says. "Can we talk for a second?"
Her voice bears the slightest tremor. But for the context of
our interaction, I would've missed it.

"Um. Sure."

My dad sits on my bed, and my mom sits next to him.
My mom turns to my dad. "Callum, will you? I don't—"

My dad clears his throat. He holds me in his gaze for a
moment and looks down at his newspaper. His voice is soft.
Same tremor as in Mom's. "Carver, Mr. Krantz called and told
us about this article in the *Tennessean*. The district attorney
has decided to open an investigation into the accident."

My pounding heart becomes a drum roll. "Did he say
anything else?"

"He said they'll probably want to talk to you now. So make sure no talking to police unless he's there," my mom says.

My mouth is parched. My palms are sweating. I can't breathe. A horribly familiar feeling. "Can I be alone for a while? I just—I need to be alone." I try not to sound frantic, even as my lungs collapse in on themselves.

They hug me and leave, gently closing the door behind them.

I fall on my bed, head swimming. Black spots form in my field of vision. I have a fleeting premonition of lying on a prison cot, having an attack.

I guess these miniature deaths are just part of my new landscape. At least I'll have plenty to talk about with Dr. Mendez at our next session.

When the worst has passed, I text Jesmyn and ask her if she'll put the phone by the piano and play for me. I don't tell her why and she doesn't ask.

It helps a little.

When she finishes, I tell her that I might be heading to prison.

Chapter Twenty-Two

It happens the most when my mind is at its quietest. While I'm drifting off to sleep. When I'm listening to Jesmyn play. When I wish it were filled with the words for my next story but instead it's a slate-gray winter sky.

I start the what-ifs. The do-overs. The replays.

It's an absence of action. I don't text Mars. What else could it be? I guess I could try to keep them from going to the movie in the first place. But that's harder to imagine because that involves my convincing them not to go to a movie they really wanted to see, with no reason to believe they'd be in danger by doing so.

I don't imagine what Mars could have done. I wasn't there. I had no control over that. I don't imagine what the driver of the semi could have done. I only have control over what I do. And in this scenario, all I have to do is nothing. Nothing is easy to do. I can *do* nothing.

So I don't text Mars. Instead, I simply wait fifteen minutes. I tell myself that they'll be there soon, and texting won't make them arrive any faster. I'm tempted, but I don't do it. I don't text Mars.

While I wait, I flip through a book I'm supposed to be shelving. As I go back to work, I hear an unholy mockery of a female voice.

"Excuse me, young man, where are your copies of *Fifty Shades of Grey*? Only the new copies, please." It's Blake. Eli and Mars stand beside him.

I grin. "You know that book involves humans and not sheep, right?"

"Oh . . . never mind then."

We all bust a gut.

"How was the movie?" I ask.

"Awesome," Blake and Eli say simultaneously, with Mars saying "Shitty."

They look at him. He shrugs. "DC's getting owned by Marvel." They roll their eyes at him.

"Imagine being such a nerd that it prevents you from experiencing joy," Eli says.

"Hey, I'm surprised you even came to the movie. I thought Jesmyn kept your balls in a little velvet-lined box," Mars says.

Ohhhhhhhhhhh, we all moan.

Eli makes a *pshhh* sound. "Bro, ask your mom, my balls are right where they're supposed to be."

We all moan louder. "Oh, *shit*," Blake says, pointing at Mars and covering his mouth. "You just got dragged, dude."

Mars starts to say something, but I put my fingers to my smiling lips. "Y'all. Chill. You're gonna get me fired. We'll assume Mars had a sick burn in response."

Eli extends his hand to Mars and they clasp hands with a slap.

Blake checks his phone. "Blade, go clock out. We have squirrels to chase and I'm about to get up in the *business* of some Bobbie's."

I pull off my green apron and start for the back room. As I'm leaving, I hear Mars say, "Fam, we need girlfriends. Not you, Eli. But the rest of us do. Chasing damn squirrels. Shit, y'all."

Their voices fade behind me, drifting upward to the sky.

That's how it was supposed to happen that day.

So I don't text Mars. I leave my phone in my pocket. I keep shelving books until they come and we talk and laugh and kneel at the altar of life without even being aware we're doing it. I wait. I don't text Mars.

And they're no longer lying broken amidst a chaos of lights and screams, their crimson blood spilling onto the dark asphalt as if it belonged there.

So I don't text Mars.

I don't text Mars.

I don't text Mars.

Chapter Twenty-Three

I'm lying under the piano while she plays, hands behind my head. From my vantage point, it's like being completely immersed in a starlit ocean. It calms my mind.

She stops playing. I still lie there. I start to rise, but she kneels, looking under the piano. She slides underneath and lies next to me, gazing upward. "Hey," she says.

"You sounded phenomenal."

"You can't tell me you didn't hear me shitting the bed on that last section."

"Can and am. What's the name of that piece? It's gorgeous."

"'Jeux d'eau' by Ravel. It's basically impossible, but I'm screwed if I play something easy, even if I play it perfectly." She crosses her legs and smoothes her sundress against her thighs. "So this is what it looks like under here."

"I'm not in it for the looks; I'm in it for the sound. You'll get dirty."

She snorts. "Who cares? I used to go frogging with my brothers. I've had so much mud between my toes."

"You went frogging?"

She sighs and rolls her eyes. "Here we go with the racism again."

"What? No. Come on. How?"

"Yes, every time I mention being country, you're so shocked because Asians can't be country."

"That's not it."

"So you're just sexist then."

"No."

"If I were a seventeen-year-old white bro from Jackson, Tennessee, would you be *at all* surprised if I told you I went frogging with my brothers?"

Shit. Walked into that. "Yes?"

"Liar. Sexist liar."

"No! It's because you're a pianist and I assume y'all are too worried about your hands." *Nice. Quick thinking there.*

She stifles a giggle and backhands me in the stomach. "That's . . . *musicianist.*"

I double over and laugh. "Ow. That hurt. Which doesn't surprise me at all, because girls *are good at hitting too.*"

"Shithead," she mutters around a smile. "So I want to hear how it sounds down here. Go play something."

"I don't play."

"Every single person on Earth has a song they can play on the piano. Do it. Git."

I feign annoyance. "Fine." I get up and dust off. I sit at the piano.

◰ ◳ ◲

Eli sits at the piano bench next to me. "This is gonna be good."

"Your face is gonna be good," I say.

"I tried with you, I really did."

"I know. I told you a bunch of times: music isn't my thing. My dad's music genes just totally skipped over me. I don't know."

"How many times did I offer to teach you guitar?"

"Dude, you tried. I admit it. It's like you couldn't stand to have anyone around you who didn't know the joy of playing an instrument."

"Fact. And another fact is that I have woefully underprepared you to hang out with my very musical girlfriend after I'm gone."

"It's not your fault."

"I was going to teach her guitar. She'd have been good."

"I don't doubt it."

Eli tosses his hair out of his eyes with a quick flick of the neck. "Stick to the key of C, dude. No sharps or flats. More forgiving."

"I'm all there for forgiveness."

"None of that made any sense to you."

"Not really."

"How did you avoid taking piano lessons as a kid?"

"Georgia gave my parents such a hard time, they didn't even try with me."

"Here's my official suggestion."

"I'm listening."

"Be funny. It's your only shot."

"That's what Blake would have said."

"Yeah, well, we know your strengths and weaknesses, Blade."

"I miss you guys."

And then he's gone.

⊡ ⊡ ⊡

Jesmyn's voice sounds distant from underneath the piano. "Okay. Wow me."

I affect my horrible British accent. "But what to play? What shall I regale you with? The Mozart? Pah. The Beethoven? Poppycock. The . . . who's another composer?"

"Bartók." She's giggling.

"The Bartók? Stuff and nonsense. No, I shall play you one of my own masterpieces—"

"Play already, you dingus!"

"Shhhhhhh . . . one of my own masterpieces entitled 'Mary Had a Little Lamb'."

She giggles. I play it haltingly, clumsily. I finish with a flourish, stand, and bow. She applauds.

I slide under the piano and lie next to her. "How was it?"

"Bravo, maestro." She pats me on the chest. "It sounds amazing under here." After a moment or two, she says in a quieter voice, "This reminds me of when Eli would play for me."

The air between us is like when a heavy wind stops and the trees become still.

"Yeah," I say, because I don't know what else to.

"Did he ever play for y'all?" Jesmyn turns on her side toward me, her hands palms-together under her face.

I turn toward her and mirror her position. "Sometimes. But I assume he wasn't trying to kiss any of us." We give each other wistful half smiles.

"I'm still not okay," Jesmyn says. "I'm better, but I'm not back to normal."

"I was coming down from another panic attack when I called you the other day and wanted you to play for me."

"You win. Are you okay?"

"Yeah. What a shitty contest to win."

"I keep crying randomly," Jesmyn says. "Like the other day my mom sent me to Kroger to buy eggs and I'm standing there in line and the line is really long so I start crying. I *never* used to cry about stuff."

"Remember how I talked about having the goodbye day with Blake's grandma? That's tomorrow."

"Wow," she murmurs. "Are you nervous?"

"Yes. I talked to her last night and she's got a plan, so I guess we'll go with it. It's hard to know how to honor someone's life."

"Yeah. You're smart and sensitive, though—you'll be fine."

"I'm not *that* sensitive."

"First of all, sensitivity is an awesome trait in men; and second of all, yes you are, and that's okay. I was trying to give you a compliment."

"Sorry. Compliment taken." The "in men" part salves the part of my ego that was wounded over being thought overly sensitive.

"What time is it?"

I look at my phone. "Four-fifteen."

"Crap. I got a student in a half hour." Jesmyn slides out from under the piano and jumps to her feet. I follow.

She faces away from me and steps backward, gathering her long, thick hair and lifting it. "Dust me off."

I balk. She waits. So I start dusting her off. I sweep her smooth, almost-bare shoulders. They're scented with honeysuckle lotion. The place where her neck meets her shoulders, even though her hair was probably covering it. I just want to do a good job. I don't do it like I'm pounding cracker crumbs from car upholstery. More as if whisking the dirt from a treasured painting discovered in an attic. Her skin is warm under my fingers, like the first day of spring when you can open your windows.

I brush off her shoulder blades. The middle of her back. The back of her left arm. The back of her right arm. Her lower back, as low as I dare go.

My pulse tingles in my fingertips. "Should I do your legs?" She could easily reach her own legs. But . . .

"No," she murmurs. "I want to walk around with dusty legs."

Interesting. "See how I didn't assume that you wanted me to because you're a girl who's afraid of a little dirt?"

She turns her head around partway so I can see her smile. "You're not hopeless."

I bend down and dust off the backs of her smooth thighs below the hemline of her dress. The minute I do, I start experiencing what we'll call "some personal growth." I'm really trying to keep this pure and innocent, and I'm not being gross about a friend, but I'm touching her legs and they're really pretty. So I conjure the image of my grandma pooping to try to nip things in the bud and avoid any potential awkwardness when Jesmyn turns around. It mostly works.

"You'll do great tomorrow," Jesmyn says out of nowhere. And that reminder works even better than Grandma pooping. "You're doing the right thing. I bet this'll help."

"I don't want to make things worse somehow."

"You won't. You done? Am I good?" she asks, letting her hair fall.

"Yeah," I say. "You're good."

␣ ␣ ␣

On my way home, Darren Coughlin calls. I pull over to answer. He wonders if I have some comment on the impending investigation. I tell him I don't and sit there and breathe and listen to my heartbeat until I'm sure I won't have a panic attack while driving.

If I had a million dollars—well, first I'd pay Mr. Krantz—but then I'd pay the rest of it for just one hour when I don't think about the Accident, about Judge Edwards, about the DA, about Adair, about legal bills, about prison, about any of it.

An hour when I can sit and let the warmth of Jesmyn's skin ebb from my fingertips' memory while my mind is as clear and tranquil as a waveless sea on a windless day.

Chapter Twenty-Four

I lie awake and the silence roars in my ears. The glowing green letters of my alarm clock read 2:45. I was almost asleep when a train woke me. Nana Betsy wasn't kidding about bright and early. I'm meeting her at seven a.m.

I try to collect my stories of him. It won't help me sleep, but I do it anyway. I line them up in my mind. I wash them and polish them.

I prepare to lay them to rest.

⊞ ⊞ ⊞

It's the third week of eighth grade at NAA. I don't know anyone because it's my first year there (it's an eight-through-twelve school). I've left all my few friends and more bullies behind at Bellevue Middle. It's weird being at a school where everybody in your class is the new kid.

I'm sitting in the back of civics and the teacher, Ms. Lunsgaard, is droning on about bicameral government and checks and balances. This is the longest hour of the day because it's the hour before lunch. I glance over at the kid next to me. He looks friendly and kind. He grins and starts making elaborate tying motions with his hands. He fits an invisible noose around his neck, tightens it, and jerks it upward, sticking his tongue out the side of his mouth.

I stifle a laugh and pantomime opening a bottle of pills and dumping the whole thing down my throat.

He doesn't succeed in stifling his laugh. Ms. Lunsgaard peers at us. "Blake? Carver? This will be on the test."

"Sorry," we mumble. We meet eyes again. Under his desk, Blake pantomimes cutting his wrist.

The bell finally rings. I'm stuffing things in my backpack. Blake extends his hand to me. "Hey, man, I'm Blake."

I shake his hand. "Carver."

"That's a badass name, dude. Sounds like a serial killer's name. The Boston Carver." He has a thick drawl. It doesn't sound local.

"Yeah, I was named after a short story writer."

"Oh."

"An *acclaimed* short story writer."

"*Oh*." He does an impressed-old-lady voice and covers his O-shaped mouth.

I laugh. "So where did you use to go to school?"

"Aw man, you've never heard of it. Andrew Johnson Middle School. It's in Greeneville."

"South Carolina?"

"East Tennessee. Way closer to North Carolina than here."

"How'd you end up here?"

"I live with my grandma, and my grandpa died a while ago, so she needed a change and she wanted me to go to a good school. So we moved here."

"Cool. You like Nashville?"

"Yeah. I wish I knew more people."

We drift out to the hall. "You wanna hang out for lunch?" I ask.

He brightens. "Sure, dude. Let's go."

We go and eat lunch. He shows me his YouTube page. I tell him about my stories. We laugh.

We laugh a lot, actually.

There was probably some period when we weren't best friends and inseparable. Days. Maybe weeks, even. But in my memory, from that day on we were as good friends as we'd ever be. It's funny how memory cuts out the boring parts. And that makes it a good story editor. Sometimes, though, you want to remember every minute you spent with someone. You want to remember even the most mundane moments. You wish you had inhabited them more completely and marked yourself with them more indelibly—not in spite of their ordinariness, but because of it. Because you're not ready for the story to end. But you only discover this when it's too late.

I reflect on that as I lie awake waiting for the sun.

⊞ ⊞ ⊞

I pull up to Nana Betsy's house at 6:54 a.m. and sit in my car until 7:01. A dog barks at me from behind a chain link fence across the street, and there's the buzzing of insects, but otherwise the neighborhood is Saturday-sleepy and placid. The air is still heavy with the humidity of summer, even though we're almost done with the first week of September. Dew sparkles on the grass that's getting a bit long. I make a mental note to return soon to mow.

Nana Betsy answers the door wearing a T-shirt with teddy bears on it, a University of Tennessee baseball hat, grandma jeans, and white sneakers. She looks the sort of tired that tattoos itself on your face. Not a sort of temporary, passing tired that you can sleep off or wash away. But a little of it disappears when she smiles.

"Blade. Come in, come in. So."

"So." I return her weary smile and step inside.

"Are you ready?"

"I think so."

"Don't mind getting dirty?"

"Nope."

"Good, because I thought we'd kick things off with one of Blake's and my favorite ways to spend a Saturday morning: going bad-fishing. Then we'll hit up the Waffle House, our favorite place for breakfast."

"Wait, you mean *bass-fishing*?"

"*Bad-fishing*. I'll explain in the car."

I help Nana Betsy load a pair of fishing poles and lawn chairs, a cooler, and a tackle box into the trunk of her creaky, peeling, brown Buick. I sink into the pillowy seat. It smells like pine and dusty tissues, and the dash is illuminated with multiple orange lights. The engine makes a squealing noise as we reverse out of the driveway. The radio, tuned to WSM 650 AM, quietly plays Johnny Cash.

"Blake came up with the name, of course," Nana Betsy says. "I'm nowhere near as quick with the jokes."

"Nobody is."

"True. Anyway, bad-fishing is just that. Bad fishing. We weren't ever any good at it. When Blake first came to live with me, he was eight. He hadn't ever done any of the things a boy that age ought to have done. Mitzi was always drunk or high. The only men around the house were her boyfriends or worse. So they'd sit Blake in front of the TV for hours and hours on end."

"That's how he got into comedy. Watching all that TV. He never talked much about his old life, but he did tell me that."

"So anyway, one day Blake says to me, 'Nana, I wanna go fishing like people on TV do.' Well, my husband Rolly loved fishing. But he'd passed on by then. So I guessed I'd better try to figure it out. I go and buy us a pair of fishing poles and some hooks, and I dig up some worms. We'll do it like in the cartoons, I reckon. So we go and spend all morning and don't catch a thing. Not a bite. But Lord almighty, we had fun—cutting up, talking, drinking root beers. We'd been a fair number of times when Blake finally says to me—" Nana Betsy starts shaking with laughter, wiping her eyes. "Sorry, it's not really that funny. But he says, 'Nana, we ain't bass-fishin', we're bad-fishin'.'"

I'd prepared myself for the experience of treading on sacred ground. But the reality is something else. I suddenly want to confess exactly why I'm not worthy to be doing this. Then Mr. Krantz's voice echoes in my head and yanks me down to reality. A partial confession only. "Nana Betsy, I'm not sure I'm the person to be doing this. This is so special."

She turns down the already-quiet radio. "It is special. It's the most special thing we could be doing at this moment. Which means I decide who's worthy to be doing it with me. And when I say you are, you are. Got it?" Her tone is kind, but with a don't-mess-with-me edge.

She glances over at me and I nod.

"What would Blake say if he were here?" she asks. "Would he say, 'No, Nana, he's not worthy to be doing this'?"

I shake my head. But I still fear that Nana Betsy's and Blake's generosity aren't enough to absolve me.

"The first time he ever mentioned you was on a bad-fishing trip," Nana Betsy says.

"Really?"

"I asked him how he was doing at school, if he'd been making friends. He had plenty of Internet fans from his web page, but that's not the same as real friends. I worried about that because he hadn't had the best social examples."

"You wouldn't have known it."

"I thought so, but here we're moving from little-bitty East Tennessee to the big city and he's thrust into this school with all these smart, talented kids. I knew Blake was smart and talented, but I worried."

"So what did he tell you?"

Nana Betsy smiles. "He says, 'Nana, I met this nice guy

at school named Carver and he ate lunch with me. We're gonna be friends!' "

"That's exactly how he said it?" It sounds so childlike.

"Exactly. I remember because it was one of those days I knew we'd done the right thing by uprooting our lives and moving out here. That was a big risk and I was scared."

And then a flash realization: *That risk you took resulted in Blake's death. If you and Blake had stayed put, he wouldn't have died.* "Do you ever regret coming here?" I ask quietly. I can't bring myself to ask the rest of the question and connect the dots.

But she seems to have done it anyway. Her eyes glaze with a faraway sheen and well up. "No. Blake died here. But if we hadn't come, he'd never have lived. He found his people here. God's hand guides our lives, and I believe he guided us to this place. I don't know why he ordained for Blake to be taken from us; he works in mysterious ways."

We sit for a few moments with silence between us like a curtain suspended from a thin thread. Then Nana Betsy turns up the radio. "We'll talk plenty today. But for now, we need to be singing off-key at the top of our lungs to old country music. Tradition is tradition."

▣ ▣ ▣

We pull up to Percy Priest Lake, park, and hike a little ways to their fishing spot. We set up the lawn chairs. Nana Betsy helps me bait my hook, chuckling. "I believe I've found the lone person on Earth worse at fishing than Blake and me."

"Lucky you."

We cast our lines and settle into our chairs.

Nana Betsy claps me on the knee and points. "Look," she whispers. An elegant blue heron glides past, its spindly legs ramrod straight behind it.

"Whoa."

"That's half the reason we'd come. We'd sit in this beautiful place and ponder God's creation."

Nana Betsy looks wistfully across the lake. She starts to say something. She covers her mouth, but she's shaking with laughter and snorting. "Of course, not even God's mighty creation was safe from Blake. Once, four or five deer walked right up to the edge of the lake to drink, not fifteen feet from us. So we watch them, and Blake whispers: 'What do you guess God was thinking, Nana? He makes these nice brown deer that blend in with everything, and then he says, No, not done yet. And he gives them these glorious, brilliant, gleaming-white asses. The most beautiful asses of all of God's creatures.'"

We laugh until we're winded.

"It's probably why we never caught anything. Couldn't shut up. Scared the fish," Nana Betsy says. And after a moment of reflection: "I think a lot about how he changed me. Did he change you?"

My mouth starts before my brain even knows it's ready. "He made me less afraid to be naked."

Nana Betsy looks slightly horrified.

"Not that way. Less afraid to be vulnerable. Sorry."

"Oh, because with Blake . . ."

"Yeah, you never knew."

Nana Betsy opens the cooler and pulls out a root beer and hands it to me.

I open it and take a sip. "Once I went with Blake to film a video. The one where he walked into Green Hills Mall shirtless."

Nana Betsy claps her hand over her face. "Oh. I wish you'd talked him out of that. Lord almighty."

"Oh, *believe me,* I tried. I was dying just following him with the camera. I was so relieved when a security guard finally kicked us out after he went into Nordstrom."

"Didn't he ask the security guard how he was supposed to get a shirt if he wasn't allowed to go into a place that sells them?"

"Something like that. Anyway, we go out to the car, and I'm like, 'Dude, Blake, aren't you embarrassed?' And he looks at me like I'm the crazy one, and he goes, 'Have you ever thought less of somebody for making you laugh on purpose'? And I think for a sec and say no. And he goes: 'Dignity is overrated. People can live without it. I know because I did. But people can't live without laughter. I'll gladly trade dignity for laughter, because dignity is cheap and laughter is worth everything.'"

Nana Betsy stares out over the lake, shaking her head slightly. She clears her throat a couple of times and wipes her nose. "He always said the first part to me. Never the second part. How much did Blake tell you about his circumstances growing up?"

"Not much. He obviously hated talking about it. I figured it was bad."

Nana Betsy finishes off her root beer, puts the empty in the cooler, and pulls out another. She looks pained. "Mitzi was our wild child. She was our youngest, and I guess we were too tired by then to be as strict as we ought to have been, so she did whatever she pleased. She got pregnant with Blake when she was sixteen. It could've been any of five men, all over thirty. She picked the one with the nicest trailer and most running cars and convinced him that Blake was his."

"So Blake never knew who his real dad was?"

"No. And all the possibilities were awful."

"Jeez."

"So they"—Nana Betsy makes air quotes—"raise Blake. Which meant sitting him in front of the TV for hours a day in the same filthy diaper while they partied and snorted meth. Sometimes they'd let me take him for the day, and I'd bathe him and feed him good food and try to teach him to talk and read and all the things he was behind on."

"Did you ever call—"

"Child Protection? My heavens, yes. The sheriff? Many times. But we're talking about a rural county with limited resources. They don't do a thing."

"Sorry. Go ahead."

"So this goes on until Blake is eight. They leave him for days. He's not attending school. Mitzi's boyfriends are slapping him around. And I've finally had it. I go get him without asking anyone's permission. I figure if the sheriff and Child Protection can't protect Blake from Mitzi, they can't protect Mitzi from me protecting Blake."

This spurs a memory. "There's another way Blake tried to change me," I say softly. "We were hanging out in my room; I don't remember what we were doing. Anyway, my mom knocks on the door to ask me a question and I get supermad—I'm embarrassed telling you this because it makes me sound like the worst kid ever."

"I'm not judging you. You said that Blake taught you not to be afraid of vulnerability."

"Okay. Well, I get supermad at my mom and she leaves, and Blake goes, 'Why are you mean to your mom?' And I go, 'Whatever, dude, you don't understand.' And he's like, 'Yeah, I don't, because if I had your mom, I'd never be mean to her. You have no clue how lucky you are, but I do.' So yeah. I'm pretty embarrassed to have treated my mom that way in front of him."

We sit for a while, smacking mosquitos, sipping root beers, and chatting, the sun hot on our backs. A couple of times we think we might have a bite. Of course it turns out to be nothing. Wind shaking our poles or something. We don't bother reeling them in to see if our hooks are still baited.

Finally, Nana Betsy looks at her watch. "Blade, I'm getting hungry. It's probably time to say goodbye to bad-fishing." Her voice cracks. "You made a very good bad-fishing companion, I must say. Second best I've ever had."

"We can come do this anytime."

She looks at the ground; out over the lake; and back to the ground, blinking fast. "Afraid not. I'm leaving."

It doesn't quite make it into my brain. I think for a second she's talking about us leaving right then. "Wait. What?"

"I'm moving home. I miss my mountains. I was only ever here for Blake's sake, to put some distance between our old life and our new life. My two sons live in Greeneville, and my older daughter lives in Chattanooga."

That shuts me right up.

"I have enough years working for the state to get my retirement. I'm putting the house on the market on Monday. I'm not asking for much. Enough to cover the funeral costs and the cost of some little place on the side of a mountain overlooking a holler. And I'll watch my stories and read my mysteries and have Sunday dinners with my boys and live quietly with my thoughts and memories until the Lord calls me home."

It had never occurred to me that Blake's death would have this particular sort of consequence. I thought its impact would be limited to grief, guilt, aching, missing. Not packing up and moving. I wonder what else will fall now from this shaken tree.

"I'm sorry."

"Don't be. I'm happy to be going home."

"I mean I'm sorry for making you move."

"We've been through this. You have no need to apologize."

But I do. I committed something so close to negligent homicide that I'm not even allowed to tell anybody but Dr. Mendez and Mr. Krantz. If I weren't guilty, why would I need to be careful about telling my side of the story?

"Okay," I say finally. I start to pick up my pole.

Nana Betsy puts her hand over mine. "No. Leave it." She pulls a piece of folded-up notebook paper from her front jeans pocket and unfolds it. She smoothes it and sets it on one of the chairs. She uses an egg-sized rock to weight the paper.

I catch a glimpse of the note, which is written in precise, neat, grammar-school handwriting. It reads:

To whoever finds these things:
Please keep them—they're yours.
They belonged to my grandson and me.
We were never much good at fishing
but we used them to make many wonderful memories.
I hope you'll do the same.
In loving memory of Blake Jackson Lloyd

I start up the path, expecting Nana Betsy to follow. She doesn't.

"Blade, do you mind going along without me for a few minutes? I need a moment or two here alone." Her voice is a scratchy whisper, the wind through long grass. She hands me the car keys.

Before I go, I watch as she lowers herself into the chair beside the one with the note. She rests her elbows on her knees and buries her face in her hands.

I do the same thing when I get to the car.

⊞ ⊞ ⊞

We've each mostly composed ourselves by the time she joins me, about ten minutes later.

"All right," she says with what seems to be genuine cheeriness (or at least temporary unburdenedness). "I could use some traditional post-bad-fishing waffles and bacon. How about you?"

"Always."

We drive to the nearby Waffle House. As we park, Nana Betsy laughs. "This must not seem like a very glorious last day for Blake. But this is what he and I loved to do together. Every Saturday morning we could, for the last few years. I'm only guessing this is what he'd have wanted for his last day, but it's definitely what I'd have wanted."

"Since I'm Blake today, I say it's what he would have wanted."

"I think if what you'd do for your last day on Earth doesn't look like a pretty normal day for you, you probably need to reexamine your life."

"I agree." I guess a Buick in a Waffle House parking lot is as good a place as any to have your notion of the well-lived life cracked open wider than the Grand Canyon.

"Let's go eat some waffles."

A blond waitress with a smoker's voice greets us. "Good mornin', Betsy! Been a while. You got a different breakfast companion."

Nana Betsy's smile fades almost imperceptibly. "Hello, Linda. Blake couldn't make it today. This is his best friend, Carver."

"Hi." I wave.

"Good to meet you, honey," Linda says. "Y'all need a menu or you gettin' your usual?"

Nana Betsy looks to me. "I'm fine with whatever the usual is," I say.

"Usual it is," Nana Betsy says.

"Comin' right up," Linda says. "You tell your grandson we missed him today."

Nana forces a smile. "I bet he knows."

We sit and Linda hustles off after pouring us cups of coffee. Nana Betsy leans over with a whisper. "I couldn't tell her. She's so sweet, and there wouldn't be any point to making her sad."

"Blake would have found this funny."

Nana Betsy's eyes twinkle. "I imagine he's looking down from heaven right this moment and laughing about the little trick we've played on Linda."

I smile and play with my fork.

"You believe in heaven?" Nana Betsy asks.

The easy answer is I used to, as casually as I believed anything relating to the Divine. It was an untested, unexamined belief, and so it dwelled comfortably in me. But now? If you came to me and said, "Listen, Blake's going to die, but that's okay because you believe in heaven, right?" my answer would have been no.

"Yeah. Mostly," I say. "But I haven't spent much of my life considering it like I am now."

"I believe in heaven," she murmurs. "I believe in a resurrection of the flesh when the dead will rise. I believe all that. And you'd suppose that'd make all this easier. Believing in my heart that I'll hug Blake again someday. It should be as easy as if I were sending Blake off to camp for the summer. But it's not."

Linda reappears with two plates piled high with waffles and a large plate of bacon. "Y'all enjoy now."

"You bet we will," Nana Betsy says.

We both look out the window at the cars passing, the people coming and going. Listen to the clink of silverware, the sizzle of the grill, the crunch of bacon. The hum of conversation and the occasional shouted order.

I feel a confessional yearning. "What do you think it takes to keep you out of heaven?"

Nana Betsy holds my gaze while she finishes her bite and takes a sip of coffee. "What do you mean?"

"I mean what if God thought I had something to do—" Linda approaches and fills our water glasses.

"Y'all good here?" Linda asks.

"Right as rain," Nana Betsy says. Linda leaves again.

I speak with a light tremor. "What if God holds me accountable for the Accident?" I want to say more, but Mr. Krantz's words resonate in my head. I've always found it baffling why criminals ever confess to crimes. Especially when they hand police the only thing they have to go on. I understand perfectly now.

"Let me tell you about the God I know." She looks out the window for a second and looks back. "My God judges a whole life and a whole heart. He doesn't judge us by our worst mistakes. And let me tell you something else. If God is someone who makes us walk a tightrope over the fires of

194

hell, then I don't care to sing his praises for eternity on some silver cloud. I'll jump off the tightrope before I'll do that." Her voice trembles as she says the last part, but it doesn't blunt the edge of her conviction.

I suddenly feel like I have a huge ice cube stuck in my throat. I try to swallow it away. I'd love to borrow her conviction, but I can't quite.

"Do you mind if I tell you a totally random story that has nothing to do with this topic?" I ask.

"Not at all."

"I remember once, Blake was over at my house and Georgia had a couple of friends over and they were listening to music with the bedroom door open. And Blake and I go into the hall, where they can see us, and we start doing funny dances. Twerking and hulaing and the chicken dance and stuff. At first they were screaming at us to go away, but by the end they were laughing so hard they couldn't breathe. Anyway. I guess it doesn't sound that funny when I tell it. Maybe you had to be there."

Nana Betsy is shaking; she has her hand over her mouth and tears are streaming from her eyes. I can't tell if she's laughing or crying. Finally she gasps, and it sounds like a laughing gasp. "Aren't most stories about the people we love that way? You had to be there."

We finish eating and stand to leave. Nana Betsy pulls yet another folded-up piece of notebook paper from her pocket and places it on the table, along with a twenty and a crisp, new hundred-dollar bill and sets an empty glass on top of it all.

"Bye now—y'all enjoy your day!" Linda says, bustling past with a pot of coffee. "See you later!"

"Bye, Linda," Nana Betsy says. "Thank you for everything. And Blake says thank you too."

Linda doesn't seem to detect the finality in Nana Betsy's voice, but I do.

We walk out to the car in pensive silence. As for me, I'm pondering hell. I'm wondering if rather than some ardent lake of fire, filled with the shrieking damned, it's an endless corridor of noiseless, windowless rooms. And inside, each one of the damned sits comfortably on a perfectly ordinary office chair, stares at the bare gray walls, and relives their worst mistake.

Again.

And again.

And again.

⊡ ⊡ ⊡

Nana Betsy planned well, because she knew we'd need some quiet by this point. So we go to an early movie, which works because she and Blake used to love to go to movies together.

It's an adaptation of *Danny, the Champion of the World*. It was one of my favorite books growing up, and I'd been planning to see it anyway. Of course, I usually saw movies with Sauce Crew or Georgia. Yet another way that my life has changed that hadn't occurred to me until now. Jesmyn might have been game. That seems probable, in fact. Possible wishful thinking on my part.

Nana Betsy and I get a huge tub of popcorn to share. "I don't blame you a bit if you can't eat another bite. I sure can't. But Blake and I always split a big popcorn and tradition is tradition."

As we sit in the dark and watch, I reflect on the mundane rituals, laid end to end, that form a life. We work to make money and then hopefully use that money to buy ourselves memories with the people we love. Simple things that bring us joy.

I don't pay much attention with my swirling thoughts, and most of the movie slips past me. Maybe I'll come see it again with Jesmyn.

Neither of us touches the popcorn.

The movie ends and Nana Betsy pulls herself out of her seat with a groan. "These movie theater seats do a number on me. Getting old is no fun."

Not getting old is also no fun.

Nana Betsy shuffles toward the exit. "I guess I won't make it to the movies much anymore. At least until the other grandkids get a little older. I don't like going alone, and Blake was my movie buddy." She opens the door to the outside, and we squint in the brilliant afternoon sun after the cool dark of the theater. I wonder for a second if this is how resurrection feels. Stepping out of darkness into blinding light.

As we make our way to the car, Nana Betsy shades her eyes and says, "I always told Blake he should try to find some pretty girl to take to the movies instead of me. He always said 'No, Nana, I'd rather go with you.' Truth be told, it makes me a little glad he never found the right girl." She starts to unlock her door.

And now I have a huge, huge problem.

⊞ ⊞ ⊞

"Yeah, well you're gayer than . . . riding a white pony through a field of dicks," Eli says to Mars. They crack up again. Eli slaps Blake's arm as I pull up to Eli's house. "Come on, bro, you must have one."

Blake sort of half smiles and shifts in his seat. "Naw, y'all got this."

"Come on," Mars says. "Do Blade. Dunk on him."

"Naw, I got nothing here."

"You're losing your edge," Mars says as he and Eli hop out.

"Your mom is losing her edge," Blake says.

"That doesn't even make sense," Mars says.

"Your mom doesn't even make sense."

We laugh, and Mars and Eli run up the walk to Eli's house.

I pull away and start driving to Blake's house. I've never heard him this quiet. I reach over and punch his arm playfully. "It's cool, dude. We just need to have a gay-joke training montage, where you're running while I ride a bike, and lifting weights while screaming gay jokes, all in preparation for your redemption from this humiliating defeat."

Blake chuckles, but his heart's obviously not in it. "Yeah."

"I'm kidding with you, man."

"Yeah."

"You cool?"

"I'm good, I'm good." Then after a few seconds: "Can I ask you something?"

"Sure," I say.

"Naw, never mind."

"Dude."

"Naw, it's weird."

"Obviously. It's you asking."

"Promise I can trust you?"

"Yeah, man. Totally. For real."

He sighs and scratches his head. He starts to say something and stops. He tries again. "How did— When did you find out you liked girls?"

I'm stunned. "Uh. You mean *sexually* or whatever? Since I was probably eleven or so. Why?" In my heart I already know exactly why he's asking.

He takes a deep, shuddering breath. As if he's about to try to escape a sinking ship. "Because. I . . . have never been into girls . . . that way. Ever."

A long silence.

I want Blake to be the one to break it when he's ready, but he doesn't, so I do. "Are you into . . . ?"

"Sheep? Naw."

We laugh.

"Yeah," Blake says quietly. "I think . . . it's guys I like." He adds, hastily, "Not you; don't worry."

"Wow."

"Obviously I like you as a friend. But not *that* way."

"Jeez, now I'm wondering if I should have moisturized or exfoliated more. I mean, I work out," I say.

"No you don't," Blake says.

"Hey. I'm sorry, dude," I say, my smile drifting off. "About every gay joke I've ever made. I didn't mean it maliciously. Mars and Eli would be sorry if they knew. They aren't really homophobic. None of us are. We just—didn't think. It was dumb of us. I'm so embarrassed."

"It's cool. I'll tell them someday, but let's keep this between you and me for now, okay?"

"Yeah, man. Of course. But I am gonna tell them to chill and knock it off next time they make gay jokes. It's shitty to joke like that anyway."

"That I wouldn't mind. It's good to get this off my chest. You're the first person I've told. Thanks for listening."

"No problem. This won't make us any less friends." And after a second: "But real quick, is it my haircut?"

▣ ▣ ▣

He didn't tell her. I figured after he told me he'd tell her. It had been a little less than a year ago. And now I have to decide whether to let her completely know Blake.

If he wanted her to find out, he would have told her.

If he didn't want anyone to find out, he wouldn't have told me.

Maybe he wanted to wait for the right moment to tell her. He would have told her eventually.

That moment will never come now.

He never told you that he was going to tell her.

He never told you that he wasn't going to tell her.

She'll be perfectly happy with her memories of him if she doesn't know.

Her memories of him will be incomplete if she doesn't know.

It will hurt her to learn that I found out before she did.

She invited you here today because you hold pieces of Blake that she doesn't.

It's the wrong thing to do.

It's the right thing to do.

Nana Betsy gets into the car and so do I. "All right, now we—"

"I should tell you something." *This is a bad idea.*

"Okay. Sure."

The words stumble in my mouth on their exit. "Blake . . . never found the right girl because he . . . didn't want to."

"Ain't that the truth. Seemed like dating was the last thing on his mind."

I wait to catch her eyes before she starts the car. "That's not what I mean."

Her expression doesn't change for several seconds. Then realization slowly dawns. She shakes her head like she's half-asleep and trying to rouse herself. "He wasn't . . ."

My heart drips cold and viscous down the inside of my chest—whites from broken eggs down refrigerator shelves. I really wonder if I've done the right thing.

She takes her hand from the keys and deflates into her seat, paralyzed. The only thing more stifling than the heat in the car is the silence. She leans forward and starts the car, and the air conditioner wheezes blessedly to life. But she sits back again and we don't move.

"I had no idea," she says. "We lived together for years. I hadn't the slightest notion."

"Me neither until he told me."

"When did he tell you?"

"Little less than a year ago."

Her face creases and she starts weeping. "Why didn't he tell me?"

"He . . . was going to. He told me." This is an unambiguous lie. But necessary to fix what I fear I've broken.

"But why wait?"

"I think he . . . knew how much your religion means to you, and it worried him how you'd react."

She fumbles in her purse for a pocket pack of tissues and dabs at her eyes. "Our religion definitely doesn't approve of that lifestyle, but I never did believe that people choose to be that way. I wonder—if maybe I'd gone and gotten Blake from Mitzi's sooner—"

"I'm pretty sure that's not how it works. I think he was born that way."

"I can't wrap my head around this. There was a huge part of him who was a stranger to me."

"It was just one part of who he was, though. You knew him as well as anybody on Earth."

"Not as well as you, I guess."

"But you know tons about him that I didn't. I think the only person who knows someone completely is that person. And even then not always."

"I pictured his future all wrong. I pictured a girl in a wedding dress and grandkids."

"You can still picture a wedding and grandkids. Just that

there'd be a tux instead of a wedding dress." *Please let me be making this better and not worse.*

"I've only ever known one gay person. My hairdresser in Greeneville. I loved him. But it was easy to tell with him." Nana Betsy blows her nose and presses her hand to her forehead. Her face crumples and her weeping becomes sobbing. "So often I let people talk awful 'Adam and Steve' sort of hateful nonsense in front of Blake and didn't say a thing. It's no wonder he was scared to tell me."

My heart keeps dripping. "I'm sorry if my telling you this hurt you. I tried to do the right thing."

Her voice quavers. "You did right. You're here to help tell Blake's story." She hesitates. "Blade, do you think he ever got to love anyone the way he wanted to?"

"I don't know. I hope so."

"Me too."

She goes to put the car in gear but stops again. "You can say no to this, but would you do a little playact with me?"

"I'll try."

"Will you be Blake and tell me so I can say out loud what I would've said? In case he can hear us?"

"I guess so. Okay. This won't be as funny as if it were Blake."

"That's all right."

"Okay. Um. Nana, can I talk to you about something?" I don't know how to do this. I guess there's no manual for coming out of the closet on behalf of your deceased best friend.

She wipes her eyes. "Yes, Blake, you can." We both laugh even though it's not funny.

"I've known this for a while, but I need to tell you I'm gay."

Nana Betsy looks skyward. "Blake, honey, if you can hear me, listen real good now." She faces me and swallows hard, and when she speaks, the tremor is gone from her voice and it envelops me like a down quilt. "That doesn't make a damn bit of difference to me. I love you more than I love God himself. So if he's got a problem with anything, he can talk to me, because I love you how you are. Now, if that's all you had to tell me, we'd best go have some of my homemade fried chicken and cornbread. Your favorite."

She nods once, like a judge pounding a gavel, and puts the car in gear, and we leave.

⊞ ⊞ ⊞

She wasn't speaking hypothetically when she mentioned the fried chicken and cornbread. We're sitting in her kitchen while she waits for the Crisco to heat up in one of her black cast-iron skillets. Another skillet is in the oven, getting hot for cornbread. A mound of flour-and-spice-dredged chicken thighs sits on a platter. A mixing bowl of yellow cornbread batter sits beside it.

My emotions roil. In some ways, this day has sharpened everything I've felt over the past weeks. The guilt. The grief. The fear. It's honed them to a razor, singing edge. But in other ways, it's removed that edge slightly and replaced it with a dull sense of absence. While the grief feels like a more active emotion—a process of negotiation—the absence resembles grief with a measure of acceptance. If grief is a pounding surf, the absence is a melancholy, gently tossing sea.

"Are you glad you did this?" Nana Betsy asks out of the blue. My face must have betrayed my emotion.

"Yes." This is largely true. The untrue part of it relates mostly to my wishing I never had occasion to be sitting in Nana Betsy's kitchen, having a goodbye day for Blake. "My therapist thought this would be a good idea." This is also not completely true. In fact, it's mostly not true.

"Goodness, a therapist? I thought this had hit me hard." Nana Betsy tosses a pinch of her chicken seasoning in the oil, where it pops and sputters. Using tongs, she carefully lowers a few pieces of chicken into the oil. They sizzle and bubble.

I guess I might as well tell her. I wouldn't have brought up Dr. Mendez if part of me didn't want to. "I was having panic attacks. I've had three so far. The first was a couple hours after I left your house on the night of Blake's funeral. The second was on the first day of school, right as I was walking in the door. The third was after I found out—" This confession is going further than I'd planned.

"Found out what?"

My mouth goes dry and I'm lightheaded. "Found out that the DA is looking at pressing charges against me for the accident."

"Do *what* now?" She turns from the stove, her mouth agape, her tongs at her side.

My voice is small—that of a kid who peed his pants in

class. "Mars's dad asked the DA to investigate the accident and see if there are any charges they can bring against me."

"You have *got* to be kidding me."

"I wish."

"What on Earth?"

"We talked to a lawyer, and he said they might be able to charge me for negligent homicide."

"How?"

"I guess if they could prove that I was texting Mars, knowing that he was driving and knowing that he would text me back and that I knew texting while driving is dangerous." My insides are a writhing ball of eels.

Nana Betsy turns to the stove and flips the pieces of chicken. "But you didn't know all that."

I'm paralyzed. I don't say anything. I don't move. Nana Betsy catches my gaze. It feels like holding my hand too close to a fire. Appropriate, since this whole conversation could burn me someday. But again, that irresistible compulsion to purge myself of the poison of this guilt.

"But you might have known all that," she says quietly.

Still frozen, in my weak voice, I say, "My lawyer told me the only way they could get me is if I confessed. And they can't make me do that. But if I confess to someone else, that's how they'll get me." I've just roundly boned myself. And it's bizarrely satisfying. Like peeling off a scab. Sticking a Q-tip too far into your ear. That inexplicable desire to jump off high places or swerve into oncoming traffic. Weird how we're programmed to get pleasure from destroying ourselves.

Nana Betsy doesn't say anything for a moment as she reaches into the oven, pulls out the skillet, swirls some bacon grease in it, pours in the cornbread batter, and returns it to the oven. She sits at the table with me. "Then I guess this conversation never happened."

"You don't need to lie for me. I deserve to be punished."

"Lie about what?"

"This is why I didn't feel I deserved to be here today."

"What's why?"

I put my face in my hands. "I'm so ashamed of myself. I hate myself for what I did."

Nana Betsy pulls my hands from my face and grips both of them. I can't look at her. My face is burning.

She waits and, when I won't look at her, says, "You made a mistake. But this thing needs at least one survivor. You owe it to Blake to survive this."

She lets go of my hands, stands, and carefully lifts the chicken out of the skillet, letting each golden piece drip before setting it on a plate covered with paper towels.

She lowers three more pieces into the oil and sits. "I tell you who really wouldn't have blamed you," she murmurs.

I shake my head slightly.

"Blake. He didn't play the blame game. I never once heard him speak an ill word about Mitzi. And you wanna talk about someone who he could've blamed? Everything I know about his growing up, I learned watching him or hearing from somebody else. Never him."

"He never told me anything bad about her."

"He didn't pity himself for the hand life dealt him. I don't guess he's sitting in heaven doing that now because he's not growing up with you."

The "not growing up with you" feels like I'm trying to digest a stomach full of cold nails.

Nana Betsy gets up to flip the chicken. "Speaking of growing up, how you doing these days? You been able to make some new friends?"

"Did you ever meet Jesmyn, Eli's girlfriend?"

"The pretty Oriental girl?"

I blush. "Asian."

Nana Betsy covers her mouth like she burped. "Sorry. Asian."

"Yeah. She and I have gotten to be pretty close friends through all this. But she's about it, friendwise. I used to be friends with Adair, Eli's sister. Not so much anymore."

"At least there's someone."

"I had my sister Georgia around and we still talk and text and stuff, but we can't exactly go to a movie together with her in Knoxville for school."

"What about your folks?"

I squirm inwardly. "I don't really talk to them much about my life."

"They seem nice."

"They are. I thought you're supposed to have your private life from your parents."

Nana Betsy turns from the stove and puts her hand on her hip. "I can tell you that ain't written anywhere."

I stare at the beige linoleum floor. "I don't know what my deal is."

Nana Betsy, perhaps picking up on my reluctance to talk about this topic, blessedly allows it to die. She pulls out the rest of the chicken, sets it on the platter, opens the oven, and pulls out the steaming cornbread.

She comes to the table, balancing one of the plates she prepared us on her forearm while holding a pitcher of sweet tea. She returns to the refrigerator for a tub of homemade coleslaw.

She says grace over the food and we dig in.

"This was the exact meal I made him to celebrate him getting into Nashville Arts. I told him he could pick any restaurant, but this is what he picked."

"I can see why," I say through a mouthful. "I wasn't even hungry."

"Save room—there's lemon chess pie in the fridge."

🖿 🖿 🖿

We eat slowly, savoring each bite as we think Blake would, and talk for hours. We treat the meal like we're taking Communion, which I guess we are, in a way. We settle into a comfortable back-and-forth of the small, ordinary things we remember about Blake.

She tells me he never killed spiders because they ate bugs he feared more.

I tell her about how Blake pronounced "library" as "liberry" all his life, as far as I knew.

She tells me Blake loved licking the eggbeater so much that if he wasn't around, she'd put it in a bowl in the fridge for him for later.

I tell her Blake was never once mean to anyone at school.

She tells me he hated raisins.

I tell her how I would let him drive my car and how excited he always got; the novelty of driving never lost its luster.

She tells me he never learned how to swim or ride a bike.

I tell her about our first argument—over whether woolly mammoths could still be alive somewhere in Siberia.

She tells me how, until he was fourteen, she used to leave the hall light on for him after he went to bed.

I tell her how every time I said goodbye to him, it cast a faint shadow on my life—muting every color—until I saw him again.

▣ ▣ ▣

It's early evening when we're done eating and talking and what remains of the lemon chess pie sits on the table in front of us. We both recline in our chairs to relieve the pressure on our diaphragms.

"Well, are you ready for the next part?" Nana Betsy sweeps some crumbs into her hand and deposits them on her plate.

"As long as it's not more food. Not that this wasn't excellent."

She smiles and gets up. I hear her rummaging around. She returns holding a pink rubber bladder. There's a mischievous glint in her eye. "Ever played with one of these?"

I shake my head.

"It's a whoopee cushion," she says. "Here." She blows it up, sets it on her chair, and sits on it with a piercing, squalling fart noise. We laugh.

"I've read about those," I say. "But I've never seen one."

"I had to order this off the Internet."

"You could probably download an app on your phone."

Nana Betsy looks sheepish. "I'm too old-fashioned to have thought of that."

"What's it for?"

"We're going to experience the world through Blake's eyes. I contacted YouTube and I was able to get the login information for Blake's site. I need you to help me make a farewell video for Blake."

I hadn't even thought of what had become of all of Blake's YouTube followers. I wondered if they had any idea what had happened.

"I have plenty of experience as Blake's cameraman."

"Then we ought to be set. First things first, though: we need to record an introduction to the video. Might as well do that here."

While I film, Nana Betsy stumbles and stammers her way through her message. "Hello, everybody. I'm Blake's grandmother. Blake has passed on and we miss him. We wanted to thank all of you for supporting him. Thank you. This next video is our tribute to Blake."

Nana Betsy picks up her keys and purse, which she empties out enough to accommodate the whoopee cushion. She inflates it and puts it inside. She does a test, squeezing it. It works. She inflates it again and replaces it. "Okay. Let's go."

We drive to a craft store. That was my idea. Blake loved the places with prim and proper employees, and a hobby store is sure to have a few who love flower arranging a lot more than fart noises.

"Whew," Nana Betsy says as we sit in the parking lot. "My stomach is full of butterflies. How was Blake able to do this?"

"Blake didn't come up with this, but he said comedy was about controlling why people laugh at you."

Nana Betsy nods firmly. Her face is more resolute. She takes a deep breath. "Then let's go control why people laugh at us. For him."

We walk into the potpourri-scented store. Nana Betsy clutches her purse at her side like it contains an explosive device—which I suppose it does. Her lips are tight. Her eyes move side to side quickly, seeking our target. I have my phone at the ready.

There are more girls in their twenties with pierced noses and purple hair than I expected. They're no good to us. I scan the store. We wander to the fabric aisle.

"There," I whisper, and nod slightly in the direction of a matronly-looking woman with short gray hair. She has her reading glasses perched on the end of her nose, and she's rolling up a bolt of flannel.

"Yep," Nana Betsy whispers. She takes another deep breath. "Oh, Lord, what am I doing?" she mutters to herself.

We approach the woman. I slip my phone from my

pocket and pretend to be engrossed in checking something, but I'm filming. Beside me, Nana Betsy swallows hard and steps forward.

"Excuse me, ma'am," she says. Her voice sounds pinched; higher than usual. Like she has a whoopee cushion stuck in her throat, actually.

The woman looks up with a dour expression and raised eyebrows. *Good choice of target.*

"Can I help you?" she asks.

"Yes, we're looking for—" Nana Betsy sets her purse on the table and reaches in, as if she's about to pull out a sheet with measurements scribbled on it. Instead, she grips the whoopee cushion and squeezes, emitting a long, sonorous, flatulent squeal. And then there are a couple of moments of complete silence, which is the perfect cutoff point to stop filming. The woman's mouth is slightly agape, and her eyes shift quickly between Nana Betsy and me.

Nana Betsy's face looks like she fell asleep in the sun and woke up five hours later. She's stammering an apology between nervous giggles and has her hand on the woman's arm. "Ma'am, I am so, so sorry. I honestly did not mean to be rude. We had to—I—"

The woman looks at Nana Betsy like she's actually ripped ass right in front of her. "I have a lot to do here, so if y'all don't mind."

Nana Betsy quickly composes herself. It reminds me of how she did at Blake's funeral. She speaks more slowly and quietly. "I sincerely apologize, ma'am. I lost my grandson a few weeks ago. He was a prankster and loved stunts where he acted the fool in public." She nods in my direction. "His best friend and I are out to have a last day to say goodbye to him. I needed to experience a little piece of his world through his eyes."

The woman's expression visibly relaxes. "I'm sorry for your loss."

Nana Betsy fumbles in her purse again and comes up with a twenty-dollar bill. She holds it out to the woman. "Please, take this. We were only trying to make ourselves look foolish, not you."

The woman shakes her head and gently pushes the bill away. "No, ma'am. I lost a nephew in a motorcycle accident a few years ago. Grief makes fools of us all."

Nana Betsy puts the bill back in her purse. "Yes it does. Anyway. I'm sorry again if I offended you."

"No apology necessary. I hope you two have a lovely rest of your night."

We walk to the car.

"That wasn't bad," I say. "The real thing works better than a whoopee cushion, though. Makes it easier to maintain the eye contact that Blake said was so essential."

Nana Betsy smiles. "At my age, you don't risk that sort of thing, even if I could manage the way Blake could."

She unlocks the car and we get in.

"Did you take a good video?"

"Yeah. Do you want me to upload the videos for you?"

"Would you? Here." She hands me a slip of paper with Blake's YouTube login information. I log in from my phone and upload the two videos we recorded.

"That was tough. I'd never want to do it again. We go about our lives doing everything we can to keep from looking silly," Nana Betsy says.

"It's fear. We're just afraid."

"He lived for that rush of doing something ridiculous to brighten someone's day. He did that over and over again—faced down the fear to make people laugh. I don't know how he did it. I almost died in there."

No one knows how anybody lives through anything. People just do.

□ □ □

The shadows are long and the light hazy and golden when we get back to Nana Betsy's house.

She seems more somber and contemplative now. Maybe shooting the video broke one last wall inside her. "I'm about beat," she says. "But there's one more thing I had planned."

We go to the kitchen, where she opens a bulging brown paper bag sitting on the counter. It's filled with large ears of corn.

She fumbles in a cabinet for a pot and fills it with water. She doesn't look at me. Something has descended upon her. "When Blake was eight, Mitzi forbade me from seeing him. She said she was tired of my getting in her business. They moved up to Johnson City, about an hour away, to make things harder." Her voice is so hushed, I strain to hear.

She puts the pot on the stove and turns on the burner. She takes a piece of corn from the sack and begins shucking it.

"Can I help you with that?" I grab an ear and start shucking it beside her.

"Please. Anyway, I'm sitting at home one night and Blake calls. I'll never forget how small and thin his voice was. He said, 'Nana, Mama's been gone for three days and I'm scared.' I said, 'Honey, enough's enough. Nana's coming for you.'"

She takes the ears of shucked corn and lowers them into the water. She sits down at the table, and I join her.

"So I load up Rolly's shotgun and put it in the car. I'm ready to take my grandson home at gunpoint from my own daughter and whoever else if need be. Can you imagine?"

"No." We laugh even though it's not funny.

"So I drive as fast as I've ever driven. When I get there . . . the smell when I opened that trailer door. I still remember it." She shudders with the sense memory. "Garbage mixed with cigarette smoke and filthy clothes and spoiled milk and rotten meat. Which is odd because I didn't see a thing in the house to eat that came from nature. Old Mountain Dew bottles and empty Twinkies boxes and crumpled-up potato chip bags lying everywhere. You hear people talk about living in a dump? This was truly worse than the garbage dump. To this day, I can't fathom how human beings lived there."

"Jesu—jeez."

"I call out to Blake, and I finally find him hiding under the bed. I put down the shotgun so's I don't frighten him. He comes out and he's filthy. He looks and smells like he hasn't bathed in a month. Which makes sense, because I try a faucet and nothing comes out. He's covered in sores and bug

216

bites. He has a hand-shaped bruise on his back and another that looks to be a shoe print."

It feels wrong to speak now, so I don't. Terrible things can be as holy as beautiful things, in their way. I have no words, besides. This story is as new to me as the news of Blake's sexuality was to Nana Betsy, and I can only receive it.

She checks on the corn and returns.

"So we leave fast as can be. I left Rolly's loaded shotgun for them as a little present. Just clean forgot it. They probably hawked it and used the money to buy meth before they even noticed Blake was gone. When we get home, it's past midnight. The grocery store's closed and I'm too exhausted to go anyway. But I want Blake to have something to eat. I don't want him going to bed hungry even one more time. I want to feed him something that grew in the soil; that soaked up the sun. So I had this bag of corn that I'd bought the day before from a farm stand. It was beautiful. We ate it warm with butter and salt. It was sweet as candy. He ate three ears."

My heart feels like it has a thin silver wire wrapped around it, cutting into it with every beat.

"So that's how we'll end this goodbye day. By eating this beautiful corn that tastes like the night Blake's life began. I hope you have room."

I do.

We butter and salt our corn and sit on the porch in rocking chairs, eating while the sun dips below the horizon and the sky dissolves to a pallid blue-pink gradient. All around, the smell of leaves and grass relinquishing their warmth.

"You wanna hear about when Blake made me laugh the hardest?" I ask this without even really knowing the answer, because sadness has so palpably seized Nana Betsy.

"Of course." She gives me a smile that leaves her eyes behind.

"So I go with Blake to one of y'all's church picnics. I don't remember if you were there. Anyway, this little kid is saying grace and he's up there with the microphone, and he's going, 'Lord, we just thank you for the grass and the trees and the oceans' and he's basically thanking God for every single thing on Earth. And of course, we're both starving. So Blake says, in this way-loud voice: 'Move it along kid. I have places to go and people to see.'" As I tell the story, I'm not certain that was the time Blake made me laugh the *hardest*— after all, that moment had a lot of stiff competition—but it did make me laugh very, very hard.

Nana Betsy chuckles softly but still exudes melancholy. "I wish I'd held on to every moment with him the way a drowning person holds a life preserver."

For a time, we rummage through the drawers of our memories, pulling out the stories that are brightest and sharpest, like knives, and setting them in a row. Rekindling fires that had burned to embers. And then we are silent and still because merely listening to ourselves breathe feels like a holy rite in Death's halls.

▣ ▣ ▣

She looks as weary as I feel. I'm hesitant to be the one to end the day, but somebody has to do it.

"Not that I want to, but I should probably go," I say, leaning forward in my rocker. "This was good. I'm glad I did this. I know Blake better now."

"It's past my bedtime, too." She puts her hand on mine, and I can detect the tremor in it. "I can't thank you enough. We did simple things today—the things Blake and I did in a normal week. But that's how I'd have wanted to spend a last day with him."

"Me too." I start to rise. "I'll be back soon to mow."

"You don't need to do that. Fresh air's healthy for me."

"I know, but . . ." I stand, the food settling in my stomach. "This all still hurts. Not as bad as it did, though."

"No," she says distantly. Some timbre in her voice sounds new. Jittery. On edge. She's fidgeting in her chair as though she wants to say something. She won't look at me.

"Nana Betsy?"

She meets my eyes and there's fear on her face.

"Carver, I have one more thing to ask."

"Sure." *She called me Carver, not Blade.* I'm now infected with her apprehension. I sit.

She exhales hard and reaches into her pocket. She pulls out another folded piece of paper. She almost drops it, her hands are shaking so badly. She unfolds it and I see a phone number. "I hired a private investigator to find Mitzi. He tracked her down a few days ago and got me this number. I haven't called her yet to tell her. I thought today would give me the strength and I could do it alone, but I'm coming up short. Will you come inside and stay a few more minutes to hold my hand while I call her?"

I push down the shadowy dread scaling the ladder of my ribs. "Yes."

Her face twists. She sobs. "She'll say, 'You took Blake from me and now he's dead because of it.' And I don't know how to respond, because she's right."

"No. But . . . No . . . that's wrong. That's ridiculous. It's because of me. Like I told you."

Nana Betsy laughs bitterly through her tears. "Oh, Blade. He would have never been in that car if I hadn't moved him here first. I'm just not ready to hear it from her. But I'll never be ready, so I guess this is it."

"It's not your fault." I meet her eyes and hope mine speak my conviction.

She finally nods. "Okay." She says it like she doesn't want to argue; not like I've convinced her. We walk inside and sit next to each other at the kitchen table, in the dark. I figure if she wanted the light on, she'd have turned it on.

She takes a deep breath. "Lord give me strength." She picks up her phone and dials. I reach over and hold her hand. She grips it like the drowning person she spoke of earlier.

I hear the phone ringing on the other end. One. Two. Three. Four. Five. Nana Betsy looks skyward. I see her murmur something. Six. Seven. Each ring is a crow pecking me in the ear. Eight. Nine. She grips my hand tighter.

And then somebody answers as Nana Betsy is lowering the phone from her ear.

She snaps the phone back up. "Mitzi? Mitzi? Is this Mitzi? Mitzi, this is Mama. *Mama.* Mitzi can you—can you turn the music down, please? Turn the music down, please.

It's not important how I got it; I need to talk to you. I know. I know, but you— Sweetie, please, you need to listen to— Because it's about Blake. *It's about Blake.*"

She's crumbling in my hand. It's like trying to grasp a handful of sand from the ocean while the waves come in.

She tries to say something else, but the words dam up in her throat. Tears course glistening down her cheeks. "I can't," she mouths. "I can't." She drops her phone hand to her lap, illuminating us in the screen's ethereal white glow. Mitzi screeches something. Nana Betsy covers her eyes and shakes her head.

I feel it impending. Something sliding off a shelf. But it doesn't fall. It sits tottering at the edge, waiting to fall. But it doesn't fall.

This. You can do this for her if nothing else. I let go of Nana Betsy's hand and slowly reach for the phone. I still hear Mitzi yelling. It would almost be comical if it weren't so very uncomical. Nana Betsy barely resists before letting me take the phone.

I raise it to my ear. "Hello, Mitzi?" I swallow hard. My legs start bouncing. My heart is laboring.

"Who the fuck is this?" Mitzi speaks with a chemical croak. I feel roaches crawling under my skin and sores on my face and my teeth decaying just listening to it. She has gangrene at the jagged edges of her voice. In the background I hear a TV or loud music and a man's voice saying something.

"This is . . . I'm Blake's friend. Carver. Blake's best friend."

"What's going on? Why's my mama calling me about Blake? How'd she get my number?"

"We're—we're calling to tell you that Blake died in a car accident a little more than a month ago." My throat throbs from restraining the deluge.

"*What?* No he didn't. This a joke?" Her words are defiant, but her voice is small. Like that of a child who's been told that a beloved toy is past repair. Or maybe like someone who's been slapped. I hear that experience in her voice too.

I shake my head and then I remember Mitzi can't see me. "Blake is gone. We had his funeral. We buried him. Nana—your mom tried to find you but she couldn't in time. I'm—I'm sorry. I'm really sorry. She wanted to tell you sooner."

"No." Mitzi's voice is smaller still. "I don't even know who you are." I hear the man's voice again, closer.

"I'm sorry." My voice quavers.

"*Jeeeeeeeeeeeeeeeeesuuuuuuuuuuus noooooooooooo.*" Her lament collapses quickly into incoherent, unshapen shrieking.

I have to hold the phone away from my ear. Nana Betsy covers her ears and rests her elbows on the table. She's sobbing and drawing ragged breaths.

When I put the phone back to my ear, Mitzi is keening a litany of *"Put her back on. Put her back on. It's her fault for taking him. I want to tell her. Put her back on. Put her back on. It's her fault. It's her fault he's dead. Oh, Jesus Lord. Oh. Oh, I can't. I can't. Oh."*

"No," I say, with as much steel as I can muster. "I won't put her back on. You'll yell at her."

Nana Betsy lifts her head and reaches for the phone. But it's a halfhearted attempt and I stand and pull away. Mitzi

222

is choking on sobs. So I fill the space. "It's not her fault. It's nobody— It's my fault. It's my fault. You can yell at me. Do it. Yell at me. It's my fault."

She wails, *"You let him get hurt. You didn't take care of him."*

"I know," I say, tears welling hot and dropping. "I'm sorry." But something is turning in me. Something is combusting and turning to anger. I can tell I'm about to say something I'll regret, and I've become acquainted with regret. "But neither did you. You weren't there for him. You weren't even there at the funeral. Your son had a good life because of your mom. He had friends and people who loved him. You should be so grateful to her. I'm—"

The line goes dead, and the only sound in my ears is Nana Betsy's subdued weeping. I slowly lower the phone and set it on the table. I feel like I've been hung from a tree branch in a sack and beaten with a stick.

"I was going to give you back the phone. I didn't want her blaming you. I didn't expect her to hang up."

She shakes her head. "Thank you for telling her."

I suddenly realize that I more or less confessed to Mitzi in the process. I should probably not do that anymore. At this moment, though, I don't really care. Let them try to find Mitzi. From the sound of things, she won't even live another twenty-four hours. Better yet, let them crucify me. It would be a relief.

Nana Betsy looks hollow and vacant. She seems to struggle to hold up her head. "I'm wore out. I don't have anything left."

"I'll go." I start for the door.

"Blade?" she calls. "Will you playact one more thing with me?"

"Yes."

"Let me really say goodbye to Blake."

"Okay." I steel myself.

She stands and faces me. "Blake. I love you and I loved the days I had with you. I have numbered every one of them in my heart. Someday, when that trumpet sounds, I'll hold you again in my arms." And she hugs me.

Words abandon me.

After a long while, she says, "This was a worthy good-bye day. I hope you agree."

"I do."

"Blake was a beautiful boy and I'll miss him."

"I will too." With that I leave.

⊞ ⊞ ⊞

My parents are watching TV in their bedroom. I hadn't told them much about what I was doing today. Only that Nana Betsy and I were spending the day together to remember Blake.

I go in and hug them longer than usual and tell them I love them. They ask about my day and I tell them I don't want to talk; I'm too tired. We'll talk about it later.

I flop down on my bed, text Jesmyn, and ask if she can talk.

While I wait for her to respond, my memories fold and replace themselves in the trunks I've removed them from. Today was cathartic in the way of a vigorous puking session. You don't feel good, exactly. Just purged of something.

Chapter Twenty-Five

"You got new glasses," I say. Dr. Mendez is wearing circular black frames.

"Yes and no," he says. "No, in that I've had this pair for a while; yes, in that generally I'm always buying new glasses I don't need. I buy glasses the way some women buy purses and shoes."

"My friend Jesmyn would say that's sexist."

Dr. Mendez smiles with a concessionary nod. "And she would be right. I need to do better."

"I won't tell."

He takes off his glasses and holds them to the light, inspecting for smudges. "The funny thing is that I never see the world any differently through new glasses. I only ever see things differently when I look in the mirror."

I tap the pad of my index finger on the tip of my nose.

He laughs. "On the nose. Fair enough. If I promised you that I did not intend to sound like such a psychiatrist right then, would you believe me?"

"I mean, it's probably hard not to. It's what you do all day."

"This is true. You're easing my worry about my short-comings while not allowing me to escape accountability. Perhaps we should switch chairs."

I half smile.

Dr. Mendez slumps into his seat and crosses one leg over the other. "So. I'm sorry I missed you a couple of weeks ago; we were on vacation. How are you?"

I draw in a deep breath and give myself until I can't hold it anymore to collect my thoughts. "Last week I did the thing I told you about. The goodbye day with my friend Blake's grandma."

"Oh? How did it go?"

"Pretty well. I guess maybe I got a little closure? I had to tell Blake's mom that he died when his grandma couldn't go through with it."

"Sounds difficult."

"It was. I almost had another panic attack when I was telling her, but I didn't."

"Good."

"Yeah. Anyway, I got to know Blake better. Told his grandma some stuff about his life she didn't know. Maybe told her more than I should've."

"Do you feel guilty about that?"

"Not that as much as other stuff."

"Other stuff?"

I look at the floor and rub my face. I want to tell him and also I don't. It's not that I'm worried about his judging me. I'm worried about his *not* judging me. And then I wonder if my panic-attack near miss just before the call to Mitzi means I'm doing better or if it means I'll backslide on any progress I'm making if I don't tell him.

So I tell him.

Everything. Every detail I can remember. I confess as completely as I did to my lawyer. More, because I add emotion, whereas with Mr. Krantz it was facts only. I tell Dr. Mendez about the DA's investigation. He takes it all in without a twitch. The occasional slight shake of the head or nod and "Mmm."

"So," he says, folding one arm under the other and tapping his lips with his index finger. He holds up three fingers. "It appears there are three components to your present emotional condition. You have grief—you've experienced loss and everything that comes with that. You have fear, over this investigation into the accident. And then, on top of that, you have guilt—you believe that you were the cause of your friends' deaths. Am I hearing you right?"

"Pretty much. I'm also afraid of what this will cost my parents: paying the lawyer."

"Okay."

"Also, one of my friends' sisters is out to get me at school."

"I see. And I'm guessing that here, the grief, fear, and guilt have a synergistic effect. One plus one plus one equals ten, not three."

227

"Pretty much."

"Mmm-hmm." He leans back and tents his fingers in front of his mouth. We stare at each other for a few seconds, listening to the clock tick; our breathing. We let the silence bloom.

"Tell me a story," he says softly.

"Like any story?"

"A story of your friends' deaths where you remove yourself from the question of causation."

"We called ourselves Sauce Crew."

He smiles. "I bet there's a good story there too."

"There is. Can I tell you that one instead?"

"Sometime, sure. But just bear with me for now."

"So you want me to tell you a story where I'm not to blame?"

"Exactly."

My mind whirls, looking for something to grab onto. Some scrap I can unravel and reweave into something. It's not happening. "I can't."

"Why not?"

"Because. That's not what happened."

"Oh, come on," he says. "You're a storyteller. You're a writer."

"Sorry to disappoint."

"Tell me a story. What's the harm in trying?"

"I like to earn things."

"You've suffered, haven't you?"

"Yeah."

"Then you've earned it. Not that you needed to."

I roll my eyes and cast up my hands. "Fine. Um. That day, instead of texting Mars, I wait for them to get to my work so we can hang out. They all live and I'm not sitting here. The end."

"No, no. Remember the rules? That narrative still turns on your actions. What you *didn't* do saved your friends. I want you to tell me a story where you don't have anything to do with the accident."

I growl deep in my throat. "Okay. The semi they rammed into wasn't supposed to be there when it was. The driver was late so . . . there it was. And if it hadn't been there, they would have lived."

Dr. Mendez frowns and nods. "Not bad. But I found myself . . . uninvested in the characters. What did you say the name of the driver was?"

"I didn't."

"Maybe that's why the story didn't quite grab me." His eyes twinkle. "You can do better."

I roll my eyes again and slouch in my chair, staring at the ceiling. When I speak, it's at the ceiling. "Fine. The truck driver's name was . . . Billy . . . Scruggs. That's a good truck driver name, right?" I still don't look at Dr. Mendez.

"Excellent."

"Billy's wife had just made him move out. She said she wanted a divorce because she was tired of his being gone on the road constantly. So he was depressed. He leaves . . . Macon, Georgia, where he lives. That's a good place for a truck driver to be from, right?"

"Billy Scruggs from Macon. Good. I want to hear more."

"So Billy is hauling a load of . . ." I look to Dr. Mendez.

He lifts his hands in an I-dunno-it's-your-story gesture.

". . . psychiatry manuals and eyeglasses to Denver." I almost want him to call me on my smartassery.

Instead, Dr. Mendez laughs and points. "Now you've hooked me."

This feels strangely good. "So Billy was never a responsible driver and he's running a little behind. He's stopped at a truck stop in Chattanooga for some breakfast. He knows he should hit the road, but he can't, because of the waitress. Her name is . . . Tammy Daniels. She's thirty-nine but doesn't look a day over fifty."

Dr. Mendez chuckles. "Fantastic."

"She's not as beautiful as she used to be and she's trying to hide it with too much makeup. But Billy still finds her beautiful. Because she only needs to be beautiful by comparison to endless asphalt and billboards and the backs of other semis."

Dr. Mendez nods. "Yes," he says softly. "Good."

"So Billy keeps trying to work up the courage to ask her for her number. She smiled and winked at him earlier, so he thinks he has a shot. He drinks cup after cup of coffee—more than he wants to—because it brings her to his table. He's wondering when he'd even see her again if he did work up the courage. Finally, he chickens out and gives up. Billy isn't only a bad truck driver—he's also a quitter. He leaves a big tip and writes 'You're beautiful' on the receipt before hitting the road."

"I was rooting for Billy," Dr. Mendez says. "Now he's late *and* he doesn't get the girl."

Somewhere along the way, I've moved to the edge of my seat without even realizing. "And plus he has to keep stopping to pee from all the coffee he drank waiting for a chance to talk to Tanya."

"Tammy."

"Oh, right. Tammy. So he's really late by now. When he hits Nashville, he's supposed to be farther down the road. But he's not. Instead, he's where Sauce Crew ran into him. In front of him is a van carrying a load of feather pillows and packing peanuts. If they'd run into that van, they would have lived. But they ran into Billy instead. Screw-up Billy."

A long silence passes. I rub at a smudge on my pants.

"In that story, you're not the cause of their deaths," Dr. Mendez says.

"I guess not. In that story."

"How do you feel after telling it?"

"Like I'm lying to both of us."

"Why?"

"Because that's not what happened."

"How do you know?"

"Because I know."

"How?"

"Because."

"How?"

I sigh. "Fine, I don't."

Another protracted, pensive moment slips by before Dr.

Mendez speaks. "Our minds seek causality because it suggests an order to the universe that may not actually exist, even if you believe in some higher power. Many people would prefer to accept an undue share of blame for a tragic event than concede that there's no order to things. Chaos is frightening. A capricious existence where bad things happen to good people for no discernible reason is frightening."

It is certainly that.

"Pareidolia," I say.

"Come again?"

"Pareidolia. One of my favorite words. It's when your mind sees a pattern you recognize where there isn't one. Like seeing a face in the moon. Or shapes in clouds."

Dr. Mendez smiles and says, mostly to himself, "Pareidolia. What a beautiful word."

"For something that isn't always beautiful."

"For something that isn't always beautiful."

Chapter Twenty-Six

Sometimes I forget they're gone for a few seconds. I'll hear something at school about an upcoming dance or theater production. I'll read about an upcoming movie or video game. Something we shared in together. There's a spark of excitement. And as quickly as it comes, it evaporates as though the air itself has some higher claim to my happiness than I do. You'd expect this would happen less often the more distance I get from their deaths. But it only seems to happen more as summer surrenders to autumn.

I've heard that people who lose a limb have a "phantom limb," which itches and senses pain as though their body's forgotten that it's gone.

I have a trinity of phantoms.

Chapter Twenty-Seven

We're inside, but we shouldn't be. We should be enjoying the perfect seventy-two-degree late afternoon. The waning summer is my favorite miniseason, with its temperate days: gentle, crisp nights with slowly singing crickets, and mornings like cool satin on your skin. I usually walk around happy for no reason at this point. Not this year.

We're at the Bellevue library. It's a new, modern building and dozens of wooden birds, carved from the trees cleared from the library site, float above us on cables. The same as we do with our memories once our lives are clear-cut and bulldozed over. We carve them into birds and hang them, as if they're still really flying.

Jesmyn sits across from me. She's watching and listening intently to something on her laptop with headphones. I'm supposed to be working on an essay about Toni Morrison for AP English lit, but Jesmyn distracts me. She's seemed pissed all day. I try to read her expression but I'm still unacquainted with all her shades.

She starts sniffling. She quickly wipes her eyes with the sides of her thumbs. I debate whether to pretend not to notice or whether to say something. I settle on saying something.

"Hey," I whisper.

"Hey," she whispers in a wobbly voice, wiping her eyes again.

"You wanna go hang outside?"

She nods and closes her laptop. She stuffs it in her bag, not making eye contact and letting her hair cover her face. I quickly gather my things and follow her outside, where she sits on a bench, her bag at her feet.

I wait for her to start, but she doesn't.

"Did I do something?" I ask.

She doesn't speak for several seconds, watching cars go by. Finally: "I want you to be completely honest with me."

"Okay." I shift uneasily.

"Have you been telling people we're hooking up?"

I feel cold and my mouth goes dry. "No. *No.* What the hell? Who would I even tell?"

"'Who would I even tell' isn't that comforting. Dudes would tell the pizza delivery guy if they wanted to brag about getting with a girl."

I'm consciously willing myself to appear truthful, which I am. The problem is that the harder you try to seem credible, the less so you seem. "Jesmyn, I *swear*. What have you heard?"

"Today, in music theory, Kerry told me that she'd heard you and I were hooking up and that we'd started even before Eli died."

Nothing strips you and leaves you lying there, naked and bruised, like finding out someone has been maliciously lying about you. I guess it's why people do it. People who hate you. A rising tide of fury and humiliation swells in my chest. "Gee, I wonder who could be spreading such a rumor."

"Adair? You think?"

"She hates the shit out of both of us."

"But why lie?"

"Because she wants to hurt us? It legitimately bums me out your mind went to me before it went to her."

"Well."

"No, seriously. Even if it were true that we were hooking up, I would *never* tell anyone."

"We're still getting to know each other."

"You should know me that well by now at least. Dude, Georgia trained me right."

Jesmyn looks slightly relieved. "Sorry. It's just this happened at my last school. I started dating this guy, and his old girlfriend started everyone talking about what a slut I am."

"See? Girls are as capable of spreading shitty rumors about other girls as guys are."

"I didn't say they weren't."

"*Sexist.*"

"Whatever."

"I'm really sorry for getting you into this." *But not too sorry.*

"Into what? Being friends? Shut up. I'll be friends with whoever I want. Adair can eat me. I just don't appreciate people lying about me." But she still seems burdened despite her defiance.

"Was that all that was bugging you?"

She fiddles with her bracelet. Her nails are painted dark gray, almost black. "No."

"Want to talk about it?"

"Only if you promise not to try to fix the problem. Guys always want to fix things."

"I promise. In fact, not only will I not try to fix things, I promise I'll screw things up worse."

She laughs. "Don't do that either. Only listen."

"Only listening."

"So I have this neurological condition called synesthesia."

"Is . . . that the thing where—"

"Where one sense triggers another sense. So when I play or hear music—or any sound, actually—I see colors."

"Oh. Wow. That's awesome. I've heard about that."

"I guess. It's awesome sometimes. Not always. Anyway, this piece I'm working on for my Juilliard audition? 'Jeux d'eau'? I was barely watching Martha Argerich performing it. It's supposed to sound crystal, cobalt blue. Like . . . blue glass set on a windowsill. That's how it sounds when she plays it. But when I play it, it sounds brownish-green. All snotty. It's gross and awful. It physically hurts to listen to myself."

"It sounds amazing when you play it."

"No offense, dude, but I have to play it for people with way pickier ears than yours."

"You'll nail it."

"Well, for the last almost two months, everything I've played sounds snot colored. It's like Eli's dying broke something in me, and now I have this weird sickly greenish-yellow photo filter over everything I do. It's horrible to have something I love so much feel so completely wrong."

"I get that."

"I don't know what to do."

In response, I'm conspicuously mum and motionless. Jesmyn gives me an expectant look.

"This is me not doing anything whatsoever to fix the problem," I mumble out of the corner of my mouth.

She laughs. A sound that's become a sanctuary to me. "Okay, you can give me a hug. That's sufficiently nonfixing."

We stand and hug, swaying slightly. "You give good hugs," she murmurs in my ear.

"Careful you don't let me fix something by accident."

"I won't."

"Sorry you're viewing the world through snot-colored lenses lately."

"Me too."

She pulls back, and maybe I'm imagining this but she lightly drags the edges of her lips along my cheek as she does so. (Personal growth, so I have to sit back down carefully.)

Jesmyn sits. "Do you think it would help me if I had a goodbye day for Eli like you did for Blake? No joking about how you're not supposed to fix anything."

I was not expecting this question, given recent events.

"Possibly. I mean, Blake is definitely quieter now in my mind than he used to be."

"Maybe we should both have a goodbye day for Eli with his parents. Might help us both."

Because of Adair, this had not even occurred to me. The idea weirds me out. "Do you want me to see if they're into it?" I'm hoping she'll say no.

"Maybe."

"What about Adair?"

"If Adair's a problem, they'll say no."

"What do we do about Adair in general? Should we try to talk to her?"

"After one attempt at it, I can't imagine that helping much."

We sit in wordless contemplation, my thoughts bubbling up and breaking on the surface.

"So," I say finally, "what color is my voice? When I talk?"

She rubs her chin and squints. "Hmmm. Usually bull-shit colored."

Chapter Twenty-Eight

I don't recognize the number on my phone. "Hello?"

"Carver Briggs?" The voice on the other end is brusque. Not the sort to deliver the news that you've been randomly selected to swim with baby dolphins while someone yells compliments at you through a bullhorn. It sounds like a black leather gun holster looks.

"Speaking," I say over the blaring klaxons in my head.

"This is Lieutenant Dan Farmer of the Metro Nashville PD. We wanted to speak with you about the car accident on August first involving Thurgood Edwards, Eli Bauer, and Blake Lloyd. We understand you were friends with them. When could you and your parents come down to the station and speak with us?"

I will my voice to stop shaking but fail miserably. "I— Actually, I'd better talk to my lawyer first."

"You're not under arrest for anything. We just want to have a conversation." He sounds palpably annoyed.

"My lawyer said I shouldn't talk to any police without him there. My lawyer's Jim Krantz."

Lieutenant Farmer's annoyance becomes full-blown exasperation—he's as terrible at hiding it as I am at hiding my nerves. "All right. You got my number on your phone?"

"Yes."

"Call your lawyer and let me know."

"Okay."

Lieutenant Farmer hangs up without saying goodbye.

I tell my parents. Then we call Mr. Krantz.

This is happening.

There's a dim, remote corner of me that actually welcomes it.

▣ ▣ ▣

The next day, after the longest day of school in my life, we're all seated around Mr. Krantz's conference table. My parents are on my left. There's an empty chair on my right for Mr. Krantz. A video camera sits on a tripod in a corner. Nobody says anything.

I hear voices; niceties being exchanged out front. The receptionist leads in two men wearing khaki slacks and sport coats. They have guns and badges on their belts. A young woman in a well-tailored suit and with an equally well-tailored professional air follows.

The older of the two men introduces himself. "Carver? Lieutenant Dan Farmer. Thanks for coming."

Oh, you're welcome! Couldn't be more excited to be here!

The younger man introduces himself. "Sergeant Troy Metcalf."

The woman steps forward. "Carver, I'm Alyssa Curtis. I'm an assistant district attorney for Davidson County."

"The whole team showed up," my dad says. He tries to play it casually, like we're people who have nothing to worry about, despite the contemptful edge in his voice (my dad's accent is a good fit for contempt). There's awkward laughter. Not from our side of the table. My stomach is full of wasps.

They take seats across from me. I stare at my sweating hands. Nobody talks. Finally, Mr. Krantz bustles in, his glasses on the end of his nose, holding a legal pad. Neither of the officers nor Ms. Curtis looks especially happy to see Mr. Krantz. But they all shake hands.

"All right," Mr. Krantz says, sitting with a grunt and looking at his watch. "I'm busy; my client's busy; y'all are busy—or at least you ought to be. So let's get this show on the road."

"Fair enough," Lieutenant Farmer says, clicking his pen. "Carver, we're here investigating the accident that took the lives of Thurgood Edwards, Elias Bauer, and Blake Lloyd on August first of this year. Why don't you tell us everything you know about the circumstances surrounding this accident?"

I swallow hard. As I'm about to speak, Mr. Krantz intervenes. He whips off his glasses and plops them on top of his legal pad. "No, no, no. You have a specific question? You ask. I'm not having my client telling you free-form campfire stories."

Lieutenant Farmer winces and squirms in his chair. "Carver, were you aware at the time of the accident that the three deceased were traveling in a vehicle?"

I start to answer, but Mr. Krantz cuts me off. "My client exercises his rights under the Fifth Amendment to the United States Constitution and Article One, Section Nine, of the Tennessee Constitution and declines to answer."

Lieutenant Farmer takes a here-we-go breath through his nose. "Did you text Thurgood Edwards immediately preceding the accident?"

"I—"

"My client exercises his rights under the Fifth Amendment and Article One, Section Nine, and declines to answer."

"Were you aware that Thurgood was driving at the time you texted him?"

I wait a couple of seconds before even trying to answer. With good reason.

"My client never told you that he texted Mr. Edwards. *You* said that. Also, he exercises his rights under the Fifth Amendment and Article One, Section Nine, and declines to answer."

Sergeant Metcalf sighs.

Lieutenant Farmer speaks softly. "Look, Carver, we're just trying to get to the bottom of this. We're not trying to trip you up."

Mr. Krantz chuckles. "Dan, you can't start playing good cop after you've already started out as the bad cop. Also, baloney. You're trying to pin something on my client—a kid—so His Honor will stand down. Let's acknowledge what this is."

"We're not enjoying this, Jimmy."

"Didn't say you were. Next question. I have a tee time."

"Carver, who have you talked with about this accident?"

Pause. Hold for—

"My client exercises his rights under the Fifth Amendment and Article One, Section Nine, and declines to answer. Next question."

"Jim," Ms. Curtis says, "Carver's cooperation would go a long way toward defusing this situation or giving you bargaining leverage down the line. Especially if our investigation eventually turns up something. Then it'll be too late."

"It would also go a long way to giving y'all the only hook you have to hang your hats on. This is your only chance to talk to Carver, so I suggest you keep things moving."

Lieutenant Farmer's eyes bore into me. As though daring me to stand up to Mr. Krantz and blurt something out. "Carver, is there anything you wish you'd done differently on August first?"

Oh, the ways that I could answer that question. Oh, the ways that question has come to define my entire existence. And my shocking, stunning answer is . . .

"My client exercises his rights under the Fifth Amendment and Article One, Section Nine, and declines to answer."

There we go.

Ms. Curtis touches Lieutenant Farmer's arm and stands. "Okay. This isn't a productive use of anyone's time." She glares at me. "I can't make any promises about how the DA will react to your lack of cooperation if we decide to go forward with the case."

Her tone chills me.

Mr. Krantz chuckles an asshole-ish chuckle. "What case?" He stands. "Folks, always a pleasure." He doesn't offer his hand. Neither do the two officers or Ms. Curtis.

"We'll be in touch," Ms. Curtis says as they start to leave.

"I expect so. And, folks?"

The two officers and Ms. Curtis turn.

"I better not hear of any back-alley attempts to trick Carver into saying something he shouldn't. No pretty young undercover officers in low-cut blouses. No forty-five-year-olds pretending to be sixteen-year-olds in chatrooms. No shenanigans; no bullshit. From here on out, my client is unequivocally and unambiguously exercising his right to remain silent. He ain't interested in helping Fred Edwards steamroll him. We understand each other?"

None of the three respond. They walk out.

Mr. Krantz looks at his watch as he gathers his things. "Sorry to be in a rush, y'all. I wasn't blowing hot air about that tee time." He claps me on the shoulder and squeezes. "You hang in there, son."

Hang in there. That's always helpful advice, especially because it always comes when you feel like you're standing at the gallows.

⊞ ⊞ ⊞

When I get home, I tell Jesmyn I plan to approach Eli's parents about doing a goodbye day. What I don't tell her is that I've decided to do this because I'm worried about two things: (1) I go to prison before I have a chance; (2) I don't go to prison and instead chew myself up from the inside before I have a chance. Either way. It's something I need to do sooner rather than later.

I'm nervous about calling them until I remind myself that I recently informed a mother over the phone that her son died. If I can do that, I guess I can do anything. Phone-wise. That still leaves Adair to be apprehensive about, but I'll leave that up to them.

I thought I would have to explain more, but I don't. I talk with Eli's mom. She tells me Nana Betsy called them shortly after Blake's goodbye day and recommended the experience as therapeutic. So they've been considering it but were worried about how to approach me. And it's perfect timing, because they have a plan to scatter Eli's ashes at Fall Creek Falls this autumn. They think he would have liked that. She tells me to invite Jesmyn. I tell her I will.

I don't tell her how I hope this will allow Eli to finally rest in my mind, because death becomes real only when people rest finally.

Chapter Twenty-Nine

"Tell me a story." It's the first thing Dr. Mendez says when we settle into our chairs. We skip the small talk entirely.

I came ready. Why not? I knew he'd wheedle it out of me eventually and I'd have to invent on the fly. "In 2001, Hiro Takasagawa was a safety engineer at Nissan. He was actually an artist—he built moving sculptures. But people didn't buy them, so he had to take a real job with his skills."

"The world is a difficult place for artists."

"Yeah. But Hiro loved his job because his parents died in a car accident when he was really young. They rear-ended a truck on an icy road. He wanted to prevent that from happening to anybody else. So he designed a safety system for cars where there was a pair of mechanical white wings—a crane's wings—folded underneath the car. And there was—a radar sensor or something on the front of the car, and if you were coming up on an obstacle too fast, the wings would open and start beating and lift the car over the obstacle. It would glide for a while and you could still steer in the air by using your steering wheel. Until you got to a place where you could land safely."

Dr. Mendez looks genuinely absorbed in the story. "The year 2001. You were very specific about that."

"So Hiro took the idea to his boss. The idea was to start putting it in 2002 Nissans. But his boss was furious. 'Takasagawa, do you have any idea how much this will cost?' He screamed. 'But it works,' Hiro said. 'I built a prototype and tested it. What are people's lives worth?' And the boss is like 'You idiot! We're running a business here. You wasted time and money with this?! You're fired!'" I'm getting into the story. I'm doing different voices for Hiro and the boss.

"What's the boss's name?" Dr. Mendez asks.

"Yoshikazu Hanawa. CEO of Nissan in 2001. Looked it up."

"Good," Dr. Mendez says quietly. "Very good. Sorry. Please." He gestures for me to continue.

I take a deep breath. "So Hiro leaves Hanawa's office and he's devastated. He thinks he failed his parents and brought dishonor to himself. So he goes and gets in his car and drives away. He intends to commit suicide. He tries to drive into the side of a building, but at the last second, a pair of gleaming white crane's wings unfurls from beneath his car. And the thing is, he wasn't driving his prototype. These just appear. They carry him up, up, over the building, into the sky. And he never comes down. He's still soaring on those wings."

There's a long pause before Dr. Mendez says: "And Mars drove—"

"A 2002 Nissan Maxima."

"Unequipped with Hiro's wings."

"It would have been too expensive."

"But if Mr. Hanawa had approved Hiro's idea—"

"Then even though Mars was texting, the wings would have carried him up over the truck."

"Billy Scruggs's truck."

"Right."

"No matter what you did or didn't do."

"Right."

"How did it feel to tell that story?"

"Like I'm still lying to myself and trying to blame someone else."

"Why?"

"Because. Hiro's story didn't really happen."

Dr. Mendez tilts his head with a gleam in his eye and I see the question.

"Fine," I mutter. "I don't know."

Dr. Mendez smiles broadly. "So. How are you?"

I chew on the inside of my lip. "I talked with the cops the other day about the accident. Well. I sat in a room with cops while they asked questions that my attorney said I wouldn't answer."

"I'm not used to praising my clients for refusing to talk, but good job."

"Why good job?"

"Do you remember what we discussed last visit? How we seek causality where there may be none?"

"You don't think I should accept blame for this right now."

"What I think doesn't matter. What matters is what you think. I'm trying to help you do your best thinking. Before you take a step that could have drastic consequences, I want to make sure you've considered other perspectives."

"I'm scared."

"Of what?"

"Going to jail."

"I can imagine." His brow furrows.

I slump in my chair. "Would it sound weird if I told you that I'm also scared of *not* going to jail?"

"Do you know why you're afraid of that?"

"Not completely."

"Is it partly because you feel it would rob you of an opportunity to atone if you weren't imprisoned?"

"Maybe."

Dr. Mendez says nothing, but his expression tells me that I should keep running down this path.

"Speaking of atoning," I say, "I'm doing another goodbye day. With Eli's parents."

"You said the experience with Blake's grandmother was valuable."

"It was."

"Having lived with that experience for a little while now, do you have any new reflections on it?"

I stare at the bookshelf behind Dr. Mendez, as if a book's spine holds the answer to his question. "It . . . made me wish even more that I'd appreciated the time I had with them more while I had it."

"That's a very normal regret to have. You don't want to live like you're constantly in the shadow of death, but unless you do that, there'll almost always be things that went unsaid or unappreciated fully. If you found the goodbye-day experience to be more therapeutic than not, I say go for it with Eli's parents."

"Yeah."

He gives me the look that precedes when he's about to reach inside my head. "But you have qualms."

"Yes."

"Why?"

"Because Eli's family is way different from Blake's grandma."

"How so?"

"Like . . . philosophically, I guess. Their world is a lot more complicated. They're both way educated. With Blake's grandma, there's God and heaven and hell and that's it. Eli's parents—I doubt they believe they'll ever see Eli again the way Blake's grandma has faith she's going to see Blake again. They're definitely not churchgoers. Also, Eli has a twin. Adair. She blames me."

"Mmmm."

"I'm not as sure where Eli's parents stand on the blaming-me thing."

"I assume, if they held you responsible, they wouldn't be amenable to the idea and that would be that."

"I guess. Another thing is that I've gotten really close

with Jesmyn, Eli's girlfriend. Ex-girlfriend. Widow-girlfriend. Whatever you call what she is."

"And that worries you because?"

"I don't want to look like I'm trying to take anything from Eli. I'm not. There are already rumors at school. I suspect Adair started them."

"This is the same Jesmyn who would have rightly taken me to task for my unfortunate sexist joke last visit?"

"Exactly. Nice remembering."

Dr. Mendez makes a triangle with his fingers in front of his mouth. "From the little you've told me of her, she wouldn't acquiesce in the giving or taking of her."

"Oh, definitely not."

"So whatever you or Eli's parents think about your relationship with her is irrelevant. She would never allow herself to be in a relationship that she didn't want. Fair to say?"

"Definitely. But we're just friends." It always sounds wrong to say that. Boners notwithstanding (let's be honest: a Kmart lingerie ad can get things moving under the right circumstances), I don't think we're anything but friends. Yet we've shared an emotional intimacy that I've never had with a friend before, so I'm not sure if "just friends" totally describes what we have.

"I understand."

"I talk with her about this whole deal more than with my parents."

"Are your parents available to listen?"

"Yeah. But I'm not a big talker with my parents. I have a hard time being vulnerable with them. It's nothing they've done. I guess . . . I don't want to disappoint them or some-thing? I just want to be independent? I like my space? Maybe I'm weird, I don't know."

Dr. Mendez shakes his head. "No, not at all. Look, I'm trained to talk to people and still, my son, Ruben—he's a lit-tle older than you—doesn't often talk to me. It doesn't make you weird."

A few moments pass.

"Allowing yourself to be vulnerable with your parents and open up to them is something we could work on," Dr. Mendez says.

"Yeah. But I have enough to deal with right now."

"I know. For the future."

"Will I ever be okay again?" I ask.

"I expect so. It'll take time and work. But someday your world will be put right. I've never found it to be a matter of purging yourself of feeling, but rather of coming to live with it. Making it a part of you that doesn't hurt so badly. You know how oysters make pearls?"

I nod.

"Like that," he says. "Our memories of our loved ones are the pearl that we form around the grain of grief that causes us pain."

I reflect on this for a while before speaking again. "I re-membered something funny and random."

"I like funny and random."

"Jesmyn's dad works for Nissan. Like Hiro. That's why they moved here."

Dr. Mendez just smiles.

Chapter Thirty

Nana Betsy sells her house in a matter of weeks. She gets enough to cover some new little place and Blake's funeral. I hope there's a little left over for Mitzi's, which didn't sound far off.

I spend a day, along with her sons, helping her move. We throw away more than we load into her rented U-Haul. Jesmyn comes by after she's done teaching and helps us with odds and ends.

When we're finished, Nana Betsy's sons start driving the U-Haul to Greeneville. She'll follow behind in her car. Jesmyn goes home to practice. Nana Betsy and I sit on her front steps once more in the cool of the burning-leaves-scented, indigo October twilight. For fifteen minutes or so. She needs to head out. But we say goodbye to each other.

She tells me the police came to talk to her about the

Accident. She says she didn't tell them anything I told her and never would.

I thank her. And my stomach opens with a dank emptiness as I think about how I've made her a liar before her God. As I think about how I'm living under a spreading shadow.

She asks me to go with her to lay flowers on Blake's grave when she returns for Memorial Day.

I tell her I will.

She asks me to have a good and happy life, full of laughter, love, and friendship.

I tell her I'll try.

Chapter Thirty-One

Two months after the Accident and I'm already getting to the point where I suspect my brain of creating false memories of them. Sauce Crew fan fiction. Where you can't remember if it's something you dreamed or something that actually happened. You believe dreams.

I have this persistent "memory" now of all of us hanging at a school playground on some temperate afternoon— perhaps during the closing days of school when spring is yielding to summer.

For some reason, one of us has a portable stereo you can hook up to an iPod. We sit on the playground equipment, listening to music. That's all. I remember nothing else.

I can't imagine when or why this would've happened. I

don't remember any other occasion besides this once that we did this. I don't remember any other details.

But my brain is convinced that it did happen.

If my brain wants to manufacture new memories of them, I'll accept it and I won't ask too many questions.

Chapter Thirty-Two

Jesmyn and I trade few words as we sit in front of Eli's house, waiting to go in.

"Is Adair coming?" Jesmyn asks.

"Let's pray she doesn't." I start to open my door.

Jesmyn laughs to herself.

"What?" I ask.

"It's not really funny. I just realized that because Eli only ever saw me in the summer, he never once saw me wearing a jacket. I love jackets. It reminded me how little time we knew each other. One season."

She's wearing a gray wool belted motorcycle jacket, with a slightly diagonal row of buttons instead of a zipper.

"He would've dug that jacket. It looks good on you."

She gives me an anxious smile. "Let's do this."

"I'm nervous too."

"At least you've done one of these."

"Still."

"I only knew him for a couple of months. I'm sure I'll still have parts of his story that you and his parents don't, but I don't want to be a disappointment."

"I doubt you'll be."

We glance at each other and I lean in and hug her. More for my solace than hers. I love nearness to her. Not in a lustful way. In the way I loved rubbing satin between my fingers when I was little. There's something inexplicably comfortable about it.

We take a collective deep breath and walk up the front steps. It's the first time I've been to Eli's house since before the Accident. The keen ache of nostalgia entwines my heart.

▣ ▣ ▣

I look around, awestruck. I've always heard that there were nice houses in Hillsboro Village, but I've never been in one. It's filled with books stacked on clean, modern, floor-to-ceiling bookshelves. They have an exposed-brick wall in their living room, and on it hang several abstract paintings. I'm clueless about art, but I could easily see them in a museum, and it wouldn't surprise me if they cost more than my house.

On one wall is a huge antique map of London. On another wall a sweeping black-and-white panorama of the New York City skyline. The furniture resembles what I've seen at a family trip to Ikea, but more substantial and luxurious.

"Man, cool house," I say.

"Thanks. I can't take credit," Eli says.

"Are your parents, like, artists or architects or something?"

"Naw. My mom is a neurosurgeon at Vanderbilt Hospital. My dad is a history professor at Vanderbilt. He researches the Cold War. You should hear this insane theory he has about the Roswell UFO incident in 1947."

I laugh. "My dad is an English professor at Belmont. My mom is a physical therapist."

"No way! We totally have parallel families."

"I have a sister."

"Dude, me too. A twin, actually. Adair. She goes to school with us. She's at dance practice now."

"Nice."

"You hungry or thirsty or anything?"

"Always."

Eli leads me into the kitchen, which is no less impressive than what I've already seen. Full of glass, steel, and granite. There's a huge wine rack, and copper-bottomed pots and pans hang from the ceiling. He opens a cabinet and starts getting out bags of chips, popcorn, and dried fruit and nuts from Trader Joe's. "Anything you want," he says.

He goes to the fridge and grabs us a couple of bottles of some cola that I've never heard of but that purports to be "handcrafted in small batches."

"Thanks." I study the label. "How do you handcraft cola?"

"Weird, huh? I picture some guy wearing a blacksmith's apron pounding a hammer into a vat of cola."

"A carpenter sawing his saw into cola."

We laugh. I grab a bag of dried mandarin oranges. We head to his room.

Here's the first indication that somebody under forty lives here. The walls are painted dark gray and covered with posters of bands I've never heard of—black and death metal bands whose skeletal, twisting-branch logos are mostly illegible. One wall resembles a museum of guitars, with four electrics and two acoustics hanging on it.

Black jeans and black T-shirts with more band names cover the floor.

I step over some. "Musician, huh?"

"How'd you guess? What about you? What's your jam that got you into NAA?"

"Writing. Fiction."

"Cool. Wanna be our scribe?"

"Sure." I pull out my laptop and sit at Eli's desk.

Eli pulls down an acoustic guitar and sits on the edge of the bed. "You mind? I concentrate better while I'm playing."

"Go ahead."

He starts fingerpicking. It's immediately clear how he got into NAA. "So," he says. "We have to predict a future technology . . ."

"And the impact it'll have on our lives."

"Dude, I'm glad we got assigned as partners. This might be right up your alley."

"Too bad I don't write sci-fi."

"What do you write?"

"Dark Southern stuff mostly."

"Nice. I'm into dark."

"Who'd have guessed?"

He laughs. "Maybe we should collaborate someday. You write lyrics and I'll do the music."

"I'm down."

"Okay. So. In the future. My mom was telling me the other day about how scientists grew a human ear on a mouse's back. It was in one of her medical journals."

"What? Creepy."

"Yeah, but cool."

"What if someday they grew, like, a full-sized human dick on a mouse?"

And that was that. The next day Eli ate lunch with Blake and me instead of Adair. And every day after that.

▣ ▣ ▣

Melissa answers the door. She's dressed for a day outside. Hiking pants, trail-running shoes, a fleece vest. Her curly, dark hair is in a ponytail. I remember Eli telling me she was an avid runner. She has much the same look Nana Betsy had—distant; haunted. "Come in. Good to see you."

"Hi, Melissa," I say. It seems wrong to call a neurosurgeon by her first name, but Eli and Adair always called their parents Melissa and Pierce, so . . .

The house is mostly as I remember. It even smells the same—Eli's mom loves these candles that smell like a mixture of black tea, tobacco leaves, and leather—opening even more doors of memory.

I see a familiar ache on Jesmyn's face. "Hey," I whisper.

"Hey," she whispers back.

We follow Melissa into the kitchen. An assortment of pastries and croissants towers on a plate. She motions for us to help ourselves. "These are some of Eli's favorite things from Provence bakery. We used to walk there every Saturday morning that I wasn't working and if the weather was good. We still go with Adair. Jesmyn, you joined us once, didn't you?"

She nods. "I had a chocolate croissant."

"We got some of those," Melissa says.

Jesmyn and I each take a chocolate croissant and start eating while Melissa wordlessly makes some fresh orange juice and sets a couple of glasses in front of us.

"Is Pierce coming?" Jesmyn asks.

"Oh . . . yeah. He was out running some errands. He should be here in a few minutes."

"What about Adair?" I ask tentatively. "Is she coming?"

Melissa sighs and pauses. "Adair is . . . tricky."

Gee, you think?

"We invited her. She declined. She spent the night at a friend's house," Melissa continues. "That's where she is now. She's not ready for any of this. It's different with twins. Pierce and I never completely understood the bond they had. How could we?"

"Will today make things tough with her?" Jesmyn asks.

Melissa turns away from us and wipes the already-pristine mottled granite countertop. "It's funny, actually. She was adamant that we go, even though she didn't want to. But we decided not to scatter Eli's ashes like we were planning on doing. Not without Adair. We'll do that another time."

Why did Adair want her parents to do this? This should make me feel better, but it doesn't. "We can call this off if you want," I say.

"No," Melissa says quietly but firmly. "I want to do it. It's good to confront feelings. You both know Eli in ways we didn't, Adair included." She picks up a mason jar full of brightly colored sand. "We're going to scatter this at the falls instead. This is one of the first things Eli ever made for me in preschool. It contains his creative energy. That'll be our ceremony."

The atmosphere is taut. Eli's family weren't cuddly types even before. So we eat, and Jesmyn and I occasionally swap supportive glances.

Five minutes or so later, we hear the front door open, and Pierce walks in, dressed for the outdoors. He also looks haggard. Bone weary. Whittled away, especially in the face. "Hello, everybody," he says. Even though I don't have Jesmyn's synesthesia, his voice sounds gray to me.

"Hi," Jesmyn and I murmur almost in unison.

Pierce walks over and gives Melissa a peck on the cheek. She gives him a narrow smile. More pressing her lips together than raising the corners.

"Help yourself," Melissa says.

"I'm fine," Pierce says.

"Thank y'all for doing this," Jesmyn says. "It's good to see you again. I missed you."

Melissa gives her a warmer smile. "We missed you too. We loved having you around."

"So," Jesmyn says, "I'm not sure how this works, but I can tell you exactly how Eli and I met if you're interested."

"We'd love to hear," Pierce says. "We have a vague idea, but only from Eli. Not from you."

Jesmyn takes a sip of orange juice and wipes her mouth. "I noticed Eli on the very first day at Tennessee Teens Rock Camp. They had us all sitting on the auditorium stage. The counselors were trying to teach us 'punk rock aerobics,' but I kept getting distracted looking at him. He was right across from me. I thought he had beautiful hair. All long and dark and curly. He reminded me of Jon Snow from *Game of Thrones*."

"I was so afraid of him getting my hair," Melissa says, "and of course he did. It was endless drama combing it out when he was little."

Jesmyn continues. "But I don't dwell because I'm there to make music, not find a boyfriend. Anyway, they assign us our bands, and of course—"

"You guys are in the same band," Pierce says. "That's all Eli told us."

"I'm like 'Whatever,' because guitarists are usually the worst. Fine, he's hot, but who cares? So we start working on our song for the showcase, and suddenly he comes over to me with this idea. He and I will play this ascending and descending guitar-keyboard line, and he'll harmonize with me. We work it out and try it. It's this warm red-orange-pink."

"Carver, you know about Jesmyn's synesthesia?" Melissa asks.

I nod, weirdly hurt that Eli's mom found out so much sooner than me. It's dumb because she's Eli's mom and a damn brain surgeon, but . . .

"I loved seeing that color, so I kept making Eli run that part with me again and again. And I never felt like he was hitting on me. He was a perfect gentleman. If anything, I pursued him. By the end of that week, we were inseparable. You should have seen how I freaked out when I found out we were going to the same school."

This story is an icepick slipping slowly between my ribs. But in a different way than the stories about Blake were. I fixate on my plate as if the answer to some mystery is written in the crumbs there. I'm afraid to look up, because I don't want anyone to ask me what I'm feeling. I wouldn't be able to say.

We eat for the next few minutes, bits of rigid small talk bobbing to the surface and sinking again. By the time Pierce suggests we head out, I'm almost hoping Jesmyn has another story of her pursuing Eli, since her first, while making me uncomfortable, seemed to relieve the tension otherwise.

We wrap up the pastries. We're almost out the door when Pierce stops us.

"Wait." His voice sounds even more leaden; rain clouds verging on deluge. "We're about to take part of Eli from his house for the last time. This is the house we raised him in. The day we brought him and Adair home from the hospital as newborns . . ." He pauses and coughs, collecting himself. He tries to start again but falters. Finally, he clears his throat and says, "Melissa was feeding Adair. So I sat out on the porch with Eli and let the wind touch his face for the first time. I saw him hear the trees moving, rustling for the first time. That's quite a thing: to see a human being first feel the wind. He opened his eyes just once, squinting up at me. I wondered how many more of the things of this world I would show him."

I hadn't considered this difference between Blake's good-bye day and Eli's: Eli's parents have baby stories.

We step out onto the porch, where the breeze has picked up, tugging at our hair.

Pierce pauses. "Everyone, the plan was to scatter the sand at the falls, but could we do a little part here?"

We all nod. Melissa has been stoic. As a surgeon who deals with death and dying every day, I guess she doesn't have much room for sentimentality. But tears stream down her cheeks.

Pierce opens the jar, reaches in, and pulls out a pinch of sand. Then he returns that small bit of Eli's spirit to the wind that once touched his face.

⊞ ⊞ ⊞

Jesmyn and I sit in the backseat of Melissa's Volvo SUV. Melissa's driving. Pierce sits beside her, cradling the jar on his lap and staring at it. The trees whip past on the interstate. Here and there, one is aflame in red, yellow, or orange finery. But for the most part, they remain a faded, weary green, the memory of summer still on them.

I catch Jesmyn's eye out of the corner of mine. She puts her hand at my side and gives a thumbs-up and raises her eyebrows. I put my hand at her side and make a "so-so" motion. Then I give her the thumbs-up and raised eyebrows. She reciprocates the "so-so."

We drive in silence. There truly is something worse than small talk.

"We loved this day trip," Melissa says finally. "It was one of the rare occasions when Eli would really let his guard down and tell us stuff."

"Maybe it's the historian in me," Pierce says, "but I can't help but contemplate the singular moments—the proverbial butterfly flapping its wings—leading to unforeseen consequences. We all decided on one of these drives that Eli should go to Nashville Arts along with Adair."

Oh, shit. This is not a good direction for the conversation. I stare straight ahead, afraid to even move, adrenaline singing in my veins. Jesmyn steals a quick sidelong glance.

Melissa's voice has a testy edge. "Well, the consequence of that was that Eli had a wonderful education and made some great friends."

"Look, Mel, can you not be so defensive? I'm merely making an observation."

"Well, I detect judgment in your 'observation.'"

That makes two of us.

"You're wrong."

"Really?"

"Yes, really. I'm not assigning a moral value to anything. I'm stating a matter of historical fact: if Eli had not gone to NAA, he never would have been riding in a car with Mars and Blake."

For a fleeting moment, I ponder how much injury I would sustain if I were to fling open my door and roll out onto the highway.

"You may not acknowledge that there are any matters of moral judgment bound up in 'fact,' but there are. Even making that observation is a moral judgment. Anyway, can we not do this"—Melissa wags her finger between her and Pierce—"in front of our guests?"

I'm shrinking in my seat. Jesmyn surreptitiously slides her foot next to mine and taps it. *I'm here,* the tap says. *I'm by your side.*

Pierce glances back at us. "Does anyone mind if we celebrate Eli's life today by being emotionally honest and open with each other? Does anybody in this car find it's healthy to bottle things up? Anybody think we'd be doing Eli's legacy a service by doing that?"

I catch a glimpse of Melissa rolling her eyes in the rear-view mirror. "It would be perfectly all right—and respectful of Eli's legacy—if we celebrated his life and didn't try to unearth the cause or causes of his death. We're not trying to figure out who built Stonehenge here."

So. Yeah. This is turning out to be pretty different from Blake's goodbye day. Being around fighting adults sucks. Being around your dead friend's fighting parents sucks worse than that. Being around your dead friend's parents possibly fighting about how you maybe killed your dead friend sucks worst of all.

Pierce starts to respond.

"The first time Eli and I kissed?" Jesmyn interjects

269

suddenly, before he can reply. Everyone shuts up. I'm relieved while simultaneously suspecting this story will make me squirmy.

". . . was after the Rock Camp showcase. We were all hanging out backstage and people were leaving. It was packed, but for some reason, by the time I went to the green room to load out my keyboard, the only person in there was Eli. He was getting his guitar and amp. And we told each other good job and somehow we kept standing closer and closer together. It was making me *so* nervous, but I loved it. How being onstage feels. And then we just . . . kissed. I don't remember who initiated it. Maybe we both did. It was a quick kiss because we heard someone coming. But I remember giggling all day for no reason. My parents probably thought I was high."

This story is indeed making me profoundly uneasy. I'm not sure why. It's not quite like guilt or grief. It's even rawer and redder than either.

But it seems to have the opposite effect on Pierce and Melissa. Pierce's face brightens slightly. Melissa laughs. "I *remember* that day because of exactly that. Eli was so giggly and goofy that we thought some of the kids had smoked up after the show. Remember that, Pierce?"

"In the car, we didn't even have to fight over the music. That was rare. I didn't think he was high on anything; I thought he was euphoric from performing."

Jesmyn has a wistful, faraway expression. She seems to be staring at the jar. "I've never kissed someone I've only known for a week. Ever. Probably never will again."

"I could tell what you two had was special," Melissa says. "You seemed to have an amazing chemistry and friendship."

"We loved being together right up until—we weren't."

I feel like I'm bleeding. Maybe healing is like surgery, where you have to open new wounds to repair old ones. I hope this is all for something.

The conversation dwindles and dies. We pull into a rest stop to use the restroom and stretch our legs, even though we've been driving for only an hour.

Pierce stands outside the SUV, still holding the jar to his chest.

I watch him staring blearily into the distance, and I realize there's something else different about this goodbye day. I don't want to confess, the way I did with Nana Betsy. Even though I sense from Pierce that he wants me to. Even though I can tell he also carries some of Adair's desire to hear me confess.

Pierce takes over driving and Melissa holds Eli's jar. I keep considering what I can contribute. What revelation I can offer. I'm coming up blank. My mind is void and my thoughts won't take shape for me to hold.

Pierce keeps shifting in his seat as if he wants to say something. "Every time I drive now, those last moments haunt me."

Melissa makes a little noise of disgust. "Pierce."

"I imagine what Eli saw in the split second before the trailer of that truck grew in his field of vision until it was all he saw."

"Please don't be morbid. Not today."

Pierce gives a bitter, sardonic chuckle. "Yeah, because

our son, Eli, who didn't own a piece of clothing that wasn't black, and who started asking for *Scary Stories to Tell in the Dark* as a bedtime story at age four, would be so offended by my morbidity."

"I'm not talking about Eli."

"Sorry, isn't that who this day is about?"

Melissa shakes her head and raises her hands in an I-just-can't gesture.

I'm going full Dr. Mendez on this. "It's okay," I say. "We—I can handle it if talking about it helps. Don't worry about me."

"I'm all right too," Jesmyn says.

Pierce catches my eyes in the rearview mirror and gives me a firm nod. Then he throws Melissa a triumphant look.

She stares forward and ignores it. "Say what you need to then." Her tone is frigid.

I've seen Pierce and Melissa sparring intellectually before. That was always part of the landscape over at Eli's. But this seems more pointed and personal. I suddenly wish Dr. Mendez were actually here rather than my attempts to channel him. He's the intellectual equal of both, and he could defuse things.

"I wonder if he had any awareness of what was happening, if his consciousness survived even for a few seconds. Or if one minute everything was bright and normal, and the next minute everything was black."

"Well, (A) how would the answer to that change your life in any way, and (B) how the hell are these guys supposed to help you answer it?"

"I'm not asking a question, Mel, I'm simply stating that I wonder. Am I not allowed to express curiosity over something near anybody who can't decisively banish said curiosity?"

Melissa starts to respond.

"Eli believed in God," I blurt. Everyone shuts up instantly. We'll be set if, between Jesmyn and me, we can keep remembering dramatic revelations every time Pierce and Melissa start to go at each other's throats. Even Jesmyn looks expectant.

"Maybe," I continue. "Sort of."

Pierce looks flummoxed. "He never expressed that to us."

"That could be because you derided religious people as idiots every chance you got," Melissa says.

"That is absolutely unfair."

I speak louder. "Once, I don't remember what we were doing. Going to a movie or something. Eli and I were talking in the car. I don't know how we got on the subject, but we started talking about God. And I knew you two were atheists, so I was surprised when Eli goes: 'What if there's a god who's so much bigger and more powerful than anything that he builds universes like ships in bottles, and no matter how far you look or reach, you can't see or touch outside the bottle? So you have no idea that God exists. You have no way of proving that God exists. But he's there. Or maybe our whole universe is just a big computer program that God is running.' So yeah. Maybe he believed in God."

"Well, he was entertaining the possibility of the existence of a god. Which wouldn't make him a theist, necessarily; it

273

would make him an agnostic." Pierce has a wounded, vexed expression. I can guess, from my experience revealing new information to Nana Betsy, what he's probably thinking.

Melissa's expression is similar to Pierce's. "Carver's *point*," she says tersely, "if I understand him correctly, was that Eli didn't necessarily share our belief system and he had constructed his own. I didn't know that about him. Obviously neither did you."

"I wish he had talked to us about it," Pierce says.

"I wish we had created an environment more conducive to that," Melissa says.

Pierce shakes his head.

"I don't think it's anyone's fault," I say. "Eli had stuff that was his and his alone. Or that he talked about with only a couple people."

"Eli and I never even really talked about God," Jesmyn says. "But he loved to consider unknowable things. We'd been dating for about two weeks when he took me to Centennial Park. It was my first time there. We sat and held each other and looked at the skyline— Sorry, I hope I'm not making y'all uncomfortable talking about PDA."

Pierce and Melissa shake their heads. I stare forward. It's not even the PDA part that's making me uncomfortable (why would it?)—it's the unspecialness of when Jesmyn and I sat at the park, watching the city lights twinkle like a constellation of human stars. It's knowing how much magic, of which I had no part, went on in the world between the people close to me.

She continues. "Anyway, Eli randomly asks me, 'If you

274

could learn the name of everyone who has ever loved you, would you want to?' "

We wait, but Jesmyn says no more.

"So?" Melissa says.

Jesmyn smiles wistfully. "I told him I didn't know. I still don't. The last thing you want is to find out that someone who you thought loves you never loved you."

"What did he say?" Pierce asks.

"He wouldn't say. I'd promised myself I'd drag the answer out of him someday."

I couldn't imagine doing this day without Jesmyn. But every time she talks about Eli, it's like the right side of my heart has been tied to the bumper of a pickup truck. And every time Pierce and Melissa talk about him, it's like the left side has been tied to another pickup. And they're peeling out in opposite directions, ripping my heart down its center.

And of course, when none of them are speaking, I'm thinking about two other trucks. The eighteen-wheeler of prosecution headed my way. And the trailer that filled Eli's field of vision in his last seconds alive on this Earth.

Jesmyn stealthily maneuvers her hand next to mine. I catch her eye. When Melissa and Pierce are both looking forward, she reaches out with her pinky and taps mine twice. *Hey. You good?*

I give her two taps back. *No. Not really. But I'll pretend I am until my facade crumbles completely and I'm naked in front of all of you.*

⊞ ⊞ ⊞

Technically Hara and I haven't broken up. We say we'll stay in touch after her family moves to Chicago, blah blah blah, but come on. We're sixteen. We're not going to be spending weekends together. So, yeah, we're pretty much broken up the minute I watch her family's moving truck fading from view.

So I'm lonely. To the point that I don't even want to text any of Sauce Crew to hang with me because I'm so afraid of being rejected. Georgia's out with her boyfriend. My parents are at some faculty thing for my dad's job. I sit in my room and try to get some writing done, but surprise, surprise, I'm not making any headway.

The doorbell rings. It's Eli.

"Dude, you look like ass." He walks in before I can invite him.

"Your mom's ass," I mumble.

"You look way worse than my mom's toned ass. So? How you doing?"

"She left a little while ago. So bad."

"Figured." With a smirk, he pulls three Netflix DVDs from his hoodie pocket and fans them like he's holding a winning poker hand.

"What're those?"

"Horrendous French horror movies. People getting skinned alive and stuff. To cheer you up."

"Nice."

"Yeah."

"But no way can we watch these here. If my parents or Georgia come home, we're boned."

276

"I didn't plan on watching them here. I came to pick you up because I figured your sensitive-poet-ass self would be too heartbroken to drive."

I smile for the first time that day and flip Eli the bird.

He grins, stuffs the DVDs in his hoodie pocket, and flips me both birds.

"Let me grab my jacket," I say.

"Grab five bucks too, because you're not sharing my Roma's."

"Don't you ever consider Roma's a ripoff even at five bucks?"

"Clearly not, dude. How shitty can pizza be?"

"Roma's is the laboratory working on the answer to this question."

Eli spreads his arms wide. "'Ey! Why-a you sayin'-a bad things-a 'bout Roma's, eh? This-a spicy pizza been in my-a family for-a generations, eh?" He makes that Italian kissing motion with his fingers.

"You are the biggest chode."

"You love this chode. Okay, less talking. More jacket getting. More Roma's getting. And more French-torture-porn watching."

For the most part, you don't hold the people you love in your heart because they rescued you from drowning or pulled you from a burning house. Mostly you hold them in your heart because they save you, in a million quiet and perfect ways, from being alone.

⊞ ⊞ ⊞

At some point during the drive, without my even noticing (shockingly, my mind was elsewhere), the sky has turned to dreary slate. By the time we reach the Fall Creek Falls parking lot and trailhead, it's begun to drizzle in that misty way where you're getting wet but it doesn't justify using an umbrella. It means the parking lot is empty. And that's good, because the last thing any normal human needs is to encounter our happy-go-lucky little band of merry travelers scattering Eli's sand at the falls.

"Well, here we are," Pierce says to nobody in particular, staring off. He puts up the hood of his parka against the rain. "Have either of you been here before?"

Jesmyn and I shake our heads.

"The first time we brought Eli here was when he was nine," Melissa says. "He was utterly captivated. He loved that we could hop in our car and drive a couple of hours and see something this majestic."

Pierce laughs. It's a hollow, rueful laugh, but it's clearly not meant to be. "Starting in junior high, he and I used to take father-son weekend trips to western North Carolina. We'd get a hotel in Asheville and spend our days hiking to waterfalls. We used to talk about all kinds of stuff." He pauses. "But obviously not everything."

Pierce takes Eli's jar from Melissa, and we begin picking our way gingerly down the slick, muddy trail. Pierce leads the way. Melissa follows behind a few paces and then Jesmyn and I lag still farther behind.

"Never really seen those two like this," I whisper to Jesmyn.

She shakes her head. "I've seen them fight about stuff, but in a more . . . loving way, I guess."

"This must be really hard on them."

"Can't blame them."

"No."

Jesmyn stumbles on a root and pitches forward a couple of steps. I'm there at her elbow. "Thanks," she says.

Almost immediately, I slip on a drift of soggy leaves. Jesmyn's hand snaps to my triceps, steadying me. I glance at her. "Karma."

The treetops are shrouded in mist, gray lace hanging tattered. Wind moves through branches with a sound like waves breaking on a beach. *A beach in November.*

I wonder if you ever get to feel the rain in prison.

"This day reminds me of a black-metal album cover," I say. "Perfect for Eli."

After a couple of moments, Jesmyn says, "This is how Eli's voice sounded. Rain on pine trees in October. Dark and green and silvery."

With a sharp twinge, I remember her joking (at least I hope it was) response when I asked her what color my voice was. I don't get to wallow in my hurt long before I notice her shivering. Her jacket isn't made for rain. I pull off my waterproof parka. "Here." I drape it over her shoulders.

"Dude, no, I'm fine. You'll be cold."

"I'm okay. I have my hoodie."

"You sure?"

I make sure Pierce and Melissa are far ahead. "I don't need any more friends dying." It's a dark joke, sure. But Eli dug dark jokes, so I guess he wouldn't mind. Jesmyn's face says she doesn't.

When we round the bend to the waterfall, the wind has intensified and the mist has thickened.

Pierce and Melissa stand a few feet apart at the edge of the pool, watching the roaring waterfall cascade into it. Jesmyn and I quietly join them. It's beautiful and terrible standing there. Being close to waterfalls always reminds me of how tiny, fragile, and finite I am.

Melissa clears her throat. "So—I'm not sure how to go about this. I'll do what feels right to me and I hope it's okay."

We nod.

She goes to Pierce, who opens the jar. She pours out a handful of the sand and holds it in her palm for a moment. The mist from the waterfall and drizzle quickly saturate it and it runs down her wrist in rivulets, dripping like rainbow tears. She covers her eyes and nose with her free hand. Her lips tighten and tremble.

She steps toward the pool. "When Eli was four, he used to come into our room on Saturday mornings and climb up on our bed. Then he'd whisper, 'Banana,' in my ear really loudly. We finally started leaving a bowl of bananas out where he could help himself. We called him our little monkey. Our little Curious George." Her voice sounds like it has a sack of stones resting on it. She steps forward again, crouches, and dips her hand into the pool, letting the water carry the sand away in a bloom. "Goodbye," she whispers.

Pierce pours out a handful of sand from the jar. He holds it for a moment, watching it run and drip as it absorbs the rain and waterfall mist. He starts to say something but stops. He tries again and stops. "All day, every day, I study and teach the history of things. Human lives laid end to end. One generation handing the torch to another generation. Fathers to sons. Unbroken threads running through it all. And—" He stops and clears his throat a couple of times. "Now I'm standing here, writing the final chapter of my son's portion of the history of my life. I never imagined that my history would include the full history of my son, start to finish. But it does now."

He walks to the edge of the pool and kneels. He lowers the sand into the pool as Melissa did. He stands and rejoins us. He talks to us without looking at us. "There's a water cycle. Water never goes away. It never dies or is destroyed. It just changes from form to form in a continuous cycle, like energy. On a hot summer day, you've drunk water that a dinosaur drank. You might have cried tears that Alexander the Great cried. So I'm returning Eli's energy—his spirit— and all that it contained. His life. His music. His memories. His loves. All the beautiful things in him. I give it to the water so he can live that way now. Form to form. Energy to energy. Maybe I'll meet my son again in the rain, or in the ocean. Maybe he hasn't touched my face for the last time."

Melissa turns to Jesmyn and me with the jar. "If you want."

Jesmyn and I trade a quick glance. She swallows hard and steps forward. She pours out a handful of sand, staring at it like she's looking for some part of Eli she recognizes. "I loved his hands. They were strong and gentle and filled with music. I loved when he would hold my hand. I loved making music with him." Her voice is small against the churning waterfall. She lowers the sand into the pool.

Melissa offers the jar to me. Pierce stares at the ground. My hand shakes as I take a handful of the sand and hold it, staring at it. My heart beats a familiar barrage, bringing a familiar constriction of breath. *Not now. Not now. Not now.* I breathe it down. The other three stare at me expectantly. I clear my throat. "Um. Once—we were a little sleep deprived—Eli and I started talking about what emotions and memories are, physically. How every emotion and memory is stored as chemicals in our brain. Love, anger . . . regret— they're all chemicals. And chemicals can break down and spoil if you don't store them in the right way. So I'm storing the chemicals that make Eli in the safest part of my brain, locked away where they can't spoil. But not so locked away that I can't get to them every single day." I lower my portion of Eli into the pool, the frigid water biting at my hand.

We take turns, each putting a handful of sand into the pool while reciting something we loved about him.

He was effortlessly funny.

When he was sad, he never used it as an occasion to make anyone else sad.

He smelled like clean, plain soap.

He closed his eyes when he played the guitar.

He played the guitar like he had been entrusted with a sacred fire.

He was ferociously intelligent.

He worked tirelessly to make himself better at what he loved doing.

We do this until Eli's sand is gone to the water.

Each time it's my turn, my mouth says one thing while my mind whispers another: *I'm sorry.*

◘ ◘ ◘

Although we're soaked and shivering, we stand, still and silent, around the edge of the pool and watch the waterfall. Melissa holds the empty jar to her breast as if it's an infant she's feeding one final time.

Jesmyn pulls her hands into the sleeves of my parka. Her face is soft in the veiled light. She has that look of wonder I saw on her face when she watched the storm, tempered this time by sorrow.

In this guileless raw moment, it's as though the rain has washed scales from my eyes that kept me from seeing; from understanding clearly.

I thought what I felt for her was ordinary fondness and affection, heightened by her being my only friend. I thought the ache when she talked about Eli was ordinary guilt and grief, heightened by the magnitude of my loss and my culpability. It is none of those things.

I have fallen in love with her quietly. A movement evading my notice. The sun crossing the sky. It crept into my heart like vines overgrowing a stone wall. It caught me like a river rising and swelling.

Maybe love, like water, returns to some unending cycle, only changing form.

There is the space of a heartbeat when I don't contemplate the consequences of this, and to hold something so verdant and alive amidst the gray and ashen makes me feel right again, as if perhaps sometimes what seems like walking into a sunset is really walking into a dawn.

Just a heartbeat.

▣ ▣ ▣

A chirping of bright voices coming down the trail snaps us out of our reflection. We head up toward the parking area. Pierce first. Melissa next. Then Jesmyn. Then me. We nod as we pass the effervescent hikers, slipping down the trail, giggling.

But it's a momentary distraction to what's now consuming me as I watch Jesmyn ahead. *You can't love her. You can't love her. You can't love her. You just dissolved Eli's creative energy in water like Kool-Aid. You have no right to love her. You can't love her.*

She turns, as if sensing my stare on her back. "I'll remember a bunch of stuff later I wish I'd said."

She waits for me to catch up so we can walk together. Pierce and Melissa are waiting at the trailhead.

"I need to use the ladies' room before we hit the road again," Melissa says. She and Jesmyn head for the women's restroom.

"Might as well too," Pierce says. He and I head to the men's restroom. We do our business and we're washing our hands in the sinks, side by side. He catches my eyes in the mirror. His are dim and gray and sunken in his skull.

"I'm glad we have a second or two alone," he says. "There're a couple of things I need to get off my chest."

Naturally I want to shit myself. Good thing I'm near a toilet. I slowly turn off the water. "Um. Yeah."

Pierce keeps looking at me in the mirror. He rubs his face. "I need to be frank with you, because I understand this to be a day for no bullshit."

"Okay."

"I'm not entirely at peace with your role in my son's death."

Hey, that makes two of us. And speaking of dying, that doesn't sound bad right now. But I channel Dr. Mendez and listen, striving for his unruffledness.

Pierce continues. "By no means am I where Adair's at. It wouldn't give me any peace to see you prosecuted and suffer legal consequences. But, Carver. Did you *have* to text Mars when you did? I study historical cause and effect all day. Do you think it's easy for me to get past this?"

My blood ticks in my chest, and I feel the something-heavy-sliding-off-a-high-shelf, but still, none of the compulsion to confess I felt with Nana Betsy and Dr. Mendez. Instead, I want to tell him about Billy Scruggs. About Hiro Takasagawa. Ridiculous. But I want to defend myself.

I open my mouth to try to speak.

Pierce holds my gaze in the mirror with his dolorous eyes. "Well?"

"I—I don't—I'm sorry. I'm sorry."

"Yeah."

I start to edge toward the door.

He turns and looks me in the face, drawing so close I can smell his metallic breath—like he's been sucking on pennies. His melancholy has melted off to a pale-blue fire. "Another thing I want to say. It's fairly obvious that you and Jesmyn have grown quite close—more than you ever would have if my son hadn't been killed. And I don't have any authority to tell either of you what to do. But I would really love it if I never had to see or hear about you getting together with my dead son's girlfriend. Because you at least deserve to not actively profit from his death." His voice strains under some emotion I don't even recognize. Maybe it has no name.

He doesn't await a response but turns and leaves.

And the heavy thing slides off the shelf. The buried-alive-fallen-through-river-ice sensation seizes me like a giant, pneumatic steel claw. I sway on unsteady legs and grip the sink for purchase.

Air.

Air.

Air.

Breathe.

Breathe.

Breathe.

My legs are too wobbly. My bones and muscles are gelatin. I sink to the muddy (I really hope that's mud) floor, leaning against a stall. I'm praying nobody comes in and sees me in this state.

Several minutes pass before I hear someone gingerly push open the door a crack.

"Carver?" It's Jesmyn.

"Yeah?" I call feebly.

"How . . . you doing in there? You good?"

"Um . . ." *Yeah, I'm great; taking in the ambience. There's a delightful bouquet in here. Earthy, mossy, with top notes of urinal cake and Pine-Sol.* I can hear Melissa saying something to Jesmyn.

"For some reason," Jesmyn says in a loud, deliberate voice, "these bathrooms reminded me of the first day of school."

I'm not feeling especially quick, but at least I catch her meaning. "Me too."

I hear Melissa saying something to Pierce. Perhaps: "He was fine before you two went in there together. Go in there and see what's wrong." Pierce responds, maybe: "Oh, come on, Melissa. He's fine; having some privacy to ponder . . . stuff."

I try to stand but slump down again.

"You alone in there?" Jesmyn calls.

"Yeah."

"Are you . . . decent?"

"Yeah."

The door opens and Jesmyn walks in. She gives me an oh-bless-your-poor-heart look and hurries to my side.

I manage a wan laugh. "Dignity, huh? Trying to beat my first-day-of-school record."

"Well," she murmurs, "you've traded smacking your head on the wall for filthy state park restroom floor."

I'm glad she doesn't tell me to breathe. In my growing experience with panic attacks, that's rarely helpful advice since you're unexcited about not breathing.

She helps me to my feet and stands at my elbow while I hold the sink, my head bowed. I manage to take a good breath or two. I have a sudden vision of Hiro, soaring above the Earth in his winged car. It's weirdly soothing. My heartbeat is normalizing, and the splotches of black are dissipating from my field of vision.

"Wow. That sucked."

"Did this happen to you on Blake's goodbye day?"

"No."

"What did he say to you in here? Or do you not want to talk about it?"

"I'd rather not talk about it."

"You wanna try to head out there?"

"Couple more minutes?"

She nods.

"Know any jokes?" I ask.

"I told my mom this scented candle she bought the other day smells like a handsome grandpa. I thought that was pretty funny."

I smile. "It is."

After a couple more minutes, I'm able to walk unassisted. The fresh, damp air smells like the beginning of all life after so long in the restroom. We walk to the car without a word. Pierce won't look at me. Not that I particularly want him to. Melissa seems to have some sense of what happened if not of the specifics.

***

The drive home is almost completely silent.

But Pierce and Melissa do tell us they've separated and intend to file for divorce. Not much you can say to that, even after Melissa offers the unsolicited reassurance that it had nothing to do with Eli's death—they'd been discussing it for a while. I find that hard to believe. I heard somewhere that some huge percentage of marriages fall apart after the death of a child.

Not that I stood any chance of redeeming myself in Adair's eyes, but now I'm finished. First her brother. Then her parents' marriage. I'm a destroying angel to her. A plague on her life. I'm the proverbial butterfly flapping its wings, but my wings are covered in anthrax.

I'm actually glad my panic attack has left me mostly too numb and exhausted to dwell on the continuing ripples extending out from the stone I've thrown in this pool.

Mostly too numb. Every once a while, I look over at Jesmyn, who—and maybe I'm imagining this—sits closer to me than she did on the first leg of the journey. I consider the day's epiphany and how it complicates things.

These chemicals. If only there were a way to drain them from my head.

***

I text Jesmyn almost immediately after I arrive home from dropping her off. I thank her for helping me through yet another panic attack. I thank her for letting me give her my parka to wear, because I didn't want to see her cold and wet. I tell her how much I miss Eli. I tell her the first part of what Pierce said to me in the bathroom. I tell her I'm glad I got to see Fall Creek Falls before maybe being imprisoned.

I tell her everything but what I most want to tell her.

Chapter Thirty-Three

My blood howls in my ears the minute the principal walks into my AP biology class, interrupting a lecture about photosynthesis. She pulls my teacher aside and they confer in secretive, urgent whispers, casting furtive glances in my direction. The principal returns to the hall.

"Uh, Carver?" my teacher says.

It doesn't come as the slightest surprise. I walk to the front, adrenaline singeing my ribs.

"Grab your things, if you would."

Everyone turns in their chairs, their stares snagging on my skin like burrs. I hear their murmurs. My face smolders. I return to my desk, grab my stuff, and walk out of the classroom, head down.

The principal awaits me in the hall. "Carver, sorry to

pull you out of class. There are a couple of detectives here who need to speak to you. If you'll come with me."

My heart shrinks to an icy steel ball. My head swims, delirious. *They're here to finally arrest me. They've found some piece of evidence. I'm done.*

I nod and follow the principal to the office. Lieutenant Farmer and Sergeant Metcalf are there. I don't say anything. Not even hello. Lieutenant Farmer holds two large envelopes. He hands one to me.

I accept it like it's full of spiders.

"Carver, that's a warrant to seize and search electronic files on your cell phone and laptop. We've faxed a copy over to your attorney. He's looked at it. You're welcome to call him or look it over."

I say nothing but open the envelope and pull out the document inside, as if I'll be able to tell whether it's legitimate. It looks genuine.

"So?" I ask.

Sergeant Metcalf holds out a bag. "Cell phone in here. This is called a Faraday bag, and it blocks transmissions to and from your phone, so don't bother trying to wipe any information from it remotely."

I pull the murder weapon from my pocket and drop it in the bag. "What am I supposed to do without my phone?" *I won't even have my phone for the Dearly show.*

Lieutenant Farmer chuckles sardonically. "For the week or two the state police are pulling stuff off it, you'll have to make do. Generations of kids before you survived without cell phones."

"Laptop too, please," Sergeant Metcalf says. He holds out a bigger version of the bag I put my cell phone in.

I pull my laptop from my bag and hand it over. "What about homework assignments I have on there? Also, I have a bunch of stories and stuff I've written."

The principal interjects. "Carver, you won't be responsible for any homework assignments that are on your computer."

"If you're concerned about anything getting wiped from your computer, don't be," Sergeant Metcalf says. "The TBI's job is to make sure nothing gets deleted from your laptop."

"Okay. That's everything. Can I—" I start to say.

Lieutenant Farmer hands me the other envelope. "This is a search warrant for your bedroom. We're heading directly from here to your house. We just spoke with your mom, and she's meeting us there. We've also discussed this with your lawyer, but you're welcome to call him."

"Can't really do that with my phone in the thingy bag." I'm aware I'm being a smartass, but their whole demeanor— this business of coming to my school—seems calculated to intimidate me. It's working and I resent them for it.

"You can use our phones," the principal says.

I call Mr. Krantz. He's headed to court. He tells me to go home, watch the officers search, and videotape it.

The principal excuses me for the rest of the day. I drive home. When I arrive, my mom is already there and some uniformed officers have just pulled up. I tell her to film on her phone and she does.

They turn over every inch of my room. They lift each

book and leaf through. Look under my mattress. Rummage through all my drawers. Go through my clothes hamper with rubber gloves on. Pull each picture and poster off the wall and look behind it. They unscrew the light fixture and peer inside. They open my vents and grope around in the ducts. I guess in case I wrote *I killed my three best friends on purpose* on a piece of paper and shoved it in there. They ask me if I keep a journal. I don't, but I only stare at them anyway, confident it's what Mr. Krantz would want me to do. They find a thumb drive and my iPod and put them in bags. They take some of the notebooks I write story ideas in.

Watching them, I feel like they're picking through my innards, tugging meat from bone. Vultures on a carcass. Their hunger: to ruin my life even more than it's already ruined.

Chapter Thirty-Four

I'm a coiled spring sitting across from Dr. Mendez. I've been dreading this visit because I know the first thing he's going to say.

"Tell me a story," he says.

"No."

His expression doesn't change. He'd be a hell of a poker player. He cocks his head and lets the silence breathe, waiting for me to explain. But I don't.

"Why not?" he asks finally.

"People tell stories to create one where none existed. There is already a story here. We know what happened."

"Do we?" Dr. Mendez is so still. Not just a passive lack of motion. Deeper than that. Actively still.

I can't sit anymore. I get up and pace. "Yes. I texted Mars

and I knew he would answer and he tried to do exactly what I knew he would do and my friends died because of it."

"What about Billy? Hiro?"

My voice is rising. It's satisfying, feeding anger to his quietude, setting this calm pasture ablaze. *"They don't exist. They're figments of my imagination. They're a lie I'm telling both of us.* I know it, and so do the police. They have my phone and laptop right now, by the way, so I hope you didn't try to call me. They searched my room. I'm going to jail."

"Did they tell you that?"

"I mean, *pretty much.*"

"I'm sorry this is happening."

"Me too."

"If I could wave a wand and make it all go away for you, I would."

"See about getting one of those wands maybe."

Dr. Mendez gazes evenly at me through his rectangular, transparent-frame glasses. "You mentioned you were going to do a goodbye day for Eli."

I stand in front of my chair and flounce down, causing it to skid backward a few inches. "Yeah."

"Did you?"

"Yeah."

"How did it go?"

"Oh. Fantastic." I punctuate "fantastic" with two acerbic thumbs-ups.

Dr. Mendez's placid smile makes me instantly regret my sarcasm and anger. "I'm sorry," I murmur.

"Don't be."

"It was a disaster."

Pause. Waiting.

So I continue. "Eli's parents . . . have issues. They haven't gotten along for a while. Now they're getting a divorce. They said it wasn't because of this, but it is. And it was super awkward being with them. Plus Eli's dad basically told me he holds me responsible. Oh, but he doesn't want me to go to prison and he doesn't hate me as much as Eli's sister, who definitely wants to see me skip prison entirely and go straight to the electric chair. And of course Eli's sister didn't go on the goodbye day but she really wanted her parents to go for some reason. It was a really weird situation."

"Drastically different, I gather, from the experience with Blake's grandmother."

"Yeah. Plus I had another panic attack. In the filthy-ass restroom. My second in front of Jesmyn."

"I'm sorry."

My legs start bouncing. "I'm sick of the panic attacks. I've been taking my Zoloft just like you prescribed."

Dr. Mendez nods and stands. He walks back to his desk, opens a locked drawer, grabs a pad, and comes back, sits, and begins scribbling. "I'm going to up your Zoloft dosage." He tears the prescription from the pad and holds it out to me.

I sit still, eying the paper. But I don't reach for it. "Will that stop the attacks?"

"If not, it'll be a step in the right direction. We'll get this figured out."

"In the meantime I sit here and tell you stories." I finally take the prescription from him.

Dr. Mendez places his prescription pad on his side table, sits back, and crosses his legs, clasping his hands in front of him and resting his elbow on his knee. "I promise you that there is method to this apparent madness. Do you trust me when I say that?"

"I guess." I can hardly hear my own voice.

"Do you believe me if I tell you that the point of our work here—these stories—is not to ask you to lie to yourself or anyone else?"

"It feels like it, but yeah."

"And it's not to suggest that we have no accountability for our actions."

"Okay."

"If I told you that I have good reason to believe this could help you, are you with me?"

"Yeah."

"I promise you: if this does not work, we will try something else."

This is one of the only things in your life not trying to destroy you. My eyes fill with tears and I look down. "Okay," I whisper to the floor.

"Tell me about Eli's goodbye day. It sounds like a confrontational experience. People. Emotions."

"Yeah."

"Were you able to confront anything you hadn't been able to previously?"

Funny how I'm fine confessing murder to him but not love. "Um. Yeah." I stare at the rug. I look up and he's watching, waiting. "I . . . realized that I might have feelings for Jesmyn."

"I imagine that raises some complicated issues."

"You think?" Dr. Mendez's calm gives my sarcasm no oxygen. "Eli's dad at one point is all, 'Oh, by the way, I see how you look at her and I don't ever want you to hook up with my dead son's girlfriend.'"

"How about emotional issues within you?"

"Obviously. That too."

He rubs his chin and taps his lips with his index finger. "I wonder if some important component of the guilt you've been harboring is related to your growing fondness for Jesmyn."

"Could be." *It's a little more than "could be," but no need to let on exactly how far this dude is up in my head.*

"Not all experiences need to teach us the same thing. It's all right if Eli's goodbye day allowed you to confront a different side of your emotional being than Blake's goodbye day."

"I guess."

"So. Tell me a story?"

"I want you to tell me exactly how to handle the Jesmyn situation."

"I wish I had a simple answer. I'm not just being coy here."

"I'd even settle for a complex answer," I murmur. "Any answer."

"I'm confident one will present itself in time. Sometimes answers arise through the process of elimination."

I give a rueful laugh. "I'm working hard on eliminating all the answers that allow me to feel like a normal, happy human being. Wanna hear something funny, though?"

He raises his eyebrows and nods for me to continue.

"When Eli's dad was saying how he considers me responsible, I didn't want to accept responsibility the way I did when I talked about it with Blake's grandma."

"What were you feeling?"

"I wanted to tell him about Billy and Hiro. Even though that's stupid and they don't exist." Tears cloud my throat.

Dr. Mendez gives me a moment to compose myself. Then he leans back and makes himself comfortable. "How about telling me a story?"

I sigh and stand in front of the open fridge of my imagination for a few seconds. "So there's this guy named . . . Jiminy Turdsworth."

Chapter Thirty-Five

Now on top of everything else, Jesmyn won't leave my thoughts. Eli's goodbye day opened some door I can't shut again.

Not that I've tried very hard.

Chapter Thirty-Six

"No, I'm sorry. You are not going to a sold-out Dearly show, with a hot girl, dressed like a sad-ass Ernest Hemingway," Georgia says.

I shrug. "Well."

"Well nothing. You're lucky Maddie and Lana and I drove in from Knoxville in time to fix this. The show starts in eight hours. We're taking you to Opry Mills Mall."

I lower my voice to a hoarse whisper; I can hear them talking and laughing in Georgia's room. "Maddie and Lana always sexually harass me."

"*Oh, puhlease.* You love the attention from college girls."

"No I don't. They always seem to be mocking me."

"They are."

"See?"

"You still love it."

I try on clothes while Maddie and Lana hoot and whistle, trying to make me blush. When we're done, I'm wearing a pair of dark-gray jeans that hurt my nuts, some brown Chelsea boots, and a black jacket. I look good, though. I have to grudgingly admit that much. And I'm excited for the show and seeing Jesmyn. Seeing her every day doesn't diminish that in any way.

Not even Maddie and Lana taking turns trying to slap me on the ass in the parking lot on the way to the car dampens my mood.

I forget about the Accident.

I forget about the DA and Mr. Krantz.

I forget about my phone and laptop sitting at the TBI, waiting for something incriminating to be pulled off them.

I forget about Blake's and Eli's goodbye days.

I forget about Nana Betsy living on a hillside somewhere in East Tennessee.

I forget about Pierce and Melissa living in separate houses.

I forget about Adair and Judge Edwards looking at me like my name was carved into their skin with a rusty nail.

I forget about the people at school whispering about Jesmyn and me.

I forget about Billy and Hiro.

I forget about the panic attacks.

I try to remember the last time I felt so good and I can't.

Jesmyn appears at the top of the stairs. I made sure to arrive fifteen minutes late. She's wearing a pair of high-waisted, skintight black jeans with rips in the knees, a black T-shirt that shows the tiniest strip of her midriff, black ankle boots, and the gray jacket she wore for Eli's goodbye day. Her bangs are cut in a straight fringe and hang a bit in her eyes. She has ornate, smoky eye makeup.

Seeing her feels like taking a rise in the road too fast, when all your organs are weightless. "You changed your hair."

"You noticed!"

"Of course. You didn't have bangs before."

"They turn out all right?"

Play it cool. "Yeah, totally," I say uncoolly.

She looks me up and down. "And hello, Mr. Rock Star Makeover."

"Georgia made me buy new clothes for the show."

"She has awesome taste. We make a great pair."

I feel a momentary fluorescence and become light-headed.

"Oh! Forgot something." She runs back to her room and returns holding her iPod.

She makes it halfway down the stairs when it hits—it's the same feeling as that of going to school dressed for a warm morning, and when class lets out, the air smells like wet stone and the wind blows hard and cold from the north. *Eli. You're heading to Eli's show with Eli's girlfriend while Eli's spirit makes its way down a river, or floats in a cloud, waiting to fall as rain. While Eli sits in an urn.*

When she gets to the bottom of the stairs, she hugs me in a whiff of citrus and honey.

She pulls out her phone and holds it at arm's length. "Squinch up."

I move in close to her and try to smile normally. She takes a picture, types something, and puts her phone in her pocket. Then she jumps, claps, and gives a little squeal. "Yay! I'm so excited for this show!"

I hope she stays in this mood. If she does, she can carry us. I'll need it, I'm sure.

We get in my car and she sits cross-legged. She grabs the aux cable on my stereo and turns to me. She has a nervous giddiness in her voice I've never heard before.

"Okay. I have a surprise." She takes a deep breath and plugs in her iPod as we pull away. She giggles and covers her face. "I can't believe I'm doing this," she murmurs.

The music starts—a sensuous, verdant electronic soundscape with driving drum machine beats. Then the vocals enter, lush and warm. The opening days of summer. It's her; I can tell immediately. It's the first time I've ever heard her sing.

It makes my bone marrow throb. It steals my breath, but not in a panic-attack way.

"Is this—"

She peeks at me, blushing from between fingers. Her nails are painted matte black.

"—you?"

She nods.

Of course she would have to be brilliant at this too. There's no respite. She's actively trying to destroy me inside. "Wow. You are *incredible*."

"Shut up! I've been working on it for a while."

305

"So—do you want to be a classical pianist or this?" I nod at the stereo.

"All of the above." She picks up her iPod. "Okay, that's good."

I put my hand over hers. "I want to keep listening."

"*Eeeee*. No!"

"Yes! In fact, I expect a copy of this." *Because this also makes me forget everything. Oh, how this makes me forget.*

⊞ ⊞ ⊞

Even though skyscrapers don't have chimneys, downtown Nashville somehow always smells of woodsmoke by mid-October. And it's perfect jacket weather. The night air tastes like chilled apple cider and the sky breathes with stars. We park and walk the few blocks to the Ryman. The crowd gradually thickens as we approach. Groups mill around, chatting excitedly.

I walk a little taller as I catch a pack of frat boys eyeing Jesmyn as we pass. *That's right, bros*. But I wish I were holding her hand.

Then: "Carver! Jesmyn! Hey!"

I look over to see Georgia, Maddie, and Lana waving. "Oh, shit," I mutter, and wave.

"What?" Jesmyn asks, veering in their direction.

"Nothing. Just—Maddie and Lana can be obnoxious."

Georgia greets Jesmyn and me with a hug. "Are y'all as completely shitting yourselves in excitement for this show as I am?"

"More," Jesmyn says.

I avoid eye contact with Maddie and Lana.

"Well, hello to you too, Carver," Lana says loudly.

"Hi."

"Hello, Carver," Maddie says as loudly as Lana.

"Hey."

"Are you gonna introduce us to your friend?" Lana asks.

"This is Jesmyn. Jesmyn, Lana and Maddie, my sister's friends."

". . . And?" Maddie asks.

"Yeah, Carver, and? Are we not your friends?" Lana asks, eyes boring into me.

I stifle an eye roll because it'll only make things worse. "And . . . my friends."

"*Awwwwwwww,*" they say in unison.

They introduce themselves warmly to Jesmyn, who gives me a look saying, *What's wrong with you?*

Georgia glances at her phone. "Okay, we're gonna grab our seats. Where are you guys?"

"Balcony," Jesmyn says.

"Cool," Georgia says. "Maybe we'll see y'all after."

"Bye, Carver," Maddie says, still being loud. She catches Jesmyn's eye and shakes her head.

I wave. We head up to the balcony.

"Those two seemed nice."

"*Seemed.* From the first second my sister brought them home from college, they've loved tormenting me. They think it's hysterical."

Jesmyn purses her lips and grabs my chin. "*Oh, you poor widdle thing. Bwess your heart.*"

I grin and pull my chin away. "Don't *you* start."

We find our seats in the balcony.

"Did you listen to that Dearly mix I made you?" Jesmyn asks.

"Of course."

"And?"

"It was awesome."

"I hear he's way better live."

I've never seen her this way. She's gleaming. I can sense her heat on my face. She cranes her neck to try to look at the stage setup.

"Sorry," she murmurs, still craning. "I'm geeking out over the keyboard gear."

"It's okay," I say quite sincerely, because the way she's positioned, I have an unobstructed view of the geography between her ear and her jaw. Suddenly, I want to kiss it so badly it makes me delirious.

But then Pierce appears on my shoulder—a cartoon demon—whispering: *You don't deserve this. This moment is not yours. She is not yours and never can be. And you can never be hers. You're borrowing this for a few hours. Both of you belong to my dead son.*

She snaps her head back to me, about to say something, but her expression changes when she sees me. "What?"

"Nothing."

"You okay? You had this Carverish look."

"Yeah . . . just thinking . . . of a story idea. About a musician."

Jesmyn's eyes dance. "I want to read it when you're done."

"Totally."

She starts to say something else, but the lights dim for the opening act.

During their set, she turns to me and says something. I'm able to read her lips, but I pretend I can't so that she'll cup her hand to my ear and put her lips to it.

"These guys are great!" she yells.

I could respond with a nod, but I opt to cup my hand to Jesmyn's ear and put my lips to it, to say, "Totally. They rock."

They play for about forty-five minutes and leave the stage. Jesmyn and I chat about nothing in particular while roadies change over the equipment onstage.

While we talk, a familiar but also new confessional yearning seizes me: I want to tell her how I feel about her. The second this hunger starts blossoming in me, though, I see Pierce's face. I see Adair's face. I see Judge Edwards's face. I see the faces of the detectives and assistant district attorney who questioned me. I see the officers turning over my room. I see Eli's face. *Here you are, man, using my ticket to go see a concert with my girlfriend after you sent the text that killed me. Why don't you tell her you're into her? Maybe you two can get together. After all, my dad didn't say you couldn't. He only said he didn't want to see it.*

Jesmyn looks at me. "You having fun?"

I hadn't realized I was staring at her; my mind was so distant. "Oh . . . yeah. Definitely."

"We'll make a music lover of you yet."

"Dude, whatever. I'm always listening to you practice and I love your music that you played me."

"I mean we'll turn you on to some musicians who *aren't* me."

"Okay, but we're going to turn you on to more books."

"Deal."

Then the lights dim again. Jesmyn bounces up and down and makes a little *eep* sound. She grabs my wrist, her fingers warm and smooth as sun-soaked driftwood, her rings cold on my skin.

It's physically painful when she lets go and joins the uproarious applause for Dearly.

He strides onstage, tall, sleek, and lean, in black jeans, black boots, and a black denim jacket with a plaid western shirt underneath. The members of his band, cool and sharp like razors, follow close behind him and take their positions on the stage, illuminated by pinpricks of white light, so it appears they're playing in a starlit sky. Dearly heads to center stage, slings on his guitar, and steps to the mic, his shaggy dark hair framing his unshaven face.

The band starts in like a tsunami. Dearly begins to sing. Jesmyn shivers next to me. She's transfixed. I understand why. The music is stirring something deep inside me, too.

A couple of minutes into his second song, Jesmyn puts her hand on my shoulder, pulling me to her. "This show would have converted Eli."

Not that I'd thought about it in advance, but that's literally the last thing I wanted her to speak into my ear.

He finishes the third song, picks up a towel, wipes off his face, and takes a sip of water. "Hey, Nashville, it's good to be home, sort of." Everyone goes apeshit. He surveys the crowd.

"Thank y'all so much for coming tonight. I see friends out there. I see people who are pretty much family. It's such an honor to be standing on this stage."

Jesmyn pulls me down again. "He's from Tennessee. Right near Fall Creek Falls, in fact."

My belly roils and creaks, turning in on itself. I try to unknot it. *Jealousy is ugly. Especially when it's directed at—* and the truth is that I don't know at whom it's directed. Dearly? Eli? All the people experiencing normalcy around me, enjoying a concert without fear that it might be the last one they see before going to prison? Jesmyn, for being able to enjoy something so unreservedly?

As Dearly thunders, soars, and bleeds through his set, Jesmyn has the same expression she had when watching the storm. When watching the waterfall. Like a symphony of colors is cascading over her. She focuses alternately on Dearly and on the impossibly hip and gorgeous blonde playing keyboards in his band.

Please just have fun. Please let her lend you her excitement, the beauty she's seeing.

Even more than I want her, I want to not want her.

My thoughts descend in a spiral—blood washing down a drain. *Where is your ability to create something so powerful? What about you could enthrall her this way? Your writing has only the power to kill, not the power to make her see vibrant color.* The music is sublime. I'm furious with myself for allowing it to evoke such malignant emotion in me. It's like being mad at a sunset.

Isn't this what you deserve? Pierce asks me with his

vacant eyes, hard and dark as gunmetal. *Enjoy my dead son's ticket. Enjoy my dead son's show. Have fun sitting beside my dead son's girlfriend in my dead son's seat.*

I watch her. Her face; her shimmering eyes that become glassy and distant during the quietest moments; her lips silently mouthing the lyrics; her movement in rhythm with the music. It's like I don't exist beside her. Some gossamer veil separates us.

Dearly finishes a song and his band exits the stage. He stands alone with his acoustic guitar. "This next song I dedicate to a friend I lost in high school."

"Oh," Jesmyn murmurs. She tenses up palpably, bracing herself.

Tears cascade down her face as he sings. I touch her back and she moves slightly toward me. The song is pulling long, scarlet threads from my heart too, making it unravel in a blue twilight. I'm able to lose myself in it until it ends. For those few minutes, my mind rests.

Jesmyn wipes her eyes through Dearly's next two songs, for which his band rejoins him. When he bids the crowd good night and walks offstage, she alternates wiping her eyes and clapping. The crowd chants for more. Dearly and the band return for an encore.

When they start playing, the crowd goes bananas. Jesmyn squeals and pulls me down to her. "They're covering a Joy Division song called 'Love Will Tear Us Apart.'"

I nod as if I'm familiar.

Even though I've spent the last hour and a half in turmoil,

I'm not ready for it to end. I want to keep watching her bathe in the colors that she sees sound.

And I'm uncertain what to say to her when the world falls silent again and we have to fill it with our speaking.

◫ ◫ ◫

The signing line is a mile long, but it's clear we aren't leaving until Jesmyn has a signed poster.

We finally make it to the front of the line, where Dearly sits behind a table, signing T-shirts, posters, records, and the occasional body part.

Jesmyn buys a poster and hands it to Dearly with trembling hands. He exudes easy confidence. I guess I would too if I'd done what he did in front of throngs of fans screaming my name.

"Hey. I hope y'all had fun tonight," he says, with a sudden hint of bashfulness as he meets our eyes.

Jesmyn laughs and smoothes her hair. "Oh, yeah, completely. It was amazing," she stammers.

The way she's all jittery and giggly and looking at him. My stomach coils again.

"We were near where you grew up last week," Jesmyn says as Dearly signs her poster.

He looks up with a slight, sad smile. "Oh, yeah? I don't go back there much."

Jesmyn tucks a lock of hair behind her ear. "So—I'm a musician too."

"Nice," Dearly says. "What do you play?"

"Classical piano. But I also write and record songs."

"Man, music was my refuge when I was your age."

"I'd love to play keyboard for you after I finish college," Jesmyn says.

Her fawning tone is making my blood froth.

Dearly twists around to a man standing behind him, chatting with a couple of beautiful women who seem to be VIPs. "Will? Hey, Will? Give me your card." The man hands Dearly a card.

Dearly turns and hands the card to Jesmyn. "When you finish college, contact Will; he's my manager. But *only* when you finish college, okay?"

"Okay," Jesmyn says, breathless. "So. One more thing. That song you played for your friend really meant a lot to us. I just lost my boyfriend, who was his best friend." She points at me.

I shift my weight uncomfortably from side to side. Trying to look casual.

"I'm sorry," Dearly says softly. "I've been there." Something else has replaced his bashfulness. "I hope you find peace eventually."

"Did you?" Jesmyn asks.

Dearly gets a wistful and distant look in his eyes. "Not yet."

"Any tips?" Jesmyn ignores the tangible impatience of the people behind us.

Dearly ignores them too. "Stick with the people you love and who love you. Stick with the music."

"That sounds like solid advice," Jesmyn says. "Anyway, amazing show. Thanks."

Dearly thanks us for coming, and we leave, making way for the next devotees in line to receive Communion.

⊞ ⊞ ⊞

"Okay, I am, like, *buzzing* right now. I'm probably going to stay up all night playing music. That was intense," Jesmyn says.

"Yeah, it was cool," I say without conviction, pretending to focus intently on the road.

"I mean, did it not blow your mind?"

"*Pshew.*" I make an exploding motion from my head.

"How is somebody even that brilliant?"

"Yeah, I thought you were about to ask Dearly to marry you." I hope she takes that as a joke, so I can say it without consequence. But even I can tell that my accompanying laugh is a bit too caustic.

If Jesmyn were a video-game character, her "exuberance status bar" would have zeroed out after that hit. "Um. *No.*"

"I was kidding," I mutter.

"So I'm some dumb groupie who just wants to get with a rock star?"

"No. I mean, you did offer to be his keyboard player, though." I should stop talking, but I can't. It's like when you pissed your pants as a kid—you knew you were doing something gross and wrong but you couldn't stop once you started.

She takes a deep breath through her nose. "Wanting to play keyboards in someone's band is not wanting to marry them. Besides, he's an adult man. With a girlfriend."

"Oh, glad you checked."

She rolls her eyes. "Why are you being shitty right now? After the best show of my life and you're seriously crapping on me."

"I'm just making conversation."

"Not the kind Eli would have made after a great show."

"I'm not Eli."

"Look, can we please stop having weirdness? I don't get what your deal is or why you're being this way, but could you please stop?"

"Fine."

We drive in strained silence the rest of the way home. At one point, we make eye contact and we trade terse, taut-lipped smiles.

There's so much I want to say to her, and so much static in my brain. I don't have a clear line on my thoughts.

We pull up to her house with my head still in a vortex.

"Okay. Well. Thanks," Jesmyn says, reaching for the door handle. "I'll s—"

"Jesmyn."

She looks at me expectantly.

"I'm—" *Don't say you have feelings for her. If you're going to do this, if you're going to succumb, use any other phrase but that.* "I have feelings for you. I like you. I *like* like you. As more than a friend."

Her expression tells me immediately that's not what she was hoping to hear. The air goes stiff.

She shakes her head and puts her hand over her eyes, bowing her head and moaning softly. "Carver. Carver."

My blood speeds. "It's not like I chose for this to happen."

"I'm sure, but I can't. You must know that. I just can't."

I'm not sure I even can. But still. I'm in it now. The only way out is on the other side. "Why not?"

"Why not? Seriously?"

"I mean, the obvious reason I know."

"Well, right. The obvious reason is *the reason*." She buries her face in both hands, muffling her voice.

"Do you not feel anything back?"

"You're my friend. I like you."

"That's not what I mean, and you know it."

She raises her hands in front of her as though holding an invisible box. "Carver, I can't. I can't deal with *this* right now. I have a Juilliard audition to prepare for. My *boyfriend*— your *best friend*—died two and a half months ago. I *am not ready* for another relationship."

"But with Eli you were ready after all of three days."

"Oh my g— Can you seriously not see how that was different? I didn't get together with Eli after my previous boyfriend had just died."

I'm crumbling; splintering. "What? What is so wrong with me?"

"There's nothing *wrong* with you."

I suddenly feel ridiculous in my new clothes. Like Jesmyn

saw right through my costume. "Is it that I'm not as brilliant as Dearly? Or Eli?"

"Your brilliance is not the problem. Not at all. I read the story you gave me."

"And of course you didn't say a word about it."

"I don't sit around telling people how brilliant they are. I show them. I showed you by the respect I've given you, which you don't seem to have for me."

"You had no problem telling Dearly how brilliant he is."

"Well, he and I don't eat lunch together every day."

"Not by your choice."

"Are you seriously jealous of one of my favorite musicians?"

I sit there with my mouth agape, trying to figure out how to answer no when the answer is yes. "No," I say. This is going terribly. But I can't stop. Some malevolent voice is telling me to burn my life down. "Eli wasn't *that* great." The words sear my lips as they leave. *What are you doing?*

Jesmyn looks at me as if I've slapped her. "Listen to yourself." She raises her index finger. "One week ago we were having a goodbye day for him. *One week.*" Her voice is unsteady and swollen with tears.

We stare ahead and say nothing. Jesmyn shakes her head. She wipes at her eyes.

"Eli would have wanted us to be together if he wasn't around anymore." I say it to myself, hoping she won't hear and make me repeat it.

She spins to face me, eyes ablaze. She points in my face with a shaking finger. "I am not a stamp collection that someone leaves in a will, got it? I am not a piece of property to be passed down."

Watch it burn. Watch it burn. "I didn't mean to—"

But she's already got the door open. She whirls to face me. "Do I need to tell you not to text me, call me, or talk to me?" She gets out and slams the door so hard, I'm surprised the window doesn't shatter.

She makes it a few steps toward her house before she spins around and returns. She opens the door. A surge of illogical, unfounded hope passes through me. *Look,* she'll say, *we're both really emotional right now. Let's forget all of this ever happened and keep being friends.*

She leans in the open door. "Another thing. You might've had a chance. *Had.* Maybe. But now?" With another window-rattling door slam, she's gone.

I sit catatonic for several moments. It's the same stupor as when I found out what had happened to Sauce Crew. In which I wonder if I'm imagining what happened, because it's too horrendous to be real.

As Jesmyn's front door stays closed and dark, the pain begins to flood in like in movies where a submarine is sinking. A little jet of water. Then another; bigger. And another. They're becoming thicker. Unfixable. Until finally, the sea rushes in, hungry and black, to claim everyone left alive.

I hate my dead friend Eli.

Even more than that, I hate myself.

◫ ◫ ◫

I make it home eleven minutes after my midnight curfew, but I don't particularly care. What are my parents going to do? Ground me from hanging out with friends?

I go into their bedroom and give them the I-haven't-been-drinking-or-smoking-pot hugs and then I head for my room. But then I hear raucous laughter from behind Georgia's door and reconsider. No way am I going to sleep.

I go out and sit on the front steps, resting my elbows on my knees. I have no idea how long I'm out there because I don't own a watch or—at the present—a phone.

The sound of the front door opening startles me. I look over my shoulder.

"Hey," Georgia says. "There you are. When did you get home?"

"Little while ago. Where are Maddie and Lana?"

"Inside. Drunk-texting exes. We smuggled a bottle of vodka home from school."

"Good, because I really, *really* can't deal with them right now."

"Hang on," Georgia says. She goes inside and comes out a few moments later with a blanket. She sits and wraps it around both of us, snuggling up next to me, shivering. "Okay. Spill."

"I don't want to talk about it."

"Jesmyn?"

"Yeah."

"You're way into her."

"Yeah."

"Obviously."

"Great."

"But she's not into you at the moment because too weird."

"Yeah."

"That all?"

"Isn't that enough?"

"Yes. But is that all?"

I sigh and squeeze my eyes shut. "I totally screwed myself. Told her how I felt. Said a bunch of stupid stuff. She's really pissed."

Georgia hugs my arm and rests her head on my shoulder. "Aw, Carver."

I rub the side of my head like I'm trying to get out a stain. "She was all I had. She was my only friend here."

"I know."

"I'm really lonely."

"I bet."

"I want to be happy again before I die. That's all I want."

We sit for a long time without speaking in the lovelorn and desperate circle of porch light, shivering and listening to the crickets' dying song in the brisk darkness. The air is heavy with dew when we finally end our empty vigil.

Chapter Thirty-Seven

I once thought heartbreak was akin to contracting a cold or becoming pregnant. It only comes one at a time. Once you get it, you can't get it again until you're done with the first round.

It turns out it's actually more like how you eat dinner until you're full. But the minute someone says, "There's pie!" you suddenly have room again in your dessert stomach, separate from your dinner stomach. You have a love heart, separate from your grieving heart, or your guilt heart, or your fear heart. All can be individually broken in their own way.

So I have all kinds of room for a new type of heartbreak.

That's what I discover the Sunday after the Dearly show, when I have all day to sit and stew and be lonely and lock myself in my room for safety until Maddie and Lana are gone. Which sucks, because I really need a day to hang out with Georgia.

I relearn it on Monday morning, when I show up to school alone. Jesmyn and I didn't always ride to school together. But we always met up to hang out for a few minutes before class. Not now.

It *really* sinks in at lunch. We *always* ate lunch together. I sit in the buzzing, pulsing cafeteria, hoping she sees me; hoping my forlornness can win her over. But she's nowhere to be found. I guess she's eating lunch in the music rooms. She said her friend Kerry and the other music nerds did that.

So I sit alone and indulge in wishful thinking, imagining her sitting there as lost as I am. At best, I can envision her giving off the faintest whiff of melancholy; so that someone asks what's wrong, and she says, "Nothing."

But at least someone cares about her enough to ask. Everyone steers clear of me. There must be some threshold for looking lonely that I've crossed. Where people sympathize with you but fear they completely lack what it takes to fill the echoing chasm inside you, so why try?

The only person who looks in my direction is Adair. She walks past with four of her friends and gives me a viperous serves-you-right glare. My solitude is nectar to her. *Don't worry, Adair, Eli's ghost is having his revenge on me for trying to get with his girlfriend.*

And so it goes. I'm starting to wonder if jail might not be so bad. Tuesday. Wednesday. Thursday. Friday. The only difference with Saturday and Sunday is nobody can see me being alone. And then repeat: Monday. Tuesday. Wednesday.

I rarely see Jesmyn, and when I do, she manages to not even accidentally look at me.

My parents can sense my isolation. I must be radioactive with it. My dad takes me to Parnassus Books and tells me to pick out anything I want. I'm not in the mood for much, though.

The police return my phone and laptop on Thursday. They drop them off at Mr. Krantz's office. I can't turn my phone on quickly enough. Maybe she texted me, unaware I still didn't have it.

Nothing.

I contemplate texting her. Calling her. Leaving her a note. Something. But then I remember her face when she told me not to.

I count the hours until my appointment with Dr. Mendez that Friday. He's pretty much all I have left. And if we didn't pay him, I wouldn't have him either.

Chapter Thirty-Eight

This is the time I'd normally be listening to Jesmyn practice. In brighter days. It's funny (and by "funny," I mean "horrendously sad")—to refer to the period when you were *only* dealing with the deaths of your three best friends, the hatred of their loved ones, and the prospect of incarceration as "brighter days."

I hear my mom answer her phone from my bedroom, where I sit, trying to read *Slaughterhouse-Five* for AP English lit.

Something in the formality of her tone pricks my ears and I strain to listen.

"Okay . . . so at five? What channel? Okay. And—okay. Should we call you afterward? Okay. I'll tell him. Thank you so much."

My mom hurries down the hallway to my dad's study, and he stops playing his acoustic guitar.

Please don't both of you come this way. Please.

I hear them both coming my way. Surely at some point, my recently overworked adrenal glands will simply explode with a little popping sound.

"Carver?" my dad says, knocking on my doorframe, my mom beside him. They're not smiling.

I turn but say nothing.

"We just got a call from Mr. Krantz. He said that in an hour, the district attorney's office is holding a press conference to talk about your case. He expects them to announce some decision."

"Okay," I say finally, my blood howling, turning every muscle to mush.

"Meet in the living room in an hour to watch?" my mom asks.

"Okay." My intestines feel like a steamroller is slowly ironing them flat.

My parents leave. I settle in for what will surely be one of the longest hours of my life. I want to text Jesmyn so badly. And I don't even know what I'd say. First I'd have to apologize. Once I cleared that barrier, if she even wanted to hear more, all I'd have to say would be: *Somewhere, someone has the answer to this question: Will Carver Briggs's life be ruined? (Correction: more ruined). And I have to wait an hour to learn the answer.*

The hour passes. I sit in the living room, one parent on each side of me.

"All right, Kimberly," the newscaster says. "I understand we're going live now to the Davidson County Courthouse, where the Davidson County district attorney, Karen Walker, will be making an announcement?"

"That's right, Peter. They're going to announce what course of action they're planning to take with regard to the car accident that claimed the lives of three teenage boys on August first. Some of our viewers will recall that this accident was linked to texting."

My mom is shaking next to me. I take a ragged breath; it feels like my lungs are full of wet cement. My pulse hammers in my temples, a headache brewing at the base of my skull.

The camera cuts to an empty podium with several microphones. The district attorney steps up to it.

"Thank you all for coming today. The accident that claimed the lives of Thurgood Edwards, Blake Lloyd, and Elias Bauer on August first, was a tragedy by any definition. The remaining question, though, was whether it was a crime as well. Over the past nearly three months, our office, in conjunction with the Nashville Metro Police Department and the Tennessee Bureau of Investigation, has diligently investigated this question. We have concluded that . . ."

My vision narrows to a laser pinpoint.

". . . this tragic accident was . . ."

I wonder what I'll do when they say it. When they tell me I'm finished. I wonder if I'll cry. If I'll scream. If I'll have a panic attack. If I'll just pass out.

". . . *not* the result of criminal conduct, and our office

will not be seeking an indictment against the fourth surviving juvenile involved. . . ."

My mom explodes in sobs. My dad exhales and buries his face in his palms, weeping. I sit completely still and mute. I'm not sure I've heard what I think I've heard, like when you watch TV half-asleep and you have to chew on each sentence to make sure you didn't imagine it.

". . . We extend our condolences once more to the Edwards, Bauer, and Lloyd families. We take this opportunity to warn young people against the dangers of texting and driving. Even when it does not rise to the level of criminal conduct, it has terrible consequences, as we've seen. Our office will continue to—"

My mom grabs me in a hug from one side. "Oh, praise Jesus," she murmurs over and over. Her Mississippi shows most at times of great emotional duress. My dad hugs me from the other side. I stare dazed at the television.

My mom's phone rings. "Hello? Oh, my goodness, yes, you have no idea. Yes. Yes, he is, I'll give you to him. And thank you so, so much. All right. All right, bye."

My mom hands the phone to me. "Mr. Krantz," she whispers.

"Hello?"

"Carver! Well? Looks like you're off the hook, son."

"Um, yeah, that's great." I try to mirror his enthusiasm.

"I knew it'd be a stretch to try to charge you. They made the right choice."

"Yeah."

"Now, you may not be completely out of the woods yet. The DA could still reconsider, so don't go talking about the accident. Also, Edwards could still file a civil lawsuit seeking monetary damages. And it would be easier for him to win that without a criminal acquittal. Anyway, I gotta run; I have a client. Congratulations and take care, all right?"

"Okay."

I hang up and draw a deep breath. I'm exhausted. I want to be alone.

"I need to go lie down," I say.

"That's fine, sweetie," my mom says, hugging me again. "I'm going to go pick up some hot chicken from Hattie B's to celebrate."

In another life, that news alone would have made my night.

I go to my room and collapse on my bed and stare at the ceiling. I cry until warm tears enter my earholes, muting sound as if I'm underwater.

I have no idea why I'm crying. I think I'm happy but I'm not sure. Happiness would be not dealing with any of this. I guess I'm relieved, but an odd disappointment tempers any relief. It's like I've been tied to a stake for days, the ropes rubbing my wrists and ankles raw; my tongue bloated and cracked from thirst. And the guy in the black hood coming with a torch to light the kindling under me turns and walks away, leaving the torch burning on the ground. And I'm still tied to the stake.

My phone vibrates in my pocket.

Jesmyn! She saw the news. She's calling to congratulate me, to tell me that if the DA doesn't consider it worthwhile to punish me, neither does she.

It's a number I don't recognize. A reporter? Did the police give out my number while they had my phone?

"Hello?"

"Carver Briggs?" asks the crisp, starchy female voice on the other end.

I really hate hearing people say my first and last names on the phone these days. I stand and pace. "Yes. This is me—he."

"Please hold for Judge Frederick Edwards."

And she's gone before I can say, *No, please, no. Anybody but him.*

I sit; my legs have turned into octopus tentacles.

I hear the other end pick up and a long breath. "Do you know the means by which I obtained this number?" Judge Edwards's voice sounds carved from granite.

"Um. No, sir. Your Honor. I don't." My voice is high and tight, like an overwound guitar string. I know I sound guilty.

"Venture a guess." Not an invitation. A command.

It feels like a bone is stuck in my throat. "From the police?"

"After Thurgood was killed, the police turned over his personal effects to me. His phone was among them. Getting your number was a matter of looking at the last number to contact my son before his death."

He lets the silence breathe, the way Dr. Mendez does. But it breathes differently: someone gathering his strength to run me through with a sword.

"Oh." What do you say to that? *Nice, good work.*

"I suppose you've heard the news."

"Yes. Your Honor. I did."

"I suppose you feel pretty lucky."

"I—I—"

And then he cuts me off, which is great, because I didn't have a good answer to that statement. "Well, you were not *lucky.* If you repeat what I'm about to tell you to anyone else, I will be very displeased. Are we clear?"

My mouth is parched. "Yes, Your Honor."

"I personally asked the district attorney not to pursue charges."

I'm dumbfounded. "Thank you, sir," I say finally. "I promise—"

He laughs bitterly. "*Thank you?* This was not a personal favor to you. Nevertheless, you are greatly in my debt, and I intend to collect."

"Okay." *Here comes the hammer.* I brace myself.

"I'm told that you've embarked on a series of 'goodbye days,' during which, if I understand correctly, you spend a day with the victim's family and have a final day of remembrance?"

"Right." *Victim's.*

"Right what?"

"Right, Your Honor."

"And you've done them so far with the Lloyd family and the Bauer family."

"Yes, Your Honor. How did Your Honor—"

"Find out? Adair Bauer contacted my office, the police,

and the district attorney's office about them. She thought we should investigate whether you'd said anything self-incriminatory. She wanted us to talk to her parents. Not a bad idea."

That's why she was so adamant that her parents do it. "Oh." And then I hastily add, "Your Honor."

"Now I want my goodbye day for Thurgood."

"Your Honor, I—"

"This Sunday you will be at my home at five-thirty a.m. You will dress for vigorous physical activity. You will also bring clothes appropriate for church. This is not a throw-on-your-T-shirt, Starbucks church. You dress the way you did for my son's funeral. Understood?"

"Yes, Your Honor."

The line goes dead.

Chapter Thirty-Nine

I feel ungrateful to the gods of fate that I'm not happier about the blade of prosecution not dangling over my neck anymore. I fantasized about this. But that was taking for granted Jesmyn's presence in my life. It was also taking for granted that, in a few days, I wouldn't be spending the day with the person who hates me the second most.

At school, a few people nod as we pass in the halls. Their expressions convey a sort of: *I'm not sure how to congratulate you for not being prosecuted, but I'm more comfortable acknowledging you now that you're not legally a murderer.*

My AP English lit teacher pulls me aside after class and tells me how glad she is for my news. My school's been fairly hands-off throughout this whole thing—pretty much just telling me when the cops were there to seize my phone and laptop. I guess they were afraid to tell me to go talk to the school counselor lest I involve him in a murder investigation.

Somehow all this makes me even more depressed. So I'm already in a bad state by my solitary lunchtime. As the lunch hour ends, I realize I've allowed myself the glowing ember of hope that Jesmyn would break down and come find me and at least tell me she was glad I wasn't going to prison.

But maybe she's not glad. Maybe that's the depth of her hatred for me now.

I go to my locker to grab my books for my next class. I open it and a fine plume of gray-black ash assaults my face as it's sucked out by the door opening. I sneeze and blink it from my watering eyes.

I'm pretty sure it's not Eli. This smells spicy and woodsy. The sort of wood that would be burned in a fireplace in a fancy home.

The Bauers have a fireplace.

The inside of my locker is covered in ash. The ingenuity to pull this off—someone must have blown it in through the door vents somehow.

I see a small, cream-colored card lying on the floor of the locker. I pick it up and ash falls from it. It's not some crappy notecard. It has an expensive heft to it. In a clean, elegant typeface, it says: MURDERER.

I can sense Adair's eyes, and the eyes of others, scorching my back. I'm staring into my begrimed locker like it contains the answer to a question, holding the card, and fantasizing about climbing in and shutting the door behind me. Waiting there until I can leave without seeing her.

"Dude, what happened?" someone asks. I ignore him and carefully, deliberately place the card in my shirt pocket. Over my heart. I hope she saw me do it.

With my eyes on the floor, I walk out of the building into the parking lot, jump into my car, and leave. I've never ditched before. You don't go to the trouble of getting into NAA only to skip class.

There comes a point when you realize that you can never make someone like you, or even stop hating you, and the only defense you have left is the ultimate one—not giving a shit anymore. But that requires the not giving of a shit, and I'm not there yet. So I'm defenseless.

When I get home, I go to the bathroom and look in the mirror.

There is still ash in my hair.

There is still ash on my face.

Chapter Forty

"So, since we last spoke, I've found myself thinking about the hapless Jiminy Turdsworth and the cat restaurant he started with the proceeds of the safety device he stole from the trailer of Billy Scruggs's truck." Dr. Mendez has a mischievous glint in his eyes from behind his steel frames.

"Sorry about the name. I was mad," I mumble. I'm suddenly embarrassed about my outburst in our last session.

Dr. Mendez waves it off. "It had a certain, say, scatological elegance. You don't think my being an adult man with a psychiatry degree means I don't find poop funny anymore?"

"No."

"How have you been?"

"Really bad."

Waiting.

I sigh. "I, um." I study the floor. "Messed things up with Jesmyn. Maybe permanently."

"Want to tell me what happened?"

"Not especially."

That even, temperate gaze from Dr. Mendez.

". . . But you're going to just sit there not saying anything until I do."

He shrugs. *Probably.*

"Well. We went to a concert together. She and Eli were supposed to go. Everything was fine. She played me some of her music on the way. It was amazing. She looked *so beautiful.* I was wearing some new clothes my sister helped me pick out. And then . . . I started getting jealous, I guess. Of how she loves musicians. Of Eli. Of . . . who knows. At the end of the night—"

I lean back and rub my mouth and look over Dr. Mendez's shoulder. He's so still, it draws the sound from my mouth.

I continue. "This is so embarrassing. At the end of the night, I tell her I have feelings for her, and she says she doesn't feel the same way, and it all goes down the toilet and I tell her Eli wasn't that great and blah blah blah. We haven't said a word to each other in almost two weeks."

Dr. Mendez nods and taps his lips, looking meditative. "Do you see yourself as worthy of being with Jesmyn?"

I start to say "of course," but catch myself. "Maybe not," I say after a few seconds' contemplation.

Dr. Mendez leans forward. "Is it possible you introduced some chaos into the relationship, perhaps to sabotage it, because on some level you felt undeserving of being with her?"

A door opens in my mind and I walk through. "Yeah. Possible."

Somehow this comforts me. It doesn't fix anything. In fact, it only makes more clear that it was my fault. But still.

"It sounded like you two were very close. If I were a betting man, I'd wager on your relationship ending up on good terms again."

"Any ideas on how I could make that happen?"

"Honesty. Humility. Listening more than you talk."

"Okay."

We stare at each other for a short while.

"So," I say. "The district attorney decided yesterday not to press charges against me."

Dr. Mendez's face illuminates. He laughs and claps. *"Fantastic!* I really need to keep up on local news better. That's wonderful!" He looks as relieved as I wish I felt.

"Yeah, it is. I mean, yeah."

"But?"

"But I ended up agreeing to do a final goodbye day. With Mars's dad."

"The judge."

"The judge who hates me."

"Hmm."

"It's this Sunday. I'm really scared."

"I bet."

"Any ideas on how I should handle it? Please actually give me an answer just this once and I'll never bug you for one again."

He takes a deep breath and laces his fingers around one knee. "Be honest. Be humble. Listen more than you talk."

Chapter Forty-One

"No, but it's weird, right? How we're totally good on last names now and we don't need to invent any more," Blake says.

"Like how in the old-timey days, people were named after what they did for a living. So John Smith was a black-smith. But yeah, we don't have 'John Programmer' or 'John Pizzadeliveryguy,'" I say.

We crack up, our laughter echoing down the hall.

"Bill . . . Walmartgreeter," Eli says.

"Amber Pornstar," Blake says.

"Jim and Linda Garbageman," I say.

"Doctor Manhattan!" Eli says.

"That doesn't really—" I start to say.

But Eli's stopped and is looking down at this short, skinny kid with an Afro, black-framed glasses, and low-top Chucks that have been drawn on with a permanent marker. He's sitting, leaning against a locker, sketching on a large pad.

The kid looks up, surprised. "Yeah . . . you into *Watchmen*?"

"Totally, man," Eli says. "Can I see?"

The kid shrugs. "Sure. Not done yet." He hands the pad to Eli.

Eli studies it, awestruck. "Bro, this is amazing. If you told me you actually illustrated *Watchmen,* I would believe you."

The kid breathes hot on his fingernails and buffs them on his V-neck T-shirt. "Well, of course I illustrated *Watchmen*."

Eli laughs and extends his hand. "It's an honor. Eli Bauer."

The kid takes Eli's hand. "Mars Edwards."

Blake and I introduce ourselves.

"Hey, we're going to my house right now to play some *Spec Ops: Ukrainian Gambit,*" Eli says. "It's more fun with four players. Wanna come?"

Mars's face brightens at the invitation. "Man, thanks." His face dims again. "I wish I could. I gotta do this church thing with my dad in an hour or so, and he's a pretty intense dude. He'd be like 'Thurgood'—that's my real name, by the way—'we do not cancel commitments or change plans ever for any reason.' "

We laugh at Mars's impression; we don't even need to have met his dad.

"You eat lunch with anyone?" I ask.

"Naw, not really. Still meeting people," Mars says.

"You wanna eat lunch with us?" I ask.

"Yeah, yeah, that'd be cool. I usually use lunch to practice sketching."

"That's fine, because we use lunch to practice being sketchy," Blake says.

The next day Mars eats lunch with us. And from then on, Sauce Crew is complete. One day he sketches a picture of me.

I frame it and put it on my wall.

I'm looking at it now; staring myself in the eyes as I lie awake, listening to my house creak and pop; listening to my humming blood.

I wish I could talk to Jesmyn. I wonder if she ever lies awake and thinks of me. I wonder if she ever misses my lying under her piano. Another phantom limb itching.

I contemplate the day stretching ahead of me like some vast unknown land enshrouded in fog. I have no idea what will happen or how it will go.

No, scratch that. I have some idea.

November. Mars and I should be immersed in the abundance of our last year together. Instead, there's this.

Penance.

Stories.

Goodbye days.

⊡ ⊡ ⊡

Not only do I want to shit myself as I pull up to the Edwardses' immaculately restored East Nashville house in the predawn dark; I feel ridiculous. I've slapped together a work-out getup of some old PE shorts, trail-running shoes I bought to use for hiking, a T-shirt, and a hoodie. I had to sneak out in these clothes because my parents think I'm visiting the Sewanee campus today. As if I'd tell them I'm hanging out with the guy who tried to put me in prison.

At precisely five-thirty, I walk up to the front door. The chill bites at my bare legs, but I can't tell whether I'm shivering because I'm cold or because I'm nervous. I knock tentatively. I hear loud, determined steps.

Judge Edwards opens the door, dressed in a pair of black running shorts with "U.S.M.C." in white lettering and a sleek, black running jacket. He makes workout gear look like a three-piece suit. He looks at his watch and glowers at me. "You're late."

My bowels are Jell-O. "I'm sorry, Your Honor," I stammer. "My clock said five-thirty exactly."

He extends his arm so I can see his watch. "Five-thirty-two."

And we're off to a great start. "I'm sorry, Your Honor. I apologize."

"I taught Thurgood to be scrupulously punctual. We do disservice to his memory by being otherwise."

"Yes, sir, Mars was always—"

"Pardon me, who?"

"Mars, sir, was always—"

"I don't know anyone named Mars other than the Roman god of war."

"Your son, sir."

"My son named Thurgood Marshall Edwards?"

"Yes, sir, sorry."

"Then let's honor his memory by calling him by his given name."

"Yes, sir."

"Let's go. I'll drive."

I had wondered if any of Mars's older brothers or sister would come. The oldest brother is a JAG in the Marine Corps. His sister is finishing her PhD at Princeton, and his other brother is premed at Howard University. I'm unsurprised to not see them coming and even less surprised not to see Mars's mom. He always said she and his dad fought a lot.

We get into Judge Edwards's sleek Mercedes that shines like black glass. The tan leather seats are firm and cold on the backs of my thighs. Judge Edwards wordlessly turns on both of our seat warmers and pulls out of the driveway.

We might as well be in the vacuum of space for all the talking we do. *Listen more than you talk,* Dr. Mendez whispers in my mind. *No problem there, doc,* I think.

After about ten minutes, we arrive at the Shelby Bottoms Greenway, a miles-long asphalt path along the Cumberland River where people run, bike, and walk dogs. I've been here a few times.

Judge Edwards parks and we get out. He goes to the trunk, retrieves a water bottle, and tosses it to me. "Drink."

I fumble it, drop it, and pick it up. I comply, even though I'm not at all thirsty. Something in his tone tells me it would be unwise to refuse.

Judge Edwards does some quick stretches. I've never noticed this before because I've always seen him in a suit, but he looks carved from gristle. There's a hardness to him that looks like all fluff and frivolity, inside and out, has been burned away by fire; consumed; withered by drought.

I mimic the motions of stretching. I have no clue what I'm doing.

"Let's go," he suddenly barks, like a drill instructor. And he's off before I'm even standing upright.

I have to sprint my fastest just to catch up with him. Even then I'm running at almost top speed to keep pace. I'm no athlete. I'm not totally out of shape because I go for walks, but I'm completely outmatched as a runner. My heavy trail-running shoes—built to withstand rough ground—clomp on the pavement, jarring my knees. My chest heaves and pleads for air. The saline, coppery tang of blood is in my mouth and on my breath. My pulse screams in my ears. I start to fall behind.

Ahead of me, Judge Edwards turns. Even in the dark, his eyes flash ardent. "*Pick up the pace*. Thurgood loved excellence. He loved to test himself. He loved to achieve. He was not a quitter. Now *move*."

I move. For what seems like hours. As if hounds are at my heels. Every cell in my body is sobbing, begging for oxygen. I'm soaked in sweat and the damp chills me. My knees throb. My feet ache. I start coughing and I can't stop. I begin to fall behind again.

Judge Edwards stops and turns around, running in place, waiting for me. He's barely winded.

I catch up to him and double over, hands on my knees, hacking up phlegm. "Your Honor, how long did you plan on running?" I wheeze. "I'm not sure if—"

"Seven miles."

Seven miles?! I almost died when I had to run a mile for PE. And that was at my own pace, not Judge Edwards's.

"How far have we gone, sir?"

"Approximately two miles."

I gasp. "I'm sorry, sir. I don't think I can run seven miles."

He bends down to meet my gaze in the dim light. His face is uncomfortably close to mine and he speaks with unshrouded menace. "Do you feel like you can't breathe? Like a rockslide has covered your chest?"

I nod.

"Does your heart ache like it's tearing in half?"

I nod.

"Does every inch of you hurt? I mean *hurt* like you want to die?"

I nod.

"Do you feel like being sick all over the ground? Like you want to turn yourself inside out?"

I nod.

He draws even closer. His breath smells like hunger and mouthwash, like he just keeps brushing his teeth without ever eating anything. "Now you understand how I felt when I received the call telling me my son had been killed." His voice quakes.

But I already know! my brain screams. *Because I felt the same when I found out.*

He stands back up, straight as a steel beam, while I wait for a coughing fit to pass and try to buy myself a second or two with a story about how Mars once bought a homeless guy lunch and then drew a picture for him to sell or trade for more food later if he got hungry.

"Once, Thurgood—"

"No," Judge Edwards says, with an I've-got-a-better-idea inflection, raising his finger to cut me off. "*Oh no.* This is not the day for *you* to tell *me* who *my* son was. This is the day for you to understand what you took from me with your recklessness and stupidity and impatience. *Now catch your breath and move.*"

Every word is agonizing. Injury on top of injury. Stubbing your toe when your feet are frozen. Rubbing off a blister down to raw flesh.

I get my coughing under control, and Judge Edwards sprints away again, with me trailing behind. Each breath sears my lungs. Every protective shell I've formed—every bulwark I've thrown up—is eroding; melting away; leaving me bare. Emotions I'd tried to bury are beginning to flood out. *He knew this would happen.*

I'm having trouble lifting each foot off the ground. My toe catches the tiniest crack in the pavement and I go sprawling, abrading away the skin on my knees and palms. I lie there, stunned by the sudden jolt that knocked what little wind I had out of me. My eyes well up with tears as I struggle to stand.

I hear footfalls as Judge Edwards lopes back to me. "Are you injured?" he asks, in a tone suggesting he's mostly concerned about my being healthy enough for him to keep breaking.

I shake my head but don't speak because of the sobs massed on the borders of my vocal cords, waiting to spill.

I stand on rickety legs. The air is cold and sharp on my newly exposed nerve endings. Suddenly, nausea overwhelms me. I make it the few steps to the edge of the path before yakking last night's dinner onto the ground. It goes out through my nose and the whole world smells like puke.

Well, Dr. Mendez, I'm doing great on the humility front. And you can't be more honest than puking in front of someone. And I'm sure listening more than I'm talking.

When I turn to Judge Edwards, he hands me a water bottle. "Drink," he says. He sounds ever so slightly sympathetic. I drink, swishing the water around in my mouth.

I hand him the bottle. "Okay," I say, hearing the fatal resignation in my own voice. "Let's go." Maybe I can run myself to death. In fact, looking at the dense, tangled woods on either side, it's not entirely implausible that he brought me out here to kill me anyway. Joining Sauce Crew would improve my life right now.

"I think that will do." He starts walking in the direction from which we came. I expect him to start running, but he doesn't.

I limp after him, tamping down my pain and queasiness.

Dawn is breaking, a luminous rose-orange silk ribbon over the black ranks of trees, but it's still cold and dark on the path, and between us we are as mute as the friend and son we came to honor.

■ ■ ■

"Bring the towel inside with you," Judge Edwards says. "And your church clothes."

I grab the towel that he made me put on his car seat, get my suit that's hanging in my car and my dress shoes, and limp into the house after him, still wheezing.

Of all of Sauce Crew, we hung out at Mars's house the least. Mars and Eli dug my house because they could ogle Georgia. We all liked Blake's because of Nana Betsy. And Eli's had the best video-game setup. Plus there was always the chance that Adair would show up with a pack of her lithe dancer friends. There was something about Mars's house that put us on edge. It felt antiseptic, cold, brutal, efficient. Blake wouldn't fart there. Not even if it was just the four of us. He'd wait until he got out in the car to let fly. "It's not the kind of place you fart in," he explained once (as opposed to in public stores and in the foyer of our school). When we did hang out at Mars's, it was in the messy oasis of his bedroom.

I stand in the entryway while Judge Edwards goes upstairs. I'm afraid to do anything without a direct order. I hear him rummaging around.

"Upstairs," he calls. "Hall bathroom."

I plod up the stairs. Even this exertion is exhausting me after the run/walk. I make my way to the bathroom.

Judge Edwards points to where he's laid things out in neat formation. "Hydrogen peroxide. Bandages. Towels. Shower, tend to your injuries, make yourself presentable for church."

I nod and he leaves. I hang my suit on a hook on the back of the door and undress. I feel vulnerable being naked in Mars's house. Especially since I would have never *dreamed* of showering at his house before. Part of me wonders if Judge Edwards plans to barge in on me midshower, yank me out, and throw me in the street, dripping and nude. *Now you see how naked I felt when you killed my son,* he'd say.

And then, as the hot water hits me, soothes my aching limbs, flushes the smell of puke from my nose, and washes the blood from my knees and palms, I wonder if he'll instead turn off the hot water abruptly, leaving me dancing and convulsing in freezing water. *Now you know how it felt when you suddenly took my son from me,* he'd say. But I finish and dry myself off. I apply the stinging hydrogen peroxide to my wounds and bandage them. I dress in my suit and tie and dress shoes and pad downstairs, feeling slightly less vulnerable. Judge Edwards is waiting for me. He's already showered and dressed in an impeccable black-gray three-piece suit, with a shirt that gleams cumulus white, and a bloodred tie.

He points to the dining room table. There's a bowl, a spoon, a container of milk, and a box of Special K. "Eat."

My stomach is completely void, but somehow I'm not hungry. Still, I sit and pour myself a bowl of cereal and eat.

Judge Edwards's study is next to the dining room. I hear him go in and sit down, and then the scratching of a pen on paper. The air is tightly wound.

Tell him who I am, Mars whispers to me in the wordless lull. *I never did.*

I can't, I whisper. *I'm afraid.*

Of what?

Of him. Weren't you?

Yeah. But I'd do it for you if the roles were reversed. What else can he do to you?

I don't know.

Tell you that you killed me?

Maybe.

What about Billy? Hiro? Jiminy?

You sound like Dr. Mendez.

He sounds smart.

"It's time," Judge Edwards says, exiting his study with a sheaf of paper in hand.

I pick up my bowl and start to take it into the kitchen.

"Thurgood always left his bowl on the table."

I halt, turn, and put the bowl back on the table.

"It drove me mad."

I pick up the bowl again.

He raises a hand in exasperation. "Leave it. Let's go."

As we walk out, I catch a glimpse of Judge Edwards staring back at the bowl on the table, lying there empty and still.

▣ ▣ ▣

My stomach simmers as we pull up to New Bethel AME Church, a large, modern brown building. It's reminding me of Mars's funeral, and that alone would do the trick even without my having tossed my cookies earlier.

"The church was an important part of Thurgood's life," Judge Edwards says, breaking the tomblike silence that has attended the entire drive. "He was part of the youth group. He sang in the choir."

"Yes, sir."

I glimpse myself in the side mirror. I have the complexion of a nice bowl of Greek yogurt. Except maybe a bit more pale green around the edges. Key lime–flavored.

We park and get out. I follow at Judge Edwards's heels as we join the bustling crowd. People greet him warmly. He doesn't look back to make sure I'm following or to introduce me. I receive some genial greetings too, but obviously as a generic guest, not as Judge Edwards's. I get kind but curious stares.

Once inside the main chapel, Judge Edwards turns to me with a residual smile from having talked with someone he knows. He banishes the smile immediately when we make eye contact, ensuring none of it falls on me by accident. He points at me and stabs his finger at a center pew.

I nod and sit on the aisle end.

"Middle," Judge Edwards commands.

I scoot to the middle. The pews fill in around me as ushers seat people. I realize that I'm pretty much in the dead center of everyone. An elderly woman dressed in purple, wearing a huge, majestic purple hat, sits at my right. A man in a sleek, shiny ivory suit sits at my left with his wife and children.

But Judge Edwards doesn't come sit beside me. Instead, he sits in a red leather armchair behind the pulpit, crosses his legs, folds his hands in his lap, and sits with a look I'm not sure I recognize.

The service begins with prayer and song accompanied by a full band. I stand on shaky legs and try to sing. I'm no Jesmyn or even Mars, but I figure I'd better do my best, since Judge Edwards is watching me. All in all, though, I'll take this over the predawn death run. I'm still concerned about why exactly Judge Edwards is sitting up there, but I guess he has to sit somewhere and obviously he's not going to sit next to me. Maybe that's where he always sits because he's a VIP or whatever.

The black-robed pastor stands and sermonizes for several minutes, interspersed with *amen*s and *hallelujah*s from the congregants. I sort of tune out. My mind needs a rest. But then he grabs my attention.

"Brothers and sisters, you hear from me every week. But today, we have a special honor. One of our most esteemed brothers, Judge Edwards, has asked to speak with you. So if y'all don't mind, I'm cutting my sermon short and offering him the balance of the time."

Scattered and eager *yeses* and *mm-hmm*s from the congregation.

A swell of adrenaline forces me to sit straighter. *This is potentially very bad. But maybe he's going to forgive me publicly. It'll be like a movie scene where he absolves me and walks down, with tears in his eyes and hugs me while everybody claps. And everything's okay. That could happen, right?*

Judge Edwards walks slowly, regally to the pulpit. He has the gait of someone accustomed to rooms full of people standing upon his entrance. He removes a piece of paper from his inside jacket pocket and sets it on the podium.

Surveying the congregation briefly, his eyes finally settle on me. And there they stay.

I do not see forgiveness in them.

When he speaks, I barely recognize him. His cadence and speech is that of a preacher—a skilled one. "Brothers and sisters, we are called upon to deal with others as Christ Jesus did."

Amens, hallelujahs, yeses, mm-hmms.

"With mercy."

Amens, hallelujahs, yeses, mm-hmms.

"With forgiveness."

Amens, hallelujahs, yeses, mm-hmms.

"With his. Own. Pure. Love."

Amens, hallelujahs, yeses, mm-hmms.

"Like him we must suffer long. But what about . . . ?"

The crowd waits fervently. Someone calls out, "Tell us, Judge!" Someone calls out "Preach, Judge."

"Justice?"

Amens, hallelujahs, yeses, mm-hmms.

His voice rises. "What. About. Justice?"

Amens, hallelujahs, yeses, mm-hmms.

"In Job, we see the question: Does God pervert judgment? Does the Almighty pervert justice?" He pauses. Lets the crowd clamor for the answer. "It may feel sometimes like he does."

Amens, hallelujahs, yeses, mm-hmms.

"You may feel as though you are called upon to give more than you can give. To bear more than you can bear. To *bleed more than you can bleed*. To cry *more than you can cry*."

Amens, hallelujahs, yeses, mm-hmms.

His eyes are burning into mine. I want desperately to look away, but I can't. That heavy-thing-sliding-off-a-shelf sensation. The falling-through-ice. I remind myself to breathe.

"But *God is great.*"

Amens, hallelujahs, yeses, mm-hmms, scattered clapping.

"God is good."

Amens, hallelujahs, yeses, mm-hmms, more clapping.

"God loves us, and so—"

Amens, hallelujahs, yeses, mm-hmms, more clapping.

"God is not *unjust.*"

Amens, hallelujahs, yeses, mm-hmms, clapping, *praise-the-Lords.*

A sheen of sweat oozes from my forehead. I'm nauseated again. Even that bowl of Special K might have been a mistake. Every eye in the worship hall seems to be following Judge Edwards's eyes to me. "Psalm thirty-seven tells us the Lord loveth judgment, and forsaketh not his saints; they are preserved for ever: but the *seed of the wicked shall be cut off.*"

Amens, hallelujahs, yeses, mm-hmms, clapping, *praise-the-Lords.*

"Wait on the Lord, and keep his way, and he shall exalt thee to inherit the land: when the wicked are cut off, *thou shalt see it.*" He's crescendoing in intensity. But no sweat on his brow.

Amens, hallelujahs, yeses, mm-hmms, clapping, *praise-the-Lords.*

"You may not live to see man's justice in every wrong you suffer, brothers and sisters."

*Amen*s, *hallelujah*s, *yes*es, *mm-hmm*s, clapping, *praise-the-Lord*s.

"You may not taste that sweet milk and honey in your days upon this land."

*Amen*s, *hallelujah*s, *yes*es, *mm-hmm*s, clapping, *praise-the-Lord*s.

"But God is watching with his all-seeing eye."

*Amen*s, *hallelujah*s, *yes*es, *mm-hmm*s, clapping, *praise-the-Lord*s.

"And he will have his justice and you will have yours."

*Amen*s, *hallelujah*s, *yes*es, *mm-hmm*s, clapping, *praise-the-Lord*s.

"I am in the justice business."

Laughter, *mm-hmm*s.

"However, I only mete out the justice of men."

*Amen*s, *hallelujah*s, *yes*es, *mm-hmm*s, clapping, *praise-the-Lord*s.

"The *puny* justice of men."

*Amen*s, *hallelujah*s, *yes*es, *mm-hmm*s, clapping, *praise-the-Lord*s.

"But be patient, brothers and sisters. For all who wrong us will one day come to account before the judgment bar of God almighty." He's almost shouting.

*Amen*s, *hallelujah*s, *yes*es, *mm-hmm*s, clapping, *praise-the-Lord*s.

"And he will have his justice."

*Amen*s, *hallelujah*s, *yes*es, *mm-hmm*s, clapping, *praise-the-Lord*s.

"And you will have your justice. Praise God almighty."

*Amen*s, *hallelujah*s, *yes*es, *mm-hmm*s, clapping, *praise-God-almighty*s.

"Praise God almighty who saw his *own son* hung on a cross but stayed his hand!" He is unambiguously shouting by this point. His eyes are a fiery red sword, pushed slowly into my belly to temper.

My mind races for a way to stave off the panic attack. It goes to Billy Scruggs. It goes to Hiro in his soaring car. It goes to Jiminy. It goes to Dr. Mendez's understanding stillness. But Judge Edwards's righteous wrath cleaves through it all. The world is a tossing ship deck. Sweat beads on my face and rolls down like tears. My chest heaves like the air is oily and I can't grab ahold of a breath. Out of the corner of my eye, I see the woman next to me glance at me in concern. I ignore her and hope she doesn't say anything.

Judge Edwards closes to riotous *amen*s, *hallelujah*s, *yes*es, *mm-hmm*s, clapping, *praise-the-Lord*s, and *thank-you*s, and sits. I put my head down and chew on my thumbnail. The man next to me turns to me and says, "Judge Edwards sure can preach, can't he?"

I nod. *He's a huge hit. And guess what—all of that was directed at me, so I suppose I'm sort of the cocelebrity of the day. Every story needs a villain, and that's me.*

The music strikes up again, and everyone stands to clap and sing. I can't do it. I slump into the exhaustion and deprivation of my panic attack for the rest of the service. Judge Edwards's eyes never leave me. He can yell at me for not participating if he wants. I can't.

It's quite a thing to sit in the middle of hundreds of nice people cheering for you to go to hell, even if they don't know they are.

□ □ □

The drive back from church is as silent as the ride there. I feel like I should say something, but *Cool sermon* doesn't quite fit the bill.

"I miss him every single day, Your Honor," I say quietly. "I loved him."

Judge Edwards laughs, cutting and caustic, and brakes in the middle of the street. The car behind us honks. He turns and regards me with the look one might give a moist dog turd served on a fine china platter. Incredulous wonder mixed with contempt and disgust. "I don't give a *good got-damn* how you felt about my son. Today is not about your *feelings*."

We drive the rest of the way back without another utterance passing between us.

□ □ □

Judge Edwards goes to the kitchen. He returns a moment later with a box of white garbage bags and a box of black.

"I presume you know where Thurgood's bedroom is."

I nod.

"Black is for charity. Anything somebody can use. The clothes, but not the shoes. He drew on them like a toddler."

Mars told us the only reason his dad let him wear Chucks was that's what Mars's grandpa had worn as sneakers.

Mars claimed it was a tribute, and Judge Edwards bought it somehow.

I stand there numbly, holding the boxes.

"White is for garbage. The artwork is garbage," Judge Edwards says.

Hearing him say that pierces like steel slivers forced under my fingernails.

"Any question, err on the side of garbage. I'll be in my study when you finish."

"Is there anything you want to keep, sir?"

"White is for garbage. Black is for charity. Do you see a third color in your hands?" His tone is as though he's speaking with a dense, recalcitrant toddler.

"No, sir."

"Any more questions?"

I shake my head and trudge upstairs. I wish I could show him how completely he's won. Physically. Mentally. Now he's trying for emotionally. And I can tell it's going to work.

I stand outside Mars's door for a moment, summoning my courage. Then I push in. The odor of unwashed clothes and stale food wallops my nostrils, like this door hasn't been opened in months. Maybe it hasn't. It's a stark contrast to the bloodless order and sterility of the rest of the house. It sounds bad, but it's not. Mars's room always kind of smelled this way. It's him. This was his island—now deserted. There's a jolt of nostalgia.

Judge Edwards made sure that even in the times he and I were apart today, I would continue to suffer.

I loosen my tie, remove it and my jacket, and lay them on

Mars's rumpled bed. I roll up my sleeves and start with the clothes on the floor.

One of these shirts might have been what he was wearing the day Sauce Crew got its name.

One he might have worn to squirrel rodeo.

One he might have spit bits of his sandwich onto while Blake showed us one of his newest videos.

Before putting them in a black bag, I press each to my face and breathe it in. Clean, joyous sweat mixed with Old Spice deodorant and Tide. I beg the olfactory portion of my brain to remember, to allow me to summon this smell again, because I will never have another chance.

Each fallen piece of clothing reminds me of a fairy-tale puppet from which the life has drained. Soon I have all the clothes off the floor in bags. Then the ones from the bed.

While pulling things from under the bed, I find a bowl of moldy peanut butter. This was Mars's favorite snack. He mixed peanut butter with maple syrup and dipped bread in it. We died laughing when we found out.

"Dude, that is the sorriest snack I've ever heard of," Eli *said between breaths, convulsing with laughter.*

"Seriously," I said, *"why don't you just eat a can of frosting?"*

"Least I ain't eating spaghetti with ketchup and mustard like y'all nasty asses," Mars said.

Blake looked at me and shrugged. "I told him about the recipe we invented. It was good."

"Dude, do not tell anyone else about that recipe ever."

I put the bowl in a white bag.

I clear his comics and graphic novels from his shelves and put them in black bags for charity.

I line the bags up in the hall so I have more room to work.

This is what we leave behind.

And then I start going through the drawers. More clothes. More black bags. The second-to-last drawer is stuffed with half-used art supplies. White bag.

I open the final drawer. It brims with Mars's drawings. I knew I'd encounter this. I'm surprised I didn't sooner. And still I'm not ready to see it. If Mars's clothes were his body, now I'm handling his soul.

I sit with my back against his bed, bury my face in my hands, and cry. I tell Mars again that I'm sorry. I sift through the drawings—page after page and notebook after notebook of character sketches. He practiced constantly. Judge Edwards was right: he loved excellence. He was not a quitter.

I find a drawing of Mars's brothers and sister.

Drawings of a couple of girls from school.

A drawing of Sauce Crew.

Then something I don't recognize. It appears to be a unified, cohesive, work-in-progress—a graphic novel of some sort. It's called *The Judge*. I leaf through. It's apparently about an African American judge who takes on the criminal underworld as a sort of superhero in a corrupt, Gotham-esque city.

My mind suddenly flashes to Hiro. But not soaring through the sky on mechanical crane's wings. Instead, I see him confronting the Nissan CEO with the idea he thinks will save people. I see him pleading his case with his hands filled with papers.

I'm done.

I'm finished being broken.

No more stories die here today.

Fear drains from me like I'm bleeding it out. I stand quickly and wait out the head rush. I collect up *The Judge* and some of the other drawings. I collect my stories of Mars Edwards. And I go downstairs on wavering legs, gravity tugging my intestines toward my feet.

Judge Edwards sits among his leather-bound volumes, typing furiously on his laptop. He hasn't even loosened his tie since church.

His eyes remain fixed to the screen as I stand in the doorway. "Are you finished?"

"There's something I think you should see, Your Honor."

He spins to me in his chair. "I asked *are you finished?*"

I hold out the sheaf of papers, *The Judge* on top. "Sir, Mars did these, and I think you should look at them before I throw them away. You'll regret it if you don't."

He stands and towers over me. His face is a raw, white-hot mask of molten rage. "*Thurgood.* His name is *Thurgood.* That is the name on his gravestone. And how dare you speak to me of *regret.*" He spits the words like venom sucked from a snakebite.

My breath abandons me. I am afraid and I want to turn and run. But I don't. *You have nothing left to lose. Tell him a story.* "He hated being called Thurgood. He wanted to be called Mars. We called him Mars. He called himself Mars. And he did this graphic novel. I think it's inspired by you. Please, sir, let me tell you—"

"*Shut up. Shut your reckless, murdering mouth.*" His saliva sprays cold on my face. He draws long, jagged breaths through his nose.

"Sir, I need to tell you—"

He stabs his finger toward the front door, so hard his sleeve makes a snap. "Get out. Now, before I decide to sue you and your parents for every penny you have."

"No." I lift my eyes defiantly to his. "I can't yet, Your Honor."

"You are officially now trespassing on my property. Leave, or I will remove you by force as I am legally entitled to do."

"Not until you hear what I have to say."

He takes a quick step forward and grabs my upper arm—the one holding the papers. They go flying. He spins me around so fast, I almost trip over my feet in my sudden dizziness. Only his bruising grip keeps me upright. He half lifts, half pushes me toward the entryway.

"Sir, please. Please. Let me make this a real goodbye day. Let me tell you about the Mars you didn't know."

"*Out.*"

"I can tell you about him; I can tell you the parts of him you didn't know. He—" My words dissolve into a yelp of pain. He's pulverizing my upper arm.

Judge Edwards reaches out with his other hand, yanks open the front door, and pushes me against the glass outer door. He's flinging me around so precisely, he manages to make the side of my body hit the door latch to open the outer door without shattering the glass. Then he pushes with the explosive force of a piston.

I fly down the two steps, catch the side of my shoe, tumble to the cement, and skid on my side. I scrape the top of my left ear. I somehow manage not to hit any of the places I injured during my fall earlier. I lie there long enough to see Judge Edwards pull the outer door shut with a rattle and then slam the front door so hard it makes the outer door pop open again.

I rise torturously. I'm bleeding from a few more places. It's soaking my pants. I've worn this suit through three funerals and one of the worst physical, mental, and emotional experiences of my life. I should burn it. Assuming I ever get my jacket back, that is.

I limp to my car without a backward glance, the dead and beautiful leaves—some as golden as the midday November sun shimmering through the trees—breaking underfoot.

⊞ ⊞ ⊞

My mom and dad are at a movie when I arrive home. I'm relieved. The last thing I needed was for them to see me walk in wearing torn and bloodied suit pants and a dress shirt with rolled-up sleeves. I didn't have a good story for how that would have happened on a Sewanee campus visit. I peel off the stained pants and stuff them in the garbage can, covering them with more garbage. I wash and bandage my new scrapes.

Then I fall on my bed and sleep dreamlessly for almost three hours. When I rouse myself, my parents are home. They ask me how my visit to Sewanee went when I go to the kitchen for a snack.

Great, I say. Looks like a cool place. It's not that I don't want to tell them what I've been through. It's that I wouldn't know how to begin.

I spend the next two hours doing not much of anything. I have a version of a depressed, anxious Sunday-night feeling. Only it's a thousand times worse than normal. As if every day of my life from here on out is going to be a Monday. I keep replaying the events of the day in my mind on a loop. Wishing I'd said and done a million things differently.

Maybe every attempt I make to lead a happy life again is doomed to fail.

I'm sitting at my desk, trying to read one of the books on my massive to-read list, when a couple of headlights attached to a sleek, shiny black car illuminate the street in front of my house. It parks right out front. My parents didn't mention visitors.

Then I look harder at the car. A wave of electric terror passes through me as I recognize it. Judge Edwards gets out, holding a bundle under one arm.

Oh no. No. No. This is not happening. Why is he doing this? He's coming to kill me. That's why. It's no longer enough to break me physically, mentally, and emotionally. He's here to literally murder me. And he'll get away with it because he's a judge.

I scurry to the entryway and watch through the peephole

as he approaches. His face is stoic and unreadable. My legs quiver so much that I struggle to remain standing. As he reaches for the bell, I fling open the door. I register his momentary surprise. It's an expression I'm unused to seeing on him.

We stand there for a moment, looking at each other like we hope the words we're after will materialize magically on each other's foreheads.

I open my mouth to speak, but he cuts me off. Softly. Gently. He pulls out *The Judge* from his inside coat pocket with his free hand. "Tell me about Mars. Tell me about my son."

Chapter Forty-Two

He's wearing a beige camel-hair coat. A navy sweater-vest with an open-collar purple gingham shirt. Khakis. Burgundy driving shoes. A tan driving cap. It suddenly occurs to me that he's wearing his version of kicking-around-the-house clothes. A calculated attempt to appear softer.

"Here," he says, handing me my neatly folded suit jacket and tie—the bundle he was carrying.

I accept them, but I'm still speechless.

My mom walks in. "Sweetie, who is—" She freezes when she sees Judge Edwards. "Sir, why are you here?"

"Ma'am, I came to see if—"

My dad enters and pales when he sees Judge Edwards. "Your Honor. May we help you with something?" When my dad gets emotional, his Irish accent thickens. Right now he sounds like he just stepped off the plane.

Judge Edwards meets his eyes with an even gaze. "I was about to ask your wife if I could borrow Carver for a few hours—if he'll allow me. To better acquaint me with my son."

"You tried to *take* our son from us." Blistering fury radiates from my mom. Thankfully, she's better at controlling it than Georgia. Even still, my dad gently touches her arm.

Judge Edwards's face conveys that he views the matter as somewhat more nuanced. However, he responds calmly. "I called for justice. I understand if we have very different views of what that means."

"He also asked the DA not to prosecute, Mom," I say. *Now I'm defending him?*

"I would *prefer* that we not spread that around too much, *as I said*." There's a trace of the old Judge Edwards in his tone.

"Sorry."

He nods, and the new, gentler Judge Edwards returns to his face.

"If that's true, then thank you," my mom says softly.

He nods.

"I know you are a judge, sir, but if this is some sort of . . ." My dad's voice trails off—deferential, respectful, but with a honed edge.

"Trick? Ruse? It is not." The old Judge Edwards tone returns. "It would mean a great deal to me, and I've had a difficult past few months, as I'm sure you've surmised."

My mom regards him with a sudden flash of sympathy. I give her a look that says: *This is an opportunity I need to take.* "If you want to, sweetie," she says.

"This is your choice, Carver," my dad says. "You don't have to go."

"I want to tell him about Mars," I say. "I know stuff about him Judge Edwards doesn't."

My parents trade wary glances but stay mum.

"This is important," I say. "What if it were someone wanting to tell you about me?"

They stand down. Judge Edwards shakes hands with them.

Judge Edwards and I leave and sit in his car for a moment. My adrenaline at seeing him come to the door is cautiously evaporating.

"You might be relieved to know that I've exhausted all of my ideas for the day. So I'm open to any you might have," Judge Edwards says.

He looks like he could use something sweet and rich, and I certainly could. "Do you like milkshakes, Your Honor?"

"Let's dispense with the 'Your Honor' business for tonight. And yes."

⊡ ⊡ ⊡

"Peanut butter and banana? What's wrong with chocolate and vanilla?"

"We could've gotten pumpkin spice instead," I say.

Judge Edwards snorts. "Worse still."

"Peanut butter and banana was Mars's favorite. You might like it too."

"They have to make everything complicated," Judge Edwards grumbles, and takes a sip. "Not bad." He takes another, holding up his cup as if in a toast. "All right. Better than not bad. I can see why these appealed to Mars." Every time he says "Mars," he trips over it.

I scan the park from the picnic table where we sit, but I don't see any squirrels. I explain squirrel rodeo to Judge Edwards.

He chuckles and shakes his head. "Good lord. Mars's grandfather marched with Martin Luther King Jr. so that his grandson could chase squirrels around Centennial Park with impunity. If that's not progress . . ."

I smile for the first time that day. "That's exactly what he thought you'd say."

The glimmer fades quickly from Judge Edwards's face. He takes another drink and savors it for a moment, gazing into the darkness. "I'm sure Mars thought I was hard on him."

"He did."

"I was hard on him. True. But understand that young black men have no margin for error in this country. I had to teach him that. I had to teach him that he can be the son of a judge, but if he acts the way young white men do— the way his friends do—he will be treated more harshly. People, police—they won't see a judge's son. They won't see a kid who worked hard and mostly stayed on the straight and narrow. They'll see another 'young thug'—the term du jour for all young black men in certain circles. They'll go through and find every picture of him wearing clothes that are too big, or flipping off a camera, or acting like a normal, rambunctious young man, and that will be all the proof anyone will need that he got what was coming to him.

"You want to know why I asked the DA not to prosecute you? I'll give you a hint. It's not because I wanted to be your new best friend. It's certainly not because I think you're blameless."

I both wanted very much to know and very much not to know.

"I'll tell you why," he says before I can respond. "I didn't want my son put on trial for his own death. And that's what would have happened."

"I wouldn't—" My voice is frail.

"You wouldn't what? Try to pin the blame on him? To save yourself from the consequences?"

"No."

"You say that now. But nobility has a funny way of disappearing when accountability raises its ugly head. Plus it wouldn't have been your call. Not really. It would have been Krantz's. And I know Jimmy Krantz very well. No. I did this to protect my son. I did this for him, not you."

I begin to deflate inside. *Maybe this was a bad idea.*

Judge Edwards swirls his straw in his milkshake. Something about the gesture puts me back at ease. "Anyway. That's not what we're here for. The point is I was never allowed to forget that I had to be hard on Mars or the world could be even harder. I see it in my court every day."

My wave of adrenaline begins to crest and subside. I'm feeling brave enough to keep pushing into potentially fraught territory. I assume my poor man's Dr. Mendez role.

"Is that why you wanted me to throw out his artwork? To forget?"

He shifts uneasily and watches his feet. "I never understood the artwork. It was not my choice to send him to art school. But when his mother and I divorced, in our agreement I got custody while she got to decide where he went to school. I thought the art school was to spite me."

"It wasn't. It was what he loved."

"I see that now."

"That's why we're here."

"Yes."

"Did he ever show you his artwork while he was alive?"

"Never."

We take sips of our milkshakes.

"I'm sure I'd have reacted badly," Judge Edwards says. "And I imagine he wanted to please me."

☐ ☐ ☐

"Dude, come on," I say. "It's more fun with two players."

"Bruh," Mars says, "I told you. Tonight I'm sketching. I have work to do."

"Come on."

"No."

"Dude."

"Dude. Do you think I'm going to make it if I don't work my ass off constantly? Think I'm the only person out there who wants to write and illustrate comics? Plus black people have to work twice as hard for everything."

"You definitely have to work twice as hard to get girls."

"Oh, all right. All right. I see how it is, funnyman."

"Mars. Just one night off."

"One night off leads to two. Two leads to three. Three leads to . . ."

"Four?"

"A hundred."

"You sound like your hard-ass dad right now."

"That's not from him. That's all me."

"He'd be impressed."

"Honestly, dude, can I tell you something?"

"Sure."

"For real, though, I don't give a shit about impressing my dad."

"Serious?"

"Yeah, man. He's never going to get or dig what I do. So why'm I gonna break my ass trying to impress him?"

"Yeah, I mean, makes sense, I guess."

"I'll tell you what I *am* gonna do: I'm gonna take all that work ethic he's always going on about, and I'm pouring it into what I love doing, and I'm making it so he can't help but be impressed someday. But I'm not trying for his approval."

"So that's why you won't hang out and play."

"Exactly."

"But it's way more fun with two players."

"Really, bruh?"

⊞ ⊞ ⊞

"Mars didn't care about that, actually," I say.

"What? My reacting badly to his artwork?"

"Impressing you."

A stormy cast clouds Judge Edwards's face. "Is that so?"

I swallow hard, remembering the ordeal of the day and not particularly wanting to relive any part of it, especially the whole "wrath-incurring" thing. But I press forward anyway. "He was pretty determined to take everything you taught him and be his own man. He . . . wasn't going to live his life for your approval. He wanted to live it for himself."

"You inferred this?"

"He told me."

"Just like that?"

"Just like that."

Judge Edwards sets his milkshake on the table, rests his elbows on his knees, clasps his hands, and stares at them, brow furrowed. His jaw muscles tense and release. He blinks fast and wipes his eyes. He coughs and clears his throat before speaking. His voice is gruff with tears. "I'm glad to hear that. Every father wants his son to want his approval. But I'm glad for his courage."

"He obviously admired you. You saw that in *The Judge*."

He sits taller. "That was something else, wasn't it? The work he must have put into that. He makes me very proud. I'm very proud that he's my son. I tried to be a good father to him."

"He knew all that. I could tell."

We pull our coats tighter around ourselves as the wind

blows from the north, carrying the mossy scent of damp leaves and rain.

"This is the kind of thing you boys did?" Judge Edwards asks.

"A lot, yeah."

"You just hung out together and talked about life and the way of things."

"Yep."

"Must've lost our damn minds, sitting on a picnic table at night, drinking milkshakes in November," Judge Edwards mutters.

"We can go if you want."

Judge Edwards takes a deep breath and closes his eyes. "No. It's pleasant. Cold. Clean. Like splashing water on your face in the morning." He pauses, starts to say something, and stops. Starts. Stops. Then finally: "I'll tell you what I wish sometimes."

I listen.

"I can't believe I'm saying this out loud."

I listen.

"When he was a baby, I would hold him on my lap and touch his hands in wonder. I would trace the lines along them. Measure his fingers against mine. Marvel at his perfect, tiny form. I wish—" He stops and looks away, blinking fast. I hear him trying to breathe down tears. He removes his hat, rubs the top of his head, and replaces his hat. "I wish I had done that once more. I wish I could have sat my son in my lap and traced the lines of his hands just one more time. My baby. He had talented hands."

"Yes he did."

We sit in a prolonged hush, punctuated by throat clearing and attempts at discreet eye wiping.

"We assume that it's better to survive things, but the ones who don't survive don't have to miss anyone. So sometimes I don't know which is better," Judge Edwards says finally.

"I don't know either."

He turns to me and wags his finger between us. "This right here. Have you done something similar to this with your own parents? Where you tell them who you are?"

"No."

"You should."

We trade stories of Mars. Some are funny. Some are not. Some uplifting. Some not. Some important. Some ordinary.

We build him a monument of words we've written on the walls of our hearts. We make the air vibrate with his life.

Until our milkshakes are gone.

Until Judge Edwards begins yawning and says that he has to be up early for court; that he's not as young as he once was.

Until it's almost my curfew anyway.

Until the wind gusts hard, bringing cool autumn rain, falling like silver arrows.

Chapter Forty-Three

He doesn't apologize and neither do I. He doesn't offer to absolve me and I don't request it. He does shake my hand and pulls Mars's drawing of Sauce Crew from his coat pocket, giving it to me when he drops me off, a few minutes before midnight.

I go in my parents' room to hug them good night. They must sense something in me. They hold me between them where they lie—warm and sleepy—and I cry like a child in their dark room. The tears are heavy, weighted with what they're carrying from me. When I finish, I'm quiet inside for the first time in months. Not happy, not free. Like flood-waters that haven't receded but are finally tranquil, all that was lost and broken drifting just below the surface under a cloudless sky.

I sit on my bed, not ready to sleep in spite of my exhaustion at the end of this seemingly year-long day.

There's something about the stillness in me that's too hushed. The way birds don't sing on a winter night and the frigid air buries every sound.

I need to try to fix one more thing.

I stare at my reflection in the screen of my black, lifeless phone. *If you survived this day, you can survive anything. And what do you have to lose?*

I pick it up and text Jesmyn, figuring she probably won't be awake. **I'm sorry. Beach in November.**

I wait a minute and there's no response. *Why would there be?* I go to the bathroom, brush my teeth, and change into my sleeping shorts. I turn out the light.

Behind my closed eyes, I see a pale white glow illuminate my room. I sit up to see my phone buzz, skittering on my desktop.

My heart pounds what must be my last reserves of adrenaline into my veins. My phone goes dark. I think about not even checking it. If it's the answer I expect, it'll leave me lying awake all night, heartache pulling me from my shallow bouts of sleep the way it did for the first month after the Accident.

But I do it. I pick up my phone.

Come tell me to my face.

Now? If the speed of a response to a text is the measure of dignity, I now have approximately zero dignity.

Now.

I dress as though I'm trying to escape a fire.

⊞ ⊞ ⊞

Around the corner from Jesmyn's house, I sit and watch the raindrops patter on my windshield and slide down in rivulets, making the streetlights flare orange like squinting at them through tears.

I spot her running in flip-flops, her jacket pulled over her head. I open the passenger door and she jumps in and slams it behind her. My car fills with the scent of honeysuckle. It makes me feverish with nostalgia. She's dressed for bed in a tank top and leggings, her hair in a messy ponytail.

Neither of us says anything. I start my car so the heater blows on her, but I don't make to turn on the lights or leave. She stares forward and rubs her arms.

"So." It must be obvious I'm trying to stall until I have something better.

"So." She shivers.

"I don't really know how to do this." A long (or at least it feels that way) silence.

"I'm glad you're not going to jail."

"Me too." I grip the steering wheel hard. "Look. I'm sorry. I was wrong. What I did. What I said. How I acted."

She takes a deep breath and releases it. "Carver, I want you to tell me right now. If we become friends again, will things be weird between us?"

"How do you mean?"

"I mean, will you constantly be comparing yourself to

378

Eli or whoever else? Will you compare what we have to what Eli and I had?"

"No." This is a lie. I won't be able to help it. But I do feel strong enough to never let her know it's happening. And for her purposes, that's as good as its not happening. I'd rather have the pain of secreting things away than the pain of her absence.

She reaches over and angles the middle vent toward her. "I'm still sorting out my emotions."

"I know."

"And I'm not sure I'll *ever* feel about you the way you do about me. If that's not something you can live with, you better tell me now."

Even though hearing this feels like my heart is being pushed through one of those Play-Doh molds, still I nod and say, "That's cool," because it is. It's better than no Jesmyn.

"No weirdness."

I nod.

"No drama."

I nod. A few seconds pass. "Eli was pretty great," I say quietly.

"Yeah. He was," she murmurs. She leans over, and we have an awkward car hug. "This sucks," she says. "Get out."

We meet at the front of the car and hug for an unreasonable amount of time in the rain, which douses us like an ablution. Now she smells like honeysuckle wet with dew. Green things becoming new and growing again.

We break the embrace and jump back into the car. I turn the heater up full blast and we rub our hands in front of the vents. She lifts her bare feet to the vent on her side. We're both giddy and giggly. That calms as we slowly warm.

"It felt pretty Beach in November when we weren't talking or hanging out," I say.

"It felt Torn-Up Song."

I cock my head in query.

"While we weren't talking, I'd go running at the Harpeth River Greenway because it always helps me blow out all my shitty feelings. So one night, after an especially bad day of practicing, I went running, and I saw these little bits of paper scattered on the path. I picked one up and it seemed to have lyrics on it. I kept picking them up and putting them together like a puzzle. It was a song somebody had torn up."

"Man, that's some Nashville-ass litter."

"Right? It way bummed me out to think about this song someone poured their heart into, torn up and abandoned on the ground. So, Torn-Up Song."

"I might have to steal that."

"Go for it."

"Was the song any good?"

Jesmyn starts laughing so hard she can't talk, and tears roll down her face. "No," she mouths.

I laugh with her.

When our laughter subsides, she becomes somber again and says, "Remember how everything was snotty green? Everything was black-blue when we were apart. Still not the right color."

"You'll get there. We'll get there."

"Can we still be Sweat Crew even with the weather getting cold?"

"I think so."

"Me too."

We listen to the rain drum on the roof of my car while a silken lull passes between us. It drapes itself over my heart like one of those days when the temperature is so perfect, you can't feel your own skin when you step outside.

Finally, Jesmyn turns to me, poised to speak, her face illuminated in a gauzy orange halo of dappled streetlight. It looks like the light is coming from inside her.

I know already I'll say yes to whatever she asks, because there's nothing I would rather do than tell her yes.

"Want a ride to school tomorrow?" she asks.

Yes.

Chapter Forty-Four

Sometimes, when I'm in nature, I imagine how placid; how idyllic it must have been before humans came along. A stillness so profound, it needs a witness. That's how I feel as I sit across from Dr. Mendez. My emotion resembles happiness enough that a smile is the only outward display that will express it.

Dr. Mendez smiles back. "You seem well today."

I lean forward, head down, and then look up at Dr. Mendez. "Can I tell you a story?"

He rests his elbows on his knees and clasps his hands, as though in prayer. "Please."

I spoke before knowing exactly what to say, but I wanted to say something. I rub my palms together. Then I rub my mouth and nose. I stare at the floor and chew the inside of my cheek. "Sorry," I whisper.

"Take your time," Dr. Mendez says.

"On, um, August first, Carver Briggs was at the bookstore where he worked, shelving books. His three friends, Mars Edwards, Blake Lloyd, and Eli Bauer, were at a movie and were supposed to meet him. They were going to go get milkshakes and then hang out at the park, which was a tradition of theirs." I swallow hard and draw a quaking breath. "They'd been friends since eighth grade."

My throat begins to constrict. I cough and wait for it to slacken. "He knew they'd be by soon to pick me—him—up, but he was impatient. So he texted them: 'Where are you guys? Text me back.'"

I begin trembling and my vision blurs with tears. Dr. Mendez sits absolutely still. I wait for a sob to die in my chest, inhale, and continue, my voice quavery but strong, somehow. "A little later he found out they were, um, killed in an accident that happened right around the time he was texting them. Mars, actually. He was texting Mars, who was driving, because he knew that Mars would text him back, just like he asked. Even though Mars was driving. And he knew Mars was driving."

I breathe down another sob. My hands shake violently. I ball them into fists and press forward. "And Carver is pretty sure he caused the wreck by texting Mars, but he's not completely sure. What he is sure of is that he didn't mean to hurt them. Ever. Ever. If he'd known what would happen, he never would have done it. And he's very sorry." I hesitate. "*I'm* very sorry."

I can't control my tremors and I begin weeping. I lean

so far forward that Dr. Mendez can probably see only the top of my head. I cover my eyes with my hand and cry like that for a minute or two. It feels so good. It feels like dream bawling. Dr. Mendez leans over and scoots the box of tissues to within my reach. I take one, wipe my eyes, and wad it up in my hand.

I finally sit upright again and slump down in my chair, exhausted. I laugh a congested cry-laugh. "Sorry. Such a baby."

Dr. Mendez's face is solemn. He shakes his head. "No." He leans back in his chair and taps his lips. He stares past me. He starts to say something but catches himself. He looks me dead on. I've never seen such a stormswept, haunted look in his eyes. "Now I want to tell you a story," he says softly. Almost as though asking permission. "I don't normally do this, but this time, I feel I need to."

I give him the "Dr. Mendez go-ahead" gesture. He smiles when he recognizes it. I see a slight tremble in his lips.

"When I was in high school, I had a dear friend named Ruben Arteaga. Anyway, one night, we're supposed to hang out, and we fight over something. I don't even remember what now. Something stupid. Something petty. We go our separate ways. I stay home; he heads over the bridge to Juarez to party."

Dr. Mendez shakes his head. He puts his finger to his lips as though trying to stop himself from talking. But he continues, clearing his throat, his voice overcast. "I wake up the next day, and, um, Ruben isn't at school. I wait for him to show up; he doesn't. I call him after school; nothing. I come to learn he was found in an alley behind some bar, badly beaten. He's alive, but barely. He holds on for a while with machines living for him. But then . . ."

A single tear slides down Dr. Mendez's cheek. "I'm sorry. This is still hard for me." His voice cracks. He removes his navy-blue-frame glasses and pinches the bridge of his nose.

I scoot the tissue box over to him. We laugh.

"Thank you, doctor," he says. He sighs and puts his glasses back on. "I knew in my heart I killed Ruben. If only I had swallowed my pride and not fought with him. If only I had stopped him from going. If only. If only. I looked to the moon and I saw Ruben's face. I looked to the clouds and saw a finger pointing at me."

"Pareidolia."

"Pareidolia."

"All the therapists in the world and I get one who understands better than anyone," I murmur.

"You were owed a bit of luck."

"Is that why the stories?"

"It was only by engaging with other stories—stories that removed me from the equation—that I was able to close this wound so I could heal. The universe—fate—is cruel and random. Things happen for many reasons. Things happen for no reason. To shoulder the burden of the universe's caprice is too much for anyone. And it's not fair to you."

"So I still have a ways to go, huh?"

"This isn't the end of a journey but the beginning. You're now where most people who lose a loved one or loved ones start. You've done the work to properly understand and contextualize your place in this tragedy, but there's more healing to come. You've beaten the infection in the wound, so now it can heal."

"I hope I feel completely right again someday."

Dr. Mendez's eyes, though teary red, twinkle. "You won't. And yet you will. I'll remember Ruben's smile, or I'll smell a cologne that reminds me of him—like a lot of teenage boys, he always wore too much. And when those memories hit me, I feel that ache. So will you. But your life will be full enough, big enough to absorb it, and you'll go on."

A few moments pass.

"Can I tell you something?" I ask.

"Of course."

I tell him I'm going to do a goodbye day with my parents someday soon. More of a hello day, actually. So they can hear my story. So I can offer them all of myself that I put behind walls for no good reason.

I tell him I believe we are stories of breath and blood and memory and that some things never finally end.

I tell him I hope, after we're gone, there's a day when a great wind fills our stories with life again and they rise from sleep; and that I write the best story I can—one that echoes in the void of the eternities at least for a time.

I tell him I hope I see my friends again someday.

I tell him I hope.

Chapter Forty-Five

Though two of Adair's dance buddies flank her as we pass in the leaf-strewn parking lot, still I stop for a moment and open myself to her. Offer myself, more like. I have nothing to tell her; I just want to give her the chance to say what she needs to say. *It's not enough that you took my brother; you also took my parents' marriage. It's not enough that he's dead; I have to see you hanging out with his girl-friend. It's not enough that you never went to prison; I also have to see you every day.*

I can receive it now, I think. Whether it was the therapy, the medication, or both, I haven't had a panic attack in a long time. I can absorb whatever she has for me and survive. Whatever comfort, whatever peace it'll bring her, I want her to have it. I try to tell her this with my face.

But she looks past me, somehow staring me down without

ever looking in my direction. Her gray eyes are as hard and hot as a fever. One from which you never become wholly well. One that takes part of you and never gives it back. One you don't survive completely.

If nothing else, I understand.

Chapter Forty-Six

Jesmyn stops playing abruptly, stands, and whoops, startling me.

"What?" I set down my laptop with my almost-completed college admission essay and slide out from under the piano to see her springing up and down, shouting.

She's incandescent. She grabs my hands. "I finally saw the blue! The right blue!"

I join her jumping and yelling.

When we settle down and catch our breath, I say, "You're done practicing for today. Pumpkin spice milkshake time."

We take our milkshakes to Centennial Park and drink them while we sit on the tailgate of Jesmyn's truck, listening to Dearly through the open cab windows, talking and laughing. We wrap Jesmyn's stargazing blanket around ourselves against the chill of the dimming autumn twilight—purple like a healing bruise—watching what leaves still cling to the trees fall spiraling to the ground, one by one.

Chapter Forty-Seven

I'm standing in line at Target, buying a Coke, when I remember, once, Sauce Crew was talking about how funny it would be if you congratulated people not on having babies but on having had sex. *You had a baby? Nice! You had sex! Congrats on having had so much cool sex!* People at church and work and stuff would say this to you.

I start laughing right there in line, laughing like I did then.

Like I did so many times.

Some days—the good ones—this is how they visit me.

Chapter Forty-Eight

Georgia's voice is sunny as she answers the door. "Hey!" I hear her talking with someone. "Carver!" she calls.

It's late-ish and it's supposed to snow, so I'm not expecting anyone. I put down my book and head for the door.

"So how long is UT on Christmas break?" Jesmyn asks Georgia as I turn the corner.

"I'm off until the first week of January," Georgia says.

Jesmyn's face brightens when she sees me. "Hey!"

"Hey! What're you doing here?"

"Surprise. Go put on your shoes and coat. We're walking to Percy Warner Park."

"Huh?"

She makes a scooting motion. "Don't ask questions. Hurry."

I comply.

Georgia insists on hugging Jesmyn before we go. "Have fun, kids. Don't do anything I wouldn't do."

"Okay," I say, "we'll try not to wake up before eleven a.m. or shower while we're at Percy Warner."

"Oh, all right," Georgia says. "We gonna do this, Carver? Right in front of Jesmyn? Huh?" She sticks her pinky in her mouth. "Do I need to hand you your ass?"

"Dude, don't!" I try to make it out the door and down the front steps, but Jesmyn, giggling, grabs me in a bear hug, pinning my arms to my sides right as I'm trying to clamp my hands over my ears. If I'm being honest, her being wrapped around me is so pleasurable that I don't try very hard to get away.

Georgia lunges forward and nails me in the left ear despite my frantically shaking my head and squalling. Then the right ear. "Had enough?"

"Yes, you gross idiot."

She gets the left ear again. "Okay. Now we're good."

Jesmyn frees me. I dry out my earholes with my sleeve. "Nasty, Georgia."

Jesmyn and Georgia high-five and Jesmyn and I leave.

The air glitters like liquid silver and the stiff wind carries the immaculate, sharp spice of faraway snow and burning wood. My breath clouds up in the bloom of the orange streetlights. "You gonna tell me what this mysterious trek is for?"

Jesmyn's expression is too enigmatic for any hints. "You'll see."

"I'm sad you'll be gone all Christmas break."

"Me too, but visiting my grandma is the best. We'll hang out plenty when I'm back."

We arrive at the park and Jesmyn leads me away from the streetlights into a dark, open meadow. The sleeping grass crackles dry under our feet. We stop in the middle.

"Here's the surprise." Jesmyn looks aloft.

I do the same. The clouds move low and fast, painted the ethereal orange-silver-pink of clouds that bring snow. They're black in the far distance. Here and there, stars gleam through a small clearing before it closes again.

"What?" I ask.

"That's the color of your voice," Jesmyn murmurs. "Winter clouds at night."

"You said—"

"I was joking. This is the color I hear you. It's better to show you than to try to describe it."

I am the color of the sky inside.

We gaze up, watching the sheer clouds drift past. A gust hums low in the bare limbs of the trees that encircle us. I glance over at Jesmyn. She has her holy-rite look of wonder. She catches me looking at her. I look back up.

Then I sense a slight tugging at my hand. I look down. Jesmyn has her pinky wrapped around mine. Her eyes are fixed skyward, but she has a faint smile. She slowly moves her fingers up mine, as if playing my hand like a keyboard, as if making the blue music—the right blue music—until our fingers are woven tightly together.

My heart moves as swiftly and weightlessly as the clouds,

carried on the wind. For a moment, I have Jesmyn's gift and my body sings a new hymn of colors I can't name.

We hold hands for a long while and stare into the blushing sky like we're reading from a page, letting the world whisper in our ears.

Chapter Forty-Nine

It's that Friday at the end of September when a storm blows in on a warm, muggy morning and it rains all day, but the rain clouds part for a crisp, bracing late afternoon and you know summer has finally lost its grasp. *That* Friday.

It's been one of those improbably perfect days when all the universe's tumblers click into place. Every joke of yours kills. Everyone's a little funnier than usual. Everyone's a little more insightful and quick. One of those days when you feel like you're going to be young and live forever. One of those days that feel perpetually like being at the top of the arc while you're swinging on a swing set.

Mars is driving. We've spent all afternoon at Eli's watching a movie and stuffing ourselves with pizza.

"You know what's funny?" Blake says, apropos of nothing, a short distance from my house.

"Your dick?" Eli says.

We crack up.

"No, my dick is normal and definitely not weird," Blake says, playing it totally straight. "It's a healthy dick."

"Oh, okay, sorry. Continue," Eli says.

"What's funny is how pretty much just adding mayonnaise to anything makes it a salad."

"Dude, *what*? That is not correct," Mars says over our hooting laughter. "This is like the time you tried to tell us that no one has ever witnessed a cat pooping."

"No, listen, you add mayonnaise to chicken? Chicken salad. Add it to tuna? Tuna salad." Blake sounds totally serious. He's thought about this.

"What if you added it to Cheerios?" I ask. "Cheerio salad?"

"I think so," Blake says.

"Mayonnaise and M&Ms," Eli says.

"M&M salad," Blake says. "I don't make the rules, dude."

"Y'all, for real, though, I've had Snickers salad before," Mars says. "At a church picnic, I shit you not. It was called Snickers salad and it was basically Cool Whip, peanuts, and cut-up Snickers bars."

"See, Mars? You actually agree," Blake says.

"Bruh, I just said it existed. I sure as hell did not say I thought it met the criteria for a real-ass salad."

"That's amazing," Eli says. "Because it's healthy for you. Just calling something salad makes it healthy."

"You know what else is crazy?" I say. "That Jell-O gets to be salad when it's pretty much the most opposite thing on Earth from leaves."

"There are some arbitrary-ass rules to salad," Mars says.

Still holding our sides with laughter, we pull up to my house just as the sun dips below the horizon, surrounding us in an embrace of dwindling light as day tips into night. Out of nowhere, I'm taken up in an unnamable ecstasy. The kind that comes from no specific wellspring and overflows before you even knew it was building in you. Everything is so beautiful, so good, you feel like you don't even need to breathe air anymore.

"I love you guys," I say, not knowing quite why. I try to pass off my abrupt turn into sentimentality as just another joke. Sometimes the best place to hide the truth is in plain sight.

A quick pause as they consider how to demolish me.

"*Awwwwww,* we love you too, Blade," Eli says, turning, reaching back, and grabbing me in a headlock from the front passenger seat.

"Group hug!" Blake shouts, and throws his arms around Eli and me as I try to squirm out of Eli's headlock. Just as I do, Mars turns from the driver's seat and gets me in a headlock, accidentally honking the horn with his butt. For the next few seconds, we romp like Mars's car is a cardboard box full of puppies. Hugging, grappling, and laughing. Hearing each other's heartbeats. Smelling each other's sweat and breath.

I open the door and escape, smoothing my mussed hair and catching my breath from tussling and merriment. Blake leans out the open door with a rubber band and shoots me squarely in the nuts.

I form a shield with both hands over my crotch to protect it from further indignity. "Okay, dudes. Later."

Blake and Eli blow kisses. *We love you, Blade,* they call. I blow kisses back with one hand still covering my junk.

They grin and wave. I wave back.

Mars speeds off.

I start toward my house, but for some reason I stop, turn, and watch them drive away.

I've never done that before. I don't know why I do it.

Maybe I wasn't ready to say goodbye.

I watch them until they disappear, fading as the day fades, into the darkness.

Acknowledgments

This book would not have been possible without my amazing agents Charlie Olsen, Lyndsey Blessing, and Philippa Milnes-Smith, or my brilliant editors Emily Easton and Tara Walker. My undying gratitude to you all.

Thanks to Phoebe Yeh, Samantha Gentry, and everyone at Crown Books for Young Readers. Thanks to Barbara Marcus, Judith Haut, John Adamo, Dominique Cimina, Alison Impey, and Casey Ward at Random House Children's Books.

My eternal gratitude to Kerry Kletter. Your book stays at my elbow when I write to remind me how it ought to be done. I don't know how I ever wrote without your friendship, brilliance, wisdom, and critical eye.

And speaking of critical eyes, I would have been sunk without yours, Adriana Mather. You know how to tell a story. It's the only thing you do better than mug making and pig raising. And I often asked myself "What would Adriana do?" when writing the character of Georgia.

Nic Stone. My Working On Excellence partner and Crown sister. I can't wait for the world to experience your brilliance soon. I am proud to know you.

Natalie Lloyd, you inspire me with the magic of your worlds and words, and you make me laugh every day.

Becky Albertalli, David Arnold, and Adam Silvera: it will never get old to me that I am friends with three of the most powerful voices ever to write for young people. Each one of you has been such a tremendous support to me. I can't thank you enough.

Amanda Nelson, you are an inspiration with your ferocious wit and intelligence.

Dr. Daniel Crosby and Amy Saville, anything I got right about Dr. Mendez was your doing. Anything I got wrong was my doing. I am in your debt.

Brooks Benjamin and Jackie Benjamin, thank you for your general radness and being two of my favorite people.

Thank you for your general hilariousness, Elizabeth Clifford.

Emily Henry and Brittany Cavallaro, I could not ask for more talented, funny, cool, supportive friends.

Matt Bauer, Matt Page, Rykarda Parasol, Corinne Hannan, Katie Clifford, Wesley Warren, Jonathan Payne, Dylan Haney, Sean Maloney, Ashlee Elfman, Olivia Scibelli, Chris and Elizabeth Fox, Maura Lee Albert-Adams, Shane Adams, Melissa Stringer, and Becky Durham, you guys are amazing and brilliant friends.

Eric Smith and Nena Boling-Smith, you two are absolutely wonderful and such amazing champions of books.

Chloe Sackur, thank you for taking a chance on a book about the son of a snake-handling preacher. I didn't get to thank you there, so I thank you here.

Stephanie Appell and the Parnassus crew. People and stores like you are the reason independent bookstores are so vital to the literary landscape. No algorithm or computer could ever do what you do. Thank you.

Thanks to my Nashville writing buddies: Jason Miller, Daniel Carillo, Ed Tarkington, Ashley Blake, Katie Ormsbee, Kristin Tubb, Rae Ann Parker, Alisha Klapheke, Courtney Stevens, and Corabel Shofner.

Thanks to my older (in publishing) writer sisters and brothers who have been so supportive: Nicola Yoon, Rainbow Rowell, Jennifer Niven, Kelly Loy Gilbert, Sabaa Tahir, John Corey Whaley, David Levithan, and Benjamin Alire Sáenz.

Thanks to my ninth-grade writing teacher Clenece Hills for teaching me to fear the passive voice.

Thanks again, Amy Tarkington and Rachel Willis.

Thanks always to the staff and campers of Tennessee Teen Rock Camp and Southern Girls Rock Camp.

Thanks to all of my Sweet Sixteener buddies, especially Nicole Castroman, Peter Brown Hoffmeister, Paula Garner, Marisa Reichardt, Riley Redgate, Amber Smith, Laura Shovan, Amy Allgeyer, Jeff Garvin, Kurt Dinan, Bridget Hodder, Julie Buxbaum, Kathleen MacMillan, Victoria Coe, Laurie Flynn, Kathleen Glasgow, Melissa Gorzelanczyk, Shannon Parker, Sonya Mukherjee, Darcy Woods, Jenn Bishop, Jessica Cluess, Sarah Glenn Marsh, Catherine Lo, Kali Wallace, Lygia Day Peñaflor, Lois Sepahban, Karen Fortunati, Randi Pink, Natalie Blitt, Kim Savage, Sarah Ahiers, Roshani Chokshi, Kathleen Burkinshaw, Meg Leder, Janet McNally, Andrew Brumbach, Lee Gjertsen Malone, Julie Eshbaugh, Parker Peevyhouse, Natalie Blitt, and Ki-Wing Merlin.

Gratitude to the amazing bloggers, booksellers, and librarians, especially Hikari Loftus, Owlcrate, Dahlia Adler, Mimi Albert, Caitlin Luce Baker, Sarah Sawyers-Lovett, Eric Smith, Randy Ribay, Will Walton, Kari Meutsch, Shoshana Smith, Ryan Labay, Sara Grochowski, Danielle Borsch, Demi Marshall, Joshua Flores, and Stefani Sloma.

Mom and Dad, Grandma Z, Brooke, Adam, Steve. I love you all.

My beautiful love and best friend, Sara. Writing while I listen to you practice is heaven to me. It is no exaggeration to say that I could not have written this or any other book without your love and support and the happiness you give me.

My precious boy, Tennessee. You are the treasure of my life. Nothing brings me more joy than watching you grow up and calling myself your father. Thank you for being my son.

About the Author

JEFF ZENTNER is the acclaimed author of *The Serpent King*. In addition to writing, he is a singer-songwriter and guitarist who has recorded with Iggy Pop, Nick Cave, and Debbie Harry. *Goodbye Days* is his love letter to the city of Nashville and the talented people who populate it. He lives in Nashville with his wife and son. You can follow him on Facebook, on Instagram, and on Twitter at @jeffzentner.